THE MAUNDRELL FAMILY TREE

Praise for *Her Little Flowers*
by Shannon Morgan

"Morgan's debut novel is a treat for fans of the supernatural. Overall, the novel provides a compelling supernatural mystery that will hold a reader's attention right up to the last page. Recommend to fans of Kate Morton and Eve Chase." —*Library Journal*

"Look for Gothic atmosphere and pleasantly creepy vibes in Shannon Morgan's story of a middle-aged woman and her extremely haunted mansion." —GoodReads, **"Most Anticipated Books of the Summer"**

"What an amazing story Shannon Morgan has delivered! With a Gothic twist, a beautifully haunting atmosphere, and a big splash of family drama, this makes an incredible read for modern ghost story lovers!" —Shanora Williams, *New York Times* best-selling author of *The Wife Before*

"Poetic prose and haunting heartbreak—a story that will stay with the reader!" —Lisa Childs, *New York Times* best-selling author of *The Missing*

"Shannon Morgan has crafted a mesmerizing tale with *Her Little Flowers*. Featuring a decaying manor filled with ghosts, compelling family secrets, and a haunting atmosphere, I was totally drawn in. From the tantalizing first page to the thrilling conclusion, this story won't let you go, and you'll learn a bit about the language of flowers along the way. A great read!" —Terri Parlato, author of *All the Dark Places*

"The book is ultimately about family bonds, loss, and forgiveness and we are given an inside look at what abuse can do to an entire family. The research about the plants was impeccable . . . What an exceptional debut." —The Book Review Crew

"Near the end, I was weeping uncontrollably." —Unquiet Things

ALSO BY SHANNON MORGAN

Her Little Flowers

IN THE LONELY HOURS

SHANNON MORGAN

KENSINGTON
PUBLISHING CORP.

w.kensingtonbooks.com

KENSINGTON BOOKS are published by
Kensington Publishing Corp.
900 Third Avenue
New York, NY 10022

Copyright © 2024 by Shannon Morgan

All rights reserved. No part of this book may be reproduced in any form or by any means without the prior written consent of the Publisher, excepting brief quotes used in reviews.

All Kensington titles, imprints, and distributed lines are available at special quantity discounts for bulk purchases for sales promotion, premiums, fund-raising, educational, or institutional use.

This book is a work of fiction. Names, characters, businesses, organizations, places, events, and incidents either are the product of the author's imagination or are used fictitiously. Any resemblance to actual persons, living or dead, events, or locales is entirely coincidental. To the extent that the image or images on the cover of this book depict a person or persons, such person or persons are merely models, and are not intended to portray any character or characters featured in the book.

Special book excerpts or customized printings can also be created to fit specific needs. For details, write or phone the office of the Kensington Sales Manager: Kensington Publishing Corp., 900 Third Avenue, New York, NY 10022. Attn. Sales Department. Phone: 1-800-221-2647.

Kensington and the K logo Reg. U.S. Pat. & TM Off.

ISBN: 978-1-4967-4391-6 (ebook)

ISBN: 978-1-4967-4390-9

First Kensington Trade Paperback Printing: August 2024

10 9 8 7 6 5 4 3 2 1

Printed in the United States of America

For Rory
My beautiful, heartbreak boy
with galaxies trapped in your head.
You are so loved.

Samhain:
A Gaelic festival
marking the beginning of winter

(Pron: Sow-win)

PROLOGUE

31 October 1990

S hadows probed the edges of the closed window. Exploratory, wheedling. Petting and fretting, searching for a way in.

Alice Maundrell eyed them without fear. The shadows were not there for her.

Her nose wrinkling, she sat opposite her mother. Though the room was set up like a hospital ward, it was not sterile and stank of that peculiar mix of odors she associated with extreme age, of throat lozenges and urine. It was not designed for comfort and held little visual stimulation, no books or magazines, no writing materials. Only old functional furniture: a metal-framed bed with a lumpy mattress emitting a disagreeable stench, two upright chairs, a trolley to one side and an old machine Alice dared not look at. The years of purposeful neglect hung heavily on the air.

"We've found her," she said without preamble.

"Wherrre?" Bitsie Maundrell whispered through the collapsed side of her mouth, a dribble of saliva running down her chin. Her pleated skin was worn smooth like crackled porcelain, green eyes moist and drooping, yet still expressing disdain for her daughter.

"She's working in Italy." Alice swallowed the lump of hatred lodged in her throat before she could speak again. "In hindsight you did her a favor by sending her away. I'm grateful she never had to come under your influence."

She marshaled her thoughts. This last meeting was a confession. Alice had no interest in redemption or atonement, only a bitter desire to ensure Bitsie's sins against many was the last thing she heard.

"Why did you hate her so much?" Alice blinked angrily; she was already going off her carefully planned script.

"Not herrr," sneered Bitsie. "You."

Alice's hands folded in her lap twitched with the urge to clench into fists. She resisted, determined not to give Bitsie a final win, to witness her ability to still wound after all these years.

"And what did I ever do to you?" she said thickly.

Bitsie's thin nostrils flared. Her mouth worked, forming around a word. "Girrrl," she spat.

"Jasper was a boy," Alice pointed out.

"Wwweak!"

Alice nodded, unsurprised. If she'd had any remaining scruples, they melted with that one slurred word. "But Theo was strong. It was always strength and power you loved."

An uncaring snort, then, "Perrrcy?"

"He doesn't want to be found." A glass with a straw sat on the table beside the old woman. "Do you want some water?"

Bitsie nodded.

"Pity." Alice deliberately moved the glass out of reach. She smiled, gleeful and spiteful, at a hiss of frustration.

Bitsie was not to be outdone in spite. She lifted one skinny butt cheek and farted. It stank. Unrepentant, she muttered, "Prunes."

Alice shook her head in mock sorrow. "And that's all you have control over now. How does it feel, Mother?" She didn't expect an answer. Conscious of the impatient shadows bunching against the

window, she pulled a turnip from her pocket. It was a slightly ridiculous vegetable, round and squat, yet it elicited the desired visceral
reaction from Bitsie. Her trembling hand crept up her throat like a
pale blind spider, horrified by the hideous face gouged into the turnip's hard, white flesh.

"Do you remember how he loved carving these each year?" Alice
murmured. "He was an innocent, a true innocent, and you were so
cruel to him." She placed the turnip on the table where her mother
could see it. "We should've stopped you. *I* should've stopped you."

"Took Rrred," Bitsie snarled.

"You can't know that, no matter how much you want it to be
him. And maybe he did, but he's beyond your control now."

Bitsie grunted. Cold, indifferent, pitiless once more. She eyed the
glass hopefully.

Alice caught the glance. "No water for you today, but perhaps
you would like some tea?" She nodded at the teacup sitting on the
trolley. It had stood there for three weeks, the liquid almost evaporated except for a thick, slimy layer of scum at the bottom.

Bitsie's growl of thwarted fury was wet, phlegmy, and turned into
a weak cough.

Leaning back, Alice waited for the question Bitsie had asked
every day since her incapacitation.

"Searrrch?"

"Still ongoing. The whole village is out scouring the island and
the maids are going through the castle again." It was the same lie
Alice always gave. An easy lie, feeding Bitsie's obsession that had
induced a stroke six years ago. And it fed Alice's sense of dark justice.

A bite of doubt itched her scalp. Bitsie was still a force of nature,
still a presence felt throughout the castle, imbuing the very walls
with her obsession like black mold. And the dead had always been
restless here. Would her mother continue to infect the ancient
stones after her last breath escaped? Alice shivered with horror at
the very idea.

Bitsie snorted her approval.

The shadows dimmed the room, moist as fine mist, humming eagerly.

Alice stood and went to the arched window. "Soon, soon," she murmured, fingers on the cold glass. The shadows pressed close, sinuous, coaxing, fickle. Beyond lay the humped Brig o' Haggs, the only way on and off the island. Tendrils of sea fog drifted off Loch na Scáthanna, shrouding its bloody waters. The surrounding Munros stood sentinel and constant, their snowcapped peaks wreathed in mushrooming clouds.

She rested her forehead against the window. The shadows clustered closer, slithering, skittering, cajoling.

How many times had she watched the bridge with desperate longing but been too scared, too indoctrinated, to escape her false illusion of safety on the island? It was too late now. The island was her prison; she would never leave it again. Countless lost wishes ached in her heart; she should have accepted his offer and blown the consequences. But wishes were useless; he was dead and she was still rattling around the castle with only her mother and the nurse for company. Come tomorrow she would be alone.

"I see them sometimes," she said distantly, watching the shadows pat the cold glass, imploring.

Bitsie grunted.

Alice faced her mother. "She's in the garden and he's in the castle. They were so close and now they can't find each other . . . Did you do something that night? I've often wondered, and lord knows you have enough malice to wish the worst on innocents."

She crossed to the trolley where Bitsie's dinner had been left by the nurse. She lifted the lid, releasing the steam of cabbage and chicken, boiled according to Alice's instructions, all color and taste leached from the food. She placed the plate and a plastic spoon on the table out of her mother's reach.

Bitsie's clawed hand scrabbled for the spoon.

"And now it's Samhain once again," said Alice, seating herself opposite her mother, smiling slightly at her impotent whimper.

"You know what that means, Mother. I've never understood your love for this particular holiday, especially knowing every tragedy on the island happened on Samhain. Perhaps it speaks to the darkness in you."

Bitsie's fumbling hand stilled. Her wet eyes narrowed with what Alice had been waiting for: fear.

"You have no idea how truly dark Samhain is," she said grimly, alert to the shadows seeping through the window she had left ajar. They slithered down the wall, across the floor towards Bitsie. "But I do."

Alice's lips curved into a smile of vengeful expectation. Some tragedies had blunted so much of her life with heartache. And some hurt not at all.

CHAPTER 1

M r. MacDonald was old. Neve was not wrong when, on entering his office, she had muttered, "He looks like a crumbly vampire."

It was the quintessential solicitor's office, seen in a hundred movies. Dry, stuffy and too much brown, from coffee-hued legal tomes along the walls to the taupe Persian carpet that was probably worth a small fortune but looked like an incontinent dog had been let loose on it. The vampire sat behind acres of desk, a vastness of rich walnut, what any self-respecting tree yearned to be when felled.

"This has to be a joke," said Edie, not for the first time, putting a calming hand on Neve's arm, who fidgeted beside her on an uncomfortable high-backed chair. "When I got your emails and letters I thought they were spam."

"It is no joke, I assure you, Mrs. Nunn," said Mr. MacDonald, his Scottish burr barely discernible. "The contents of the will are quite clear."

"You have the wrong person. I don't know this Percy. I've never met a Percy in my life!" It was a plea for sanity as Edie's carefully reconstructed world lurched sideways with the dry words of a dead stranger.

Mr. MacDonald cleared his throat, his eyes sliding back to the sheath of legal documents in front of him. "You are Edwina Nunn, née Standish? Raised in St. Jerome's Orphanage of Hammersmith, London? Wife of the late Joshua Nunn?"

"Yes," said Edie testily. The unexpected mention of her childhood residence raised a quick flash of images: the dark, turreted building squeezed between two factories, crying babies, childish laughter in the asphalt playground, the purposeful flat-slap of the nuns' sturdy shoes echoing through huge dormitories crammed with beds. "But the nuns picked a random name and surname like they did for every other baby left on their doorstep. I am not the one you're looking for. It's all a dreadful mistake."

The solicitor's cool façade cracked slightly. "There is no error on our part. These are the known facts given to us by Lord Maundrell, and we, at MacDonald, MacDonald and MacDonald, have done our research most assiduously. If I may say, the Maundrell family went to great expense to find you. They would not have done so on a whim."

"Why?" said Edie. "If they gave me away, why would they want to find me again?"

Mr. MacDonald pulled at his upper lip, thrust into deep water with emotional sharks swimming below him. "I cannot say."

"Who cares?" whispered Neve, staring at her mum as though she'd grown a unicorn's horn. "He wants to give us a castle. We should definitely let him *give* us a castle."

"It's not ours." Edie's stomach knotted with trapped anxiety, pinned to her seat by the solicitor's emotionless gaze.

"I assure you, Mrs. Nunn, Maundrell Castle is legally yours. You are the last living Maundrell. You and—er—" He nodded at Neve with the glazed expression of an older generation confronted by the alien younger generation, especially one with bright pink hair.

"Neve—Neve Nunn," said Edie, pitying the old man. Neve was not for the fainthearted in appearance or temperament.

"Er—yes, Miss Nunn, of course." His attention slid back to Edie. "We were fortunate to discover the orphanage had not discarded a couple of your belongings after you left at sixteen, and we were able to take the precaution of running DNA tests. Now if I may continue?" His thin, dry lips creased into the approximation of a gentling smile when Edie gave no further protest. He shuffled the papers on the desk into a neater rectangle. "As the question of your illegitimacy has been cleared up sufficiently by Lord Maundrell, I see no other impediment, legal or otherwise, to you taking your inheritance. Although sadly the castle does not come with much in the way of funds."

"Illegitimacy?" said Neve, perking up from the slouch of boredom she had lapsed into. "Why was Mum sent to an orphanage in London if she was born in Scotland? Aren't there orphanages here? It kind of feels like spite, sending a baby away as far as they could."

"I cannot say, Miss Nunn." The solicitor bent his head towards the will quickly to discourage further interruptions from Neve.

As his dry words flowed over her, Edie swallowed against the scream building in her throat. It came straight from her aching orphan heart. It didn't matter where she'd been sent. These Maundrells hadn't wanted her was all she needed to know. Being illegitimate didn't bother her; it was one of the many theories she had spun over the years.

With a stern self-admonishment of *do not cry!* she pulled the tattered threads of her customary common sense together and focused when Mr. MacDonald cleared his throat, hesitant.

"Finally," he said. "Lord Maundrell's last codicil involves the Maundrell Red."

Edie stared at him blankly.

"You have heard of the Maundrell Red?" His hesitancy slipped into uncertainty.

"No."

"I have," said Neve, surprising both Edie and the solicitor. "Tik-Tok," she added with adolescent defensiveness. "It's a cursed diamond. Like the Koh-i-Noor and the Black Orlov."

"That is correct, Miss Nunn," said Mr. MacDonald, nodding at Neve with grudging approval. "However, unlike the two you mentioned, the Maundrell Red was discovered in the Kimberley diamond fields of South Africa, not India, by your ancestor, Lord Ernest Maundrell. It has, however, been missing for many years."

"Yeah, I heard that too," said Neve. "Looks like the curse followed us too if we are Maundrells as you say." She slumped back in her chair again, slipped her phone out of the pocket of her jeans and glanced down at its screen.

A hunted expression navigated Mr. MacDonald's long, lined face at another potential emotional pit opening in front of him. "We did, of course, learn of your husband's tragic accident two years ago. You have our deepest condolences from everyone here at MacDonald, MacDonald and MacDonald."

Edie nodded, weary of condolences though kindly meant. Joshua. God, she missed him. He would have pissed himself laughing at all this absurdity. Her throat tightened with unshed tears, his death was still a crushing ache, gaining the family she'd never believed possible, then torn away too soon by a cruel flick of fate, leaving Neve and herself behind like the punch line to a sick joke.

"As I was saying," said Mr. MacDonald, "though it is missing, Lord Maundrell was quite insistent that should the Maundrell Red ever be recovered your legal claim to it could not be disputed."

That got Neve's attention. "Who else has a legal claim?"

"There was an instance, many years ago," said Mr. MacDonald in careful tones, "where an unverified claim was made. It was resolved by the Maundrells themselves."

"Oh," said Neve, losing interest.

He paused, eyeing her uncertainly in case she interrupted again, then continued with, "Lord Maundrell has left a personal note he asked be conveyed to you at the reading of his will." He pushed his spectacles farther up his nose and read, *"My dear Edwina. I wish we could have met, but time has a way of catching up with one and mine has run out. I would that I could atone for my—our—family's cruel abandonment of you, but an apology will need to suffice. No words can make up for what you have lost, and I can only hope you, unlike most of our family, have found some modicum of happiness.*

"I have left what remains of my fortune to my husband, who gave me immeasurable joy in my life, but even if I could legally have given him Maundrell Castle, I would not. Though you will inherit the castle, I urge you to sell it as quickly as possible. It is cursed. It will only bring you pain and tragedy as it has to every member of the Maundrell family. Signed *Lord Percy, Archibald Maundrell, on 21 March 2021, Santorini, Greece."*

"God, that's cheery," muttered Neve.

Edie ignored her and said, "That's it?"

"I fear so, though Lord Maundrell was most insistent I convey his feelings to you." Mr. MacDonald placed his folded hands over the neat pile of papers in front of him. "You will both have questions. I shall endeavor to answer them as best I can."

"Who were my biological parents?" Edie asked hoarsely.

The solicitor's dry expression puckered with discomfort. "Unfortunately, everyone who might have given you the answer is now deceased."

"You don't know?" said Neve, straightening from her slouch.

"I fear not."

"Was Percy my father?"

"To the best of my knowledge, no." The admission was wrenched from the solicitor, who, like all of his profession, refrained from absolutes if they could. "It is my understanding that Lord Maundrell left the castle when he was seventeen and never returned."

"So I was born in the castle?"

"As far as I am aware."

"Where is it?" asked Neve.

"It is in an area called Sutherland in the western Highlands.

A most beautiful area I am led to believe, though I have not been there myself."

"Who is living there now?" asked Edie.

"The caretaker, Mr. Fergus MacKenzie, has been retained by the Maundrell estate as a presence on the island."

"Wait, what island?" said Neve, with an excited glance at her mother.

"Ah yes, of course. Maundrell Castle is situated on an island in Loch na Scáthanna. The loch, island and surrounding area are all part of your estate." Mr. MacDonald slid a thick folder across the vast desk. "I have enclosed copies of the various deeds and entitlements to the Maundrell estate for perusal at your leisure. We will retain the originals if you wish to extend use of our services. We have served the Maundrell family for centuries since Lord Henry Maundrell acquired the castle and land in 1750. We do hope we will continue to serve you faithfully into the future." There was a well-mannered request in the solicitor's voice.

Edie nodded helplessly, picking up the folder with excessive caution as though it were laced with poison, then sat in a stupor of mixed emotions as Neve asked questions until she ran out of steam.

Mr. MacDonald hid his relief well as he ushered the Nunns out into the gray October day.

CHAPTER 2

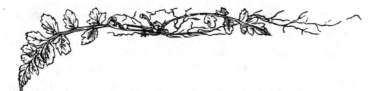

Edie and Neve loitered on the pavement outside the offices of MacDonald, MacDonald and MacDonald. Edinburgh felt like a different world from their little house in Hampshire, as far south in England they could get in a straight line. St. Giles' Cathedral loomed solid and lovely opposite them, oblivious to the flocks of tourists flowing up and down the Royal Mile.

Clutching the folder to her chest, Edie shook her head, dazed. She had traveled all the steps leading to this moment, but none of them made sense. How was it possible she had inherited a Scottish castle from a family she hadn't heard of a couple of hours ago? Family. An alien word with the bittersweet aftertaste of grapefruit from the little she had learnt of the Maundrells.

Watching the tourists, Neve said, "So some rich uncle you've never met—"

"Or heard of," said Edie, needing to stress this fact. "And I'm not sure he was an uncle either. He could've been a cousin or a brother. The vampire didn't say."

"So a relative you've never heard of," Neve continued blithely, "pops his clogs and gives you a Scottish castle. This sort of shit doesn't happen except in movies."

"Language," Edie reproved with absentminded mildness. "But you're not wrong."

"Are you all right?" Neve didn't look at her mother, still in that awkward stage where showing concern was a sign of weirdness or weakness or both.

Of course she wasn't all right. Edie felt oddly numb. She longed to hug Neve and be hugged but resisted the urge, knowing it wouldn't be reciprocated. She hadn't adjusted to this almost-adult Neve had morphed into these past couple of years. No longer the little girl who had considered Edie the center of her world, now a startling, sometimes frightening stranger, with a will far stronger than her own. Neve looked so much like Joshua it sometimes stunned Edie with such intense heartache she needed to sit down. Thick brown hair— which Neve had recently dyed bright pink, despite threats of losing her mobile until the color grew out—and quick brown eyes above high cheekbones. Edie wasn't sure where Neve's lips came from, the upper plumper than the lower, giving her a sensuous pout. She had inherited none of Edie's freckles, fair skin and fairer hair.

"I'll be fine," said Edie gruffly.

Silence yawned between them, awkward with too much unsaid.

"So we're going to see our castle," said Neve. It wasn't a question.

Her new castle-owning situation made Edie hesitate. Though the hunger to discover her family bit marrow-deep, her orphan's dream in reach, the idea of traveling up to this castle terrified her, feeding into her fear of rejection. She needed time to process a whole world of unresolved pain, to peel away the numbness cushioning her core, in a safe place, a known place.

"Perhaps another time," she said warily, stomach clenching in anticipation of an argument she knew she would lose.

"No! We go see our castle. It's a castle, Mum! A genuine, holy fuck castle!"

"Neve! Language! God, anyone would think I'm raising a savage."

"We've been given a castle! Aren't you the least bit curious to see it?"

"Of course, but we were only up here for the night. The October break isn't long enough for more. You have to be back at school in a week."

"That's still loads of time."

"And I only have two days off work. I can't afford to take off more time."

"Stop being so practical, Mum!"

"What's wrong with being practical? One of us has to be."

"It's boring. You can phone the agency and tell them you need more time . . ." Neve grabbed Edie's mobile held loosely in her hand.

"Neve!" cried Edie. "What are you doing? Give that back!"

Neve ignored her, tapping at the screen in a blur of thumbs, and handed the phone back.

Edie's heart sank at the curt text Neve had sent:

Taking the week off. Family business.

"I get a say in this too," said Neve, "and I say we go see our castle. I googled it while you were talking to the vampire. The nearest town is called Lochinver, about a five hour drive from here. If we leave now we can get there before dark."

Three dots bobbled on the screen as Edie's employer composed a message. Then:

Hope everything's okay. We'll manage.

"Hah!" said Neve, reading the message upside-down. She walked down the steps into the flow of tourists, not waiting to see if her mother followed.

Edie didn't count to ten as she usually did when confronted with the stubbornness Neve had inherited from Joshua, doing everything as though they might not be here tomorrow. She hurried after her daughter, not wanting to lose her in the crowd.

Neve's five hours turned into seven and counting. The roads from Edinburgh started off well, dual carriageways that gradually got narrower and twistier the farther north they drove. Those whittled down to potholed single-track lanes meandering through tight glens between heather-clad mountains reflected eternally in deep, secret lochs and over zigzagging passes dodging sheep that strayed wherever they felt like it. Towns became villages so small Google Maps couldn't find them. Farmhouses gave way to occasional ruins of old crofts and forgotten churches with overgrown graveyards of long-buried Highlanders. Then only vast moors remained with spindly, wind-worn birch growing in unlikely places and moss colonizing every rock and tree, giving the barren beauty a false, green softness.

Neve spent the first half of the journey going through Mr. MacDonald's folder, exclaiming out loud, "Loch na Scáthanna means 'Lake of Shadows'!" And, "There's more than one island, but our castle is on the biggest." And, "Our castle was built by the Macleods of Haggs." And, "Our castle is really old, Mum. Like *really* old, a thousand years and more . . . There's some touristy crap here about our castle."

Edie lost count of the times Neve said "our castle" as though saying it often enough cemented their ownership.

As the miles passed, Neve lapsed into silence after her initial excited chatter. Entranced by the increasingly remote Highland scenery, she hadn't turned to her mobile for entertainment except to put AirPods in her ears and listen to music.

The silence gnawed at Edie, allowing unwelcome thoughts. She gripped the steering wheel so hard her fingers cramped as they headed towards the reality of childhood dreams, long squashed for their impossibility. Why had she been discarded like a dirty rag? It hadn't been for a lack of finances if these Maundrells had Scottish castles lying about. And there had been that almost throwaway comment by the solicitor of her illegitimacy being sorted out. Was that really such a big thing in 1970? Or had her biological parents simply not wanted her? After living with the possibility for half a century, it still hurt. It was one thing to be given up for financial reasons or something equally pressing, quite another to know she had been born a regret, a mistake.

Tears slid down her cheeks. She brushed them away angrily. It was ridiculous. She hadn't known the two people who had created her. Why should she care that they hadn't wanted her? Yet she did. And her childhood could've been worse; she hadn't experienced abuse or unkindness at the hands of the nuns. No love exactly, but regulated care by industrious, well-intentioned women in white, prayers and saint days. She hadn't rebelled against her fate, too reserved and fearful of repercussions, mostly of a divine nature.

As she drove through one increasingly remote glen after another, her go-to reaction was still fear.

Fear was something she understood ever since she left the safety of the orphanage's walls, armed with a small, mostly empty, suitcase, a little money and a letter of recommendation. There hadn't been many opportunities for a sixteen-year-old girl with only GCSEs, so she took a job as a live-in carer for an old lady. On the peripheries of the old lady's family, it had sunk in what family meant. The casual intimacy through long familiarity, the easy acceptance, the reliable support, the inside jokes that weren't funny to anyone else, a sense of belonging, of being rooted in something bigger than herself, and mostly unconditional love.

Though she had been desperate for the anchor of kinship through blood, fear had prevented Edie from forming attachments. For who would want a girl who came with nothing, unmoored and alone?

Until Joshua.

She had been drawn to his warmth, his humor, his devil-may-care attitude, his confidence in himself. And for the first time in her life Edie hadn't feared, not with Josh at her side, her safety net. Josh had been her undoing. Fear had not prepared her for the ringing of the doorbell, the solemn faces of the two police officers, their hollow words that Josh was dead, dead, dead.

She would never surrender her fear again.

Blaming hormones and tiredness and the fact that her arse was wedge shaped from sitting in the car too long, she dreaded Neve's eye roll if she saw Edie crying. Breathing deeply to relieve the tightness in her chest, she focused on the serpentine road wending up yet another pass littered with tumbles of granite boulders like a giant child's playground. She had every intention of stopping at the next sign of human habitation for the night.

"I think we're on the wrong road," said Neve, peering over the dashboard as far as the constraints of her seat belt allowed.

"Story of my life," muttered Edie, readjusting her grip on the steering wheel. She ignored her daughter's snort of disdain.

"And we haven't had signal since we left Lochinver," Neve added, looking at her mobile where the blue dot on the GPS had stalled on the outskirts of the little town.

Crowded silence filled the car as Edie concentrated on the road, her heart lurching over each blind rise and sharp switchback, her gaze forced down to another stark glen far below.

Not Neve. Her eyes glittered with excitement; Edie worried it was a sign her daughter would become one of those daredevil sorts who jumped off mountains on the end of a rope, or worse, out of an airplane tied to a piece of fabric.

"We're definitely going the wrong way," said Neve when the road shrank to two strips of tar snaking up another steep, heather-clad pass.

"We have another hour or so of daylight; we should go back to Lochinver. It wasn't that far back," said Edie, thankful for the longer twilight Scotland enjoyed, being so close to the Arctic.

"No, Mum! Don't be such a wet fish. It can't be much further. And there's nowhere you can turn round. I haven't seen one of those *Passing Places* signs for ages."

Crowded silence returned as Edie slowed the car to a crawl. In the fading light, she *felt* the vast remoteness around her, like driving through a land the gods had forgotten.

"This is fucked up," Neve muttered, peering out the window at the sheer drop on her side.

"Neve! Did I just hear what came out of your mouth? How many times do I have to tell you to mind your language?" It was a sad reality of parenthood that once a battle had been picked, she started to sound like a broken record.

"You swear all the time," said Neve, not taking her attention off the tight bend of the next switchback.

"I'm an adult," snapped Edie, "and I never swear in front of you!"

"Then I'll be sure not to swear in front of *you!*" Neve snapped back.

"Wrong answer. You are not to swear at all! You're only fifteen!"

Neve slouched back against her seat, arms crossed and scowling. But in seconds she was upright and watching the road again with that worrying sparkle.

Cursing under her breath, counting to ten, twenty, a hundred, Edie regained her composure, wishing she'd had a child in her twenties to avoid hitting her daughter's adolescence during menopause. The two did not play nicely together, especially in poor light on a road that was no road, and with the creeping conviction they were very lost on a Scottish mountain with no end.

"Holy fu-ahhh— Father Christmas." Neve caught Edie's gimlet eye and herself in the nick of time, as they crested Haggs Pass.

The track meandered between the arms of mountains folding away into the haze of distance, washed blue by the deepening twilight. At the far end of the glen lights of a small village twinkled beside a long loch, its waters black with the approach of night, dotted with islands. Beyond that the sea rolled steadily over the curvature of the earth. And on one of the islands rose— "Our castle!" cried Neve, grabbing Edie's arm excitedly. "I can see our castle!"

October 1965

"**Y**ou'd best be about yourself and find the wee man," said Mrs. Macleod when Lottie walked into the castle's vast kitchen.

Lottie snapped out of her daydream. "Why? What's Mungo done this time?"

"Not a thing, bless him. The doctor's here."

Lottie's face fell. "Again? But he was here only a couple of days ago."

"Aye, so he was. But it isnae for the likes of us to wonder at the goings on above." Mrs. Macleod was a well-nourished woman with a blaze of red hair tied in a messy bun under the stupid cap Lottie's grandmother insisted the housekeeper wore. She nodded at the ceiling, lips tight with disapproval, then picked up a fearsome knife and took out her uncharacteristic anger on a pile of harmless carrots. "Now be off, lass, and find the wee man afore herself upstairs has something to say about it."

The kitchen was a sprawl of tables and ovens. The walls were lined with dressers and doors leading to the cellars, the buttery, and bakery. A pile of turnips sat on a table at the far end; Mungo must've been here

19

earlier, for some of the turnips had been badly carved with faces in preparation for Samhain at the end of the month. Mungo loved Samhain.

Samhain was celebrated differently upstairs, following the traditions of Halloween her American grandmother insisted on: carved pumpkins, the halls decorated with fake skeletons, and the recording of a terrible witch's laugh that always frightened Lottie when she entered the Baronial Hall. But downstairs Mrs. Macleod ruled, and the older, darker Samhain was followed with turnips and apple dooking and guising and—

"Be about yourself, lass!" said Mrs. Macleod again.

"But—"

"Nae buts! You ken what'll happen if herself upstairs finds you here and not searching for the wee man."

Lottie sighed and did as she was told, thinking she would be searching for Mungo even in death, for it was all she seemed to do. Stepping out into the walled garden the kitchen faced on to, she sighed again. Her parents sat in the orchard where the old apple trees grew like petrified goblins.

Were other families as complicated as hers? she wondered. Jasper and Vida Maundrell sat on facing benches; two black Labradors lay at their feet. Her parents were stiff and distant, neither looking at the other, the shadow of Mungo's mother between them.

Lottie knew all about Uncle Theodore's scandalous marriage to the housekeeper's daughter, Greer Macleod, eloping to Gretna Green, then Theodore going off to war and getting himself killed and leaving Greer pregnant with Mungo. It was an open secret her father had been in love with Greer too, and her mother could not compete with the remembered perfection of a dead woman.

The ill-fated marriage had been short, but its effects were still felt twenty years later and complicated the already-complicated relationships of her family. There was Mrs. Macleod the housekeeper, who was Mungo's grandmother, but also loosely related to Lottie through Greer Macleod's marriage to Uncle Theodore. There was "herself upstairs," Lady Elizabeth Maundrell, or Bitsie to those who were in favor. Bitsie was the matriarch of the Maundrell family who also happened to be both Mungo's and Lottie's grandmother.

Families were too complicated, Lottie decided. She avoided her parents, quietly stepping through the arched gate leading to the Nine Hags, a circle of nine misshappen stones. She knew she was supposed to love everyone in her family equally, but some were harder to love than others. If pressed to decide whom she loved most the answer would come easily: Mungo.

She passed Mr. Macleod, groundskeeper, and husband to Mrs. Macleod and as equally distantly related to Lottie.

"Keep going, lass," he muttered. "I saw the wee man head into the grotto not a half hour back to have his chatter with the Witch. He could still be there."

Lottie smiled vaguely, not surprised he knew she was looking for Mungo, and wandered down to the rose gardens. She dawdled amidst the late roses, their fragrance clinging to the last of the year's heat. She loved Mr. and Mrs. Macleod most next she decided, although there was her brother Percy. But no, she definitely loved Mr. and Mrs. Macleod more. She didn't know this new Percy who had come back from school. This was a cool Percy, not the fun Percy she remembered as a child. School had changed him.

She wished she had gone to school too, instead of having a tutor. It was a wistful dream; the island was her prison as much as it was Mungo's. She had not set foot on the mainland since she arrived ten years ago.

The problem, Lottie decided, as she bowed to smell a blown rose, was the island had too much history. It was everywhere; the castle, of course, hunched in the center like a gray, tooth-edged beast. There were ruins aplenty, from the old foundations of St. Columba's monastery to the Viking longhouses near the Nine Hags. There were no fewer than four graveyards from different eras and occupiers of the island. And that was no small thing considering the island was little over a hundred acres.

Stop daydreaming, Charlotte! *Lottie rebuked herself in the stern, exasperated tones of her grandmother, and forced herself to head towards the grotto.*

She paused on the path, hoping to hear Myrtle Bruce weeping. The ghostly bride who, according to Mrs. Macleod who had it on good authority from her great-grandmother who'd been a tweeny maid at the castle then, had been the loveliest of brides soon to wed Edward Maundrell. But Edward had had a duplicitous heart, and on the eve of their nuptials Myrtle had discovered he longed for another. In her despair she had wept into the well. The Witch heard her sorrow and the two made a pact. But the Witch was as faithless as Edward Maundrell, and on their wedding day, which had also been Samhain, the Witch had struck and the newlyweds hadn't made it out of the chapel. All that had remained of Myrtle and Edward were desiccated husks, their shrunken arms out-stretched towards the chapel doors, desperate in death to moisten their withered frames in the cool Scottish mist.

To this day, stories persisted of Myrtle heard weeping in the grotto. But the only time Lottie had heard any weeping was when she had seen her aunt Alice come out of the grotto, eyes red and sniffling.

The grotto was a grotesque neo-Gothic structure, like an igloo made of newly hardened, prickly lava, all cracks and crinkles, with three arched entrances. It had been built by the Victorian Maundrells, who'd outdone themselves with the formal rose gardens, then failed miserably with the grotto.

Lottie told herself she hated the grotto for its unlovely aesthetics, but truly she feared it. She almost believed she could see shadows seeping from the arched openings like a noxious vapor.

It was not surprising the island was called the Place of Shadows, for they moved oddly here, slithering and skittish. Sometimes they felt protective, sometimes curious, but on Samhain they felt predatory.

The shadows were a taboo subject. Everyone knew about them, had seen them, had felt their creeping touch, but never spoke of them aloud. Lottie was undecided about the shadows. Some said they were the Witch's pets; others said they were the souls of the departed; others yet said they were a curse inflicted on the island centuries ago. Lottie knew a lot about curses.

She held her breath as she stepped into the grotto. The walls had a circular ledge for seating with a few scattered cushions. It wasn't larger than an average sized room, yet it retained the echoing quiet of a cathedral. In the center, between two carved Pict stones, was the spring surrounded by a low wall that everyone called the well, but no one dared drink from it.

Unlike the grotto, the well felt old. It squatted like a poisonous spider in the unnatural gloom. Acid-green algae and lime-pale lichen grew over its low, pitted walls as though leprous.

Her courage firmly in hand, Lottie released her held breath before she passed out and stood directly in front of the well. The water was black and deep, many said bottomless, with the chill of a crypt and an odd haze hugging the surface. From it had sprung a web of legend and myth. Trembling from cold and fear, she forced herself to peer into the dark water where the Cailleach, known locally as the Witch in the Well, slept in the summer, only rising on Samhain to bring snow, ice and misery to the world.

Mungo wouldn't have lingered here. Ever since Mrs. Macleod told them of the Witch when they were small, Mungo came to say hello every morning before going on his way. Now he could be anywhere on the island.

Still Lottie lingered, hoping to catch a ripple of the surface to give some indication the Witch was more than superstition. But not so much as a feathered wrinkle disturbed the water, and she was uncommonly disappointed by this.

Her gaze traveled to the Pict stones. According to Mrs. Macleod they were curse stones, though she had been hazy when questioned who they cursed and why. Taller than Lottie, they were cut from pale stone not found on the island, their edges uneven, nibbled by time. Etched deep into the stones were pictograms no one could decipher, a confusion of circles within circles, lines going nowhere, something that might represent a snake, waves, and possibly a cross.

The shadows crept around Lottie like malicious whispers, taunting, teasing. She stared at the pictograms until her eyes watered. Had they shivered and changed shape?

Her bravery seeped away and she ran out of the grotto. Shadows scuttled after her before dissolving in the sunlight.

Breathless, though she hadn't run far, Lottie slowed and walked down to the boathouse to give Mungo more time.

Loch na Scáthanna sprawled before her, its waters a brooding red, deepening to burgundy in places where the gentle breeze brushed against its surface, then sharpened to cerise in shallower water. The heathered slopes of the Munros slid into the loch to meet their purple reflection so Lottie could not distinguish where the mountains ended and the loch began. On a clear day like today, she could see the blue shimmer of the Minch beyond the loch, a reminder that another world existed out there. She had spent hours watching the ever-changing colors of Loch na Scáthanna, a name given by the Blood Druids—Irish druids once feared and revered throughout the Celtic world two thousand years ago.

Mungo often came down to the boathouse to watch the water eddy around its stilts. It could occupy his attention for hours if the mood took him. But Mungo was not in the boathouse.

Lottie started back up the path, walking slowly but quick enough it appeared she was doing what she was told. The path leveled out along the cliffs before descending to the only serviceable beach on the island. The pebbles dug through her shoes as she crossed to the base of the cliffs to another of Mungo's secret places. The honeycomb of shallow caves echoed hollowly though there were no waves to create a sound—unless Mungo was here and bellowing as loudly as he could.

She loitered on the beach, throwing pebbles into the loch, stippling the smooth surface with long streaks of flying droplets. As she so often did, Lottie pictured the Roman fleet legend claimed had sunk in the loch, a claim verified in a few old documents discovered years ago. It was said the ghostly fleet was cursed to sail the loch for all eternity, though Lottie had never seen it.

Ghosts abounded on the island, and Lottie believed in them all. She knew all the stories and where they had been sighted. She was ever hopeful of seeing blood dripping over the edge of the cliffs from the Haggs Massacre that, according to Mrs. Macleod—the font of all the island's lore—had turned the waters of Loch na Scáthanna red. Her gaze rose to the ruined watchtower where a ghostly Highlander had often been spied. To her eternal disappointment, she saw not so much as a peculiar glimmer.

She returned to the cliff path and dawdled in the rose gardens as long as she dared, then cursed silently when Aunt Alice tripped down a path and sat on a bench. She lifted her face to the sun like they were sharing a secret, before bending over her notebook to write.

Alice was a thin woman, all bones and freckles, her face pinched in perpetual worry. Not surprising for someone who lived in the shadow of her formidable mother, Lady Elizabeth. Truly Alice was a mouse of a woman. A sneaky mouse, thought Lottie, then chided herself for her unkindness.

She slipped behind a rosebush, knowing Alice would report back to Bitsie if she saw Lottie loitering when she should've been searching for Mungo. Everyone reported back to Bitsie. And if it wasn't something Alice wanted her mother to know, it would be written in her diary. Alice, though quiet as a sneaky mouse, was observant and saw everything that went on in the castle.

Lottie sidled backwards until she hit a path that led away from her aunt. On tiptoe, heart in her throat, she darted past the Italian fountain where a heroic Hercules wrestled the Hydra, from whose many serpentine mouths water squirted onto the lily pads below. Below the lilies, coins glimmered for wishes never granted.

Once on the lawn, Lottie sped past the dead. The Maundrells' grave-yard overlooked the loch beside the family chapel, where the ghost of Myrtle Bruce had frequently been sighted, wearing her wedding day finery that became her funeral finery. Lottie liked reading the epitaphs to Mungo; the Maundrells had the odd tradition of writing their own, usually humorous, epitaph. She had never understood this peculiar need to laugh at death, especially her family who had mostly been blessed with no sense of humor at all.

Just beyond were the Viking cairns, their rounded grassy slopes like huge green slugs in the sunshine. Bitsie had once commissioned an archae-ological expedition to open a couple of the cairns. It had been so exciting. For months, Lottie and Mungo had watched as the chambered tombs slowly revealed their buried secrets. It had all been going swimmingly until one of the entrances collapsed and Mungo was heard screaming within. To this day no one knew how he managed to trap himself inside. Their grandfather had still been alive then and sent the archaeologists packing, much to Bitsie's fury that had shrouded the island for days.

Lottie shivered, the air chilling like a cloud had passed over the island though the sky was clear. She turned, sensing she was being watched. No one was there, but she was sure the shadows had scuttled away out the corner of her eye. She scurried on quickly.

"Oh!" she gasped as she entered the laburnum arch that meandered through the wild garden beyond the cairns. She backed out, hoping her exclamation hadn't been heard.

"It's all right, Lottie; it's only us," called Percy. He and his school friend, Ashley Templeton, sat on one of the benches lining the tunnel.

Red-faced, she re-entered.

Lottie had spent many hours poring over the magazines she had nicked from her grandmother, who had them posted at great expense from London. She was always careful to take the ones a few months old to avoid notice of their disappearance. At night, by torchlight under the bedcovers, she drank in pictures of Elizabeth Taylor, whom she considered the most beautiful woman in the world. She longed for the flawless perfection of Sophia Loren, wishing she hadn't been cursed with what her mother called a pleasant face of pale skin covered in freckles and mousy hair. Lottie hated her freckles.

But mostly she admired the men, beautiful men unlike any who came into her world. Until recently. She had been astonished when Percy arrived home, metamorphosed from the gangly blond boy she remembered to a striking adult. And he had brought home his impossibly handsome friend. Now they *looked like movie stars. But where Percy had the blond, blue-eyed intensity of Peter O'Toole, Ashley had the dark, brooding menace of Sean Connery . . .* Well, maybe not menace, *Lottie conceded to her hapless infatuation, but he had Connery's beauty, and that ridged dimpling smile.*

Ashley was smiling at Lottie now, causing her heart to pulse in a highly irregular fashion that sent a deep flush to her freckled face.

She was distracted from her embarrassment by the tin soldier Ashley was turning over between two fingers like a nervous tic. "That's Mungo's," she said in surprise.

Ashley nodded. "He gave it to me."

"Oh. He must really like you."

Ashley smiled and Lottie's heart exploded with happiness. She stared at him gormlessly, then flushed again when Percy raised an amused eyebrow.

Mustering her last shreds of dignity, she squeaked, "I need to find Mungo," and scuttled down the laburnum arch.

She overheard Percy say, "I think you have another admirer," and died a little inside. The magazines had not told her how to deal with love, or boys, especially boys her brother brought home from school who looked like gods. How was she supposed to act around them, or indeed speak to them at all?

"She's a sweet kid," Ashley drawled.

Kid? Kid! Lottie's heart shriveled in embarrassment. She was fifteen! Hardly a kid! She was . . . well, she was—

"Charlotte! Dear God! Look where you're going, you stupid girl!"

Hands gripped Lottie's shoulders, long nails digging in.

Lottie swallowed her gasp and looked up at Lady Elizabeth Maundrell. She was only Bitsie in the privacy of Lottie's head, and lived in a constant state of mild terror of the woman. "Sorry, Grandmother, I—"

"You were not looking where you were going as usual." Bitsie released Lottie and shook her hands as though she had picked up something unpleasant from the contact.

Bitsie, at sixty, was as beautiful and cold as a Venetian mask. A sterile beauty, all clean, straight lines, tall, with a perfect angular figure she maintained by eating as little as a hummingbird, and blond hair cut in a severe shingle bob. Always exquisitely dressed, she wore the emerald chiffon and taffeta outfit that brought out the green of her eyes. She hadn't seemed to have aged from the photos Lottie had seen of Bitsie with famous people when she had been the sought-after American heiress doing a five-year European tour, the darling of the press and every man with a title and no fortune of his own. That had all changed with the end of the war. But Bitsie's change in circumstances was never discussed within her hearing.

Lottie's eyes were drawn to the broach pinned to Bitsie's breast.

The Maundrell Red. The rarest of diamonds, a Fancy Red, and the largest at 5.1 carats. Shaped like a drop of blood, it was a thing of beauty nature seldom revealed, crafted by human hands into an object so extraordinary it took Lottie's breath away. Yet she feared it too. The diamond was cursed, haunting the Maundrells with tragedy ever since one of Lottie's ancestors had dug it out of the dry African earth.

Bitsie followed Lottie's gaze. Her fingers fluttered to the stone, an unconscious caress, as though she feared it had fallen off.

Reading Lottie's mind, she said, "I do not fear the curse." Her American accent was sharp and crisp, not even slightly modulated though she'd lived in Scotland for the latter half of her life.

"I wish you would," said Lottie meekly. "I don't want anything horrible to happen to any of us . . . or you," she added as an afterthought. Her caution was pointless.

Bitsie's fascination with the Maundrell Red was powerful; a talisman, admired and coveted, lovely and deadly. Lottie had observed her in quiet moments, staring into its crimson depths, stroking its cold facets with far more affection than she'd ever shown to her family. Lottie was quite certain her grandmother would kill for it.

But as much as Bitsie was obsessed with the stone, she was not above using it for control. She had been planning her death for years and used the diamond as leverage, hinting who she might leave it to, to gain some advantage over whomever was opposing her will at the time. She didn't only do it to the family, of course; there was the doctor . . .

"Where is Mungo?" she demanded. "I sent word you were to find him over an hour ago. There's no need to keep the doctor waiting without purpose."

Lottie held back her scowl; Bitsie would've kept the doctor waiting for as long as she liked if the purpose had suited her. *"I have been looking for him," she only half lied. "I'm still looking in all his usual places. I was about to go into the woods."*

Bitsie wasn't listening. She glared over Lottie's shoulder, face pinched with fury.

Her stomach rippling with disquiet, Lottie turned to see Percy and Ashley pull away from each other. In those few moments of unbridled observation, her small world unraveled into confusion. Love was there in the brushing of hands, in darting glances, in soft smiles neither could wipe. She understood instinctively this love was secret, taboo.

Bitsie's eyes deepened to emerald hardness. "I will destroy them!" she hissed. "It is a crime! I shall not allow them to bring that sort of sordid shame to our family."

Lottie's terror of her grandmother ratcheted up to painful dread in her chest. Percy's secret was currency, leverage to maintain control over him. The last time she had seen Bitsie so angry was when Mungo stole the Maundrell Red two years ago and hid it for more than a week before Lottie persuaded him to return it to their grandmother.

"Please don't hurt them," she whispered.

The full force of Bitsie's attention reverted to Lottie. "I will deal with your disgusting brother as I see fit. And his . . . friend." She spat the word like a curse.

"But you *invited* Ashley here," said Lottie. She sucked in a breath of horror, her confusion untangling. "You knew. You knew, that's why . . . What are you going to do, Grandmother?"

"If you breathe a word of what you saw," Bitsie hissed, gripping Lottie's arm, "I will destroy everything you love!"

She released Lottie when they heard Vida Maundrell calling for Mungo. Smoothing down her chiffon dress, she said, "Go help your mother find the idiot. And don't forget our agreement, Charlotte. You know what will happen to him if you do."

CHAPTER 3

A humming stillness hung over the island, a tight, breath-sucking, expectant atmosphere. Edie's skin crawled as she stepped out of the car, certain if she turned around quickly and suddenly she would come face-to-face with the numen of this place.

"This is well creepy," said Neve with a delighted shiver.

Edie nodded. She rubbed her arms fiercely; it was far colder than it had been in Edinburgh.

In the blue twilight, the castle menaced. Three stories high, its granite walls were softened by ten rounded towers, positioned in a symmetrical square. It was a solid, no-nonsense building. Not a frill or molding enhanced the stark walls.

The island was bigger than it had appeared from the mainland, the castle taking center stage. From it stretched acres of ankle-high grass that still received the occasional mow. Beyond that nature had reclaimed the formal gardens, a creeping wilderness to the edges of the island. A small, shadowed wood of stunted oaks, like something out of an Arthur Rackham illustration, climbed a tiny mound of tossed boulders near the humped bridge they had recently crossed.

There were other buildings, a row of small cottages near the wood, a walled garden abutting one side of the castle, a chapel in the distance, an old watchtower teetering on the edge of the cliffs, and a few grassy mounds that hadn't formed naturally.

The loch stretched out long, still and dark, wedged between steep mountains like protective arms all the way to the sea at the far end.

Edie turned in a slow circle, unable to believe she *owned* all of this.

"I bet those are all Munros," said Neve. She, too, was turning circles, spinning in her excitement.

Edie waited for an explanation. When none came, she asked, "What's a Munro?"

"I read about them on the way up here. The Scots call mountains Munros if they're over three thousand feet."

"And this is a thing because?"

Neve shrugged. "It's a Scottish thing, and I'll bet they all have cool names like Crookshanks or Skiddadoo or something. We have to climb them."

"You're on your own there, kiddo. My climbing days are long over."

"Yes, I can tell."

"Neve! Why are you being so bitchy today? That was bloody rude and hurtful." Edie glared at her daughter, still unsure how to handle this new streak of nonchalant cruelty. In the hope it was due to grief or adolescence, she tried to ignore it, but she was reaching her limit. "Wait until you hit menopause," she muttered. "Then we'll have another chat about weight gain."

"Sorry," said Neve, not terribly contrite, and took off through the long grass, laughing like a small child.

"Don't get too close to the edge!" cried Edie, hurrying after her.

"Stop worrying, Mum!" Neve went right to the very edge of the cliff and stared down into the water. "It's a weird color. Like red wine."

"A very dark red wine," said Edie, panting slightly as she caught up, resisting the urge to snatch her daughter away from the edge. "Like a Shiraz."

"You would know. You chug enough of the stuff."

Edie counted silently to ten, before she could respond with, "One of the delicious hazards of living in Italy for three years."

Neve redeemed herself by hugging Edie, crying, "I can't believe we have our very own castle!"

Quite breathless by her daughter's mood swings, Edie relished the hug. They were so rare these days.

Neve looked over Edie's shoulder, seemingly content to remain in her mother's embrace, and said, "I hope there's lots of ghosts. An old place like this is bound to have loads."

Edie raised her eyebrows. "You might not like what you're wishing for if you met one."

"Ahem!"

Edie and Neve startled. They turned to the man standing a few meters away. He was in his sixties or seventies, it was hard to tell with all the facial hair, from which peered two small blue eyes, the nose of a drinker, but no mouth Edie could see, yet he was talking.

"Thir's a muckle o' ghaisties an' ghoulies roamin' th'halls." He glared at the castle and shivered like he'd walked over his own grave. Clearing his throat, he said, "Ye'll be th'noo wans, nae doot. L'wyer fella phoned t'say ye'll b'heidin' oop oor wy."

Edie and Neve stared at him blankly.

He snorted and jangled a set of keys at them. "Ye'll b'wantin' th'kys."

"Who are you?" demanded Edie.

"F'rrgis M'Knzee. Grindskepper."

"Right," said Edie, throwing a warning glance at Neve, who had caught a fit of the giggles.

"Yer kys." He jangled the keys vigorously at Edie again. "Ye'll b'wantin' thim fo' th'cassel."

Fascinated by the old man and his delightful incomprehensibility, she accepted the keys with an uncertain, "Thank you."

"If yer needin' summat, Am tha'wy tae th'wee c'ttage. Firs' on th'lift." Mr. MacKenzie's jaw worked, fluffing up his beard. He muttered something, quick and garbled, that sounded like "b'weir th'de'il an' th'hag" and stomped off across the lawn.

"Not one word," said Edie as Neve stifled her giggles. She was relieved to see someone else was on the island. It was sinking in how very remote and very alone they were here in the back of beyond.

Grabbing their jackets and overnight bag meant for a one-night stay in Edinburgh, they walked towards the castle.

Neve waved her mobile about, then scowled when she looked at the screen. "No signal."

"How will you survive?" said Edie dryly.

"I will," said Neve. She switched on the mobile's torch now twilight had darkened to deep purple. "I'm starving," she said as they passed through a vast gatehouse into an overgrown grass quadrangle in the middle of the castle, with ivy infesting the walls.

"You'll have to survive on Mars bars tonight. I saw a small shop in the village we drove through. We'll stock up tomorrow."

They found a door that matched a key and stepped into a vast, stale darkness.

Edie sucked in her breath. An unexpected spike of chilly air probed her skin like fishhooks, far colder inside than out, and curiously dry.

"Doesn't feel very friendly, does it?" said Neve, stepping closer to her mother.

"No." Edie didn't consider herself particularly fanciful, but her first impression was the old building resented their intrusion.

She felt along the wall, hoping the Maundrells had put in electricity, with the added doubtful hope it hadn't been cut off. Her questing fingers found a light switch. It was one of the old sort, bronze and round with a little lever.

She hesitated before flicking it; if no one had lived here for decades the wiring would be old and probably eaten by rats. On the other hand, she had no desire to knock about a creepy castle in the dark.

Biting her lip, she sent up a general prayer to random saints not to electrocute herself, and flicked the switch, hurriedly removing her finger. A worrying buzz came from the walls before a yellow glow spread geriatrically from the four chandeliers.

They absorbed the sheer size of the Baronial Hall in silence. Displays of archaic swords and muskets fanned out across the paneled walls beneath a vaulted ceiling. There wasn't much else except a throne-like chair on one end, facing a great hearth with an ornate mantelpiece.

"What's all this?" said Neve, moving to a table beside the door covered in piles of pamphlets. She picked a couple up and frowned. "They're tourist brochures. I thought this place hadn't been occupied for ages."

"So did I. Let's see what the vampire has to tell us." Edie opened the folder she'd been gripping tightly and scanned through the reams of tightly printed information. "So not completely unoccupied," she said. "In the last ten years some effort was made to rent the place out. It's been a hotel . . . Oh. No. It was meant to be a hotel, but the people left after a year . . . Then someone else rented it six years ago with the idea of turning it into a museum." She nodded at the brochure table. "That's what those must be for. That crowd didn't last longer than a year either."

"Why?"

"It doesn't say."

Neve, like a visiting tourist, picked up brochures and booklets.

Edie regarded her with mild surprise. "What are you doing?"

"It's free stuff. I'm taking it."

"But it's ours anyway."

Uncaring, Neve shoved the tight wad of brochures into the back pocket of her jeans.

Edie shook her head; her daughter's moral compass seemed

worryingly pointed in the wrong direction. "Right," she said firmly. "Time to find a couple of beds. There'll be plenty of time for exploring tomorrow."

Four doors opened off the hall. After a quick look, they picked the one leading to a stone spiral staircase, its treads worn into grooves by countless footsteps over the centuries.

"You can hear that, right?" whispered Neve as they wound their way up the corkscrew stairs, a faint click-clacking matching their footsteps.

"Like someone's following us?"

"Yeah." Neve peered down the black pit of the stairwell. "I hope we haven't woken up something nasty. This place doesn't look like it's got friendly ghosts like Casper."

"Oh, stop it!" said Edie as they came out onto a hall running the length of the castle.

"This is unexpected," said Neve after finding a switch that lit up a design unlike the Baronial Hall in every possible way.

An art deco geometric pattern ran the length of the walls and ceiling, garishly yellow and green with matching light fittings and enormous vases positioned between arched, stained-glass windows. It hurt Edie's eyes, like stepping into a mathematical equation.

One hallway bled into another, each a different color scheme, without finding a single bedroom after poking their heads through doorways. Signs of the museum that never happened were in the arrows on the walls and names above lintels proclaiming the Blue Room, the Grey Lady's Room, the Japanese Room and Lady Elizabeth's Room. Each was filled with cabinets of letters, photographs and write-ups tacked on freestanding boards for the tourists who never came.

Smothering dust hung in the air, adding to the neglect permeating the castle, crumbling gently in the uninhabited lonely hours. Yet Edie sensed it had not been a quiet dormancy. With each room they entered, her unease grew that something watched them from the shadows, peeped out from under dust sheets, and listened from the walls.

Neve had dropped ghosts into Edie's head. While she was almost certain she didn't believe in them there was no need to scare herself unnecessarily, and she switched off the lights as they left each room, not wanting to come back by herself to do so later.

Another floor, another mathematical equation in blues and reds.

"A bedroom!" cried Neve thankfully.

White with splashes of pink and uninspired paintings, it held all the impersonality of a hotel room and the broken dreams of the previous occupants. For this Edie was grateful. She hadn't relished the idea of motheaten four poster beds surrounded by moldy curtains where her recently acquired ancestors had lived and died.

Neve darted through a door leading off it. "And it has a bathroom! This is my room as it's pink."

Edie stood in the doorway and said, "You're sure you don't want to stay with me tonight?"

"Why?"

"It's a big, scary castle."

Neve rolled her eyes. "I'm fifteen! Stop treating me like a baby." And she closed the bedroom door in Edie's face.

Edie rested her forehead against the door. She sometimes thought the hardest trial of motherhood was learning to let go and accepting her little girl was forging ahead into her own story of which Edie was only a side character.

Opening the next door along, she found another en suite room in white and green.

She tiredly took off her shoes and padded across unblemished carpets to the bathroom. Deciding to brave a cold shower in the morning, she brushed her teeth, got into her pajamas, climbed into bed and switched off the light.

Leaning back against the pristine pillows, Edie burst into tears. She reached across the bed where Joshua would've lain. Grief had no constancy with the distance of time, but the long, empty hours beyond midnight were always the worst. A survivor of another apocalyptic day, she felt isolated in the vast darkness, disconnected from humanity in the loneliness of her own thoughts.

Determined not to think of the emptiness beside her, she listened to the unfamiliar building. For a place abandoned for decades, it was alarmingly noisy. Creaks and scurries in the corners of the room, a click-clacking hissed under the door, the curtains shivered as though someone hid behind them releasing quiet breaths, a disembodied cry of a distant nocturnal waterbird on the loch.

Night sweats beat sleep. Cursing menopause, she kicked the duvet off, still unused to her body heating up without warning or outside influence. Lying in a puddle of instant sweat, she wondered what she was supposed to do with a castle. It wasn't a practical home for two women to live in alone. Too big, too expensive, too remote. The only alternative was to sell it as her newly discovered, albeit dead, relative, Percy Maundrell, had suggested—no, strongly encouraged.

Why had he written to her at all? Why encourage her to sell? There had been hatred in his letter. Hatred for this place. Something was wrong with this whole situation; an out-of-the-blue inheritance just didn't happen. It had been her experience when something appeared too good to be true it usually was.

Cold again, Edie wrapped the duvet over herself and considered her birth dispassionately. The vampire seemed to think she had been born in the castle, so she was in the right place to do some digging. She could talk to Mr. MacKenzie, and maybe the people in the village. In a small, secluded place like this, someone was always watching and might know something.

There could be paperwork somewhere, though she doubted it. She had been left on the steps of the orphanage, a foundling without a name, wrapped in nothing but a blanket. As she had so many times before, she pictured the cold street outside the orphanage and a woman hurrying away, head bowed and covered in a disguising cloak, her retreating footsteps an echo in the night. A clandestine abandonment didn't leave a paper trail.

As she grew heavy with the weight of exhaustion and spent emotion, the cold air susurrated around her, fading then swelling, a whispered lullaby of *flofloflofloflo*. A tepid coolness brushed against her skin, exploring the contours of her face. She sensed an edge of desperation in the whispers, a yearning, an echo of dreams. It felt like only seconds had passed when her eyes snapped open to find Neve leaning over her, shaking her shoulder frantically.

"I've seen a ghost! Wake up, Mum! I've seen a ghost!"

"Ha-ha," muttered Edie, and glanced at her watch. "It's three a.m.! Go back to bed. I'd only just fallen asleep."

"Mum! I'm not joking! I walked right through her. I heard this noise, like scratching at the door. So I went to open it, thinking it was you . . . And I walked right through her!" Neve leapt into the bed and clung to Edie like a child waking from a nightmare.

"Through who?" said Edie drowsily, breathing in the scent of Neve's hair, relishing the close contact her daughter had been at pains to limit these past couple of years, knowing it would end when Neve remembered she hated her mum, and reverted back into the sullen creature she had become. But for these few precious moments Edie dared to hug her daughter tightly.

"This woman, only she wasn't there. I saw her coming down the hall; then she walked through me and floated on as though I wasn't there. It was horrible!"

"Did you feel anything?" Edie asked, curious despite her need for sleep.

Neve paused from burrowing her face in the crook of Edie's shoulder, and drew away, frowning. "No. Not a thing."

"I'm sure it's nothing to worry about. It was only a ghost."

"Only a ghost? Only a ghost! Are you even listening to yourself?"

Mother and daughter stared at each other and burst into hysterical laughter.

"There's more," said Neve. "There are things outside. I saw them on the loch. Boats, Mum. Old boats, like Vikings or something. I saw them from my bedroom window . . . I couldn't sleep," she added to explain still being awake at an ungodly hour.

"Mmmm . . ." said Edie doubtfully. One ghost she could almost swallow as the overactive imagination of a teenager who had had rather a lot of shocks in the past twenty-four hours. Two, not so much.

"Go and see for yourself," said Neve when Edie didn't immediately leap out of bed.

"For Christ's sake," Edie muttered. She levered herself from her sleepy warm nest and glared out the window with her arms crossed. "There's nothing— Oh!"

A sea mist had stolen over the loch with the night and there, riding on the still water, was a fleet of ships shivering in and out of existence, as though woven from cobwebs.

If motherhood had taught Edie one thing it was to hide fear behind a calm mask, though her heart fluttered within her rib cage like a trapped bird. She had never had cause to wonder how she would react if confronted by something supernatural and was rather proud of herself for not grabbing Neve to make a run for the car, screaming hysterically.

Her fear deflated somewhat when, after a few moments, the fleet didn't *do* anything. No ghosts leapt off the ships to create spectral havoc; no fearsome ethereal beasts were unleashed. The fleet rode the still loch and did nothing at all.

"They're not Viking," she said. "I think they're Roman galleys."

"You can see them too?" said Neve, relief loud in her voice.

Edie nodded.

"You're not scared?" Neve eyed her mother with newfound respect.

Edie paused, then shrugged. "No, I suppose not. They're out there and we're in here. Nothing is coming off them, so . . ."

"Oh, I hadn't thought of it like that . . . What about the one I walked through? That scared the crap out of me!"

"That is another story," admitted Edie, not thrilled with the idea of sharing the castle with ghosts.

"Well, I'm not sleeping by myself tonight," said Neve as Edie climbed back into bed and pulled the duvet up to her chin.

"Switch the light on," said Edie after a moment. While she was not as terrified as she thought she would be, light banished shadows and ghosts liked shadows.

Neve complied and the two lay side by side, staring at the ceiling in silence. Neither commented on the click-clacking beyond the closed door, measured, hollow, like claws on marble, pacing the halls with the pent-up menace of a caged lion.

"I wish Dad was here," said Neve after a while.

"So do I."

CHAPTER 4

"Mum! Wake up! You have to see this!"

Edie opened a bleary eye. "What time is it?"

"About six."

"In the morning?" Edie bolted upright. "And you're already up? Are you okay? Do you feel sick?" Then the memory of last night hit her. "Please tell me it's not another ghost."

Neve pulled a face. "I'm fine and no ghosts. Now get up and come look."

Grumbling, Edie hauled herself out of bed and joined Neve at the window. "Holy fuck," she breathed.

Barely disguised by thin, shredded mist, the loch was a treasure trove of reds. There, a ripple of garnet. There, a smudge of jasper. There, a dazzle of ruby. The loch's surface was smooth and still as the skin of a drum, hazily reflecting the surrounding heather-clad mountains.

Blood-drenched dripped into Edie's mind, yet it was a beauty so utterly unique she couldn't tear her eyes away from it.

"Language," said Neve with reproving mockery. "Whatever would the nuns think if they could hear you now?"

"That is not remotely funny."

They stood shoulder to shoulder, captivated by the view before Neve spoilt it by saying, "I'm starving."

"We'll go into the village later when that little shop opens. In the meantime we need to find the kitchen and see what we're working with."

They got dressed in their remaining clean clothes, and hurried through the empty halls, walking close together. Neither commented on the footsteps trailing after them, fading a couple of seconds later than their own.

The kitchen was vast; a necessary size to feed the hundreds of people who had once lived here. Scarred tables ran down the middle; ovens lined the walls; a couple of huge open hearths still had metal rotisseries that could roast an entire cow. A quick exploration of the doors leading from the main kitchen revealed a labyrinth of well-stocked cellars and a butler's pantry with an intriguing little door at its far end that demanded future exploration.

Edie opened one of the old fridges that gave off a loud, comforting hum. "How thoughtful," she said. The shelves were stocked with the basics.

"There's bread," said Neve, peering into a lonely bread bin. "Looks fresh, and there's a toaster, so toast it is." She eyed the pint of milk Edie had taken from the fridge, then the loaf of bread. "I think someone's been living here, *is* living here." She nodded at the milk bottle. "That's only half-full, this is not a full loaf, and there's a couple of dishes in the sink."

"Mr. MacKenzie maybe?" said Edie. Unlike the rest of the castle trapped in a dusty time warp, the kitchen did seem to have been used recently. The Nespresso machine was an instant giveaway.

"No, he said something about a cottage somewhere."

"There's nothing about anyone else living here in the vampire's folder," said Edie. "The only person who is supposed to be on the island is Mr. MacKenzie."

Neve shrugged, but Edie didn't share her lack of concern. She sat down, thoughtful and uneasy. Last night someone had been in the castle and she had been totally oblivious to their presence. Ghosts who hadn't harmed them were one thing; a living, unknown human was quite another. It could be an axe murderer hiding out here in the middle of nowhere. Her first concern was Neve, who for all her adolescent confidence was still only fifteen and vulnerable merely by being a girl.

"What are we going to do with all this space?" said Neve, and crunched on a slice of toast.

"We're not keeping it. We have a life in England, not Scotland. What about school and all your friends? We'll give the castle a bit of an airing, sort out the garden and put it on the market."

"No, Mum! It's *our* castle!"

"A castle needs a lot of money to maintain. Money we don't have. I've been through everything Mr. MacDonald gave us. Not much money comes with the castle and the land. There's barely enough to cover Mr. MacKenzie's wage for a few more years."

Neve bit down on her toast savagely, fleeting expressions crossing her face from anger to a thoughtfulness that worried Edie.

"I'm surprised you want to stay here, considering what we both saw last night," she said gently. "Money aside, you won't want to live in a haunted castle. That's probably why the previous tenants left. A lot of money had been put into their newly fledged businesses. I could see it in our rooms, everything is brand-new, the hotel didn't have a single guest and the people who planned a museum never opened to the public."

Neve opened her mouth, hesitated, and nodded slowly. "It's always irritated me in horror movies when people stay in a house knowing it's haunted. I always thought I would run like hell, yelling for the ghostbusters, but now . . ." She looked around the kitchen with a definite proprietary air. "This is *our* castle. It's a dream come true. Who doesn't want their very own castle? And you did say the ghosts didn't do anything to us; they're scary, but if all they do is roam about and leave us alone, I think I can live with that."

"So far," said Edie, and crunched on her toast to hide her scowl. She didn't share Neve's acceptance of harmless ghosts. Even with pale sunshine peering through the kitchen's windows, the castle pressed down on her unpleasantly. She was unable to squash the fanciful notion that the old building didn't want her here.

Chewing slowly, she watched Neve, who was fiercely thoughtful again. Something was coming, an idea, something outrageous no doubt. She repressed a sigh, hoping she'd have the strength not to cave to Neve's whims as she so often did. She loved her fierce daughter with all her being, but sometimes she was a little afraid of her. Neve had emerged from her womb, fists waving, already fighting the world, armed only with a powerful voice and a contrary nature. She had the power to change the world for the better or totally destroy it. There would be no half measures for Neve, and Edie could imagine her as both hero and villain.

It wasn't two minutes before Neve's face brightened with an occurring idea. "We need to find that diamond."

Edie's jaw dropped. As outlandish went, this was well out in cloud cuckoo land. "The one that's been lost for decades?"

Neve nodded enthusiastically.

"Don't be ridiculous. I am not going on a pointless treasure hunt while we're here. And even if I were so inclined, what makes you think we'll find it when others haven't? I'm pretty sure this place has been thoroughly scoured."

"But we're here now, and we can go wherever we like. Last night I saw the museum had an exhibit about the Maundrell Red. I could start there; it might tell me what has been searched and we can try everywhere else."

Fifteen years of experience told Edie the beginnings of an obsession were percolating from the obstinate gleam in Neve's eyes. But perhaps this was one obsession that could work to her advantage. "I tell you what, you look for the diamond and I'll get a start on giving this place a good cleaning."

"And if I find it we stay?"

"We'll see."

"Whenever you say 'we'll see' it means 'no,'" Neve grumped.

"No, it doesn't. If you do find it we will definitely weigh up our options, okay?"

"Fine," muttered Neve sullenly.

No one was about when the Nunns drove across the humped bridge to the village, but curious eyes watched from behind twitching curtains. Edie considered driving straight through and over Haggs Pass, back to sanity and civilization.

Her fleeting indecision was quelled by Neve's narrowed, knowing gaze, and she pulled up in front of the little shop. Neve sat in the car, fuming that she was old enough to stay at the castle by herself, but Edie had no intention of leaving her alone with the possibility of an axe murderer lurking about.

The moment they returned, Neve leapt out of the car and ran across the lawn. Edie followed slowly and surveyed her little kingdom with a sinking heart. She had set herself a mammoth project that couldn't be done in a week. It needed an army of gardeners, carpenters and cleaners and probably electricians and plumbers, as she was certain the wiring and plumbing had not been updated since originally installed.

Neve appeared from nowhere, her earlier fume replaced by the excitement of exploration. "There's a stone circle, Mum! We have our own stone circle!"

"God, I hope we don't get any druids coming up here."

"Druids? Like those tie-dye freaks who dance around Stonehenge in the noddy?"

Edie bit her lip to hide her smile. "Where do you come up with these ideas?" she wondered aloud. "And I doubt modern druids have much in common with the old druids. I think they were more like spiritual leaders."

"Dammit, I would've paid good money to see idiots dancing around in the nod." Then she was off again.

Edie walked down to what had once been formal gardens. Roses scrambled everywhere, a thorny, knotted confusion disguising paths and a rather lovely fountain of Hercules wrestling the Hydra above stagnant water. A few valiant lily pads hid rusted coins.

Just when she was starting to think she would find a sleeping princess somewhere, she stopped and shivered.

The stomach-clenching stillness hung heavily on the air like a soundless cicadas' drone. In the silence she noticed an absence of nature's background noise. No birdsong. Not a fluting blackbird or screeching seagull, the most persistent of birds. No buzz of insects, no secret scuffles and skitters of little creatures amidst the feral roses. There wasn't a single midge Scotland was notorious for. And though the sun shone it was cold, a deceptive cold rising from the ground, seeping deep into Edie's marrow.

Yet the island felt different from the castle, like two worlds inhabiting the same space. With the loch spread out like a vast spill of red wine and the Munros looming stark and sentinel, there was a lingering sadness, a wretchedness that had nothing to do with the neglect of the grounds. The castle, however, from the moment Edie had stepped within its walls, hadn't felt welcoming. It felt oppressive, predatory. She didn't want to use the word *evil*, but that was what circled her mind.

She turned swiftly, sensing she was being watched, but it was only Neve running up to her.

"I found weird little hills over there! One has a little doorway."

Edie followed Neve's pointing finger. "Barrows," she said, eyebrows rising in surprise.

Neve glanced at her questioningly.

"Burial mounds. Maybe Viking or earlier."

"Why?"

"Why what?"

"Why Vikings or stone circles? Why the castle? It's an island in the middle of nowhere. It's not any more special than that island over there." Neve nodded at another island farther in the loch. "What is so special about *this* island that people built castles and stone circles and barrows?"

Edie wasn't surprised; the island had a feel to it, wild, unmoored from reality, an oasis of otherness. It was there in the breeze drifting off the loch soft as moth wings murmuring secrets to a flame, there in the breathing tightness that wrapped around her like cobwebs, there in the unnatural silence that hushed birdsong. It felt like hallowed ground steeped in human tragedy.

"Come on!" cried Neve. She grabbed Edie's hand and dragged her up an entangled path. "We have our own church! And you *must* see the graveyard."

A small family chapel perched on the edge of the cliff beside a graveyard smothered by thick grass and nettles.

Neve darted amongst the graves, yelling, "Listen to this one: *Now I know something you don't*, and, *I'm dead, leave me alone* and *Here I lie and rot, because I was a drunken sot!*" She turned in a circle, hands on hips, nodding in satisfaction. "I'm starting to like these Maundrells . . . It's weird to think all these dead people were related to us."

More than weird, it felt alien. Edie didn't feel like she belonged to these people, this history. Yet she assumed her biological parents must be buried here, the secret of her birth taken to their graves.

Neve stopped in midcircle and frowned. "Who's that?"

Edie looked up from two headstones side by side that read: *Mungo Maundrell. Beloved* and *Charlotte, Elizabeth Maundrell. Together in death as in life.*

She hurried over to Neve, who peered down at a small, pebbled beach. A man crouched at the water's edge.

Swallowing her apprehension, Edie said, "Stay here. I'll go see who it is."

She quickly found the path leading to the beach, then slowed to a tiptoe over the pebbles. A few shallow caves in the cliffs echoed hollowly though the loch was still and silent. Stomach tight with trepidation that she was about to confront the axe murderer who'd been living in the castle, she approached the man cautiously, gripping the car key in her pocket between two fingers as a weapon. She would poke his eye out if he gave so much as a menacing sneeze.

"Hello?" she said, cursing the frightened waver in her voice.

He turned and smiled lazily. "Hey."

They stared at each other until Edie's face grew hot with awkward embarrassment. Clearing her throat, she said, "Who are you?"

He stood up. Edie took a step back, her hand gripping the key sweaty and slick.

His smile widened, creating dimples. "Cameron, your friendly trespasser. You must be the new tenant." His voice was deep, his Scottish accent a gentle roll, and comprehensible. Edie didn't think he was from around here.

Her tension eased, charmed by his accent and scruffy good looks. "Um . . . New owner actually."

His eyebrows rose. "Is that a fact? Must've cost you a pretty penny."

"No, I inherited it."

"Ah." He hunkered down again, picked up a plastic vial lying amidst the pebbles and filled it with water from the loch. He lifted it to eye level, then screwed on the cap.

"Why do you say you're trespassing?" she asked when he said nothing else.

He threw a self-deprecating grin over his shoulder. "I dinnae have permission to be here, and as this is all private land—your land as it turns out—I'm wilfully trespassing."

"But *why* are you trespassing? What are you doing with those little bottles?"

"Testing the water. I'm a microbiologist."

"What's wrong with the water?" Edie eyed the water with concern. It was red, granted, but she hadn't thought it might be diseased—and if water were ever to look diseased this was it.

"Nothing. It's healthy, though I widnae drink it if I were you; it has a high saline content." He looked across the loch where the last tendrils of mist hung stubbornly above its surface. "It's a fascinating place," he said. "The locals believe it's red with the blood of the Macleods after the Haggs Massacre, but it's down to nothing so macabre."

"It isn't?" said Edie cautiously, wanting to ask about the Haggs Massacre. She didn't, not wanting to sound ignorant either.

He stood and faced her. He was a few years older than Edie. Tall, topping six foot by a good two inches, with a mess of brown hair shot through with gray. His eyes fascinated Edie, pale and tawny as a lion. Not for the first time she thought it was unfair men often aged better than women.

"Loch na Scáthanna is salt water, not fresh," he said. "About three hundred years ago the entrance to the Minch silted over and the water had nowhere to go but up." He pointed to the sky. "And because of high evaporation levels, the water became increasingly saline until a certain little halotolerant organism called Dunaliella algae was one of the few things that could live in such a high-saline environment. It's little Dunaliella that turns the water red, as it needs beta-carotene . . . and I lost you somewhere around halotolerant." He grinned at Edie, whose interested expression had slipped into blank incomprehension before halotolerant. "It's an occupational hazard, I'm afraid; I get excited about tiny things."

"No!" said Edie, thankful he couldn't see her blush had spread down her body, setting off a hot flush. "It's very interesting." She knew nothing about algae. Until this moment she'd had zero interest in learning more and now felt like an idiot.

"In layman's terms, algae blooms turn the water red . . . and it's my personal theory the peat found in all Scottish water has given it a darker redness. I've always thought it looked like blood."

"Yes, that was my first thought when I saw the loch." Now she was certain he wasn't an axe murderer, she smiled and held out a hand. "I'm Edwina. Edwina Nunn."

"Not a Maundrell then?"

"No. Well, I am biologically it seems."

His eyebrow quirked like a lazy question mark. "You've an interesting story to tell there."

"I suppose I do." Unable to control her blush under his intense gaze, she babbled a version of the past twenty-four hours, editing out the ghosts.

"What do you do when you're not inheriting castles?"

"Nothing nearly as exciting as microbiology. I'm a personal care aide," she mumbled, embarrassed to admit her occupation.

His interest died instantly. "Guess someone has to do it."

Edie hated herself for feeling ashamed. She liked to think her job was an important one, especially to the people she cared for. It felt good to be needed, and caring had come with a couple of perks. She had been fortunate to care for a severely autistic boy and live in Italy for a few years. It had been one of the highlights of her life, and ever since she had kept her passport up-to-date on the off chance she got a similar opportunity.

"Speaking of castles," she said, steering the conversation away from further embarrassment, "do you know why this one was abandoned? I got some information from the lawyers, but they didn't give specifics."

"Only what I've heard from the locals in Haggs, but they're a close-knit lot and dinnae take too kindly to strangers."

"Did you meet any of the Maundrells?"

He shook his head regretfully. "Sorry. An auld lady still lived here when I first came up, but she widnae speak to me. When she died I asked the estate for permission, but they were quite adamant I wisnae allowed anywhere near the place."

"But you came anyway?"

Cameron grinned with a delightful boyishness. "I'm not very good at doing what I'm told. The auld lady hardly ever came outside; I doubt she even knew I was here. And the hotel crowd and museum fellow didnae care and left within a few months. These past few years I've not seen a soul on the island apart from old Fergus and he disnae come out of his cottage much. He has too deep an appreciation for our fine whisky."

"Why did they leave?" asked Edie. "The hotel and museum people. They put a lot of time and money into their projects. It's crazy to up sticks and leave like that."

"Is it?" His gaze flicked up to the castle, the tops of its rounded towers visible above the cliffs. His cheeks creased into teasing dimples. "So you havnae met them yet? The ghosts?"

Edie's reply never made it past her lips when a terrible scream rent the air. She paled. "That's Neve! The axe murderer's found her!" She took off at a run.

October 1965

"I hate her! I hate her! I hate her!" Lottie raged, stomping away from her grandmother.

She had never understood Bitsie's spite. Her father said she was bitter because she had never had to strive to achieve anything. Lottie disagreed with this nuanced viewpoint after she found gossipy articles in her grandmother's old magazines.

Bitsie, the socialite, heiress to an enormous fortune, and darling of the press, had lost everything after the First World War. It was widely speculated she married Rupert Maundrell for his fortune to recoup her own. A pair as unsuited as Lottie's own parents.

But Bitsie hadn't reckoned on Rupert Maundrell, a man who hated London's false society, and a backbone when he'd been pushed too far. He swept his new bride up to the wild Highlands of Scotland. And the tabloids' snide laughter followed them.

Bitsie, undaunted by her new remote location, decided to bring London to her with a ball to end all balls. A Halloween ball, of course, a *throwback to those hosted by the Blairs in America each year, the biggest social event and tickets coveted by all. The guest list was a veritable who's who of the wealthy and famous.*

The press arrived by the cartload, and that had been Bitsie's final social undoing.

Lottie could imagine the scene now, the castle decorated as garishly as only her grandmother knew how, the gardens snipped and pruned, tables heaving with food all brought up at great expense from London—Bitsie would never have accepted anything from Edinburgh—a champagne fountain with a dash of Angostura to look like flowing blood, and spooky ice sculptures. And Bitsie standing proudly in front of the castle, already in her costume—the same one she always wore—flaunting the infamous Maundrell Red, a wedding gift from Rupert.

How long had it been before Bitsie had realized no one was coming? For not a single car or person crossed the Brig o' Haggs. Not the gossips who frequented even the most boring party in London, not a single one of Bitsie's rivals—and there had been many—not one old suitor or fair-weather friend cared enough to see the backwater Bitsie had been reduced to.

And the press was there to witness and record Bitsie's humiliation, wasting no time getting back down to London to broadcast it. For months afterwards the tabloids chattered of little else.

Bitsie could have escaped witnessing the worst of her disgrace, but she was both sadist and masochist, ensuring every newspaper and magazine was posted to the castle, to be ripped up in weekly fits of rage. The Maundrells never threw anything away, not even scraps—which is perhaps why they clung to their wealth after the First World War when so many, like Bitsie, lost theirs. Lottie had found those ripped up magazines and newspapers, had taped them all together and read them with dark glee.

Bitsie's shame and ostracism from a society she'd adored, coupled with the toll of isolation, twisted her into a bitter creature. Lottie sometimes wondered if her grandmother's obsession with the Maundrell Red was because it was a symbol of the person she had once been, feted and cherished, with the power of a fortune behind her. Her craving for power never abated, reduced but concentrated to a small island that rarely featured on the most detailed maps.

Lottie didn't feel at all sorry for her grandmother as she entered the woods.

It was her favorite place on the island. Sitting on the highest point, it was little more than a tumble of jagged granite rocks cushioned in centuries of moss and lichen, from which grew stunted oak trees so ancient their branches entwined and twisted like a multiarmed single organism.

At fifteen, Lottie told herself, she didn't believe in magic anymore, but there was something magical about the woods. A part of her still expected to spy fairies peeping from under the rocks, or a goblin playing his flute as he leaned against a gnarled oak festooned in horsehair lichen, or a nest of pixies picnicking under the boulders that looked suspiciously like a dolmen.

Unsettled and angry, she was quite breathless as she clambered over the mossy rocks, thankful her mother's voice calling Mungo had receded, heading away from the woods.

Lottie was a born worrier. She worried about Percy and what their grandmother might do to him. She worried about Ashley Templeton, who had always been kind to her and Mungo; kindness was a rare commodity in her family. She gulped down a sob that she had misconstrued Ashley's kindness for interest.

But mostly she worried about Mungo . . . and there he was, crouched below an oak so crooked its branches swept the ground, creating a cage of sorts—or a hiding place. He crooned to himself, concentrating fiercely on what he was burying, his red hair its usual rat's nest, a beacon of color amidst the green and gray. At twenty, he was a tall, somewhat podgy man, but to anyone who knew him he was no more than four mentally and did everything with the same intensity of that age.

"What are you hiding, my Magpie?" whispered Lottie so as not to startle him.

Mungo looked up, his blue eyes, set wide apart in a round face, brightened with delight. "Lottie!" he exclaimed, unable to keep his voice below a bellow. He held up something sparkly, pleased with himself.

"*Mungo,*" chided Lottie. *She crouched beside him and took the necklace away from him. "What have I said about taking things that don't belong to you?"*

"Ant Alice gi' tae Mungo."

"Mmmm . . ." she murmured skeptically, holding up the gold chain with a sapphire pendant.

"Ant' Alice gi' tae Mungo," he insisted, watching the pendant swing like a pendulum, transfixed by the motion.

Lottie wasn't sure whether to believe him or not. Mungo could be quite manipulative in his own way, but he wasn't very good at lying. "Why would she give this to you?" she wondered, giving him the benefit of the doubt.

But Mungo wasn't listening, too intent on patting down the musty earth; a buried treasure Lottie would have to retrieve when he wasn't around.

She put the necklace in the pocket of her trousers, with every intention of asking Aunt Alice why she had given it to Mungo at all, and sat on a moss-soft rock, dreading what she had to do.

Of all the stories on the island, Mungo's was the saddest. An orphan from birth, and vulnerable in ways others weren't. There had been little love for a child like Mungo.

His mother, Greer Macleod, had done two things right in Bitsie's opinion; she had provided an heir, and died doing so. Lottie sometimes wondered if Bitsie hadn't somehow engineered Greer's death. She had no proof for her suspicions but a deep knowledge of her grandmother and the lengths she would go to get her own way in all things.

Bitsie had never got over the horror of her first grandson being mentally handicapped. Mungo would've been thrown into an asylum there and then if their grandfather hadn't fought to keep him on the island.

Ironically, it was Mungo's diagnosis that entwined Lottie's future with his. After swallowing the doubly bitter pill of losing her favorite eldest son in the war and having her grandson declared an imbecile, Bitsie had been forced to accept her despised middle child, Jasper—Lottie's father—as heir to the Maundrell fortune. Lottie remembered little of the move from London. Her earliest memory of Maundrell Castle was waking up to a pair of blue eyes watching her intently, then a storybook being thrust into her hands with the command, "Read tae Mungo!"

After her initial fright at finding a strange ten-year-old boy in her room, she had read the same story again and again as he demanded until she loved Mungo for his belly laugh and his strangeness, and he loved her for the patience and kindness he had rarely received.

It didn't take long before she was Mungo's world, and he was hers. With the help of Mr. and Mrs. Macleod, she had slipped into a role as his de facto carer without being aware of it. The Macleods helped as much as they could, of course, but theirs was a precarious position being servants first and family a distant second.

It worked out for a few years until Lottie and Mungo's grandfather died and there had been no one with the strength to stop Bitsie from putting Mungo in an asylum as she had longed to do. How Lottie had begged her not to . . . and she hadn't. The price had been Lottie's soul.

Mungo put a hand over his brow and squinted up at the sky as though he could read the time like he'd seen Mr. Macleod do hundreds of times. "Is time fo' Mungo's bath." It was an echo of Lottie's daily announcement at four o'clock, yet it was not yet noon. Mungo had no concept of time.

"Not yet, my Magpie," said Lottie regretfully. "But soon."

"Is soon fo' Mungo's bath." Satisfied with his own reasoning, Mungo gave the earth a final careful pat, then stroked a hanging mossy branch with gentle fingers. Back and forth, back and forth. He hummed, low and toneless, content in the cool quiet of the woods.

Stiff with guilt, Lottie let him be for as long as she dared. She had struck a bargain with the devil and there was no going back; she could not allow Mungo to go into an asylum. Her mum had worked in places like that when she still nursed in London and had told Lottie horror stories she would never forget. Mungo would shrivel and die in an asylum. At least on the island he had freedom to roam in relative safety. The price they paid for his freedom was a few minutes of pain every few weeks for Mungo, and a lifetime of guilt for Lottie, who was forced to ensure Mungo endured his treatment with a minimum of fuss. Bitsie had couched their "agreement" and Lottie's part in it as for Mungo's own good. Lottie knew better; it was all about control. Bitsie used Mungo to control her, well aware he was Lottie's weakness.

As she did every time the doctor arrived, Lottie thought to hide Mungo. For someone with a limited mental capacity Mungo was exceptionally good at hiding himself when he didn't want to be found. She had learnt how to manipulate Mungo to save himself when he wasn't aware of danger.

"Shall we play a game, Mungo?" she asked, leaning forward as though conferring a secret.

Mungo twisted his head, without looking at her directly. Back and forth, back and forth went his fingers over the moss, but he stopped humming.

"Shall we go into the walls to find the Piper?"

"Piper . . . Aye, Wully play pipes, Lottie. Hurt Mungo."

"I know, so maybe we must go into the walls and find the Piper and ask him to stop playing so you don't hear him at night?"

Back and forth, back and forth, fingers moving faster, no longer gentle, pressing into the springy softness. "Pipes a' night, Lottie. Hurt Mungo. Stop Wully, aye."

The only person who heard the ghostly pipes in the walls was Mungo. Many a night, Lottie had stayed up with him hoping to hear them too. She never had. Perhaps it was Mungo's fear of Wully Macleod, but of all the ghost stories Mrs. Macleod had told Lottie, it was her least favorite.

Mungo cocked his head, squeezed his eyes shut, and listened. Lottie listened too, her heart sinking.

"Is Lottie's mum," he said. "Is Mungo's ant Vida, but Mungo no call Ant Vida Ant Vida coz Ant Vida go lek this." He scrunched his face up like he'd smelled something terrible right under his nose.

It was a good mimicry of her mother's expression whenever she had to deal with Mungo, for Vida Maundrell had never made it a secret she wanted nothing to do with Greer Macleod's only child.

Lottie jumped to her feet and took Mungo's hand. "Let's hide! Quickly!" He obediently allowed her to lead him deeper into the woods.

They scrambled over the mossy rocks, climbing as high as the small wood allowed. On the far side the stunted oaks thinned and the Brig o' Haggs was visible. A sudden desperate thought struck Lottie; if they could get to the bridge unseen they could run into Haggs. No one would think to look for Mungo in the village as he had never been known to cross the bridge. They could wait until the doctor got fed up with waiting and come ba—

Lottie shrieked as Mungo's hand was wrenched from hers.

She turned to the two white-clad orderlies manhandling Mungo. Beyond them stood her mother, tight-lipped with impatience.

Vida Maundrell had once been an attractive woman, able to pull off her dark hair cropped short like a skullcap with large dark eyes and a figure suited to the tight-fitting nurse's outfit she wore when attending the doctor. But disappointment had etched deep, bitter lines into her face so she looked older than her forty-one years.

"Nae, Lottie, nae!" Mungo moaned, struggling against the orderlies' stronger grips as he was dragged towards the castle. "Nae go! Dinnae let 'em hurt Mungo. Dinnae, Lottie, dinnae . . ."

Lottie burst into tears.

"Oh, snap out of it, Charlotte," said her mother in exasperation. "Dr. Kincaid is trying to help him, not hurt him. But the way you two carry on, you'd think he was killing Mungo. Really, you are too much sometimes."

"Mungo's heid! Mungo's heid!" he shrieked, face streaked with snotty tears.

"Stop it!" cried Lottie, hanging on to one of the orderlies' arms. "Can't you see you're scaring him?"

"What the hell is going on?" said Percy, out of breath, having run from the laburnum arch with Ashley on his heels.

Lottie turned to her brother. "Please stop them!" she begged. "He doesn't understand. He hates it. You know it; you all know he hates going to the doctor. Please stop them from hurting him!"

Before Percy could say anything, Aunt Alice came running up from the rose gardens and demanded to know, "What is all the commotion about?" Then, "Oh," when she took in the orderlies struggling with Mungo and Lottie crying as she tried to grab hold of an orderly's arm.

Everyone froze when the sound of a motor engine cut through the clear air, eclipsing Mungo's screams.

"Get him inside now!" snapped Vida Maundrell, her tone controlled yet furious. She glared at Mungo, who howled long and loud, all restraint lost. "The doctor can deal with him."

"No, Mum!" shouted Lottie, refusing to be part of the unspoken agreement not to air family drama in front of strangers. She turned to the orderlies. "Please don't do this," she begged. "Can't you see he's terrified? You know this is wrong."

"I'm sorry, lass," muttered one, his face jagged with distress. "We're trying to be as gentle as we can."

"Control your sister!" Vida snapped at Percy.

For a moment Lottie thought he might disobey their mother; then his face tightened. He grabbed her, hugging tightly. "Don't make a fuss," he whispered as she struggled in his embrace. "The sooner it's done, the sooner it's over."

"Coward!" Lottie hissed. "You know what that man does to Mungo!"

"Yes, but Mum has explained it all to me. It really is for his own good. Don't you want Mungo to get better?"

"Not like this!"

"Lottieeeee!" Mungo moaned as he was dragged away with Vida Maundrell following. Then he slumped between the orderlies like a rag doll.

Percy loosened his grip when Mungo and Vida were in the castle.

"Let go of me!" Lottie yelled, stumbling as she pushed Percy away. "I hate you! I hate you all! You're all—you're all hateful!"

"Sort yourself out, Lottie," said Alice, not unkindly. "It really won't help any of us if Mother hears about this, it really won't."

Lottie glared at her aunt, but Alice was watching the dark green Morris Minor trundling over the Brig o' Haggs, her face soft and bittersweet, lips curved with anticipation that seemed a little much for the arrival of the greengrocer.

Although she didn't like Alice much, Lottie felt some sympathy for her since her illness last year. It had certainly proved convenient for Bitsie to have a doctor at her beck and call to make familial inconveniences disappear.

But in that moment, Lottie didn't care. Not about Alice trapped under Bitsie's influence. Not about Percy and Ashley and the danger they had put themselves in. She hated them all. She hated them for what they allowed the doctor to do to Mungo because of their terror of Bitsie. She hated her mother even more for not only turning a blind eye but actively participating in what could only be described as torture. But mostly she hated herself for her powerlessness.

Tears streaming down her face, she turned and fled back into the woods.

CHAPTER 5

Cameron caught up with Edie quickly. "Axe murderer?" he asked, not at all out of breath, while Edie's were already explosive little puffs before she'd reached the cliff top.

"Someone's been living in the castle," she gasped.

"Ah." Cameron grinned easily. "That would be me. I didnae think anyone would mind seeing as no one's lived there for ages."

Another scream. Edie put on a burst of speed she hadn't thought her lungs could manage and sprinted down a rose-infested path.

"Neve!" she yelled, then pulled up short in front of an ugly black structure. "Neve?" she called again, and cautiously entered the odd building.

With exaggerated care, Neve turned to Edie and Cameron. "Mum, something's touching me," she whispered.

Establishing no axe murderers hid behind the two peculiar carved stones on either side of the low well, Edie approached her daughter warily. "I can't see anything."

"It's on my hair."

Edie inspected Neve's head. "There's nothing in your hair. Was it a spider?"

"No, and it's still there!" Neve cried shrilly. "Get it off me!"

Edie brushed a hand over Neve's hair. She sucked in her breath, fingers cramping in the iciness surrounding her daughter's head.

"Whatever you are," she hissed, her skin stippling with goose bumps, "get away from my daughter!" She yanked Neve towards her, hugging her tightly.

The dark, dank space had a subterranean feel, more like a cave with prehistoric art than the neo-Gothic foible of a wealthy Victorian. It felt weirdly organic; the seeping walls vibrated as though breathing softly in and out, in and out. On the edge of hearing came humming. It seemed to come from the well itself.

Cameron chuckled as he stepped past the Nunns and peered into the dark water. "It's probably the Witch," he said.

"What witch?" said Edie at the same time Neve said, "Who the hell are you?"

"Cameron. You must be Neve—nice hair by the way—and the Witch lives in there." He nodded at the well, its knee-high walls lush with festering patches of lichen and algae. "She's well known in these parts." He grinned broadly. "Cannae you feel it? It's always a little uncanny in here."

Edie nodded grimly and hugged Neve tighter, who was shivering uncontrollably. "Let's get outside," she said, and led her daughter out to the rose gardens before stopping.

"Feeling better?" she said, stroking Neve's cheek worriedly, not liking the paleness of her skin.

Neve nodded, on the verge of tears, and slipped back into Edie's embrace. "It was horrible, Mum. I saw these shadows . . . Don't you dare laugh!" she snapped at Cameron, who was finding the situation amusing. "They were—" A full-body shiver. "I saw them creeping into that place; then I saw the well and those—god, have you seen those awful stones?"

"Pict stones," supplied Cameron, rocking back on his heels, still grinning. "They certainly are creepy. Supposed to be curse stones though no one's managed to translate them."

Edie and Neve flinched at the word *curse*; there had been too much talk of curses. Edie was starting to wish she had never heard of the Maundrells or their castle, much less own it.

"The carvings were moving," Neve whispered. "I could see them out the corner of my eye. And the well had this weird haze over it, like a hand was stirring the air." She shut her eyes briefly. "It sounds mad, doesn't it? Then something touched me. It was all over me and I was so cold. It was horrible!" She buried her face in Edie's shoulder.

"The Witch's shadows," said Cameron. With an exaggerated glance around, his voice dropped to a spooky whisper, "They're her familiars that creep out to do her bidding."

"And what is her bidding?" said Edie through tight lips, failing to see this as a joke.

"Depends who you speak to. Some say you can make a blood pact with the Witch in return for your heart's greatest desire. Others say she's a cursed soul who demands blood sacrifice as the old Picts and Celts once did on Samhain. But look at any legend about this island and you'll see her hand in it. She brings tragedy and despair to anyone who dares trespass here and disnae give her due homage. You've heard of the Cailleach?"

The Nunns shook their heads.

"A nasty creature. One of the auld Celtic gods, the Hag who brings storms and winter. But in summer she sleeps in her well until Samhain." He nodded at the rounded black dome visible through the thicket of roses. "That well is another mystery. It's considered sacred, has been for hundreds of years. Personally I believe it's because it's a freshwater spring surrounded by salt water, which in itself is peculiar. The locals wilnae go near the place, but who's to say this isnae the well spoken of in legend? Maybe the Witch *is* the Cailleach."

"Are you taking the piss?" said Neve.

Cameron laughed. "A little . . ." He wrinkled his nose. "Well, maybe a lot, but you two are taking this way too seriously . . . And we havnae even mentioned the ghosts in the castle."

"We met a couple of them last night," said Neve defiantly. "They weren't that scary."

Cameron raised an eyebrow in surprise. "You have?"

"Yeah. I walked right through one, and Mum and I both saw the Roman ships."

"Oh," said Cameron, nonplussed. "I've been coming here for years and I've not seen any except the monks, and I had shared a bottle of whisky with auld Fergus not long before, so more likely whisky ghosts." He grinned ruefully, revealing a dimple.

"Ghostly monks?"

He nodded at the chapel, its bell ringing gently in the wind gusting across the loch, sharpening its surface into carmine ripples. "Aye. St. Columba built a monastery here. You can still see the foundations— And I'm guessing from your blank expressions you have no idea who St. Columba was?"

Edie and Neve shook their heads.

"He was an Irish saint who performed miracles all over Scotland, and one of them was here on your very own Loch na Scáthanna. The story goes he fought off a water horse with the power of prayer." His eyes narrowed on the castle, his flippancy slipping into disquiet. "There's more ghosts here than you could poke a stick at," he murmured. "And the castle is something else. Disnae matter where you are, it feels like it's watching you."

Edie silently agreed. It was impossible to be unaware of the castle; hatchet gray, it cast its presence wide like the feral scent of a stalking predator. A few wisps of cloud scurried around its squat towers as though fearful to go near it.

"Well," said Edie with false brightness, worried about Neve's ashen pallor. She itched to grab her hand and run for the car. Instead she forced a smile. "Thank you for charging up here to the rescue. It was kind of you, but I've had enough of ghosts for one day."

Cameron smiled back, then winked at Neve. "A pleasure. I'll see you two around." He started towards the cliffs, stopped and turned back. "Before it gets awkward, there's the question of living arrangements now you know I've been wicked and living in your castle rent-free. I promise I'm not an axe murderer . . ." He raised a hopeful eyebrow.

Edie glanced at Neve, who shrugged.

"It's fine. The place is huge and we're only here for a week, so you're welcome to stay."

"And I can continue my research?"

Edie nodded, a blush stealing up her throat when he gazed at her intently. "Yes, that's fine too. Go wild."

He lifted a hand and disappeared down the cliff path.

"He seems to know a lot about the place," said Neve doubtfully as she and Edie made their way up to the castle.

"He's been here for a long while." Edie quickly told her what she had gleaned about Cameron.

"He's not bad looking as old blokes go. A bit like an old Han Solo."

"Was he? I hadn't noticed," lied Edie, reddening.

Neve snorted her disbelief. "I saw you checking him out. You were doing that thing with your hair when you're nervous . . . You should go for it."

"Go for what?"

"Him. Old Han Solo."

"Don't be ridiculous. I love your father."

"Dad's dead, Mum. You're not. And Han Solo was definitely checking you out too."

Edie frowned. "And you'd be okay with that?"

Neve shrugged. "I'm not saying bonk him on the first date."

"Neve! Really, some of the things that come out of your mouth."

"What? I've done sex-ed at school; it's no big deal."

"Even so." Edie worried her lip for a moment. "But you'd really be okay if I met someone else— Not now," she added hastily, "but one day, maybe?"

"It's got to be better than crying yourself to sleep every night . . . I can hear you, Mum. Our house has thin walls."

"Oh," said Edie, mortified Neve had heard the grief she had been at pains to hide, not wanting to burden her daughter when she was grieving too. "Well, maybe one day. I don't think I'm quite ready yet."

Neve stopped and looked up at the castle soaring above them in dark and sullen splendor, biting her lip. "Do you want to leave?"

"Uh-uh, I'm not falling for that one. You were the one who got a fright today, so you first."

Silence, then a deep sigh. "I hate that you were right. I love the idea of ghosts, but I'm not sure I love the reality."

Edie could've hugged her daughter for her honesty but instead said, "We can leave right now. Nothing's stopping us. We can be packed and in the car in less than ten minutes."

But the earlier shock dulling Neve's eyes was already brightening to a sharp glimmer. Edie knew her answer before she said, "No, I want to stay. We can't give up this opportunity. Ghosts or no ghosts."

"Or witch," added Edie.

"Yeah." She shivered at the recent memory. "I'm never going near that horrible place again."

"Well, if we're staying, we need to get on. There's a lot of cleaning to do."

"Later for that!" Neve dashed towards the gatehouse, throwing over her shoulder, "I'm going to find that diamond." She raced across the Inner Ward, disappearing through the door leading to the Baronial Hall, ignoring Edie's wail of, "Neve! You little bugger!"

Edie huffed in annoyance but didn't follow Neve, not wanting to admit she was reluctant to go back inside. She turned thankfully to a movement in her periphery vision, thinking it might be Cameron or Mr. MacKenzie.

She froze, heart lurching. A strange man loitered near the barrows.

Stepping closer to the bulk of the castle walls, she watched him pull at his bottom lip thoughtfully, then glance around before ducking through the small opening in one of the mounds.

"Oh no, you don't," muttered Edie. Feeling braver knowing Cameron was in screaming distance, she stomped through the long grass with proprietary irritation.

There were three barrows in a row. One had a short walled track leading to a primitive doorway. Slung low and narrow, the side jambs were two menhirs, propping up the lintel. It didn't look safe, yet it had been standing for at least fifteen hundred years if they truly were Viking barrows.

"Hello?" she called into the gloomy opening, with no intention of entering a burial chamber occupied by a strange man. Hand in her pocket, she gripped her car key once more. "Whoever is in there, come out now. You're on private property." Cursing the warble of panic in her voice, she backed hurriedly up the short path when the man bent low and squeezed out, squinting in the sunlight.

He stopped and blinked slowly at Edie. She stared back with nervous defiance. He was middling height, stocky and weathered with a high forehead, an upper lip plumper than the lower mostly covered by a neat beard. He showed no embarrassment at being caught trespassing red-handed.

"Hamish Macleod," he muttered as though responding to a question.

Edie straightened her shoulders, determined not to be intimidated. "Mr. Macleod, I would appreciate it if you moved off the island. It is private property."

"Just Hamish. Too many Macleods about without causing confusion," he said. His accent, though strong, was more intelligible than Mr. MacKenzie's. His gaze traveled to Edie's car parked in front of the castle, to the village and the mountains beyond. "Saw your wee car pass through the village last night. Takes a brave woman to venture over Haggs Pass at night."

Edie opened her mouth, then bit back a retort, belatedly hearing the backhanded compliment. "What were you doing in there?" She nodded at the barrow.

"Being nosy." He grinned without shame, revealing very white teeth through his beard. "I always like to pay my respects to the wee folk that live in the cairns."

"Cairns?" said Edie, sidestepping the mention of wee folk. Though she wasn't surprised in his belief in the supernatural; in a tiny remote place like Haggs it had likely been ingrained into his psyche from the cradle.

"Aye." He slapped the stone doorjamb. "These are cairns, burial mounds. Viking maybe, could be Pictish." He eyed Edie curiously as though she were a rare tropical bird that had strayed off course into the Highlands. "You'll not be best pleased to ken you're the talk of the village. It's not often we get strangers in these parts."

"And you thought it your civic duty to come check us out?"

Hamish chortled with a mischievousness that changed his face into something a little familiar. "Aye, something like that. I run the greengrocer along the way."

"I think I met your wife this morning," said Edie, feeling surer of herself now she could place the man in context with Haggs and the one person she'd met there. She relaxed her fingers around her car key.

"Lorna? She's my sister, though you widnae think it to look at her. Night and day we are."

A self-conscious blush spread up Edie's face when Hamish stared at her again as though trying to commit her face to memory, no doubt to regale everyone in Haggs with their meeting later.

"Well," she said, half turning away, "I don't mean to be rude, but I have a lot to do."

"Sure, sure," said Hamish, not taking the hint. He ran a hand down the stone doorjamb like it was an old friend. "Always liked the auld cairns," he said. It was a conversation opener, forced and awkward.

Edie bit back a sigh, certain she was about to hear about the wee folk living in the cairns. More weirdness to add to the ghosts and whatever lived amidst the roses. "Very interesting, I'm sure," she said politely. "Lots of history about."

Hamish made a noise that sounded very much like, "Pssshht! The Highlands are awash with history, but occasionally something interesting pops up."

"Like the barrows—cairns."

He shook his head. "These are two a penny hereabouts. The Vikings left far more interesting things behind."

Against her better judgement, she asked, "Like what?"

"There's the brochs, of course. Fortified roundhouses," he added for Edie's benefit. "Plenty of them about, and they left whole cities up Orkney way. And bog bodies have been found over the way in the Hebrides, though they're afore the Vikings were about."

Edie wrinkled her nose. "Bog bodies?"

"Aye." He stamped on the ground that even at its driest had a slightly spongy texture and never felt fully firm. "It's the peat hereabouts. It's a natural preserver. Peat can mummify humans or animals given the right conditions and time." He leaned against the doorjamb, settling in for a chat. "Of course, now most people come for the recent history. The natter in Haggs is you're here to have a poke about for the Red." He held up his hands when Edie opened her mouth to deny this. "There's nowt wrong with having a poke about; we've all done it at some stage. Why, my father and grandad were paid to find it when it went missing. Them and the whole village. Great hullabaloo to hear them tell it. The auld woman was obsessed with finding it to her dying day."

"I'm not here to have a poke about. I own the castle and the island." And the village, but she kept that to herself, deciding it would not be prudent to mention it.

He wasn't awfully surprised. "So for once auld Fergus had the truth of it."

"Fergus MacKenzie?"

"Aye, he was in the pub last night telling anyone who'd buy him a pint. Probably one of the best nights of his life, getting bladdered on everyone else's expense."

Noting the derision in Hamish's tone, Edie felt rather sorry for Mr. MacKenzie. "Well, now you know," she said tartly. "It's been lovely to meet you, but I really must be getting on." And she turned and walked away, giving up any pretense at politeness.

"A word of warning," he called after her.

Sure he was going to warn her about the ghosts, she turned and forced a smile. "Yes?"

"You'd best keep your eye on auld Fergus. There's stories about him that would make your ears curl into your heid."

Edie frowned. "He seems harmless enough."

His lips pursed into another, "Pssshht. You cannae trust a MacKenzie," he said darkly.

"O-kay," said Edie. "I'm sure Mr. MacKenzie's intentions are good, but I really must be getting on." She took off determinedly again.

"Another thing . . ."

Turning to Hamish again, she didn't bother to smile. "Yes?"

He wasn't looking at her, but up at the castle. "You be careful in there, you and the wee lass. Something isnae right with the castle."

"I've heard of the Witch in the Well," said Edie, heading him off before he could get going again.

Hamish hunched his shoulders, his brow drawn low. "The Witch never made the place feel like it does now. When I was a lad the island felt uncanny, sure, eldritch, our Lorna would say; she has a love of fancy words." His eyes sidled to Edie, then back to the castle. "Feels evil now, like the devil himself has found a new home more to his liking."

Edie paused, having thought something similar herself. In the breathless silence between one thought and the next, she sensed the castle's attention on her. Hamish's words felt like a warning, an omen that at any other time she might have scoffed at as farfetched and superstitious nonsense.

She nodded and hurried towards the castle, desperate to check Neve was all right.

CHAPTER 6

Edie found Neve in one of the museum rooms, sitting cross-legged on the floor, absorbed in an old book. Relieved she was safe, Edie didn't disturb her but stepped quietly back into the hall to the nearest window.

Hamish Macleod still loitered by the cairns. In no hurry to leave he mooched over to the Maundrell graveyard, before slipping into the chapel. He came out a while later and sauntered towards the Brig o' Haggs. There, he turned to the castle.

With a drawn-in hiss, Edie ducked away from the window when he gave a mocking salute, wincing in embarrassment that he'd seen her spying on him. Standing well back, she continued to watch him until he had crossed the bridge, certain Hamish Macleod had been searching for the diamond.

Tapping a nervous finger against her teeth, she was reluctant to remain in the castle. It wasn't any quieter during the day than it had been last night. Murmurs and soft rustlings and what sounded like faint sobbing dipped and rose within the walls. From the far end of the corridor came an echo of click-clacking footsteps, stopping and starting like something was pacing.

"Stop it," she muttered to herself. Putting this burst of imagination down to talk about the Witch and vague warnings, she forced herself to walk down the hall in measured steps, deciding to have a good explore.

As she entered one dust-sheet shrouded room after another, down long halls and up corkscrew staircases, the magnitude of the place truly sank in. Trying to ignore the footsteps stalking her, she counted more than fifty bedrooms, half as many sitting rooms, odd little nooks and a room that looked like a dilapidated hospital room. All signs of human occupation were old and faded; dusty memories of laughter and heartache leached into the air to dance with the dust motes. Forgotten lives still resonated in the small things: a child's toy discarded on a bed, an open piano with the stool askew as though someone had just popped out of the room, an empty wine bottle and a glass with lipstick kisses tucked behind a curtain. Each find was intimate, a snapshot capturing the past.

"Oh!" she murmured in surprise when opening the topmost door of the Clan Tower.

The suite of rooms had been lived in. No dust, bed rumpled, the duvet thrown carelessly, a jumper tossed over the back of a chair, a mix of salt and cologne faint on the air. The furniture was heavy, dark and scuffed, the decor feminine in pinks and creams.

Tense as a greyhound, Edie listened to the castle, straining to hear the stalking echo. In the dusty silence, she breathed deeply until the unease coiling in her chest lessened and she tiptoed into the room.

Feeling like an intruder, she opened the wardrobe to discover men's clothing on old wooden coat hangers. Specimen bottles, some filled with brackish water from the loch, littered the table under the window with a glorious view of Loch na Scáthanna sprawled around the island like a vast pool of blood captured in the cupped hands of the Munros, and the abandoned rose gardens looking ever more like something from a dark fairy tale.

It didn't take a huge leap of conjecture to realize Cameron had been staying here, but curiosity overrode her guilt for snooping.

Two doors led off the bedroom, one to a dated bathroom, the other to a spacious sitting room. On the faded wallpaper glared a few brighter squares where paintings had once hung. Only two remained, reminiscent of Degas, that Edie thought deserved more than a cursory glance to ascertain their provenance and value. But it prompted the suspicion that someone had been helping themselves to the valuables left in the castle. Cameron? Mr. MacKenzie? Hamish Macleod? Someone else from Haggs? It would be impossible to ascertain; the castle would not be difficult to break into, and she doubted Mr. MacKenzie's presence had been much of a deterrent.

A desk under the window was covered in more specimen bottles. Her fingers hovered over the ornate handles of the drawers. Her snoop's guilt allowed her to open it only a fraction. Surprise overcame guilt and she pulled the drawer fully open to find children's toys; trick cards, a cup and small balls, a set of rings she couldn't pull apart. When she found a black and white magician's wand, Edie smiled. Cameron spent his spare time learning magic tricks. She rather liked him for it.

Another drawer revealed a pile of old posters of B-rated horror movies from the eighties; the rest were empty except for an old lipstick that had rolled to the back.

A pile of books rested beside an armchair pulled up in front of the fireplace; stale ash still lingered from the last time it was lit. After a quick flick through the titles, Edie noted they were all ghost stories, mostly of the Highlands.

A title caught her eye: *The Ghosts and Ghoulies of Loch na Scáth-anna*. She skimmed through the tales of blood and bone, of shadows with teeth and claws. All impossible, yet here in this castle, on this island squatting in a loch run red with blood, they weren't so hard to believe.

Putting the book back exactly as she had found it, Edie stood in the middle of the sitting room, sensing Cameron's long habitation, his masculinity stamped on every surface. Yet once, she thought, this had been a woman's room; small forgotten touches from the lipstick in the drawer to a woman's dressing gown still hanging on the back of the bathroom door.

Stepping quietly back into the bedroom, she picked up a framed photograph from the bedside table of a man holding a baby in the small garden of a terraced house. He was slickly handsome, his pale eyes blazing with fatherly pride.

Assuming it was Cameron with his father, she went to put the frame back where she'd found it, then sucked in her breath at the sudden spike of iciness brushing against her skin. The frame tumbled to the floor.

She wasn't alone.

The air was freezing, hostile, slithering around her in pinching wisps. She wanted to run, but her legs had taken root. Her chest hitching painfully with fright, she licked her suddenly dry lips and whispered, "Who's there?"

Not daring to move, the wispy cold nipped and bit her exposed skin. A corner of her mind not stupefied by terror, thought she was being assessed and had been found wanting.

The air slowly, slowly warmed. Edie turned her head to the open door as *click-clack-click-clack* faded away down the hall.

With belated bravado she shouted, "You can't hurt me! You're a ghost; you're dead!"

Deadeadea . . . echoed back to her, a normal reverberation one would expect in a huge empty place.

Picking up the framed photo with trembling hands, relieved the glass hadn't cracked, she put it back on the bedside table carefully and muttered, "I will not be scared of a ghost."

She walked out of the room with a deliberate lack of haste to prove to herself she wasn't scared. Each time she sped up, she forced herself to slow down. But not a single click or clack shadowed her when she finished her exploration in the library.

Though not much of a reader, Edie liked the room immediately. Once a chapel in one of the rounded towers, all that remained was a recessed altar under the stained-glass windows of a religious nature. Around the walls curved bookcases rose three stories, disappearing into the gloomy ceiling. A ladder on wheels attached to brass railings ran along the spines of books faded to a uniform taupe, like they've been soaked in day-old tea.

Deciding the library was as good a place as any to start cleaning, Edie got the items she needed from the laundry and an old feather duster that many ostriches had died for, to set about her self-appointed task.

Using the ladder, she was surprised its wheels did not squeak, and suspected Cameron had spent time in here to while away lonely evenings. Soon a cloud of ancient dust swirled about her. It was dull work; the titles she read as she moved around the room were duller, and in no particular order. Livestock diseases nestled beside old Mills & Boons. Fishing snuggled up to Scottish lore, legal tomes beside ghost stories, and heraldry leaned against poetry.

She was almost up to the third floor when she found the castle's old accounts, detailing the day to day running expenses going back centuries. Thinking to call it a day, she looked up at the uppermost shelves. Old-fashioned diaries frowned down at her.

Clinging to the side rail of the ladder, Edie pulled out a diary at random. As she had already snooped through Cameron's room, her guilt was muted at reading another person's diary, though it smacked uncomfortably of voyeurism. But it was the first thing she had found that might lead to a clue to her parents' identities.

She flicked through the pages, wrinkling her nose at the tight lines of copperplate writing of an Ernest Maundrell. Her hand slowed as she returned the diary to its slot.

A whispering rustle like leaves shifting in a breeze broke the silence of the library.

Floflofloflofloflo . . .

"Neve?" Edie called, dread knotting her stomach that whatever she had met in Cameron's room had caught her unawares. "If that's you playing silly buggers, it's not funny."

When Neve didn't appear wearing a smirk for scaring her, Edie climbed down the ladder and stood still, listening intently.

The whisper grew brittle, abrasive, scratching up into the high ceiling, yet sounded nearby.

She darted behind the altar, then backed up quickly against the wall.

Mother says I'm fat and boys don't like fat girls . . . appeared on the altar in front of Edie's terrified eyes.

As soon as the line faded another appeared.

Mother says I'm fat and boys don't like fat girls . . . Mother says I'm fat and boys don't like fat girls . . . Mother says I'm fat and boys don't like fat girls . . .

A childish handwriting, unformed, large and looping.

It stopped as suddenly as it had started.

Heart beating too fast, Edie listened hard to the silence. She reached out, sensing something near her, a presence unseen. A coolness brushed against her face. A tentative touch, hesitant as though fearful of being repulsed, not threatening and hostile like before.

"Mum!"

"Jesus!" Edie squawked, peering over the top of the altar at Neve. "Don't sneak up on me like that!" She glanced around cautiously. But whatever had been there had been frightened off by Neve's arrival.

"I didn't."

"Is everything all right?" said Edie, noting Neve's ashen pallor. "You haven't had another . . ." She paused, not wanting to say anything about ghosts or witches, and ended up with, "Episode?"

Neve scowled. "I didn't have an episode. I know what I felt in that place—it's called the grotto, by the way. I found a bunch of plans of the castle and the grounds."

"So why do you look as though you've seen a ghost?" asked Edie as she came out from behind the altar.

Neve gnawed at her lip before saying, "I think this diamond really was cursed."

"O-kay?"

"I've spent all afternoon reading stuff about it. It's horrible the things that happened here. And not so long ago either . . . Are you all right?" she asked, belatedly noticing Edie's own paleness.

Edie glanced at the altar. "I've just had a weird experience. I saw *something* writing on the altar; then it disappeared." She hesitated to tell Neve about her experience in Cameron's room. That had scared her, but the last thing she wanted was to scare her daughter after her earlier fright.

Neve didn't notice her caution and exclaimed, "Or someone!" with too much satisfaction for Edie's liking. "Ghost writing! That's a new one. I found a room all about the ghosts in the castle. Han Solo was not wrong; there are literally hundreds, but nothing about ghostly writing. Did you speak to it?"

"No!"

"Why not?"

"It might answer back."

Neve looked around the library. "Did you at least find anything interesting in here?"

"Not really. Dust mainly. Some diaries."

"You've always told me not to read other people's private stuff."

"They're all long dead, so they won't care." Edie blushed, not daring to tell Neve of her snoop through Cameron's room. She had taught Neve to respect other people's privacy and would never live it down if she found out her mother had been doing the exact opposite.

"And they could be ghosts now. They'll come and haunt you for reading their private stuff . . . Maybe one is the Grey Lady."

"The Grey Lady?"

"That's the ghost I walked through last night. No one knows

who she was, and all she does is walk along that hallway, then disappears into the wall."

Edie shivered. Unlike Neve, she wasn't happy about living in a castle full of ghosts. Even now she felt they were being watched, the air tightening around them with reproachful shadows. She hurried her daughter out of the library.

CHAPTER 7

"It's the biggest red diamond ever discovered," said Neve, shoveling a forkful of pasta into her mouth.

Edie nodded, stabbing her own pasta harder than it deserved, and pushed it around her plate. She had no appetite for dinner and instead took a sip of the red wine she had found in the cellar.

"And ever since it's been found," continued Neve, her voice dropping to a whisper, "the most terrible things have happened on the island. Even before it was discovered terrible things happened here. And all on Samhain, Mum. Every single one. That's only ten days away."

It wasn't only Neve who shivered and squinted at the shadowed corners of the kitchen. Edie couldn't shake the feeling someone or something was watching and listening. She took another sip of wine to mask her apprehension.

She smiled with false brightness to erase Neve's worried frown. "As we are only here for a week, it shouldn't affect us. What else did you find?" she asked as a distraction.

It was the wrong question. Neve's frown didn't fade but tightened.

"A Roman fleet really did sink in the loch. I found a letter from some old Roman bloke called Quintus something who saw it all. Had a lot to say about shadows. All the legends have a lot to say about shadows. And there was a bit about St. Columba, pretty much what your Han Solo said."

"He's *not* my Han Solo!"

"Whatever . . . And he was also right about those stones in the grotto. They're Pictish curse stones. No one really knows who was cursed, but there's a theory about a Pict queen who pissed off a lot of people and got herself and her people massacred . . . and there was a whole lot about the clans. The Highlanders took their feuding way too seriously. This area belonged to the Macleods of Haggs; they were a vicious bunch, fighting with everyone else. There was some hundred-year blood feud between the Macleods and the MacDonalds; then the MacKenzies came onto the scene and massacred the Macleods. No wonder there's so many ghosts."

"Not just ghosts."

Edie squawked in fright, flinging a bit of pasta across the kitchen, and whipped around to Cameron on the threshold. He stamped his boots on the threadbare welcome mat and came inside, grinning like he was bursting to share a secret.

"Hi," she said, a guilty blush stealing up her neck that not long ago she had been rummaging about in his private things. She shoved a forkful of pasta in her mouth to hide her embarrassment.

"Hey yourself." He sat at the table uninvited.

"Would you like to share dinner with us?" said Edie. "It's only pasta, but you're welcome to it."

He waved away her offer. "I ate at the pub."

"What do you mean not only ghosts?" Neve demanded. "You talking about the Witch?"

"Not just the Witch. There's trows too." Cameron's voice deepened with teasing laughter.

"What's that?" asked Neve.

"A sort of goblin or troll, depending who you speak to." He leaned

across the table, nicked Neve's empty glass with a raised eyebrow and
helped himself to the bottle of wine Edie had opened. "They live in
the Viking cairns."

Edie snorted her disbelief. "Ghosts I can just about swallow, but
trolls? Really?"

"Why not?" Cameron winked at Edie, his gaze lingering.

Unnerved by his attention, her whole body flamed, not sure she
was reading him correctly.

"I would kill to see a trow!" said Neve.

Edie broke eye contact with Cameron and turned to her daughter. "Really? Trolls? Goblins?"

Cameron's lips twitched to hide his smile. "You could leave offer-
ings for them at the cairns in the morning and you might get lucky."

"Don't wind her up," said Edie. "She's had enough frights for one
day."

"I'm fine!" snapped Neve.

"Speaking of the cairns, I saw you there earlier," said Cameron,
shifting his gaze back to Edie.

She flushed, now certain of the promise in his eyes. She twirled a
strand of hair around a finger, then stopped when she caught Neve
watching her with a knowing smirk.

"You were talking to someone?" Cameron prompted.

"Oh. Yes. I met one of the locals from Haggs. I think he was
having a bit of a snoop." Edie bit her lip in reflected embarrassment.
Who was she to call Hamish Macleod a snoop when she was guilty
of the same?

"Fergus is doing a stellar job as usual to keep strangers away," said
Cameron dryly.

"You don't like him?"

"It's not a question of like or dislike, more of trust. He has a reputation. He certainly landed with his arse in the butter here."

Edie frowned. It was the second time she'd been warned about
Mr. MacKenzie's reputation. As she had only met the man once,
her mind boggled at what sort of reputation. Was he having it away

with the barmaid at the pub? Or maybe he was smuggling? Loch na Scáthanna certainly lent itself to smuggling remote as it was, and with valuables in the castle to pick and choose from. Or was it something darker, dangerous? Had he hurt someone? She glanced at Neve, always her first concern.

Her mouth opened to interrogate Cameron further, then snapped shut. Skin crawling, she stared at the door leading into the kitchen. The click-clacking came fast and hard towards them, stopping behind Cameron.

He froze, the wineglass hovering in front of his lips, staring at a point behind Edie.

"There's—" began Edie. She stopped when Cameron shook his head warningly.

Slowly he lowered his glass and whipped around in his seat. "Get away!" he hissed.

The lights dimmed.

Breathing shallowly, her stomach squirming with dread, she licked her dry lips, her skin itching as though all the moisture had been sucked from the air.

"Mum," Neve whispered, her voice reedy with fear. "Something's in here."

"Shut up!" snapped Cameron, standing abruptly. Shoulders rigid, he squinted into the shadows. "I ken you're here, you auld bat," he said tersely.

Edie and Neve swiveled in the direction of his hard gaze.

In the frugal light Edie thought, for a moment, the air darkened, shaping into an indistinct figure of a tall, angular woman before a rushing hiss curled around the table.

The lights flickered, brightened, and the sharp *click-clack-click-clack* disappeared the way it had come.

In the ensuing silence, Cameron topped up his glass, drained it and said, "Dinnae assume all the ghosts in the castle wilnae harm you," and stalked out of the kitchen.

Open-mouthed, Edie and Neve regarded his retreating back.

"You saw—"

"Yes—"

"What—?"

"I don't know," said Edie, draining her own glass for Dutch courage.

"Why did Cameron call it an old bat?"

"I don't know, love," said Edie, her chest as tight as a drum. She picked up the plates, scraped the uneaten food into the bin, and washed up to stop herself from freaking out in front of Neve. When she felt more in control, she said, "Come on, it's bedtime."

Neve didn't resist an early night as she usually did. She stood with alacrity and walked close to Edie as they left the kitchen.

As they climbed to the first floor, Neve grabbed Edie's arm, forcing her to stop. "Did you hear that?"

Their eyes rose to the ceiling and the rush of scampering, scrabbling racing above them, down the long, geometric hallway, fading into the distance.

"Like scurrying feet. Little clawed feet," said Edie.

They looked at each other in dismay. "Rats!" they chorused.

"Big rats," said Neve.

"And lots of them."

"Maybe they're ghost rats."

Edie gave her an old-fashioned look of disbelief.

"It's not me! It was St. Columba and the Witch in the Well. When he died the island lost his protection and the Witch sent a plague of rats." Neve's eyes widened with horror. "What if those were the rats?"

"Now you're being ridiculous," said Edie, and walked determinedly down the hall. "If we have rats, which is not really surprising, then we'll need to get pest control in here." She added it to the growing list of problems she needed to sort out. But rats she could deal with; whatever had been in the kitchen worried her far more.

Neve rubbed her arms as though cold. "It's all well and good inheriting a whopping great castle, but I didn't sign up for ghost rats."

"They're not ghost rats! And even if they were, they didn't seem bothered by us."

"Well, they bother me. I've changed my mind; I am not living in a haunted castle."

"We're *not* living in a castle, haunted or otherwise," Edie reminded her.

Neve snorted. "We need to get rid of them. Get a priest in or something."

"A priest? What good will that do?"

"I don't know. They can flick holy water about and bring good juju or something."

"I don't think that will work; a priest's remit doesn't extend to rats."

"Why not? If there's ghosts, there must be gods and devils and stuff."

"I don't believe in gods and devils. I had enough of all that at St. Jerome's."

"You must believe in ghosts now."

Edie nodded, she certainly did believe in ghosts now, but she couldn't stretch her belief to gods and devils. Unlike the nuns, she would need visual confirmation of those too before she went that far.

"Do you want to stay with me again tonight?" she asked when they reached their bedrooms.

Neve hesitated, then shook her head. "I'll be fine."

Edie swallowed her own dread, wishing her daughter wasn't quite so brave. "Okay. Good night."

She hurried to her room and had a quick cold shower and washed her knickers, thinking she'd have to raid the closets she'd seen filled with clothes during her exploration of the castle. She had just hurtled into bed to warm up when her breath caught in fright at another passing rush of scrabbling in the ceiling. She counted to ten, twenty, expecting the bedroom door to fly open with a gibbering Neve, but her door stayed resolutely closed.

Her nerves stretched thin, the night settled around Edie. Alone with a tangle of impossible thoughts of what was inhabiting the castle and her skin prickling with sudden sweat, she knew sleep would not come. Sighing, she picked up the vampire's folder and tried to immerse herself in the dull legal documents.

Floflofloflofloflo . . .

"Jesus!" Edie yelped, her head snapping up.

Whispers rustled around the room, an urgent hushing lullaby. She got out of bed slowly, watching the wall where the words . . . *Mother loves Theo more than Jasper and me . . .* appeared, then faded away. It was the same careful, rounded script of a child she had seen in the library.

Floflofloflofo . . .

Another wall, another line: *Mother said I am not to call her Mummy . . .*

Father bought me the most beautiful dress. It's red with blue stripes. Mother said I was not to wear it as it clashes with my pasty complexion . . .

Mother says I'm fat and boys don't like fat girls . . .

Over and over the words patterned the walls, writing over themselves before dissolving into alphabet soup. Snatches of loneliness of an unhappy little girl left an ache in Edie's heart and a sour taste on her tongue. It was no wonder women were conditioned to believe they were on earth to please men when their mothers enabled that way of thinking.

Edie pressed her hands flat against the cold wall. "Who are you?" she breathed, creating condensation against the paint.

She stood still for a good, long minute listening for the faint scratching, but the walls remained bare, the air silent. "I'm going mad," she muttered, and turned back to the bed, a hysterical giggle trapped in her throat that she had spoken to the walls and had expected them to answer her.

Floflofloflofloflo . . .

Edie swiveled in time to see . . . *Alice, Gladys Maundrell, nine years, three months and seven days old . . .*

"Hello Alice," she whispered, her chest tight with pity for young Alice, whose mother sounded dreadful.

A suggestion of warmth cupped her cheek. Eyes wide, she dared not move as it slipped over her skin, slowly, gently, questing, like a blind person feeling the geography of her face.

Floflofloflofo . . .

Beware . . . Beware . . . Beware . . .

"Beware of what?" Edie whispered as the warning faded from the wall.

The bedroom door burst open.

"You're awake!" said Neve thankfully. With a quick, puzzled frown at her mother standing rigid in the middle of the room, she darted to the window and beckoned urgently. "She's still there!"

Edie felt her cheek. It was cold. It took her a moment to regain her equilibrium and join Neve at the window.

"Oh!" she said. Down in the night-shrouded gardens a girl flitted about the roses like stolen moonlight.

"I've been watching her for ages. She keeps looking up at the castle like she's scared of it . . . I wonder who she was."

"She could be Alice."

"Who?"

"Alice, Gladys Maundrell." Edie quickly told Neve about the ghostly writing.

"Shit!" said Neve, round-eyed. "And she touched you?"

Edie nodded, not bothering to rebuke her daughter for her language. It was a battle she feared she was losing.

Neve turned back to the window. "Well, I don't think that's your Alice. She looks like she might be my age, and your Alice was only nine."

They watched the ghostly girl until she vanished down towards the beach. Neve didn't need to be asked if she was staying with Edie again. They climbed into bed together. Edie switched off the bedside light.

As the dark pressed against them a distant *click-clack-click-clack* penetrated the thick walls. Edie switched on the light again and lay with the covers drawn up to her chin.

Neve's breathing didn't slow into sleep. In silence the Nunns listened to the castle, tensed, waiting for something else to happen.

The night was still as a tomb. Whatever roamed the halls terrified the living and the dead into acute silence but for the regular skitter of little clawed feet. Rats, ghostly or otherwise, feared nothing.

Minutes passed. Edie's primal fear of small scurrying creatures was no small thing, searching the shadows of the room for mean red eyes looking back at her.

Hours passed. Sleep did not come. Cold leached the air until Edie's breaths were puffs of vapor. There wasn't a single creak in the ancient building, not a single gurgle or groan from mysterious pipes in the walls, not a whirr or buzz from a machine, no dripping from the showerhead through the open door leading to the bathroom. Sometime long after midnight the ghastly click-clacking faded deeper into the castle until it was little more than a hollow ticking. Eventually Edie switched off the light.

Almost immediately, Neve's disembodied voice quavered, "Mum? There's a man standing beside the bed."

Edie quickly switched on the light, leapt from the bed and picked up the vampire's folder on the bedside table as the only available weapon. "Where?" She stared about wildly, ready to damage something fiercely with the written word.

She lowered the folder, her racing heart slowing to a gallop. "Nothing's here. I think you're overwrought."

"He was here!" snapped Neve, sitting up and waving her hand about in the air beside the bed. Her eyes widened. "He's still here!" she whispered. "I can feel him . . . Switch off the light!"

Edie climbed back into bed warily and did as Neve bade. She squinted into the dark, waiting for her eyes to adjust. "Nothing's there," she whispered after a long while.

"Yes, he is. He's looking at me." After a moment, Neve tensed and whispered, "Did you hear that?"

"Hear what?"

"He's speaking to me."

As Neve spoke, the darkness curved into the shape of a man. He was big with a thatch of messy hair and wide-spaced eyes. He gazed at Neve expectantly.

On the edge of hearing came a distant bellow, an echo of longing and lost wishes, a homesickness for someone encapsulated in a name: "Lottie."

"Go away!" Edie yelled, unable to bear the tension any longer. "Get the hell away from my daughter!"

The ghost stared at her in astonishment. Then he glanced over his shoulder at the *click-clack-click-clack* coming from the hall, gaining pace, louder, closer. A frightened gasp, "Lady is comin'!" and he stumbled through the wall.

Edie and Neve sat bolt-upright, listening to the ghost's shambling footsteps fading away, stalked by the terrible click-clacking.

The night reclaimed its silence.

"Sod this." Edie switched on the light.

"You scared him, Mum!"

"I didn't scare him; something else did," said Edie through tight lips.

"You saw him?"

"Yes, and I heard him." She flopped back down on the pillows. "I've had enough. I am not having strange men in our room, ghosts or otherwise. We're leaving tomorrow."

"No! We had a deal. You said I could have a stab at finding that diamond. I'm staying!" Neve crossed her arms, defiant.

"You will never find it. Look at the size of this place." Edie waved a vague hand around to incorporate the enormity of the castle. "And have you thought that it could all be nonsense? The Maundrells probably sold it years ago and put the story about that it was lost for tax evasion or an insurance scam, or they sold it secretly to pay for death duties. There is no bloody diamond, and we are not staying here with weird men coming into our room. That was the last straw!"

"He wasn't doing anything, Mum," said Neve reasonably. "He looked upset."

Edie threw her hands in the air. "Of course he's upset! He's a bloody ghost. He's dead. Who wouldn't be upset by that?"

Neve rolled over, showing her back, ending the discussion.

"This is over, Neve," said Edie. She burrowed under the blankets, adding, "We are leaving tomorrow."

Edie awoke with a gasp, disorientated, a whisper edging into her dreams. Gray dawn light stole through a gap in the curtains. She reached for Joshua from habit, his side of the bed still warm. For a moment her heart leapt; then she drew back her hand, remembering Neve had slept there.

Floflofloflo . . .

Springing out of bed, Edie stared around wildly, and whispered, "Hello . . . Alice?"

The words were barely out of her mouth when Alice's scrawl flowed across the wall: *Jasper has made friends with Greer, Mr. and Mrs. Macleod's daughter. Mother is furious, but it's the happiest I have seen Jasper. He has something Theo doesn't. Jasper is so silly with his jealousy because Theo doesn't care what Jasper does . . .*

The writing was urgent, fast, disappearing as soon as it appeared, as though Alice had been waiting impatiently for Edie to wake up.

Last night Mother called Jasper the 'spare' in front of Greer to humiliate him. Theo laughed when Jasper cried, but I wanted to cry too, because I am also a spare . . .

The handwriting changed, maturing from a little's girl's careful script to the controlled steadiness of an adult.

Jasper is in love with Greer. I wish I were as pretty as Greer. Maybe Mother would love me then . . .

"Oh," whispered Edie. "This is a diary." She stepped closer to the wall where . . . *I saw Theo kissing Greer in the laburnum arch! Poor Jasper, he will be so mad when he finds out. And Mother will be mad when she finds out Theo is kissing the housekeeper's daughter. I did not know keeping secrets could be so exhilarating . . .*

Mother found out Greer is pregnant! What a to-do . . .

Edie sat on the edge of the bed, now wide awake, fascinated by the unfolding love triangle between the beautiful Greer and Alice's brothers, Jasper and Theo.

Mother has been impossible these past three days since Theo and Greer snuck away together. She doesn't know I saw them leave . . .

Theo and Greer are married! They eloped to Gretna Green, and there's nothing Mother can do about it. Jasper is devastated. He loves Greer so much . . .

Theo received his call up papers in the post this morning. Mother nearly had a fit and Greer cried. She is always crying. I am not sure if it's because she is pregnant or because Mother has been cruel to her from the moment she and Theo returned from Gretna—

Edie tensed. Something had startled the ghost writer. *Or scared her,* she thought when a few seconds later she heard *click-clack-click-clack* prowling the hall.

Sensing Alice's cool presence nearby, Edie whispered, "What are you afraid of, Alice? Why did you say last night I must beware? Beware of what?"

It was an age before a single word bit into the wall. Deep, gaunt, ugly: *Mother.*

Long after the dreadful pacing had faded along with Alice, Edie sat in the quiet of her room, stomach clenched so tight with trepidation she thought she might vomit, dark thoughts chasing across her mind.

There was something furtive about Alice's writing, quick stolen snatches. And Alice had been terrified of whatever had been outside the room. The ghost of Alice's mother? It was worrying that the idea of another ghost no longer bothered Edie . . . until another dark thought occurred to her: *Could a ghost hurt another? Could they hurt the living?*

The castle's withered marrow resonated with human tragedy. What had happened here? To Alice and her mother. The Grey Lady. To the man who'd spoken last night, and the girl in the garden.

Shaking herself free of gloomy contemplations, Edie got dressed and peered out of the window. Melancholic clouds obscured the Munros, hanging low over Loch na Scáthanna, its bloody water a rusty garnet.

She spied the stringy figure of Fergus MacKenzie walking determinedly into the rose gardens. He paused beside the fountain and glanced up at the castle. His shaggy face squinched with unease, as though sensing Edie's attention, and he ducked down behind a thicket of roses.

Edie pulled back from the window and waited. It wasn't two minutes before Mr. MacKenzie's head bobbed up again. He looked around furtively, darted over to the fountain and plunged his hands into the murky water. He was quite obviously searching for something.

Thoughtful, she went in search of Neve and quickly found her in the museum, sitting amidst piles of old papers and books.

Worry gnawed at Edie as she watched Neve from the doorway. She wanted to leave but knew from her daughter's determined expression nothing she said would dissuade her. It was a terrible self-acknowledgment to realize her will was weaker than her child's. For a moment she wished to go back ten years to the warm, squidgy girl who would curl up bonelessly against Edie for hours, content merely in their proximity.

"You just don't give up, do you?" said Edie.

Neve looked up briefly. "No. I would've thought you'd be happy I'm showing diligence. You're always saying I should show some, so I am."

Edie pulled a face, not bothering to point out Neve's version of diligence tended to become obsession. "Only when it suits you. And

I don't think you're the only one looking for the Maundrell Red. I spotted Mr. MacKenzie being most secretive around the old fountain in the garden."

Neve snorted. "That would be a stupid place to hide a diamond." She stood up, looking smug, and walked to a wall covered in a family tree with a crest at the top. "Come and look at this. I think I may have found something."

Edie had always regarded family trees with sadness, lives lived and since forgotten but for a few dry words linking blood to blood. Her blood.

"What am I looking for?" she asked, noting her name was definitely not on the family tree. The last entry was in 1965; five years before Edie's birth.

"The weirdest thing of all. Every single Maundrell died on the thirty-first of October."

"Samhain," said Edie, frowning.

"Yes. Three hundred years of Maundrells all dying on the same day. That can't be a coincidence."

"And it's my birthday," said Edie. She'd never made a big thing of her birthday, an unnecessary annual reminder of her abandonment on the steps of the orphanage when she'd been only a few hours old.

"So it is," Neve murmured thoughtfully.

October 1965

No one came looking for Lottie after she ran back into the woods. She knew they wouldn't, but a small part of her wished someone had so she wouldn't feel quite so alone.

She scrambled over the rocks until she found the spot where Mungo had buried his treasures earlier. Digging into the recently disturbed soil, she pulled out grimy tin soldiers and smiled through her tears.

They had belonged to their grandfather. Rupert Maundrell had been a kind man. Though no match for the powerful personality of his wife, Bitsie, he had tried to protect Mungo nonetheless. Lottie still felt the loss of her grandfather, an ally and confidant when life in the castle had grown unbearable.

Their grandfather had played a game with Mungo, placing tin soldiers all over the castle for him to find, then watching the sheer joyful excitement when Mungo found one. After their grandfather died Bitsie, with casual cruelty, had told Mungo never to touch the tin soldiers again.

But Mungo remembered. Taking the soldiers was his own small rebellion. Sobbing in the quiet of the woods, Lottie put his treasured memories back in his hiding place. He had many secret places all over the castle and island, but only Lottie knew where most of them were.

It was late afternoon when she crept out of the woods. She paused on the gravelled driveway leading to the Brig o' Haggs. Freedom lay on the other side. So often she had dreamt of packing a bag and stealing across the humped causeway in the dead of night. But her dreams were fleeting; she only had to think of Mungo's round face to know she couldn't leave him.

Lottie headed towards the castle. She scowled when she spied Alice walking down to the rose gardens, and changed course, following her to the bench she had been sitting on earlier to pick up her diary.

"Aunt Alice," said Lottie, her voice hoarse from crying.

Alice started guiltily. "Oh, it's just you, Lottie," she said, her worried expression slipping into relief, but her eyes darted around the garden as though expecting someone else to appear.

It didn't take a great leap of intuition to know that someone was Bitsie.

"What do you want?" Alice asked impatiently.

"Why did you give Mungo your necklace?" Lottie held the necklace out to her.

Alice snatched at it. "I did nothing of the sort! I hadn't known he had taken it."

Lottie saw the lie in her aunt's shifting eyes. It made no sense. Why would she give something of value to Mungo, then lie about it?

"But no harm done," said Alice, lips pressed into a nervous thin line. "You found it and that's what matters." She smiled slightly. "It will be our little secret."

"Why does she hate us so much?" said Lottie, the question popping out of her mouth without thought.

Startled, Alice straightened, her expression shuttered. "I don't know what you mean."

"Yes, you do. Grandmother hates us all, even you, but especially Mungo."

Alice settled on the bench, making a fuss of her skirt, hoping Lottie would go with the question unanswered. She sighed loudly when Lottie remained where she was. "Mother can be difficult sometimes, but she loves us in her own way."

"No, she doesn't!" snapped Lottie. "She hates us. I've seen the way she looks at us all. She can barely look at Mungo. Don't lie to me, Aunt Alice."

Alice closed her eyes against Lottie's glare. "It's because of Theo, I think."

"Uncle Theodore?" said Lottie. "But he's been dead for twenty years."

"And Mother adored him." Alice's eyes slitted open, thin nostrils flaring. "Theo was the perfect son. He could do no wrong, and Jasper and I were unnecessary. Spares!" she spat, a damaged trove of bitterness and envy in the rigidity of her posture. "I sometimes hated him!" Her lips spread wide in a mirthless grin. "Yet he was the one who betrayed Mother, eloped with a servant's daughter, then got himself killed in the war, leaving an imbecile for her grandson." She leaned forward earnestly. Lottie took a step back.

"Mother can't believe her perfect son produced a child like Mungo. She blames Greer, of course." She quivered with a lifetime of repressed fury and resentment. "And Mother means to make Mungo's life a living hell for Theo's betrayal . . . She hates you too. More than you can ever know."

"Why?" cried Lottie. "I've done nothing wrong!"

"You're Jasper's child. You and Percy. Jasper succeeded where Theo failed. Mother resents you both because you were normal while Theo created . . . Well, Mungo."

It was so irrational Lottie flinched. "I hate her! I wish she were dead!" she burst out, more tears threatening to spill.

Alice laughed with real amusement. "If wishes could kill Mother would've been dead years ago. But be careful what you wish—" The words faded on her lips when a scream erupted from the castle.

They both looked at the storm-gray building threatening the sky like a fist.

"I imagine that's something you'll want to deal with," said Alice, relieved to end the awkward conversation. She picked up her diary and scuttled away.

Lottie raced to the castle and slipped in through the Clan Tower. She ran down long corridors, her footsteps muffled by ghastly carpets of psychedelic hopscotch, past walls and windows an eyesore of mismatched colors. All Bitsie's choice of decoration when she'd married into the Maundrell family, determined to put her stamp on the castle and rile the family who didn't like change. Only the Baronial Hall and the kitchens had survived her purge.

A stitch in her side, Lottie darted up the spiral staircase to the top floor of the Corbie Tower. Relieved to see the orderlies had already gone down to the kitchen for a cup of tea once Mungo was in with the doctor, she leaned against a wall to catch her breath.

Over the pounding of her blood through her head, she became aware of a hissed conversation. She sidled along the wall to peek around the corner at her two least favorite people.

Lottie couldn't decide whom she hated more: her grandmother for numerous reasons, or her mother, Vida, for encouraging the terrible treatment of Mungo. Both strong women, it was odd as mother and daughter-in-law they didn't despise each other in the often natural order of families. Though not linked by blood, they were cut from the same psychological cloth, with a mutual understanding of the other's motives. They were far more like mother and daughter than Bitsie and Alice were.

Yet their usual amity was strained. They faced each other with hostility.

"He's my son!" snapped Vida.

"And my *grandson!" Bitsie snapped back, emerald eyes boring into Vida's returning brown glare.*

"Even so, ECT is not proven to cure"—Vida swallowed her distaste —"certain proclivities."

"His proclivities are an abomination! Can you imagine what people would say if they heard your son—my grandson—was a sodomite?"

Vida flinched as though she had been slapped. She shook her head and said, "You're asking too much. It is one thing to use ECT as a cure for the mentally defective; clinical studies have proven it is beneficial. But it's quite another for an otherwise healthy man—"

"Men," corrected Bitsie. "It takes two to do what those two do together, and I have the Templetons' blessing. They are as worried about their son's . . . relationship," Bitsie's thin lips crinkled around the word like she'd sucked a lemon, "with Percy as I am."

Vida blinked in astonishment at her mother-in-law. "How long have you known?" she said faintly.

"A few months, and I'm damned if I'll allow their secret to become public knowledge. We are Maundrells, and I shall not have it. The Templetons are of the same opinion."

Vida sighed, then nodded. "Very well. But it's not me you have to persuade."

"The doctor will do as I say," Bitsie sneered. Her beringed hand rose to the Maundrell Red gaping like an open wound against the green of her outfit.

Scowling, Vida crossed her arms defensively. "He isn't completely your man, Bitsie. You may have promised him all sorts of things, but he swore the Hippocratic oath. Putting a perfectly healthy man in unnecessary danger goes against all his training."

Bitsie smiled coolly, but not wide enough to form lines. "Everyone has a price, and I know more about the doctor than he would like."

"What's that supposed to mean?"

"It means the handsome Dr. Kincaid has lied to us."

Lottie leaned back against the wall, feeling quite ill. She needed to warn Percy and Ashley of the danger they were in.

While her mother and grandmother were intent on each other, Lottie crept to the door across the hall, opened it quickly and quietly, and slipped into the room.

Once a guest bedroom, it had been converted into a medical facility.

Beside the high bed in the middle stood a trolley with a machine covered in dials and knobs that Dr. Kincaid was presently twisting.

Mungo lay on the bed. Wires connected his head to the machine. Eyes squeezed tight, he moaned quietly, his whole body twitching.

Lottie had been ten when the doctor first came to the castle. She had disliked him instinctively. He was handsome in an Anthony Perkins sort of way. Tall, dark hair slicked back, and strange pale eyes the color of cider. He was always impeccably dressed as though he were at the castle to attend a dinner party.

She had pestered him with incessant questions, which he had answered in exasperation to get rid of her. But he had shown her the machine, a convulsator for electroconvulsive therapy, the latest technology from Sweden, as proud of it as though he had built the horrible thing himself.

But for all her questions, she had discovered little about the man himself except what he had let slip last year, that his wife had recently given birth to a son. It wasn't much knowledge for a man who had been coming regularly to the castle these past five years.

Dr. Kincaid hadn't yet noticed Lottie had snuck in. With a hand on the doorknob to make a quick escape, she watched him warily, gauging his mood.

Her heart sank at the tight lines around his mouth when he turned to Mungo and snapped, "For god's sake, will you shut up? I havnae even given you a particularly high dose!"

"Mungo's heid!" cried Mungo. "Hurt. Mungo's heid hurt!"

Dr. Kincaid leaned closer to Mungo. "It's not often I get angry with my patients," he hissed, tightening the straps around Mungo's twitching hands. "But right now I could break your arms without conscience or guilt for the performance you put on earlier."

He looked up at Lottie's gasp of horror. "What are you doing in here? I thought I made it perfectly clear last time that you were not to enter this room under any circumstances while Mungo was undergoing treatment."

Mungo's eyes rolled to Lottie with such relief she almost started crying *again. "Mungo's Lottie . . ." he moaned. He looked terrible with the wires attached to his head like Frankenstein's monster.*

"He's had enough for one day," she said, trying to keep the quaver from her voice, knowing the trouble she would get into when Bitsie found out she was in here.

The doctor raised a sardonic eyebrow. "Do you think so? And what qualifications do you have for your diagnosis of the situation, mmmm?"

Hating that she was fifteen and had no authority whatsoever, she straightened her shoulders and snapped, "You and I both know this will never make him better. You've been doing this for years and it's never worked!"

Dr. Kincaid hesitated, then shrugged. "Your grandmother may be a god almighty bitch, but she does pay well."

Lottie's eyes narrowed. "But I know what you're really after," she said, rather astonished at her daring. She clung to her lack of caution, and added with a sneer that would've done Bitsie proud, "She'll never give it to you, you know. She's obsessed with it."

His cheeks twitched, jaw tight with fury. "Yesterday, I widnae have believed you," he said through gritted teeth.

Lottie opened her mouth, then shut it against what she had planned to say in her head. "You wouldn't?"

"Never make a bargain with a devil," he spat. "It goes against their nature to keep their word." Without looking at Mungo, he turned one of the dials hard to the right.

Mungo screamed. His body arched and slammed back down on the bed.

"Stop!" Lottie shrieked. "You'll kill him!"

Dr. Kincaid gave a sharp bark of unamused laughter. "You're the only one who will care if I do."

Lottie rushed to the bed, slapping the doctor's hands away as he tried to stop her from ripping the wires from Mungo's head. She sobbed in her haste to get the hateful wires off him, the hateful straps, desperate to get him away from the hateful room, the hateful doctor.

The moment he was free, Mungo reared up from the bed with a toneless roar of terror. He staggered towards Dr. Kincaid, arms open wide as if he intended to crush the man in a bear grip.

Everyone forgot how big Mungo was; though he had the mind of a child, he had the strength of an adult. The doctor's eyes widened with alarm at Mungo bearing down on him.

Panicking, Lottie glanced over her shoulder, hoping to see an adult who could help, but instead saw shadows seeping under the closed door. They spread across the floor slowly and thickly, up the walls, creeping into corners, dimming the room.

"Get away from me or I'll have you slapped into an asylum so fast your head will spin!" shouted the doctor, stumbling away from Mungo.

"Mungo!" cried Lottie. She raced around the bed and stood between him and the doctor. "Look at me, Mungo," she said urgently, reaching up to cup his face in her hands. His skin was slick with sweat, mouth open in a soundless scream with saliva dribbling down his chin.

"Please don't do something stupid," she whispered. "Look at me, Mungo. Listen to my voice." She was vaguely aware of the door opening and the room filling up with people. She ignored them all. "Look at me, Mungo," she said, keeping her voice calm though her heart was beating so fast she felt light-headed. "Please, Mungo." Out the corner of her eye she saw the shadows hovering above the room like a curious cloud.

Mungo's soundless roar stuttered to a hoarse cry, then stopped altogether when his wild eyes were drawn down to Lottie. "Mungo's heid," he whispered, and burst into gulping sobs.

"This is not you," said Lottie, forcing a smile. "You don't want to hurt anyone, do you?"

"Guid boy, Mungo," he whimpered. "Nae hurt Doc-ta. Guid boy, Mungo."

"You are a good boy, my Magpie," said Lottie, and wrapped her arms tight around his waist, feeling every tremor passing through him. He stood in her tight embrace, neither returning nor pulling from it.

"What the hell is going on here?" Bitsie's American accent cut through the charged atmosphere like lightning.

Dr. Kincaid straightened from his crouch by the far wall and smoothed down his jacket. "He's been impossible to treat today," he said, glowering at Mungo.

"No!" snarled Lottie, turning on the doctor. "Your pet gave too high a dose." She took Mungo's hand. He was as docile as a lamb now, holding his head and blinking rapidly.

"Nonsense," scoffed the doctor. But he was staring at Bitsie, something dangerous in his expression, daring her to castigate him.

Bitsie raised an amused eyebrow. "Did you really think that would work, Dr. Kincaid?" she said. "If you were to kill him during his treatment I would not mourn the loss; if anything, you would be doing me a favor. But his death would terminate our agreement."

"You're the devil," he said hoarsely, shaking his head in disbelief.

Bitsie smirked. "Devil I may be, but what does that make you?" She turned and walked out of the room.

The doctor's bravado rushed out of him like a deflating balloon. He had gambled and lost. No one won against Bitsie.

"I'm taking Mungo now," said Lottie, glaring at her family.

They were all there apart from Bitsie. Vida stood in front of Dr. Kincaid, arms crossed protectively as though fearing Mungo might truly attack the man. Aunt Alice, eyes bright with excitement at the brittle atmosphere, faded into the background behind Percy and Ashley. Jasper had just stepped into the room and frowned at everyone.

Lottie glanced at Percy, hoping for an ally, but he was watching Ashley's face blanch with horror as he took in the bed and the convulsator for the first time.

"Don't be ridiculous, Charlotte," said Vida. "He's just begun his treatment."

"Nooooooo . . ." escaped from Mungo. He let go of Lottie's hand, staggered past Jasper, who stood at the door, and took off down the corridor in a blundering run.

"Oh, for god's sake!" snapped Vida. "I suppose I'll have to go after him again."

But Lottie was already racing out of the room. "Hide him, Lottie," whispered her father as she passed him.

Glancing over her shoulder, Lottie's heart lurched with panic. Dr. Kincaid and her mother were stalking after her with determined expressions. Above them shadows flowed over the ceiling and the walls in a scratchy, humming, jostling confusion.

Lottie hurtled down the spiral staircase after Mungo.

CHAPTER 8

"Come and look here," said Neve, taking her reluctant mother's hand and dragging her to the next room lined with display cabinets.

"This was the beginning of an exhibition about the Maundrell Red," she said, leading Edie to the first cabinet. "An Ernest Maundrell found it in South Africa—"

"Ernest Maundrell? I found some of his diaries in the library."

"There's a few here too," said Neve. "Anyway, he and his valet or manservant, or whatever the hell you call it, a Lachlan Macleod, found the Maundrell Red in Kimberley. They brought it back to Scotland and a few months later Ernest's son died under mysterious circumstances. And get this, one of the maids saw shadows slipping into his room and the next morning he was dead."

"On Samhain?"

Neve nodded. "And that was only the start of it." She darted out of the room, saying, "Now come and see this."

Edie dutifully followed her daughter to the adjoining room.

Neve stood amidst yet more cabinets and opened her arms wide.

"Now this is all about the night the diamond disappeared in 1965, and the very next day three people died, also on Samhain."

"Where are you going with this?"

"I'm not sure." Neve frowned at the room. "It must've been taken by someone on the island."

"Right," said Edie doubtfully. "And if it was taken by one of the people that died? The dead have a habit of taking their secrets to the grave. Plus, the entire place has been searched and it's never been found."

"But maybe they were all looking in the wrong place. Just hear me out," said Neve, putting up a hand when Edie opened her mouth to quibble. "I found a bunch of old wills belonging to a Lady Elizabeth Maundrell. There's a lot about her. She was a dreadful woman, a class-A bitch . . . Anyway, when she married Rupert Maundrell, he gave her the diamond." She picked up a wad of documents and waved them at Edie. "She made about thirty wills, but the only thing she ever changed was who would inherit the Maundrell Red from her. So what if one of those people got tired of waiting until she died and took it?"

"That would make a weird sort of sense if she was one of the people who died," said Edie.

Neve pouted. "She wasn't unfortunately as that would've fitted my theory perfectly . . . But what if someone took the diamond and hid it somewhere hoping to retrieve it, then there were the deaths and the police arrived and the thief never had a chance to come back for it?"

Edie shook her head. "You're taking thinking out of the box to a whole new level."

"Maybe, but after those people died, the only people still on the island were Lady Elizabeth and her children. Everyone else left that night or died."

"So?"

"So it's a starting point."

"A very tenuous one.

"And not a particularly original one," Neve admitted. "The museum people had already done some of the research. There's another room with the possible culprits. But if I can figure out who might have taken it, or *not* taken it, it will narrow the field."

Edie sighed. She was fed up with Neve's flights of fancy. "That's enough! The diamond's gone, and we are leaving today."

"No! I am not going anywhere! You promised, Mum!"

"And last night we had a strange man in our room!"

"He was a ghost!" A crafty expression crossed Neve's face. "I thought you wanted to find out who your parents were."

"That's a low blow!" snapped Edie, a prickle of tears in her throat. She had sculpted her life around Neve, a fluid molding, ever adapting as she grew. But Neve was butting against the shape of Edie every chance she got, resisting the safety Edie had cushioned her life with. Now each sharp word, each pushback, each casual unkindness, ravaged Edie's heart like a starving cat's fangs. And Neve knew exactly which buttons to press, exploiting Edie's desperation to protect her against her desire to know who her own parents had been.

"Is this a bad time?"

Neve and Edie whipped around to Cameron leaning against the doorframe.

"I—no," said Edie, her face heating up. "We were having a silly argument about nothing."

"Would you like to go for a walk?"

Edie blinked at Cameron's abruptness. "I—we—that is—"

"Mum would love to go with you," said Neve with saccharine sweetness.

Edie scowled at her.

"I'll be fine by myself," Neve added, grinning wickedly at Edie's discomfort.

Pushed into a situation she wasn't sure she was ready for, Edie forced a smile. "That would be lovely." With a backward glare at Neve, she followed Cameron out of the room.

He led the way, walking fast like he was trying to elude his own shadow. Edie hurried to keep up, relieved to get away from the cloying atmosphere prowling the long halls like a dark miasma.

It wasn't much better outside. Clouds hung low over Loch na Scáthanna, shadowing the waters to a deep burgundy. A light dusting of early snow clung to the Munros like icing sugar and cold mist rose from the ground. As the delicate tendrils curled around Edie, she shivered in the humming silence. Not for the first time, she thought the island was a place of regretful sorrow. It clung to the air, seeped up from the earth, and threaded through the Nine Hags visible in the near distance, huddled together for comfort.

"Are you all right?" asked Cameron, watching her look around as they walked. "If you're worrying about the Witch, she wilnae regain her powers until Samhain," he teased.

"I'm getting a little sick of hearing about this witch," muttered Edie.

"Then we'll change the subject . . . What were you two doing back there? Looked like dull work."

Edie grimaced. "Neve has got it into her head she can find this diamond that's been missing for ages."

"The Maundrell Red?"

Edie looked at him in surprise. "You've heard of it?"

"Everyone's heard of the Maundrell Red. The most cursed diamond in history and the cause of umpteen legends. Had no end of treasure seekers coming to search for it."

"Treasure seekers?" said Edie. Her thoughts flittered back to her meeting with Hamish Macleod. Now the cairns would've been a good hiding place for a diamond.

"Aye. Loads of them. Especially after the auld lady died. Anyone can slip Fergus a bottle of whisky and he'd allow them to have a bit of a search. But they mostly dried up these past years."

"Mmm . . . I think I may have to have a little chat with Mr. MacKenzie about that."

"It would be a waste of time." Cameron paused, choosing his

words carefully. "We may not always see eye to eye, but to be fair to the old boy he has been a steady, if pissed, presence on the island. He's done right by your lot mostly. A lot more right than the Maundrells deserved."

Surprised by his dark tone, she asked, "You didn't like the Maundrells?"

"Not many people in these parts do. From what I've heard the Maundrells were a strange lot who kept themselves to themselves and their secrets closer. Some of your lot were right bastards. Especially that Lady Elizabeth. The villagers still spit if her name is mentioned."

Wishing she'd thought to study the Maundrell family tree Neve had found, she felt a little foolish asking, "I don't suppose she had a daughter called Alice?"

Cameron's eyebrows shot up in surprise. "She did. Why do you ask?"

"I—um . . ." Edie faltered. How did she explain about the writing on the wall without sounding like she was insane? "I—um—saw something she had written about her mother," she said. "And she did sound awful." She caught her bottom lip in her teeth and stole a glance at the castle, sensing its attention on her. Shrouded in mist, it looked like something out of *Brigadoon* if it had been written by the Brothers Grimm.

"Well, I didnae know Alice, not to speak to, but she was still living in the castle when I first came up here . . . I'm surprised you dinnae know all this."

Edie grimaced, not sure why she felt ashamed she knew nothing of her past. "I grew up in an orphanage in London," she admitted. "The first I heard of the Maundrells was when I started getting letters from their lawyers. But they didn't tell me much. All I know is I was born in the castle, and even that I'm not completely sure of."

"Now there's a thing." Cameron laughed to himself. "When you told me before you'd inherited the place, I'd thought you were some distant relative the solicitors unearthed. You hear it sometimes in these auld families when they die out; the black sheep son sent off to Australia in the year dot, and turns out he was the only one who kept the line going. The blood a bit diluted, but that's probably for the best." He hesitated, glancing at Edie sideways. "This is a delicate question, but did the solicitors tell you who your parents were?"

"They didn't know."

"Well, it widnae be Alice," said Cameron. "I've spoken to the locals in Haggs a lot about the Maundrells . . . I'm curious about them," he added at Edie's sharp look.

"How do you know Alice wasn't my mother?"

Cameron pressed his lips together, hesitating again. "What I've been told is she never left the island."

"What? Ever? Not even to the village? Not once?"

"So I've heard."

"Why not?"

"This is only hearsay, but the gossip is Lady Elizabeth kept her whole family firmly under her thumb, especially Alice. Never allowed her to marry or have any contact with the outside world."

"Why would Alice allow that?" said Edie, aghast.

"I doubt Alice was a match for her. From all accounts Lady Elizabeth was a force to be reckoned with, not someone you crossed twice. I've heard her called the devil more times than I can count."

"Oh," said Edie, crushed that an avenue of possibility had closed before it had really opened.

"I widnae feel too sorry for Alice," said Cameron, mistaking Edie's frustration for sadness. "I doubt she was much better than her mother."

"Do you know how Alice died?"

He grinned. "Ask anyone in Haggs and they'll tell you the Witch's shadows got her."

"Ha-ha," muttered Edie. "Not even remotely funny."

"The Witch's shadows hardly ever are. They almost always bring death."

Edie nodded, raising a half smile at Cameron's teasing tone. "The Maundrells did seem to have a habit of dying a lot."

"So they did." He eyed her sideways again. "I wonder if you've noticed anything about their deaths."

"That they all occurred on Samhain?"

He nodded.

"It is weird," Edie admitted. "This whole place is weird. It gives me the creeps. I wanted to leave today, but Neve is being stubborn."

"Well, a treasure hunt will appeal to most teens. You should let her get on with it. She seems a determined lass."

"She certainly is," said Edie darkly. "I thought she'd want to leave after the ghosts we saw last night."

"More ghosts?"

"Yes. A young girl in the garden we saw from the window, and a man came into our room. He stood over Neve and called her Lottie. Then he ran away as though something had frightened him. And anything that frightens a ghost scares the hell out of me— What?" she said when Cameron stopped abruptly.

"A girl in the garden, and a man who spoke to you?"

Edie nodded. "Yes, it's no weirder than Roman fleets and ghost rats in the walls— Did I mention the ghost rats?"

Cameron shook his head.

"Well, it seems we have a plague of ghost rats, maybe something to do with your St. Columba."

"I've heard of the rats. I thought I'd heard of most of the ghosts on the island, but the other two are new to me."

"They are?"

"Sure. But this place is rank with ghosts; there's bound to be a few that havnae been seen."

Edie hesitated to tell him about the ghostly writing of Alice Maundrell. The writing had felt personal, intimate, meant only for her. She was vaguely flattered a ghost had singled her out to share the pain she had endured when alive. Instead she asked, "What happened last night? In the kitchen," she added when he raised an eyebrow.

"Ah," he murmured. "I would like to say it was because I was pissed and I was winding you two up, but . . ." He flashed her a sheepish grin. "Promise you wilnae laugh?"

"Of course not."

"Well, there are . . ." He faltered and tried again. "I think mostly I'm scaring myself, but every night I hear noises, feel cold spots in a room or like someone's watching me. It helps if I shout at them."

"You called it an old bat. I thought you might know what or *who* it might have been?"

"Nothing more than institutionalized misogyny." He grinned to take the sting from his words. "I just had a feeling it had once been a woman."

"So why do you stay if the castle scares you? Why not find somewhere in the village? You could do your research as easily from there."

Cameron looked around at the island. "I could, but the thing is I've never actually seen anything definitive, just weird chills and creepiness. Maybe if I had I might have left . . . screaming my heid off probably." He grimaced ruefully. "Plus, living in the castle comes at the right price. Free." He started walking again in a purposeful direction.

"Where are we going?"

He gave her an easy smile. "I didnae ask you to walk with me for the pleasure of your company—although that is an added bonus—I wanted to show you something."

He really shouldn't smile like that, Edie thought as she lifted the hem of her shirt and sweater to let the cold Scottish air cool the sudden flush of her skin that may have been a hot flush or the heat of his smile. She followed him into the woods, hoping she wasn't red in the face.

The ancient weight of the woods settled around Edie the moment she stepped into its shadows. The trees were bowed and gnarled with age, smothered in spongy moss, and dripping with horsehair lichen that grew from scatters of jumbled rocks. It felt sacred, blessed, a place filled with ancient secrets.

Cameron stopped beside a pile of rocks that looked like a lop-sided dolmen but had been crafted by nature. An old oak crouched above it, its branches clawing the ground like a gnarled giant hand.

He hunkered down and dug about in the moist earth, then pulled out a little tin soldier. He brushed off the dirt and laid it on his palm. "There's a whole battalion hidden here."

Edie picked up the soldier. Its bright red and black paint was pristine even after its long hibernation in the earth. "I've seen some like this before, in one of the rooms in the castle. It's filled with battle scenes."

"Looks like some of the soldiers were stolen. I can picture a wee lad in here, hiding his stolen treasures, perhaps staging battles amongst the rocks."

Edie smiled, liking his imagery. Her smile faded. A little boy who hadn't come back for his treasures. From all she had learnt in the past couple of days, that did not bode well for the treasure burier. But Cameron's discovery did give her pause. The island had been searched for years; why had the soldiers not been found?

It didn't take a great leap of conjecture to guess Neve and Mr. Mackenzie were not the only ones searching for the Maundrell Red. And what did it matter anyway? It wasn't as though any of them would find anything.

Cameron's head was close to hers. He turned slightly and leaned towards Edie. His breath was warm on her lips; then his met hers. A mere brushing of skin on skin, a suggestion and a query at Edie's hesitation before his mouth opened over hers.

Edie drew back, flushed with guilt. What the hell was she doing? She was married, for god's sake!

No, you're not, said a sad little voice in her head. *Not anymore.*

The woods closed around them, tight, watchful, expectant. "I—I shouldn't—" she murmured.

She frowned and turned to listen, breaking the spell.

"Sounds like your daughter's calling you," said Cameron, leaning back on his haunches.

Edie stood so fast she hit her head on a branch, knocking some sense into herself. What was she doing, she berated herself, kissing strange men she'd just met? What would Joshua think?

"I'll go see what she wants," she muttered, and scurried out of the woods.

"Mum! Mum!" Neve came racing out of the castle, then screeched to a stop and warily eyed Cameron, who had followed Edie. "Oh, I'd forgotten about you."

"Neve!" exclaimed Edie with a horrified glance at Cameron. "Don't be so rude."

Neve shrugged and nodded at the castle meaningfully. "I need to show you something. Right now!"

Lips tight with embarrassment, Edie said to Cameron, "I'm so sorry. She's not usually this rude."

But Cameron was laughing. "Dinnae fash yourself. I'll be sure to pay her back in kind one day." He grinned broadly at Neve, winked at Edie, said, "I'll see you soon," and sauntered off towards the cliffs.

"What is wrong with you?" Edie hissed when Cameron was out of earshot. "I can't believe how rude you were."

Neve ignored the reproach and grabbed Edie's arm, hauling her towards the castle. "Come and look!" she cried excitedly. "There are secret passages in the walls!" She brandished a large, crumpled paper at Edie. "They're right here, on the plans of the castle!"

"Not so secret if they're on the plans," said Edie sourly. "They were probably built for the staff to move around the castle without being seen."

"Stop being so practical, Mum! This is a real find." She led the way into the kitchen. Letting go of Edie, she hurried across the expanse and disappeared through a doorway. Her head popped out a moment later. "Come on, Mum!"

Edie counted to ten silently, then followed her daughter into the butler's pantry in time to see her disappear through the door at the far end. With misgiving, she stepped through into a dark passage.

The ground was uneven, covered in small stones and rat and bat droppings. Some light entered the gloom from arrow slits that sliced the floor into thin ribbons. The walls were roughly hewn and every few meters were crude drawings of a plague mask with the eyes gouged out.

CHAPTER 9

"What is it?" said Neve, coming back to Edie.

"A plague mask. Like doctors used to wear in the old days."

"That sounds suitably horrible," said Neve with ghoulish glee. "I wonder who drew them."

Not sharing her daughter's delight in the new discoveries, Edie stared at the crude drawings, the withered silence biting into her skin like restless spider mites. There was rage in their execution, gouged deep into the stone.

"It stinks," said Neve, wrinkling her nose. She took off down the passage.

Edie followed slowly, uneasy and alert.

Doorless openings lining one side had Neve darting into each tiny empty room with hopeful enthusiasm. The passage was narrow and wrapped all the way around the castle like a noose. The odor of dust and ammonia clung to the stale air, making it hard to breathe. Sensing they were being followed, Edie kept glancing over her shoulder, certain there was a turbulence of newly awakened shadows scuttling to hide between the dim strips of light.

They came back to the point where they had started.

"That was rather anticlimactic," said Neve. "I was kind of expecting to find a couple of skeletons, or a Viking helmet or something."

"This was built long after the Vikings," said Edie, rubbing her nape, still feeling they were being watched. "And I've had enough of skulking about in here. It's time for lunch."

They turned to leave, then froze.

"You can hear that, right?" whispered Neve, moving closer to Edie.

"Yes. Sounded like bagpipes."

"We're in Scotland. Makes sense."

"In the castle walls?"

"Could be coming from outside."

The mournful piping skirled through the passage, enveloping the Nunns in a lonely lament as though the piper were playing right in front of them.

"Ooh! I'll bet it's Wully Macleod!" said Neve, squinting hard into the striped gloom.

"Who?"

"He was this piper who escaped after the Battle of Culloden and came here to hide. But the MacKenzies found him and killed him, and ever since his music has been heard in the castle."

"Another ghost?" said Edie doubtfully. Really, there were too many ghosts in this place.

"Ghost music. No one's actually seen Wully, but I found a book in the museum with the legends of Loch na Scáthanna, which said he made a pact with the Witch in the Well."

The lament swelled around them, shrill, then soft. As the music faded, it was replaced by the echo of a sob and running footsteps.

"Mum!" Neve whispered, a quaver in her voice. "Something's coming."

"Stop Wully . . . Mungo's heid! Mungo's heid!" The cry quivered along the walls, rooting Edie and Neve to the spot.

"You heard that?" whispered Neve, clutching her mum's arm tightly.

Edie nodded, her mouth too dry to speak.

Running towards them, a figure flickered in and out of the bands of light and shadow. It stopped in front of Edie and Neve in a tremble of surprising warmth.

"Stop Wully! Mungo's heid!"

Undeniably a ghost, the man stared at them in astonished fright, hands clutching his head, panting as though he had been running through eternity. The Nunns stared back.

He was so vivid. His messy hair quite red, the blue of his eyes bright. Edie thought if she reached out to touch him, he'd feel solid, like he hadn't realized he was dead.

His terrified eyes swiveled to the walls. "Lady!" he bellowed.

Neve overcame her shock first. She followed his gaze to the crude drawings. "Is that Lady?" she whispered with only a slight tremor in her voice.

"Lady!"

"What are you doing?" Edie hissed.

"Talking to him. It's the ghost from last night. I think there's something wrong with him."

"Speak to him. See what he wants."

Impressing Edie with her composure, Neve smiled gently at the ghost and said, "Hello there."

He regarded Neve with expectant longing; then his face creased and he burst into gusty sobs. "No' Lottie!" he wailed. "No' Mungo's Lottie."

"No, I'm not Lottie," said Neve. "Are you Mungo?"

"Mungo want Lottie!" A horrible tremor ran through him, his head turning slightly to listen.

Edie heard it a moment later. A rapid *click-clack-click-clack* coming towards them. Her blood ran cold. She whipped around, peering down the long passage, but nothing wavered in the banded light.

"Mum," Neve quavered, pulling at Edie's sleeve. She pointed to the wall beside Mungo.

Every hair on Edie's body stood on end. Etched with grinding slowness into the stone another plague mask appeared, each grating line and curve hitting her exposed nerves like nails drawn hard down a blackboard.

"Lady is comin'!" Mungo shrieked, and vanished.

Before the mask was complete, Edie grabbed Neve's arm and hustled back through the butler's pantry into the kitchen.

Neither spoke, not daring to voice the clamor in their heads. Edie listened for the click-clacking she was growing to recognize with dread. But all she heard was the loud hum of the old fridge.

Edie found her voice first. "Let's get out of here."

Neve didn't need telling twice. They ran out of the castle, not stopping until they reached the cliff edge.

Mist still smothered the loch, champagne pink. Not a sound broke the hush of the island. A slight breeze winnowed through the mist, setting it to dance in ribboned shapes. But as quickly as it came, the breeze disappeared and the mist settled once more, moist and thick.

"We definitely saw it," Neve said, more to herself than Edie. "It scared Mungo."

"Yes."

"And who the hell is Lady?"

"Another ghost?" Edie hazarded.

Neve ran a hand down her face, pulling her eyes down to show veined lids. "Whoever heard of a ghost scaring other ghosts? They're all dead."

"With unresolved issues."

Neve was quiet for a long time, lost in her own thoughts, then turned to Edie. "What is wrong with Mungo? He was odd as ghosts go."

"Not odd," said Edie, who had watched the ghost of Mungo carefully. "I think he is—was—autistic."

"An autistic ghost?"

"After everything I've seen here in the past few days, I'm not the least surprised."

"Why can he speak to us, but the others haven't?"

"I don't know. They're ghosts. They can do as they please."

"He seemed so *real*. Far more than the other ghosts we've seen. And kind of lost."

"Maybe he died recently. I think I saw his grave." Edie nodded in what she thought was the direction of the Maundrell graveyard.

"Hardly a big reveal, Mum. It's well known ghosts haunt the places where they died."

"Well, I wish they would go and do it somewhere else," Edie grumbled. "But if he was autistic in life, maybe it has something to do with that? The autistic boy I looked after in Italy struggled to understand abstract concepts."

"There's nothing abstract about death; it's pretty definitive."

"Yes, but the concept of death is confusing for autistic people." Edie squinted into the mist, then brightened. "It's not too late; if we leave now we can still make Lochinver in time to find somewhere to stay the night."

"I'm not going anywhere," said Neve, her lips tucked down into the stubborn line Edie knew too well. "None of the ghosts have hurt us. And I want to find that diamond. We had a deal and you need to stick to it." Then she dashed towards the castle before Edie could stop her, quickly swallowed by the mist.

Edie didn't bother to call her back; she had lost the battle before it had begun. She pressed her palms to her temples. The ghosts might not have harmed them, but they were certainly giving her a headache. For a brief, blessed moment her mind was utterly blank, until a thought presented itself as they do so often when not consciously thinking of any particular thing. She stared sightlessly into the suffocating paleness, turning the thought over.

In a remote place like this, it would be hard to hide a pregnancy, more so a birth, which tended to be noisy. Surely there had been whispers in the halls of the castle, a local scandal perhaps?

There had to be someone she could ask. She had two options, one living, one dead. The second was the crazier of the two. Alice never left the island, but something might have reached her ears. Except she was dead, even if she was sort of communicating.

The first option had more possibilities by the mere virtue of being alive. Edie cast around for a reason to disturb Mr. MacKenzie. She spun around to the castle, little more than a gray haze in the near distance, hunched like a dark omen.

Clammy fingers of mist brushed against Edie's skin. She pulled her jacket tightly around her, shivering. She hadn't given much thought to heating and the castle was cold; it would only get colder with the approach of winter.

She hurried through the seeping mist to the cottages huddled on the far side of the island in a tight row. Edie knocked on the only door with a fairly recent coat of paint. She hugged herself tight as she waited, trying to ignore the vibrating hum rising up from the earth, as fragile and menacing as a lucid dream, twisting on strands of mist stretched thin as violin strings plucked by an invisible hand.

She knocked again. No answer. She knocked on all the other doors; then she stalked off with grim determination to find Mr. MacKenzie.

"Whit dae ye want?"

Edie spun round and hurried back to him. "I thought you were out."

Mr. MacKenzie grunted, peering at her below shaggy eyebrows. Not even the odor-subduing mist could mask the whisky fumes.

"It's getting cold," said Edie. "I was wondering if there was central heating in the castle."

The old man spoke fast, his regional accent strong. By listening carefully Edie smoothed out the hard consonants into something she could understand when he said, "There is, but there's no oil. You'll need to order a truck."

"That doesn't really help us now."

"Aye, it disnae," he agreed, scowling at the mist. "I widnae be surprised if we're in for snow."

"A little early for snow, isn't it? It's only October."

He hunched into himself and muttered, "The Hag's a contrary creature like all women. Sometimes she comes out fast and fierce; other times she comes slow and gentle."

Edie didn't know whether to roll her eyes at Mr. MacKenzie's obvious belief that the weather was controlled by a supernatural being, or to raise her eyebrows at the sexist remark. She did neither.

"Is there any wood?" she asked. "There are fireplaces in all the rooms."

"Aye." His eyes dimmed with something like fear when they flicked to the castle. "I'll bring a load to the kitchen for you and the lass," he said gruffly. "Two loads maybe."

"Thank you," said Edie, thinking furiously how to broach the subject of furtive births. "Mr. MacKenzie?" she cried, as he stepped back into his cottage.

His head popped out through the closing door. "Aye?"

"I was wondering," she gushed. "Um—how long you've worked on the island?"

His face scrunched until he looked like a shaggy goblin. "Near twenty year now." The door started to close again.

"Oh," said Edie, deflating. "Wait!"

The door opened a fraction.

"Did you—? I mean, are you from around here?"

He puffed out a gusty sigh of annoyance. "Aye. Haggs born and bred."

The alien sound of an engine broke the unnatural silence of the island.

"You've a visitor sounds like," he said, and slammed the door shut before Edie could ask him anything else.

Huffing, knowing she had handled the conversation clumsily, she turned and marched down to the castle.

A geriatric green van was parked outside the entrance to the kitchen. It was something Joshua would've loved, though she didn't know the make of it, knowing next to nothing about cars in general.

It was also empty.

Edie slipped into the kitchen cautiously. Hamish Macleod loitered at the far end.

"Hello," she said.

He jerked in alarm, then grinned sheepishly. "The door was open," he offered in explanation for his uninvited presence. "It's Hamish. Hamish Macleod," he added.

"What can I do for you, Mr. Macleod?"

"Just Hamish," he reminded her, and nodded at a box on the table in front of him. "Thought you might need a few provisions. Not sure what would suit, so I brought options."

"Oh!" Edie colored slightly, embarrassed by her unkind thoughts of Hamish. She mustered an awkward smile. "That's kind of you."

He shuffled his feet, equally embarrassed. "Well, Lorna said you two were alone here in the castle; it's only right we offer our services as we did for the Maundrells afore."

"Ah," said Edie. Not a grand gesture of kindness after all, but a marketing tactic.

Shoving his hands deep in his pockets, his gaze slid to the walls as though expecting to see dripping blood. "My uncle used to deliver to the castle. Every Wednesday, regular as time. I remember as a bairn the auld van going over the Brig o' Haggs. Wisnae allowed to go with, mind. The Maundrells were an odd lot. Didnae like strangers."

"No one seemed to like them," said Edie, a little sad for the Maundrells. *They can't all have been bad.*

Reading her mind, Hamish said, "They weren't all bad. We were grateful to them. There's not much call for customers in Haggs and the Maundrells paid promptly. Cannae say the same for others in the village. And we'd see the auld lord from time to time down the pub. He was well liked. No airs and graces to that one."

"Percy?" said Edie. "I thought he left the castle when he was a teenager."

"Nae, the auld man, Lord Jasper. He would have been Percy's father if I've my facts straight. There was a bit more to the title, but we all called him Lord Jasper."

It was the first time Edie had thought of the title that went with being a Maundrell. The vampire hadn't mentioned anything, so she assumed she didn't have to be Lady Maundrell due to her illegitimacy. And for that she was thankful.

"When was this?"

Hamish frowned at her abrupt tone but said, "When I was a bairn. Not so regular afore he died, ooh, must be a guid twenty years ago now."

"Did he ever go to Haggs before 1970?"

"Bit afore my time," said Hamish.

"Did he make any"—Edie searched for an appropriate word— "friends?"

"Friends?"

"Yes." She blushed. "Female friends."

Hamish pulled at his bottom lip. "He was a friendly sort. You mean—?" He was blushing now.

"Yes."

"Mmmm . . . There's not much choice of women hereabouts, except maybe Agnes at the Stagger Inn." Hamish pulled a face. "Not auld Agnes. Cannae say there's a man alive as would take her on willingly."

They stared at each other, the air thick with their shared discomfort. Hamish looked away first.

"Well," said Edie with false brightness, "thank you for the provisions."

He grunted, his eyes sidling back to her, narrowing as though he were trying to place her.

"Was there something else?"

He blinked and cleared his throat. "Nowt that cannae wait." He nodded at the box. "Pop whatever you dinnae use back at the shop." With a last look around, he grinned awkwardly and shuffled through the kitchen with a, "I'd best be off or Lorna will have my guts for garters if I'm too long away."

Edie followed him out to his van.

He got in and shoved the key in the ignition. The van made a dreadful noise and a puff of black smoke erupted from the exhaust. Hands gripping the steering wheel, he stared through the windscreen for a long while.

"Mr. Macleod—Hamish, is there something else?"

"Not as such . . . well, Lorna is worried about the two of you here all alone in the castle."

"Why would your sister be worried about us?"

His jaw worked; then all in one breath he said, "It's nearing Samhain, and she said if you wanted to step along our way for the night, you'd be welcome. It's not safe for two women alone here on Samhain."

Edie was touched. "Thanks for the offer, but we'll be leaving before then."

"Is that a fact?" With an awkward half smile, he put the old van into reverse, grinding the gears and muttering curses.

Edie watched the green van limp across the Brig o' Haggs, not sure what to make of the man. He was nosy and endearingly awkward. She smiled. She rather liked Hamish Macleod.

Her thoughts turned to Jasper Maundrell as she walked back into the castle. One of her parents had to have been a Maundrell; her illegitimacy suggested the other hadn't been. She'd been assuming her mother had been the Maundrell, but there was a fifty-fifty chance it had been her father. And she knew a little about Jasper Maundrell, courtesy of her ghost writer.

Mr. MacKenzie had been like speaking to a brick wall, so option two it was. She needed to find Alice.

CHAPTER 10

For two days, Edie hunted a ghost.

While Neve holed up in the museum and obsessed over finding the Maundrell Red, so Edie obsessed with finding Alice, convincing herself the ghost writer could provide the answer to her parents' identity. She didn't see much of the living. Mr. MacKenzie had been true to his word and delivered two great piles of chopped wood to the kitchen door, then made himself scarce. But occasionally she saw Cameron from the windows. She told herself she wasn't watching out for him, though her blush called her a liar. It had been so long since a man other than Joshua had kissed her, and her thoughts circled back to it constantly. She rather hoped Cameron would seek her out again, then felt guilty for hoping.

She wasn't the only one prowling the halls. The fear that had been her savior through childhood, granting her a cloak of invisibility from the curious stares at her charity clothes, her home-hacked hair, the nuns always by her side, hadn't prepared her for the malevolence leaching from the castle walls, and the constant *click-clack-click-clack* following her. This was a primordial fear, stapled to the marrow of her bones, fear of what lurked in the shadows, of night-mares, of claws and blood.

As she peeled away the secrets that had moldered quietly in the lonely hours of the castle's long dormancy, she wasn't surprised to discover more ghosts, each adding another layer of tragic history.

A wailing baby in the early hours. A Highlander hanging from the rafters of the Baronial Hall. A horde of roaring Vikings nearly scared Edie to death one evening and sent her running away like a frightened hare before they disappeared over the edge of the cliffs. Neve had her own ghostly experiences with a maid dressed in an old-fashioned uniform one afternoon in the museum rooms and a well-dressed gentleman walking across the Inner Ward. Each encounter added to the gloomy knowledge that these had once been people who had lived, loved, hated and died in the castle.

The most frequent specters were Mungo and the girl in the garden. Edie often heard Mungo running through the castle walls or caught a glimpse of him as she turned a corner, startling them both, before he vanished. At night, when sleep would not come, she sat on the broad windowsill in her bedroom with the window slightly open to cool her night sweats and watched the girl flitting about the rose gardens.

The ghost girl hardly varied from her routine, searching for something into eternity. She was fading, little more than a pale sil-houette, as though she had forgotten who she had once been. Per-haps she would eventually fade until she was nothing more than a strange feeling or a cold shiver on a warm day. It was only when the girl looked up at the castle that she became more defined, wearing an expression of such terror it tore at Edie's heart. Whatever the girl had feared in life gave her no rest in death, and that something was in the castle, perhaps watching as Edie watched. But of Alice there was nothing.

It was late on their sixth night at the castle that Edie, weary from stomping fruitlessly around the castle after a feckless ghost, entered the museum rooms. Neve sat cross-legged on the floor surrounded by boards and paper and books. She had finally succumbed to wearing the clothing Edie had scrounged from a closet, and looked rather like a hippie in checked flared trousers and a blue corduroy jacket. The clothing, though dated, was clean and the sort of expensive quality that lasted years.

"Come on," she said. "It's time for bed. We've got an early start tomorrow if we want to make it down to Edinburgh."

Neve looked up, unfocused and glaring. "The Maundrells were bastards!"

"You are not the only one to think so. And I'm sure some of them were. I'm one too."

"I don't mean like that. I mean nasty, cruel, selfish, horrible people! You will not believe what they did!" Neve breathed deeply to rein in her fury, then said, "I think I may have found someone who had a genuine claim to the Maundrell Red."

Edie sighed, resigning herself to an even later night. "Let's hear it then."

Neve jumped up and hurried over to a board. "In 1965, when the diamond was stolen, there were ten people on the island. I've gone back into each of their pasts, more as a process of elimination than anything." She took down an old sepia photo of two men standing side by side, staring stoically and unsmiling at the camera. They wore bush hats with flat-topped acacia trees in the background. "This is Ernest Maundrell and his valet Lachlan Macleod in South Africa. And this—" Neve took down another photo of a man and woman dressed in servants' uniforms in front of Maundrell Castle, "is Ainsley and Leana Macleod, who were both working here in 1965."

"And?" said Edie.

"And the real mystery isn't Ernest but Lachlan. These two found the diamond and brought it back to Scotland. But when Ernest's son dies, he blames the Maundrell Red." She frowned at the photo of Ernest and Lachlan. "It's kind of weird, but Ernest was scared of the diamond. This was before he even left Africa. He was talking about someone called a *sangoma*—I'm not sure what that is."

"I think it's a witch doctor."

"Oh, that makes sense then. So this *sangoma* tried to stop them taking the diamond from Africa because it had some sort of power."

Edie snorted her disbelief.

"Well, we're seeing ghosts, so who's to say there aren't other supernatural powers floating about, and after what I felt in the grotto the other day," said Neve with a sudden shiver. "Anyway, Ernest and Lachlan went back to Africa, taking the Maundrell Red with them. Then Ernest pops his clogs and Lachlan brought his personal effects back home including the Maundrell Red." Neve drew in a deep breath after talking at breakneck speed. "And Lachlan claimed he had been promised the diamond on Ernest's deathbed, but he had no proof of it."

"How did you find this all out?" asked Edie, impressed with what her daughter had achieved in just under a week.

"Some of it was already here in the museum, and I've been plowing through Ernest's diaries, but I haven't finished them all yet. He was one of those old colonial types, all elephant and tiger hunting in India, and prospecting and lion hunting in Africa. He got around, did old Ernest . . . But what I'm trying to tell you is that until his dying day Lachlan Macleod claimed the diamond belonged to him. And it really did, Mum!" She pulled out a wad of paper from a pile on the floor and waved it at Edie. "The museum lot didn't find this! It's Ernest Maundrell's will dated *before* he returned to Africa in 1901. No other will was found in his effects after he died, and the will states very clearly he had left the Maundrell Red to Lachlan Macleod for a lifetime of service and stalwart friendship—Ernest's words, not mine."

Edie took the will from Neve and read it, then looked up. "Where on earth did you find this?"

"That's the best part. It was in a book of poetry amongst Ernest's diaries. I think it belonged to his wife. There's a dedication to a Winifred, and he was married to a Winifred. And she was using his will as a bookmark, so she must've known, but the bastard Maundrells kept schtum and never gave the diamond to Lachlan." She picked up the photo of the servants in front of Maundrell Castle. "And this bloke was Ainsley Macleod, Lachlan's grandson, and guess where Ainsley and his wife were on the thirtieth of October 1965 when the Maundrell Red went missing? Right here, working as groundskeeper with his wife as the housekeeper!"

"Yes, all right, very clever." But it was impossible not to be hooked by the puzzle Neve had posited.

"Well, it is, because the museum people never made the connection between Lachlan Macleod and the Macleods who worked here," said Neve, preening. "They don't even have the Macleods on their list of possible thieves."

"Technically they wouldn't have been thieves if you're right and the diamond belonged to them anyway."

Neve nodded gloomily. "Which is a right bastard."

"Did you say the diamond was stolen on the thirtieth of October, not the thirty-first?"

"Yeah. I thought that was a bit strange. I kind of expect everything dreadful to happen here on Halloween. Although something dreadful did happen the next day with three people dying, so . . ."

"I don't suppose you've found out who my biological parents were while you've been going through all this stuff?" said Edie hopefully. Neve had been far more successful in her search than she had been.

"No. The most recent birth on the island was in 1945; a boy, Mungo Maundrell."

"Mungo? The same as the ghost in the passages?"

Neve nodded. "He was one of the people who died in 1965. And you were right, he was autistic, quite severely so. I found a couple of doctors' reports about him. They were not polite about autism in those days. Mostly he was called an imbecile or similar. Poor bugger."

Poor bugger indeed, thought Edie sadly.

After a great deal of cajoling and finally threats, Edie got Neve to her bedroom. It was long after midnight when she stepped into a hurried cold shower to cool the building heat of a hot flush.

She switched off the water, shivering, certain she'd heard the bedroom door open and close.

"Neve?" she called.

Her chest tightening with disquiet when she received no answer, she stepped out of the shower and wrapped a towel around herself. Would Cameron come into her room uninvited? Had he knocked and she hadn't heard?

She stared through the open doorway to her bedroom, then almost laughed in relief when *floflofloflofloflo* echoed into the bathroom, followed by a scritching like a spider trapped in a matchbox.

She tiptoed into the bedroom to catch . . . *Greer is dead* . . . scribbling across the wall above the bed. It faded into . . . *Mr. and Mrs. Macleod are devastated. Mother outdid herself in cruelty. She told them Greer managed to do two things right today; she provided the Maundrells with an heir and she died doing so. I really hoped Mrs. Macleod would slap Mother. She looked like she wanted to. I like Mrs. Macleod. She has always been kind to me, and I am sorry Greer is dead. Mother told the Macleods they would not be allowed to see Mungo* . . .

Edie pulled the towel tightly around herself, shuddering in the cold night air creeping in from the loose windowpanes, but not daring to take her eyes off the scratching writing.

Mungo is only a baby and already I pity him. I will write to Jasper tonight to tell him about Greer. I would rather he hears from me, for I know Mother will either not bother to tell him until he returns home or tell him in the cruellest way she—

Edie's head whipped to the door as Alice's writing ended abruptly. *Click-clack-click-clack* sounded loudly, pacing the hall outside. She glanced between the now blank wall and the bedroom door, her mind swirling, connecting snippets of hearsay and fact into an upsetting deduction. Alice had warned Edie to beware of her mother. Alice's mother was Lady Elizabeth. Mungo was terrified of something or someone he called Lady. Could it be that whatever stalked the halls, scaring the other ghosts, was the ghost of Lady Elizabeth?

As she breathed shallowly and slowly, a tiny part of her, the brave bit she kept well hidden, wanted to yank open the door and confront the ghost. She stayed put, knowing she was no match for Lady Elizabeth, living or dead.

The pacing outside disappeared quite suddenly. Edie released her pent-up trepidation in a gushing sigh. Everyone accused the Witch in the Well of every misfortune that had occurred on the island, but she wondered if maybe the Witch was blamed unfairly, that Lady Elizabeth, whose presence hung like a diseased miasma over the castle, wasn't the cause of some of them.

She dithered in the silence, wanting to confirm what Alice had written. But she had a long drive ahead tomorrow, she needed to get some sleep, and she did not love the idea of creeping around the castle with a ghost that scared her as much as Lady Elizabeth did. And they would come back during the next school holidays; Edie knew Neve would insist on it and she would cave as she always did. To be fair, she had her own unresolved search to finish.

She dithered some more, laying out her clothes for tomorrow and packing the overnight bag.

"Shit!" she muttered, knowing she wouldn't sleep until she checked, and shrugged on her jeans, shirt, jumper, and jacket, putting on her shoes without socks. She contemplated waking up Neve to walk with her to the museum rooms but resisted the urge. She was the adult in their relationship, for god's sake! The unsettling niggle that Neve was far braver than her gnawed at her worth as a parent. Angry at her own timidity, she stole out into the dark corridor before she could talk herself out of it.

Switching on lights as she went, Edie listened for click-clacking footsteps as she hared down the stairs to the museum and the Maundrell family tree. She quickly found the names she was looking for: Theodore, Jasper and Greer. No longer dead names but brought to life through Alice's scrawls.

"So young," she whispered. Theodore had been eighteen and Greer just seventeen. Though Theodore had died somewhere in France, both died on the same day in 1944. 31 October. Samhain.

The next generation had three names. Mungo Maundrell, son of Theodore and Greer, and his cousins, Charlotte and Percy, children of Jasper Maundrell and a Vida Hayes. There were no death dates except for Mungo and Charlotte. The family had stopped updating the family tree in 1965.

She stared at the names until her eyes watered. It felt strange to think of this family in relation to herself. But it was warming too, a little glow shimmering in her chest. Here were her ancestors, people who had shaped her genetically. Perhaps she might have liked them, even loved them if given the chance.

But if her surmising was correct, there were only three possibilities for a name here to belong to one of her parents. Lady Elizabeth would have been sixty-five when Edie was born, too old to have a child. That left Jasper, Vida, and Alice.

According to Hamish Macleod, Jasper had been a regular at the pub in Haggs. It was entirely plausible he'd been having an affair with someone in the village and Edie had been the regretted by-product discarded at an orphanage. The same applied to Vida. There was also the possibility Jasper and Vida had had another child, but Edie couldn't think of a reason why they might have abandoned their child if they were married and already had children, *especially* if one had died.

And then there was Alice. Alice who had never left the island. It was possible someone had come to the island, but from all Edie had gathered about the Maundrells they seemed an eccentric family who had valued their privacy an awful lot.

She tapped her teeth with a fingernail thoughtfully. There was another possibility, of course. The Macleods who had been working at the castle. She quickly scrapped that idea; the Macleods would've been a similar age to Lady Elizabeth, and equally too old to have children.

A stealthy footfall from the corridor scattered her musings.

Alarm squeezing her chest, she listened to the night. No click-clacking sent her fleeing to her bedroom, but she had heard something.

Visions of an axe murderer remerged. Then her more sensible self chided her for being melodramatic, insisting it was probably Cameron.

Even so Edie's skin crawled as she crept to the door and peered up and down the hall.

It was empty.

She stole along the corridor to peek around the corner. Her fingers hovered over the light switch of the unlit corridor, then paused as torchlight flickered at the far end and disappeared down the stairwell of the Hollow Tower.

Almost certain it was Cameron, some of Edie's panic faded into curiosity. Why was he skulking about by torchlight when he could've switched on the main lights as she had done?

Curiosity overwhelmed her fear. Edie scurried down the darkened corridor, one hand on the wall. She slipped down the pitch-black stairwell of the Hollow Tower in time to see the torchlight disappear into the library. High on adrenaline, Edie felt the urge to giggle hysterically. No one who knew her would believe practical, logical Edwina Nunn would creep through a haunted castle in the middle of the night. She was far too sensible and fearful for midnight escapades.

Gathering her failing courage, she stopped in the library's doorway. It was dark and so silent Edie's breathing was the only sound. She felt along the wall and flicked the lights on.

"Hello."

She shrieked. Her eyes flew up to Cameron on the ladder.

"You—You—Christ, you gave me a fright!" A hand to her racing heart, she said, "What are you doing here in the middle of the night . . . in the dark?" with a pointed look at the torch in his hand. It wasn't switched on.

Cameron pulled out a book and glanced at the cover, taking his time. "Cuidnae sleep, and I didnae want to wake you. What are *you* doing here in the middle of the night?" he asked, putting the book under his arm before climbing down the ladder.

"Same as you, couldn't sleep," said Edie defensively, conscious her thin, fair hair was frizzled from her shower and her jeans were rucked up around her knees from being pulled on when damp.

"You should be more careful wandering around in the dark here," he said, stepping close to her. His face in shadow, his amber eyes glowed, giving him a predatory look at odds with the smile curving his lips.

"Can you feel it?" he whispered, his gaze traveling around the library.

"Feel what?" Edie whispered back. She was certainly feeling something as heat bloomed up her throat and face.

"The castle. It feels like it's alive, and it disnae want us here."

All thought evaporated as he ran a hand up Edie's arm to her bare neck.

"You can feel it," he murmured. "You're shivering."

"I'm cold." Again, the defensive tone.

"Mmmm . . ." He raised a disbelieving, mocking eyebrow.

The air curled around them, their breaths mingling as Cameron leaned towards her. So close, so solid, so there. Was she a fool to hope he might kiss her again? Did she want him to? Her breath hitched a notch, faster, uneven, her stomach clinching in anticipation, eyes fixed on his lips. Of course she did.

Floflofloflofloflo . . .

Edie turned her head to the sound, Cameron's lips brushing against her hair.

He stepped back, frowning, his control of the burgeoning situation slipping with Edie's distraction. "You all right?"

Floflofloflofloflo . . .

Edie's eyes flicked to the altar, the bookcases. She peered down the corridor behind her. Her nape prickled uneasily. There was an urgency to Alice's whisper, a warning.

"Did you hear that?" she asked. "A scratching?"

Cameron listened, then shook his head. "No, but many a wee ghaistie goes bump in the night here."

The intimacy of moments before had broken, and awkwardness crisped the air between them.

"Well—um—" said Edie, her whole body a messy hot blush of embarrassment. "I think I'm going to bed."

"I'll walk you to your room."

Grateful for his midnight gallantry, she switched off the library lights and followed Cameron into the passage.

Floflofloflofloflo . . .

Edie put on a lick of speed, eyeing the walls. Cameron didn't question her haste, except to raise an eyebrow, and matched her pace. She was very aware of his arm brushing against hers occasionally, their footsteps a tandem echo.

Floflofloflofloflo . . .

"I'll leave you here," said Cameron when they reached the stairs winding through the Clan Tower. "Will you be all right finding your way to your room?"

Edie turned from her scrutiny of the walls, belatedly hearing more than a question of solicitude, an unspoken, more intimate promise of something more.

She opened her mouth, then shut it again, aware of *floflofloflo-flo* curling around her like a distressed cat seeing things humans couldn't with their witch eyes. She focused on him briefly. Did she want something more than stolen kisses in a haunted castle? Could this be the start of something that could survive the rigors of reality beyond Haggs Pass without the dark romance surrounding Loch na Scáthanna?

She thought not. His honey-hued eyes were lit with a promise that would last the night, not something that could survive the cold light of day.

Knowing her fragile heart wouldn't handle disappointment, she said croakily, "I can find my way from here. Thanks."

Cameron gave her a long searching look, then nodded. "Guid night then." He disappeared into the stairwell's maw, taking the stairs two at a time.

Edie ran down the corridor, her chest squeezing with worry, following Alice's *floflofloflo* . . . fluttering ahead of her like a wounded bird.

October 1965

Lottie knew where Mungo would go. *The same place whenever he managed to escape Dr. Kincaid. Maundrell Castle had a multitude of hiding places, but some had been* built *for hiding.*

She hurried through the little-used door in the Chapel Tower, her breath little hiccups of panic, sure she was being followed. The library dimmed around her. A cloying, saturated darkness brushed against her face, her hair, her throat, the shadows curious to see what manner of creature she was and why she ran.

With a spurt of speed up the worn stone steps on the far side, she slipped into the passages between the walls.

They weren't secret passages, but few used them. Built by the feared and vicious Macleods of Haggs five hundred years before, they threaded through the vast walls of the castle on all three stories, linked to each other by tight, spiral staircases. The walls were roughly hewn, the floors uneven and coated in centuries of dust. Little light filtered through the arrow slits.

According to Mrs. Macleod, who had it on good authority from her grandmother, the Macleods had built the labyrinth of passages to confuse intruders so only a true Macleod could find their way in or out of the castle. Lottie's grandfather, Rupert Maundrell, had had a more prosaic theory that the passages had been built so soldiers could defend the walls without fear of the enemies' archers in battle. Lottie tended to favor her grandfather's version, for he had been a soldier for many years and had known of such things.

The passages still served the same purpose: to hide Macleods from siege or attack, and Mungo, who was half a Macleod, had been subject to both.

Through the thick walls Lottie heard the faint cries of Dr. Kincaid and her mother calling Mungo. She should've felt safe, for few knew Mungo came into the walls, yet she couldn't shake the stifling awareness of being followed, perhaps her own fear given life.

Mungo's running footsteps and trailing sobs echoed towards her. Her heart aching for him, she hurried through the checkerboard of light and shadow and caught up to him between the curved walls of the Hollow Tower. She paused to watch him warily, for he was at his most unpredictable after a meltdown, though he had never once tried to harm her.

His shoulders shook as he calmed down to sighing hiccups before she approached him cautiously. Together, they peered out of the arrow slit at one of the loveliest views of Loch na Scáthanna. The setting sun lit the water with an inner glow like it hid the entrance to hell. The Munros' heather-clad slopes had darkened, sliding into the loch like black lava, and beyond, the Minch had been set on fire.

"*Doc-ta,*" *Mungo hiccupped.*

Dr. Kincaid stormed across the lawn towards the rose gardens. His urbanely handsome face creased into something ugly and feral, something desperate.

"*Silly, silly doctor,*" *said Lottie with a great deal of satisfaction.* "*He won't find us in here.*"

"*Silly doc-ta,*" *Mungo mimicked, and took another shuddering* breath before finding Lottie's hand in the dark, and they watched in silence as everyone came out to search for Mungo.

As the last glimmer of sunlight disappeared, lanterns were lit and bobbed across the island like little swinging comets. At first only Mungo's name was called, but as the night wore on, Lottie's name echoed against the Munros' mighty slopes too. But the majestic mountains kept the two fugitives' secret, their peaks obscuring the emerging stars as the world spun on its axis.

Lottie's attention was drawn to the grotto. Shadows slunk from the three entrances like strands of cobweb. They reared and multiplied into vulpine shapes emerging from their lair to sniff the air in search of prey, then prowled through the roses, vibrating with avid expectation.

The shadows were early; it was still a week to Samhain. The last time they'd emerged early had been shortly before her grandfather died. Lottie ground her teeth, her spine tingling with an awful foreboding. Something would soon happen. Something horrible. But the comforting bulk of Mungo kept away the worst of Lottie's fearful imaginings of what Samhain might bring.

"Ant Alice," said Mungo. He, too, watched the grotto.

Framed palely in the entrance, Alice glanced over her shoulder, fearfully, furtively, then hurried through the rose gardens.

Worried they'd be discovered, Lottie slid down the wall, pulling Mungo down with her. They leaned against each other.

"Is time fo' Mungo's bath," said Mungo after a long silence punctuated by their names called. It was long past his bedtime, but some routines were imprinted into the concrete of his mind.

"Not tonight, my Magpie," said Lottie, who had no intention of letting Mungo out of the safety of the walls until she knew Dr. Kincaid was off the island. There would be consequences for her actions, those she could cope with, but there would be repercussions for Mungo too, and she wanted to delay those for as long as possible.

"Mungo want ice cream," he said hopefully.

"Not tonight, my Magpie."

He sat quietly for long minutes with only the occasional hiccupping sigh, pulling each of Lottie's fingers gently, over and over.

She leaned her head against the stone wall, tired, tense and watchful, listening to a scrabbling of claws she hoped was only rats and not something willed up in nightmares.

"Doc-ta fight Lady," said Mungo in what passed for a conversational tone for him.

Lottie's eyebrows shot up in astonishment. "Dr. Kincaid fought with Bitsie?" she confirmed, well acquainted with Mungo's descriptions of the family.

He nodded and wiped his snotty nose on his sleeve. "Aye. Lady."

"What were they fighting about?"

Mungo's face crunched with confusion. "Glass."

"Glass?"

"Aye. Glass." On Lottie's palm he drew a teardrop with his finger.

With no idea what Mungo meant, she said, "Glass what? Glass windows? Stained glass? Or do you mean grass? No, that makes even less sense."

"Lady say Doc-ta no' wor-wor . . . wort . . ."

"Work? No, word? No." Lottie frowned. "Work, word, were, worth . . ."

"Worty," said Mungo, nodding.

"Worthy?"

"Aye. Lady say Doc-ta no' worty," he got out to his own satisfaction.

"Worthy of what?"

"Glass."

"I don't know what you mean by glass, Mungo. You'll need to be a bit more specific than that."

But Mungo had lost interest and rocked back and forth, crooning monotonously to himself. He reached out a hand to stroke Lottie's hair so gently she barely felt it.

"Read tae Mungo."

Lottie didn't bother to correct his verb choice, a story was a story to him, so she told him his favorite: the legend of Blacklaw Castle.

"*Some places breed evil,*" *she whispered verbatim in the singsong tones of Mrs. Macleod, for they'd heard the story many times,* "*and some places are evil themselves. James Grey, the new sheriff of Haggs, was bred evil.*"

The shadows in the dusty passage were febrile, curling around Lottie and Mungo's faces, their hands, their drawn-up knees, as though they, too, wished to listen.

"*Sent to the Port of Haggs by Edward Longshanks when most of Scotland lay under English submission,*" *she whispered, keeping an eye on the shadows,* "*James Grey hated the land and its people. And the Macleods hated James Grey so well they could not bear to say his name aloud but spit a curse for the lashes on their backs and the spoilation of their wives and daughters.*

"*At that time the English were constructing Blacklaw Castle on the island to protect the seaport of Haggs. The building was taking too long for James Grey, and he lashed the Macleods something terrible, forcing the men and women to work all hours.*

"*But every night the Macleods would pass the well on the island, a bottomless well, home to the oldest of spirits that guarded the loch, and one by one they dropped their whispered curses into the dark water with a drop of their blood until the well bled red.*

"*So it went on for a year and a day, until the night James Grey forced the Macleods to work on Samhain, angering the spirit of the well. She had been listening to the Macleods' curses and accepted their pact of blood. On that dark, dark night when the veil between worlds was at its thinnest, she crept from her watery home and found James Grey and his men.*"

"*Silly Nglish,*" *said Mungo with satisfaction, his fingers playing with Lottie's hair, intent on each word she uttered.*

"*Yes, they were,*" *said Lottie.* "*As a crone bent and worn, she confronted the Englishmen, promising to build Blacklaw Castle and the bridge to the mainland before the end of the night in return for a day of their lives to be taken when she chose. Recognizing her power, the*

Englishmen decided none would miss one day of their lives, and they agreed.

"In an instant the island was shrouded in a vast shadow that none could penetrate and none could leave.

"For the next one hundred and one years, the isle of Loch na Scáth-anna vanished but for one day each year on Samhain. Then Blacklaw Castle would appear, fully formed and built solid, and the Brig o' Haggs would unfurl, twisted ropes of sand, along which a single Englishman would cross. The moment his foot touched the mainland, the bridge and island vanished back into shadow and the Englishman crumpled to dust, leaving neither nail nor bone behind.

"For the Englishmen were fools; they did not understand the Witch was a fickle creature, interpreting pacts as she saw fit. And for their cruelty to the Macleods, the Englishmen paid with their lives."

When she finished the whispered story, she started another, whispering in the dark until Mungo's hand grew heavier on her head, then stopped moving altogether. She smiled at him in the gloom. He had fallen asleep sitting upright with one hand on her head.

Gently she put his hand in his lap and curled up against him for warmth, for he always ran hotter than anyone else, a human hot water bottle.

The castle was not a quiet place; it ticked and groaned around the two runaways. Somewhere in its depths Bitsie paced the halls, her stiletto heels a distant click-clack-click-clack. Lottie's grandmother didn't have to do much to make her presence felt. There had been times when Lottie thought she heard Bitsie approach and turned to flee, then stopped in confusion when she never appeared.

The shadows elongated and shrank along the walls, a turbulence of black on gray, telling a shadow-story if Lottie squinted through her eyelashes.

Slowly, slowly her lids grew heavier, her thoughts sluggish, and the shadows stole into that uncertain space between waking and sleeping. In fractured lucidity, Lottie accepted the shadows' tale as they merged into a woman with the proud bearing of a queen. Long-limbed and strong, *in a long kilt, her exposed skin was painted in intricate whorls of blue. Others appeared, similarly clothed, similarly decorated in blue. A family, a tribe, from babies to the elderly, settled around a fire.*

Lottie walked amongst them; she recognized the island though shrouded in thick mist, but not as it was now. There was no castle, no cairns, no chapel, no watchtower, no Brig o' Haggs. The oak forest, so small today, covered much of the island, the trees young, strong and tall. The Nine Hags stood in a glade in the wood, the stones newly hewn, covered in pictograms traced in blue. A path led from the stone circle to a small pond. It took a moment for Lottie to recognize it without its retaining wall, unsheltered by the grotto. Where the castle would one day stand was a stone tower crowned with thatch. Smaller dwellings huddled around it, enclosed by a wall with watchful guards walking along it.

The peaceful scene fragmented into hell at a warning shout from the walls. From boats that had snuck through the cloaking mist, fearsome kilted warriors leapt. Lottie shrieked as a fierce battle raged across the island. It was short, bloody and savage. The tribe was rounded up. One by one they were decapitated. No one was spared, not a baby, not an old woman. The last to lose their head was the tall woman. She stood proud and snarling as the axe swung through the air and connected with her neck.

As is the way of dreams, the scene of blood and death blurred. Lottie was not surprised to find herself standing in the grotto. Beside the well stood the tall woman painted in blue. She beckoned Lottie urgently to come closer.

Lottie muttered in her sleep, turning towards Mungo, and the well and the woman fractured and re-formed into more pleasant dreams.

Dawn poked long pale fingers into the passage when Mr. Macleod tapped Lottie on the knee to wake her up.

He crouched in front of her, his whiskered face haggard in the sharp light of the lantern he held up. "It's off to the kitchen for you and the wee man. Grannie Leana is that worried about him. Been up all night fretting."

"Has the doctor gone?" asked Lottie through a yawn.

"Aye. But he'll be back. His sort always comes back like a bad penny."

A faint click-clack-click-clack drifted down to them. Mr. Macleod and Lottie looked up at the ceiling.

"She's a darkness, that woman," he said, scowling.

Lottie understood exactly what he meant. Bitsie's spite had sunk deep into the bones of the castle, into the peat and stone of the island, and they were all trapped in her fine-spun web, helpless against her malice.

Tired and drained, Lottie was horrified when tears streaked down her cheeks once more. All she seemed to do these days was cry.

"Come now, lass. None of that," said Mr. Macleod, not unkindly. "Grannie Leana has some porridge for you and the wee man hot on the stove, so you'd best be up and get about yourself."

"What are we going to do?" she sniffled. "Mungo was in such a state, and I can't bear it when he's in pain. He's so scared of Dr. Kincaid."

"We ken . . . You've a guid heart, lass, and there's always those who'll use that against you." He glanced at Mungo, who still snored the whistly snore of deep sleep. "I wish we could do more for our wee man. If we'd got our due maybe it could've been different, but there's nowt gained crying over spilled milk."

"What was your due?"

Mr. Macleod grinned like it was a silly question. "The Red, of course. Our histories were entwined long afore Mungo was born, lass."

Lottie's eyes opened wide in questioning surprise.

He snorted. "I suppose herself upstairs wilnae be telling you the truth of it. It goes back to your great-grandad."

"Ernest Maundrell? What's he got to do with anything? Didn't he die in Africa?"

"He did, aye, but what herself upstairs disnae like to tell freely is my father was out with Ernest in Africa when he discovered the Maundrell Red and he promised the stone to my father on his deathbed."

"Then it should be yours," said Lottie, though she had no idea of the legality of such things.

"So you would think. But your great-grannie, Lady Winifred,

widnae hear of it, and when herself upstairs came along . . ." He shrugged. *"You and I know she'll not be parted from that stone until her blood runs cold and she's buried six feet under."*

Lottie wanted to rant at the unfairness of it all; how different Mungo's life would've been if the Macleods had had the means to take him in and care for him with love. That went a lot further to someone like Mungo than material wealth. But she was too tired to rant, and instead said, "It's probably just as well, otherwise the Maundrell curse would've passed on to you."

"Pffff! Dinnae go believing in all that, lass; the Maundrells were cursed long afore that stone was pulled from the ground. Now up you come and we'll get the wee man moving."

Mungo always slept heavily and took an age to wake up. He held Lottie's hand and followed her as docilely as a sleepwalker as she and Mr. Macleod made their way through the walls, slipping out through the butler's pantry and into the kitchen.

Percy and Ashley sat at a table with Mrs. Macleod, nursing mugs of tea in tired silence. They looked up when Mr. Macleod entered with Lottie and Mungo trailing behind him.

"Mungo!" Mrs. Macleod hurried from her chair and hugged her grandson tightly. "You're safe . . . Where were they?" she demanded of Mr. Macleod.

"In the walls. They're fine, Leana."

"Grannie Leana," said Mungo sleepily. "Mungo want p'ridge. Mungo want honey. Lots o' honey fo' Mungo."

"You'll get what you're given and be happy for it. Now sit yourself down and put your bib on."

With Mungo under Mrs. Macleod's fretful care, Lottie slipped onto the chair beside Percy and waited until Mrs. Macleod moved to the bank of ovens to ladle out thick porridge into chipped bowls and Mr. Macleod disappeared down to the cellars to get some honey for Mungo.

She started to warn her brother of what she'd heard the day before, but he got in first.

"That was quite a stunt you pulled yesterday, Lottie. Grandmother *was livid when she heard you two had run away again. Where have you been all night?"*

Lottie ignored the question. She checked to ensure Mrs. Macleod was occupied with Mungo, then whispered, "I need to speak to you . . . both of you," she added, with a nod at Ashley, who still looked impossibly handsome and disheveled with lack of sleep.

Percy frowned. "What is it?"

"Bitsie's up to something," said Lottie before she lost her nerve. "She saw you and Ashley—" She blushed, not sure how to put into words the intimacy she had witnessed.

Ashley and Percy stiffened and shared a worried glance. "Saw us when?" said Percy warily.

"In the laburnum arch yesterday," said Lottie with similar caution.

The two men deflated slightly.

"She was really angry," continued Lottie. "And I overheard her talking to Mum about it." She launched into a quick recap of everything she remembered of the overheard conversation between Bitsie and Vida Maundrell.

"Mum would never allow her to use that machine on us," said Percy firmly.

"It sounds like my parents have already agreed to it." Ashley took Percy's hand under the table, lacing their fingers tightly together.

It hurt Lottie to see it, her infatuation still gripping her heart. She looked away, at Mungo, who was eating as messily as ever, getting porridge all over himself, the table and the floor. He finished the bowl and held it up saying, "Guid boy, Mungo." Mrs. Macleod filled it up for him again.

"I told you it was strange your grandmother invited me to stay," said Ashley quietly to Percy. "You said she didn't do anything unless it benefited her in some way. Now we know why I'm here. And if she's got permission from my parents . . ." He let the relevance sink in without needing to finish the sentence.

"I won't allow it!" Percy stared at Ashley with such intensity Lottie's face heated up with embarrassment.

"Won't allow what?" said Jasper from the doorway, his Labradors sitting obediently at his feet.

The three started guiltily.

"Your mother is what," spat Percy, misdirecting his venom for Bitsie at his father.

Jasper sighed and leaned heavily on his cane. "What's she done now?"

Percy opened his mouth, then closed it when Ashley put a hand on his arm and shook his head warningly. Percy stood up and muttered, "I'm sure you'll hear soon enough." He pushed past his father and stormed out of the kitchen.

"I'm sorry, sir," said Ashley, and followed Percy.

Jasper watched them go, then turned to Lottie. "It seems I have missed something."

Lottie put on her most innocent face. "I don't know what that was all about," she lied.

Jasper smiled wearily, looking every one of his thirty-eight years. Though he was a good-looking man in a thin, scholarly way, the trauma of the war had left him prematurely aged, with a limp and lifelong pain. He spent much of his time trying to subtly undo the damage Bitsie caused, well aware what a horror his mother was.

He limped past Lottie and put his hand on Mungo's shoulder. "Glad to see you're safe, my boy," he said.

Mungo glanced up briefly, grinned with porridge dribbling down his chin, before returning to the task of eating breakfast with messy enthusiasm. He chortled when the Labradors put their paws on his lap and stretched up to lick the porridge off his face. "Silly Hash, Silly Brown!" He laughed, still trying to shove a spoonful into his mouth around the dogs.

Jasper pulled the Labradors off Mungo, and watched him for a while, his face creased with sadness. Lottie thought he was seeing Greer in her son. The dead left flawed memories that the living smoothed with time into something perfect, unblemished. These were the memories Bitsie still cherished of Uncle Theodore, as did her father of Greer. Though

Greer had been dead for two decades Lottie understood her father still loved her as he never had Lottie's mother.

It's a terrible thing to understand the truth of your parents' relationship when in your teens. Lottie understood too much about her parents; she had observed the undercurrents and knew their causes. But what she understood most was her mother and father were totally unsuited for each other and should never have married.

CHAPTER 11

Floflofloflofloflo . . .

"Alice?" Edie whispered, a fearful warble in her voice as she raced down the corridor. The air kinked, heavy with her incomprehensible panic that Alice was leading her, warning her, and Edie's first thought was always Neve.

Floflofloflofloflo . . .

Edie barely paused in her headlong flight as the words appeared on the wall alongside her . . . *I am spending more and more time in the grotto as Mother rarely goes there . . .*

A little farther on . . . *I don't like the grotto. It has a peculiar atmosphere . . .*

. . . Sometimes I see shadows above the well out the corner of my eye but when I look properly it's still an old well, nothing more . . .

Floflofloflofloflo echoed down the stairwell corkscrewing through Blacklaw Tower.

Edie leapt up the stairs, following the curling words . . . *I overheard*

the maids talking about a girl from the village who made a pact with the
Witch in the Well to make a man fall in love with her . . .

Out of puff, Edie's worst fears were realized when the writing
scrawled across the corridor leading to the bedrooms . . . *Mr. and*
Mrs. Macleod said I should avoid the grotto. But I am too old for fairy
tales, and Mother scares me far more than a witch . . .

As the word *witch* faded, the lights dimmed. She eyed the lights
worriedly, hoping the geriatric electric supply wasn't going to die on
her now.

An insistent *floflofloflofloflo* pressed against her as she wrenched
open the door to Neve's room.

Neve had left her bedside light on. The sharp scritching bit into
Edie's skin, her terrified gaze on the wall above Neve's sleeping head . . .
The Witch . . . The Witch . . . The Witch . . . Beware . . .

Trembling, Edie turned to the window at a new sound, a succulent hissing. Shadows slithered around the loose windowpanes. They
didn't act like shadows should in the presence of light. They oozed
like black vinegar in oil. Down the walls, across the floor, seeping
moistly towards Edie.

Frozen in the doorway, a swelling scream wedged in her throat as
the shadows sent out exploratory fingers, a pitter-patter creeping up
her jeans and jacket. Petting her throat, her face, her hair.

Repelled, breath hitching, Edie kept absolutely still. Darkness
undulated across her body, unholy and lush, before slipping back
onto the floor and rippling towards the bed.

Galvanized by panic, she lunged towards Neve to shake her
awake, screaming, "Get away from my daughter!"

Neve slept, insensible to Edie's screams and the shadows extend-
ing into moist ribbons to explore her face, snagging in her hair.

"Get off her!" Edie swatted at the creeping darkness, but she may
as well have been fighting her own shadow. They continued to fret
and nuzzle, pinching and stroking in turns.

"Neve!" Edie whispered urgently, tugging at her daughter's

sleeping dead weight, trying to drag her off the bed. Whimpering in terror, she threw herself bodily over Neve.

With a strength Edie hadn't known her to possess, Neve sat up, shifting Edie as though she were as light as dandelion fluff. The shadows settled across her shoulders in a mantle of midnight.

Neve swung her legs off the bed and stood. She took a step forward like a marionette, jerking towards the door. The shadows swarmed around her, stroking her skin, cajoling her forward.

Edie tried to take Neve's arm. The shadows shifted in a menacing hiss, pressing clammily against her chest in warning.

Helpless, tears slipped down her cheeks, as Neve shuddered and juddered into the hall. Not knowing what else to do, Edie followed.

Neve lifted her arm like an automaton to lower the door handle leading to the Blacklaw Tower stairs. The shadows swirled thickly around her, coaxing her downwards step by step. She sleepwalked into the Baronial Hall with Edie following as closely as she dared without the shadows turning their attention to her.

"Nae, Witch!" The bellow echoed around the hall. "Nae hurt lassies!"

Startled, Edie squinted into the darkness. "Mungo?" she whispered.

"Nae, Witch!" Mungo stumbled into the gloom and stopped in front of Neve with his arms wide. He had been a big man in life and towered over Neve.

Edie scuttled towards him, hoping he could help.

He took no notice of her. "Nae, Witch!" he bellowed again. "Nae hurt lassies!"

Neve and the shadows continued slowly across the hall. She lifted a lifeless arm, opened the door and stepped out into the cold night.

Mungo took a shambling step forward, gazing at the expanse of the Inner Ward beyond with a heart-wrenching longing. He took another step, another, almost on the threshold.

Click-clack-click-clack rushed in from all directions. Speeding out of the walls, clattering from the doors, erupting from the vaulted ceiling.

Mungo spun round, clutching his head, and moaned, "Nae, Lady!"

Edie crouched low, hands to her ears to block the rising whine pulsating around the hall. The air parched weirdly, tight against her skin, lips chapping. The desiccated air winnowed visibly like an angry whirlwind. It hissed up to Mungo, forming into a shimmering mirage of a vast, opaque plague mask wearing a flat-topped, wide-brimmed hat.

Mungo took a step back from the threshold, eyes squeezed tight, sobbing, "Nae, Lady! Dinnae hurt lassies . . ."

The beak opened, lengthened, stretching towards him, susurrating *redredredred* like sand in an hourglass. It snapped once, right in his face. The crack resounded around the hall. It gained a life of its own, snickering up into the vaulted ceiling, to chortle like a thousand ravens from the distant rafters, raucous with terrible mirth.

Mungo screamed. It was the scream of a child's nightmares, of the innocent confronted by evil. It broke Edie's heart.

With an eye on Neve making slow, jerky progress across the Inner Ward, she surprised herself by taking a step towards the mask and yelled, "Leave him alone, you fucking bitch!"

The mask shrank slightly and clattering laughter filled the hall, the beak snapping in time, faster and faster.

"I know it's you, Lady Elizabeth!" Edie shouted, carried away by a spurt of courage she hadn't been aware she had. "You leave this poor boy alone!"

The mask swiveled to her, then back to Mungo. It snapped its beak again and lunged at him. Mungo screamed in terror, and he and the mask vanished all at once.

The air still withered with the menace of Lady Elizabeth. A moan slipped from Edie, not daring to move. *Pooorrr boooyyy* crooned into her ears. *Pooorrr boooyyy . . .*

Edie's courage failed. She ran, chased by clattering laughter.

She stumbled into the Inner Ward and through the West Gatehouse after Neve. The frigid night repressed the fragrance of late roses and fading lavender to little more than a crushed wish.

Onwards Neve jerked through the wild gardens, along one path, down another. As she neared the cliffs, a new spine-tingling thought penetrated Edie's terror with visions of her daughter being pushed into the burgundy waters of Loch na Scáthanna.

"Neve!" she pleaded desperately. "Please wake up . . . Get away from me!" she shrieked as the shadows darted towards her with a warning hiss.

Edie sobbed with relief when Neve veered away from the cliffs along another path. Her relief was short-lived.

"No, no, no," she moaned when the silhouette of the grotto appeared ahead amidst the briars like a poisonous toad that swallowed Neve. The shadows snaked and twined, weaving themselves into a tight mesh of sharply thorned vines across the entrance.

"Neve!" Edie yelled. It shouldn't have been possible, but the shadowed thorns cut at her arms and snagged on her jumper as she tried to push through the gossamer mesh.

Her breath came in little panicky sobs as she darted back along the path and down another, forcing her way through a tangle of rosebushes, barely noticing the vicious thorns digging into her skin. She broke free and flew down another path, panting hard.

"No!" she screamed as the entrance ahead started to weave another tight mesh. She put on a burst of desperate speed and ran full tilt ahead.

Thrashing amidst the scratching, puncturing shadows, Edie fought like a wildcat trapped in a snare, shrieking for Neve to wake up.

She was never sure afterwards what she did to break through; one moment she was snarled up in something impossible, the next she was stumbling into the grotto.

Neve stood beside the well. She clutched a jagged rock and sliced through her palm. As she raised her cut hand above the water, Edie thought she saw a figure standing beside Neve. A tall woman, strong and proud, etched with blue.

"Dinnae let her blood touch the water!" Cameron shouted as he burst into the grotto.

Edie leapt forward. The moment her arms closed around Neve the woman disintegrated into the shadows seething above the well in thwarted torment.

Cameron dragged them both bodily from the grotto, not letting go until they were in the rose garden.

"What the blazes?"

They all turned to Fergus MacKenzie racing towards them, following the beam of a powerful torch.

Edie took her daughter's face in her trembling hands. "Neve," she whispered, her voice cracked from shouting. "Are you hurt?"

Neve blinked. "Mum? You're okay!" Her relief was deep and heartfelt. "You were screaming . . . They were all screaming . . ." Then she noticed where she was, flinching at the sight of Mr. MacKenzie and Cameron. "What's going on? You were— You were—" She shook her head in confusion.

"You don't remember anything of the last half hour?" said Edie, keeping the urgency from her voice. "The shadows? They were—" Her throat closed around the impossibility of what she'd witnessed. "You don't remember leaving the castle?"

Neve frowned. "I had the weirdest dream." She rubbed her arms, the cold night air mottling her bare skin with goose bumps. "Did I sleepwalk?"

"You've never—" Tears bunched in Edie's throat, quite trembly with a need to hug her daughter and smother her in kisses. Reining in her maternal instincts, she forced herself to speak calmly. "Tell me about your dream."

Neve scrunched up her face. "There was a battle—here on the island—but it didn't look like this. It was horrible. People screaming and blood everywhere. Then it all disappeared and a woman appeared . . ."

Conscious the men were listening intently, Edie murmured, "Was she tattooed?"

Neve nodded slowly, still not quite awake. "She was covered in blue tattoos. She wanted me to go outside and do something, but I wasn't sure what. So I followed her. I think Mungo was there too." She shut her eyes briefly to grasp the fading dream, and shook her head. "Can't remember. Then I heard you screaming in the grotto, Mum. I thought the axe murderer had got you. But when I got there, that woman was there. And the stones . . . God, those weird stones were moving. Then the woman gave me a knife." Neve looked down at her hand as though expecting to see the knife. "Oh!" She was still gripping the rock tightly, its ragged edge cutting into her palm.

"What happened next?"

"Nothing. I woke up." She smiled weakly. "I think I've been reading too many ghost stories." Her eyes skittered in embarrassment to Cameron and Mr. MacKenzie. "What are you two doing here?"

"I heard your mum shouting," said Cameron.

"Aye," said Mr. MacKenzie, nodding. "Skirling fit to raise the deid."

"Sounds like the Witch was forcing you to make a pact with her," said Cameron, lips quirking into a teasing grin.

"Bollocks," Neve muttered.

"You cannae force a pact with the Witch," said Mr. MacKenzie. "Has to come without persuasion." He eyed the grotto. "It cannae be the Witch. It isnae her time to wake. Samhain isnae on us for a few more days."

"Winter *can* come early," said Cameron wryly. "And she is supposed to be the Cailleach, the bringer of winter and storms."

"That's as may be for some," muttered Mr. MacKenzie, and shoved his hands in his pockets, huddling into his coat.

If Edie hadn't experienced what she had, she would've scoffed at all this talk of witches and pagan goddesses. But she *had* seen it. She could still feel the clamminess of the shadows that kept her away from Neve, the scratches on her arms and legs beginning to sting.

Her clothes were torn, but now she couldn't say whether it was from the shadowy briars that had blocked the grotto or the rosebushes she had scrambled through to find another entrance.

"The Witch can go stuff herself. We're leaving!" she said shrilly with a sudden, desperate urge to be home in their small house in England. It wasn't a castle, but it was ghost- and witch-free.

"You cannae," said Mr. MacKenzie, his eyebrows beetling together. "The way out is too dangerous in the dark."

"Fergus is right," said Cameron grudgingly. "If you're set on leaving, you'd best wait until morning. The roads are barely passable in daylight; it would be suicide at night."

Edie opened her mouth to argue, then shut it. She hadn't forgotten the hair-raising journey to get here, an experience she didn't think she could cope with right now. Her hands trembled with delayed shock. She needed a quiet, brightly lit place to fall apart before she ventured over the daunting Haggs Pass.

"I'll see you two up to the castle, if you like," said Cameron.

Edie nodded. She glanced worriedly at Neve, but she appeared more sheepish than frightened that everyone was making a fuss of what she still seemed to believe had been a dream.

"Well, I'll be off," said Mr. MacKenzie, and he stomped off into the dark, torchlight dancing ahead of him.

Cameron fell in step with Edie as Neve went slightly ahead towards the castle. A feathering of snow drifted around them, dreamy swirls of tiny stars, each perfect and ephemeral, and deceptively abundant.

He held out a hand, capturing a snowflake. It melted instantly on the warmth of his skin. "Looks like Fergus is wrong and the Witch is waking early," he said, an unsubtle dig at the groundskeeper's fervent belief in the Witch and her powers. He eyed Edie sideways. "This is going to sound peculiar, but did *you* see anything strange?" He hesitated. "The shadows acting weirdly?"

"Like they had a mind of their own?"

He nodded. "Something like that."

Edie bit her lip, not wanting to sound like a basket case, not sure how far Cameron's credulity went. She nodded. "They were controlling Neve," she murmured low so Neve couldn't hear.

"I've had a similar experience."

Edie gave him a sidelong frown. "Like the ghostly monks you saw after a skinful?" she snarked.

Cameron laughed softly, not at all offended. "Could've been. There's not much to do here at night but drink. Not until you two arrived to liven things up."

Feeling slightly guilty for disparaging someone else's experiences with the supernatural so recently after her own, she asked, "What happened?"

He grinned, embarrassed. "It was years ago, but on Samhain I usually go across to Haggs and listen to the auld boys in the pub telling their stories about the Witch. So one year I decided to see what all the fuss was about. I went to the grotto, cut my hand open and dropped a bit of blood in the well as a lark, demanding my heart's desire in return."

"And?" asked Edie, intrigued.

Cameron pressed his lips together, no longer flippant. "The water turned red." He grimaced. "It was probably the whisky and the talk, but the shadows were sort of dancing around me, trying to push me towards the well, like they wanted to drown me in it. And it wisnae just the shadows; those auld Pict stones were doing something uncanny. The pictograms were—" He shook his head, unwilling to go on.

"What did you do?"

"I ran like hell all the way back to the pub, sat in a corner and got thoroughly bladdered."

Edie surprised herself by laughing. "And what was your heart's desire?"

Cameron grinned. "Now that would be telling."

CHAPTER 12

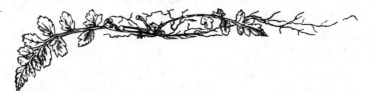

Edie, Neve and Cameron sat in the kitchen with every light on in the castle until it was lit up like a joyless Christmas tree decorated with black and bloody baubles and dripping intestines for tinsel, more suited to the darkness of Krampus. The gentle snow flurries had morphed into white demons, goaded by the rising wind to howl and whistle around the castle. Clots of tormented snowflakes streaked against the windows to settle on the sills, the cold hissing through cracks and under doors.

Edie found a musty old quilt made from frayed scraps of material that smelled faintly of dog to wrap around Neve, who wore only pajamas. Shoulders and chest stiff with worry, she watched Neve frowning into her cup of tea, occasionally opening and shutting her mouth, her frown deepening.

"I'm going to leave you two here for a bit and have a look around to make sure everything is okay," said Cameron, draining his mug. "I wilnae be far if you need me."

Edie nodded, wishing he wouldn't leave, but not wanting to sound needy by asking him to stay.

The shrieking wind filled the silence when he left.

"Are you okay, love?" said Edie when she couldn't bear the silence any longer.

Neve didn't answer at first. "I feel weird, like I'm bruised all over. I keep going over the dream, trying not to forget it, but it's already disappearing. It's the weirdest dream I've ever had."

Edie took Neve's hand, the wound still oozing blood. She stood and rummaged around for the aging first-aid box she had seen when investigating the cupboards previously. She contemplated the tube of Germolene that had expired ten years ago, decided not to risk her daughter's health with it, and used a clean, damp cloth to wipe away the drying blood.

She waged a silent war with herself as she wrapped a bandage around Neve's hand, before the honesty she had always tried to offer her daughter won. "It wasn't a dream," she said, snipping off a piece of elderly plaster and fixing the bandage in place. "It was real. I followed you from your room to the grotto. And I saw the woman too. It was so brief . . ." She shook her head. "I might have imagined it. I was pretty worked up by then . . . Don't look at me like that," she said, her throat tight against the threat of tears. "It was the most terrifying thing I've ever experienced."

"You're not going to get menopausal on me, are you?" said Neve warily as tears of self-directed disgust squeezed from Edie's eyes.

"I *am* menopausal, and I'm tired, and I had the most terrible fright tonight. I couldn't do anything . . . I was useless," she whispered, rubbing her cheeks angrily. "The shadows were all over you and it didn't matter what I did I couldn't make you wake up or get them away from you. I'm your mother; I should be able to protect you from anything, but I couldn't—"

"I don't think dealing with a witch is in the parenting handbook," said Neve, not unkindly. She fiddled with the frayed ends of the bandage, not wanting to look at Edie. "Mungo was trying to help me, wasn't he?"

Edie nodded, surprised by Neve's easy acceptance that the dream had been real. But perhaps it shouldn't be surprising. They had been living with ghosts for a week; a witch living in a well was merely another horror to add to the growing list. One that could slip into dreams was a little more worrying, however.

"He was yelling at the shadows," she said, and filled Neve in on what had occurred in the Baronial Hall. "He was scared of the mask," she concluded. "More than scared. It terrified him. And I'm sure this Lady is Lady Elizabeth. Alice is scared of her too."

"Lady Elizabeth stopped him from leaving the castle?"

"That's what it looked like."

"Why? And why a plague mask?"

"I don't know."

They contemplated their own uneasy thoughts.

"There's something else," said Edie after a long while. "Alice warned me you were in danger, through her diary."

"Mmmm . . ." murmured Neve, wrinkling her nose pensively.

"What?" said Edie when Neve didn't say anything further.

"Why is Alice writing to you?"

Edie hesitated, hurt by her daughter's unflattering tone. She didn't want to be derided for her foolish hopes, that perhaps Alice had singled her out because their connection was personal. "I suppose she wants to tell her story to someone."

"But why you in particular?"

"I don't know."

"And why like a diary?"

"I think it's the only way she can communicate. Diaries are powerful things. All those emotions, dreams and yearnings trapped in dry pages."

"And secrets."

"Yes," said Edie. "Maybe Alice had one she wished she hadn't taken to her grave and is trying to tell someone what it is."

Neve nodded noncommittally and lapsed back into thought.

Edie watched her, waiting; Neve's preoccupied silences were usually followed by something outrageous.

It didn't take long before her eyes glimmered. "Mr. and Mrs. Macleod," she said distantly, then a muttered, "Shit, I'm an idiot." She shot up, grabbed Edie's hand and flew out of the kitchen, ignoring Edie's cries of, "Slow down!"

They hurtled through the corridors to the museum. The rooms were freezing; the fire Edie had lit earlier was nothing but wet ash from snow falling down the chimney. Neve stopped briefly in front of the Maundrell family tree before dashing over to a board covered in names, photos and jotted notes.

"What have you thought of?" said Edie, eyeing her daughter curiously. Though she considered the search for the Maundrell Red futile, it was a relief to have something to occupy Neve's mind.

"I keep circling back to the Macleods," said Neve. 'They were more tied up with the Maundrells than I'd realized. I think Alice's Mr. and Mrs. Macleod are the same two who were working here in 1965. If I'm right, Greer must've been their daughter, and Mungo would've been their grandson." She stared in hard thought at the board. "Does that give the Macleods another motive to take the Maundrell Red? Their daughter dies, but they aren't allowed to see their grandson because of horrible Lady Elizabeth. They took the Maundrell Red for revenge maybe? Double revenge because really it should've been theirs anyway." She darted back to the family tree. "And then there's Jasper Maundrell who was in love with Greer, but his brother stole her away. He was here on the night it went missing, but I'm not sure that works for a motive. I found some letters Jasper wrote to Greer before she died. He hated his mother. He could've taken the Maundrell Red to spite her." She shook her head. "It amazes me no one murdered Lady Elizabeth instead of stealing her diamond."

"Jasper could've taken it for financial reasons," said Edie.

"No, he became heir to the Maundrell fortune after Theodore died so he would've been minted anyway."

"As Theodore's son Mungo would've inherited, not Jasper."

"Except Mungo was autistic. From the little we've seen of him I don't think he had been able to take care of himself, let alone a vast fortune."

"True," said Edie slowly. It occurred to her that no matter who of her three options was her parent, she was related to Mungo either way. They were cousins. "Could Mungo be at the center of all this?"

"Speaking of Mungo," Neve murmured. "He's here, behind you."

The ghost stood at the window, peering outside wistfully. He took no notice of Edie when she walked quietly to stand beside him.

"Mungo's Lottie," he whispered with a hiccuping sigh like a child after a storm of tears. "Mungo's Lottie gone."

Edie didn't know what to say, not sure if he was talking to her or himself. Life could be horribly cruel to the most vulnerable in society. It was upsetting to think what Mungo's life must've been like; severely autistic, tossed the terrible fate of navigating through his short life without the care of his parents. She hoped his Lottie had loved him as much as Mungo appeared to love her.

The wind and snow hadn't let up, but there was a paleness in the chaotic dark, a gray smudge in the east. It wouldn't be long and they could leave the island.

"He's been coming in here quite a bit," said Neve softly, coming to stand beside Edie. "Doesn't say anything. He looks out the window or crouches down in the corner and watches me like he's building up the courage to talk to me."

Edie's lips quirked with sadness with the realization that Mungo was lonely. She couldn't think of anything lonelier than being a ghost and felt oddly guilty they would be leaving him soon.

The three stood at the window, two living, one dead, watching the pale smudge brighten, lulled by exhaustion and the wind keening around the castle's towers, searching for a way in.

"What's that?" whispered Neve, frowning at a bruise of condensation on the darkened window.

A line appeared with a rubbing squeak like a finger dragging hard through the moisture, the sound chafing up Edie's spine.

Mungo trembled, mesmerized by the line as it curved up on itself to form a sharp beak, then struck out in sharp edges of a wide-brimmed hat. The final flourish were two round circles for eyes, crossed out savagely.

The moment the plague mask was complete, Mungo shrieked and vanished.

It leered at the Nunns, a trickle tracing down from the point of the beak.

"We're leaving right now," said Edie, grabbing Neve's arm and backing out of the room. Once in the corridor they ran.

Nothing followed, no click-clacking, no clattering laughter, as they raced up the spiral stairs in Blacklaw Tower.

They were barely on the third floor when *floflofloflofloflo* fluttered around them. Edie pulled to a stop, heart pumping, gasping for breath.

"What is it?" said Neve.

"Alice." Edie hurried along the corridor, scanning the walls, with Neve on her heels.

Floflofloflofloflo . . .

"There!" Edie darted up to the fading writing . . . *I was SEEN today!*

"What does it say?" said Neve, staring fiercely at the wall.

"You didn't see it?"

"No."

Floflofloflofloflo . . .

"Alice?" Edie rushed down the corridor. "There you are," she whispered to the blooming words . . . *He told me I was beautiful! I was so shocked, knowing I am plain as can be, that I simply stared at him. I hope I did not scare him or appear aloof. It's so hard to tell what a man thinks. No. It must've been a joke . . .*

As though aware Edie was leaving, Alice's words flowed over each other in hasty, panicking flurries, desperate to communicate her secrets in the only way she knew how.

"Is she writing?" asked Neve, her eyes darting between Edie and the wall. "What is she saying?"

"I saw D again today," Edie read aloud. *"He smiled at me as if I were the highlight of his day. How is this possible? I cannot believe this is happening . . . D kissed me! It was long and slow and somewhat wet, but I felt like I was drowning in the taste of him. If Mother knew she would kill me . . .*

"A secret romance," whispered Edie as the words scribbled farther down the corridor. She frowned when the next thing Alice wrote seemed random, like she was flipping through her diary, searching for anything that might pique Edie's interest. *"Mungo has taken the Red!"*

"What?" cried Neve. "Mungo—"

"Shush, she's still writing . . . *'No one can find it, not even Lottie who knows all his little hiding places. He's such a magpie for shiny objects; I'm always finding Father's old tin soldiers lying about, which drives Mother mad . . .'"*

"If Mungo—" began Neve.

"There's more . . . *'Dr. Kincaid is furious at the Red's disappearance. It was rather loyal of him to take on so, although he is such a toady it was probably for Mother's benefit to curry favor. But while everyone was searching yesterday, I heard them having an argument. I could not believe my ears! Mother has promised the Red to Dr. Kincaid if he should cure Mungo of his imbecility! Why would she feel the need to bribe him in such a way? And with the Maundrell Red too . . .*

"'The Red has been returned! Lottie found it, of course. It was a great relief, for Mother has been unbearable all—'"

Alice's wild scrawl disappeared abruptly. A moment later Edie heard *click-clack-click-clack* from deep within the castle. Lady Elizabeth was prowling.

Edie waited, tensed, but nothing else appeared. Alice had been scared off.

"Mungo took the diamond?" said Neve, eyes round with shock. "I never thought—"

"And it was found again," said Edie before Neve got any ideas about charging back to the museum. Conscious of the furious click-clacking coming nearer, she hustled Neve down the corridor, saying, "We need to leave before the snow settles."

Edie's room was an icebox. She hoisted the overnight bag onto her shoulder, took a last look around to ensure she hadn't left anything and stepped out into the corridor.

Floflofloflo . . .

Edie's head snapped around to the words *Don't leave . . .* already fading from the wall above her bed.

"I'm sorry, Alice," she said thickly around the lump in her throat. "I wish I could help you, but I have to think of the safety of my daughter."

She closed the door sharply against the desperate *floflofloflofloflo . . .*

The island was the center of a freezing maelstrom as the Nunns hurried out of the castle, the hissing snow stinging their cheeks, their eyes streaming.

Their car was a hump of white; snow caked the windscreen and banked up against the tyres.

"Quickly!" cried Edie, unlocking the car, and relocking once Neve was seated.

Neve peered through the snow-speckled windscreen. "Are we seriously going to drive over Haggs Pass in a blizzard?"

"Yes," said Edie firmly. "If we don't leave now we could be stuck here for a long while. Put your seat belt on."

She fumbled the key in the ignition in her haste, her whole body a tangled ball of frayed nerve endings in her urgent desire to leave while they had a chance.

Nothing happened.

She turned the key again and again, with not the faintest responding mutter from the engine.

"Shit!" Even though she was certain she had switched off the lights when they had first arrived, Edie checked anyway. They were all off. The fuel gauge showed they had enough to get to the nearest petrol station in Lochinver.

"What's wrong with the car?" said Neve.

"I don't know."

"So what do we do?"

Edie pressed her lips together and glared at the castle, convinced plague masks had appeared in every window to watch the Nunns leave.

A quick drum of her fingers on the steering wheel before she glanced over her shoulder at the Brig o' Haggs. "We'll walk. I'm sure we can find someone in the village to help us. Maybe Hamish— The bloke from the shop," she added when Neve frowned at her in confusion.

Neve's gaze swiveled from her mother to the snowstorm raging around the car, then back to her mother. But Edie's fierce expression discouraged any voiced doubts. She got out of the car with a muttered, "This is ridiculous."

The wind was an animal howl; the relentless snow fought every step they took down the driveway. But Edie was determined. She would not stay on the island another minute longer, and she battled forward.

The Brig o' Haggs appeared like a humped serpent, a blurred outline not of this world. Through its many arches the garnet red of the loch had paled to milky coral, the pebbled shingle along its edge a froth of salt and snow.

Neve pulled up sharply when they neared the bridge. Snow swept across it in furious gusts. "This is madness!" she shouted above the wind. "We should go back to the castle!"

"Absolutely no!" Edie shouted back, high-pitched, on the verge of hysteria.

Neve stared at her with unflattering consternation. "It's fucking cold, I'm fucking wet and I think you've gone fucking mad!" She pointed at the bridge. "And there's no way in fuck I'm walking across that in the middle of a blizzard!"

Edie brushed snow away from her eyelashes. Everything in her being was telling her to get off the island, get Neve away as quickly as possible, get back to their lives and routine, away from the madness infecting this place.

"This is crazy, Mum!" Neve yelled. "We can't walk about in the middle of a fucking snowstorm!"

"Language!" snapped Edie, her stretched nerves getting the better of her.

"If ever there was a time to swear, this is it!"

Edie grimaced. Neve was not wrong. All that stopped the cursing explosion huddling in her throat was her daughter's presence. She turned away from the bridge. A semblance of sanity reasserted itself. She wasn't thinking straight. All they needed was someone to start the car and they could leave safely.

Her thoughts flickered to Hamish Macleod again, but their options were limited to the island.

"We need to find Cameron or Mr. MacKenzie," she said, and sped up the driveway with Neve close beside her.

They hurried around the castle. Trees bowed before the wind, the Nine Hags looked like a huddle of snidely gossiping old women encrusted with snow. Everything was white and unsettling, the mundane distorted into frights and fears. Edie stormed up to Mr. MacKenzie's cottage and rapped on the door. She knocked again and again.

"He's not in," she said, as she and Neve huddled in the temporary shelter of the small porch.

"So we're not the only idiots wandering about the island in the middle of a blizzard," muttered Neve.

"He's probably gone to the castle. And Cameron should be there too. I can't imagine he'll be down at the loch today," she added, realizing she hadn't seen him since he'd left them in the kitchen. A guilty blush stole up her throat that he might have returned and found them gone without saying good night. Her blush burnt hotter, for she hadn't given either Cameron or Mr. MacKenzie a moment's consideration and had planned to leave without saying goodbye.

The Nunns took off towards the castle, crisscrossing the paths of the rose gardens, all sullen and white.

Neve put a hand on Edie's arm. "I can hear voices," she said, nodding at the dome of the grotto swelling up before them like a purulent blister.

The voices rose and fell, an ebb and surge of fury, matching the storm's wrath.

"They're having quite a row," said Neve.

"It's nothing to do with us," said Edie, and dashed down the path, shouting, "Hello?" at the entrance to the grotto. She had no intention of entering the place again.

Cameron and Mr. MacKenzie poked their heads out. "I thought you two would be long gone by now," said Cameron.

"There's a problem with that," said Edie. "Our car won't start."

Cameron and Mr. MacKenzie glanced at each other, then away as though they couldn't bear the sight of each other. Mr. MacKenzie peered up at the howling snow, seemingly surprised to find himself in the middle of a snowstorm.

"It'll be the Witch," he said with a satisfied nod that pissed Edie off. "She disnae want you to leave."

"Sod the fucking witch!" she yelled. "I am sick to death of her. I want off this wretched island!"

"I can have a wee gander at the car." Mr. MacKenzie nodded contemptuously at Cameron. "This one disnae ken a camshaft from a fan belt."

Cameron glared at him. "Guid luck with that!" he snapped, and stormed off down a path, leaving Edie and Neve open-mouthed in astonishment.

"You'd best be leery of that one," muttered Mr. MacKenzie, watching Cameron until the swirling snow veiled his retreating figure. He wriggled his eyebrows meaningfully, then stomped off down another path.

Edie shook her head in disbelief. It appeared there was little trust or love lost between the two men, as she had received a similar warning from Cameron about Mr. MacKenzie. Trust seemed in short supply on the island.

"The whole island's gone mad," said Neve wonderingly. "Ghosts, witches, shadows and now two grown-up men acting like drama queens. What the hell was all that about?"

Edie shook her head. "I have no idea."

October 1965

*C*onfined to her room for a week in the Belfry Tower, Lottie was feeling sorry for herself. She spent the dragging days watching the sunlight glitter off Loch na Scáthanna like rubies from the window, imagining herself as a captive princess and her grandmother as the wicked witch.

The restless nights were worse, tricked into seeing shadows creeping from the grotto and ghosts populating the island like a spectral carnival. It didn't take more than a breeze to ruffle through the rose gardens and Lottie was craning out of the window hoping to glimpse monks floating through the ruins of the old monastery or watching the crumbling watchtower, eager to spy the Highlander everyone said was the sole surviving Macleod of the Haggs Massacre. Mr. Macleod always scoffed at those stories; he had seen the apparition with his own eyes and swore blind the Highlander wasn't a Macleod but a MacKenzie of Kintail by the tartan the ghost wore—and Mr. Macleod knew of these things, so Lottie believed his version most.

But the early hours of morning were worst of all when a sea mist rolled over the red waters and the air felt electric and tasted of tin as though a storm approached. Lottie was reassured daily by Mr. Macleod—through Mrs. Macleod when she brought up Lottie's meals—that there would be no storm, and neither Mrs. Macleod nor Lottie questioned his meteorological knowledge, for he could gauge a week's worth of weather merely by squinting at the sky.

As the days grew shorter, the air grew fretful, tightening around the island like a garrotte as it always did at this time of year. Tomorrow was Samhain. Everyone felt it, of course, but Lottie thought this year Bitsie felt it most of all. All week she heard her grandmother stalking the halls, the click-clack of her heels on the stone floors echoing to every part of the castle with the shock and recoil of gunshots.

There were some advantages to Lottie's confinement. From her high vantage point, she could spy on her family's routines and private moments with unbridled curiosity.

Mr. and Mrs. Macleod were always the first to start their day with a short walk from the servants' cottages to the walled garden. There, Mr. Macleod brushed a kiss against Mrs. Macleod's proffered cheek before they went their separate ways. Soon afterwards Mrs. Macleod hurried out to the Viking mounds with a saucer of milk and yesterday's bread crusts for the trows that were said to guard the dead in the cairns.

Lottie knew she shouldn't wish a moment of her life away, but as she watched Mrs. Macleod she wished with all her heart that Samhain had already passed and they were cut off from the world by deep winter, the island snuggled under a thick eiderdown of snow. Then she and Mungo could sit in front of a fire in the kitchen, sipping hot cocoa and munching gingerbread dripping with butter—Mungo's favorite—with Mrs. Macleod in her usual chair, her knees covered with a patchwork quilt Lottie and Mungo had made for her a few years before. It was an eyesore of frayed confusion, but Mrs. Macleod treated it as if spun from the finest silk, knowing the love that had gone into the search for bright scraps and every prick of the needle. Mr. Macleod would sit at the kitchen table nursing a chipped mug of whisky and a late-night cigarette, listening to Mrs. Macleod, her voice low, barely a whisper, telling the tale of the Trows of Loch na Scáthanna.

"Let it not be said," Mrs. Macleod would say, "that the trows of Loch na Scáthanna were ungrateful at Álfablót, though their gratitude can come in forms most surprising.

"On that auspicious night—which we know as Samhain—when the crops had been harvested and the cattle were fat from summer grazing that the Norsemen would hold their secret rites of elven sacrifice. A hallowed occasion not broken even for the laws of hospitality. The Norsemen understood the need for blood sacrifice to appease not only the elves, but the gods of this new land where they'd settled."

"Witch!" Mungo would bellow excitedly. "Witch! Mungo's friend!"

"Shush, Mungo," Lottie would hush gently. He had heard the story a hundred times but still listened as if for the first time.

But Mrs. Macleod would smile at him. Lottie sometimes thought she saw her eyes grow wet with the memory of her daughter, Greer, for Mungo was all Mr. and Mrs. Macleod had left of her. There was fierce love in that smile, as fierce as the Highlands, as fierce as its people. There, in the warmth of the kitchen, Mungo was surrounded by those who loved him most.

"But . . ." Mrs. Macleod drew out the word once Mungo had settled once more, bribed with another piece of gingerbread. "It wisnae so quiet a night for the Pictish clans, though just as auspicious, who lived high in the passes above Loch na Scáthanna. For them it was a night of celebration, for revelry and fighting.

"On this night so long ago, the Picts grew bold in their revelry, and came down from their passes as guisers and mummers, their masks fearsome and bodies blackened. Such was their mischief they came knock, knocking, knocking on the doors of the longhouses on the island.

"But fearing Odin's wrath more than the mischief of the Picts, the Norsemen didnae open their doors and didnae bear arms to protect their homes. They knew well the terrible luck that would befall them all should they step out on the night belonging to the elves.

"The terrible noise of the guising Picts aroused the wrath of the

neighboring trows, the mound-dwellers who lived in the howes of the Norsemen. Dirt-covered, ragged of hair and wild of face and claw, the trows crept out and set the howes to glow with an eerie light.

"Cussing and shrieking for quiet on this night, the trows danced wildly about the Picts. But the Picts paid them no mind and went battering against the Norsemen's doors. Within, the women wailed prayers to Odin for salvation, and the men hid below the windows, weapons held uselessly in their hands.

"In their fury, the trows scurried to the place where the water was black and pitiless. They called on the ancient one who lived there, the Veiled One so pale and cold."

"Witch!" bellowed Mungo in delight, cross-legged and bouncing.

"Aye, so it was. But in those times she was not as we ken her now," said Mrs. Macleod "Though it was not her time to wake, she heard the fury of the trows, and she saw the plight of the Norsemen who understood the ways of the auld country and the new, and she saw the disrespect of the Picts.

"But it was still too early for her to rise with snow and ice. So she nodded to the trows afore sinking back into the bottomless well. The trows took the enchantments bestowed upon them by the Veiled One and called to the waters of Loch na Scáthanna.

"From its depths whispered a slithering shadow. It crept up the cliffs and pressed clammy fingers to the gnarled faces of the trows, who danced their fury and pointed to the Picts. The shadow spread quickly across the island like a vengeful mist, touching all who dared be abroad on this hallowed night. And one by one the Picts burst into sprays of blood and brain and bone, adorning the longhouses in gory bunting."

"Ewww!" Lottie and Mungo said on cue with ghoulish appreciation.

"Aye," said Mrs. Macleod. "And with their night's work done, the trows crept back to their cairns, the shadow slipped back into Loch na Scáthanna, and the private rites of Álfablót continued once more."

But Samhain was still tomorrow, time keeping its steady course as Lottie watched Mrs. Macleod walk back from the cairns, carrying the saucer from her offering the day before.

Next to appear were the three maids walking over the Brig o' Haggs, giggling until they set foot on the island. Their smiles darkened to frowns and, almost on tiptoe, they disappeared into the kitchen. The Maundrells no longer kept the staff they had a decade ago. None lasted long, unable to bear the island's remote, bleak atmosphere or the oddness of the Maundrells.

Not long after Mungo came out of the kitchen, still wiping his mouth from a hasty breakfast before running wild across the island. He was supposed to be locked in his room for the week too, but Mrs. Macleod had let him out from the first day after an almighty argument with Bitsie that was probably heard over in Haggs. Lottie sometimes wondered if Bitsie wasn't a little scared of Mrs. Macleod, for she seemed so incorruptible and Bitsie had little to use as leverage over the housekeeper.

On Lottie's second day of confinement, Ashley and Percy yelled her name not long after daybreak. She leaned out of her window with complete disregard for the fact that she was three stories up. Mungo was with them, walking in circles in that odd hopping gait of his as though he were playing hopscotch with himself.

"There she is," said Ashley, touching Mungo's arm gently.

Mungo stopped his circling, waved madly at Lottie and started circling again, faster and faster.

"He's been showing us where he hides his treasures," Ashley shouted up to her.

"Is he all right?" she asked anxiously.

"He asks for you all the time," said Percy, "but he's all right."

Mungo stopped circling and grinned up at Lottie. "Ashy an' Pessy go boat wi' Mungo!" he bellowed. "Go boat wi' Mungo!" He patted Ashley on the head, mussing up his hair.

"We're taking Mungo out on the loch," said Percy. "We'll keep an eye on him until you're out."

"He's scared of the loch," said Lottie.

But Lottie was proved wrong. She saw them half an hour later on the red water, the boat rocking as Mungo tried to take the oars from a laughing Ashley. After that she saw the three together every day, forming *a bond while she was locked away. She was ashamed of her jealousy; Mungo was her person and she was his. It hurt that he didn't seem to miss her at all.*

And then there had been Aunt Alice's peculiar behavior. All week Lottie watched her pacing the cliff path from the boathouse to the Brig o' Haggs, speaking to herself, hands animated with sharp jerky movements to reinforce her thoughts. Lottie was fascinated; her aunt rarely did anything interesting or out of the ordinary.

At noon on the fifth day of Lottie's incarceration, the greengrocer's Morris Minor van putted across the humped bridge as it did every Wednesday. She rarely considered her family from an outsider's perspective, but she supposed they must appear odd, for the Maundrells dressed as they liked, acted how they liked and did as they pleased as long as it fell within Bitsie's perceptions of appropriate upper-class eccentricity. Alice was no different, decked out in a bright pink party frock unsuitable for the cooling weather, but like Bitsie, Alice was always beautifully turned out, though no one but family saw them.

Lottie wasn't the only one watching the van's progress. Alice stopped on the cliffs, her expression shifting from impatience to relief. She glanced up at the castle fearfully before scurrying along the path to meet the van as it drove onto the island.

A dark head popped out the driver's open window before Lottie's view was blocked by Alice. The two were having a tense conversation if the rigid set of Alice's shoulders was anything to go by.

"Alice!" Bitsie's sharp voice cut through the air. She strode out of the East Gatehouse looking like thunder.

Alice turned, guilty panic scrawled across her face, and scuttled away from the van. The greengrocer continued down the driveway to the castle and reversed up to the kitchen door.

Bitsie had a carrying voice, for which Lottie was grateful as she shamelessly eavesdropped.

"How many times do I have to tell you ladies do not speak to the help?" Bitsie snapped before she had reached her daughter.

To Lottie's astonishment, Alice eyed her mother with none of the

*subservience that usually characterized their mother-daughter relation-
ship. If anything, Alice looked defiant.*

*Perhaps Bitsie noticed the shift in Alice's demeanor too, for she leaned
towards her and hissed something Lottie couldn't hear. Then she turned
on her heel and stormed back to the castle. Alice glared at her mother's
retreating back with pure hatred.*

*Lottie was thoughtful as she pulled herself back into her room and sat
on her bed, puzzled by what she had seen. True, Alice had been a little
peculiar since her illness last year, the euphemism everyone had used
after she got herself into trouble.*

*It had been a terrible time. Bitsie's fury had shrouded the castle in a
fuming pall, setting everyone on edge. At first, she had screamed to know
who the father was, but no amount of threats had persuaded Alice to
give up a name, and for that alone she deserved some respect; it was no
small thing to resist a personality like Lady Elizabeth Maundrell.*

*Then had come brooding silence. Everyone had walked around on
eggshells while Bitsie paced the halls and Alice hid in her rooms.*

*Afterwards, everyone said it was for the best Alice lost the baby,
though never in her hearing. It was the only time Lottie had been grateful to have Dr. Kincaid in the castle for Mungo's treatment. According
to Bitsie, he had saved Alice's life and her reputation; not surprisingly
Bitsie considered the latter of more importance. That had happened on
Samhain too.*

*Lottie speculated that perhaps the greengrocer was acting as a go-
between for Alice and whomever was the father of her lost baby. Though
how Alice had met a man at all was a mystery, for she couldn't remember a time when her aunt had gone off the island.*

*She whiled away the rest of the afternoon watching Mr. Macleod
mowing the grass, counting the minutes until Mrs. Macleod knocked at
the door at six with her dinner on a tray. The housekeeper always slipped
her a treat and news of Mungo.*

*It wasn't five when the knock came. As the door swung open, Lottie
sang out, "You're early!" then, "Oh! Mum," unable to keep the disappointment from her voice.*

Vida Maundrell looked her daughter up and down and tut-tutted. "Get dressed," she said without preamble. "And wear something decent, for heaven's sake. Not those dreadful trousers you're so fond of. We've all been summoned to the Hall."

"Why?" said Lottie. A summons to the Hall was serious. "What's happened?"

"I've no idea. Your grandmother asked me to send for you."

Relieved to break the tedium of her confinement for even half an hour, Lottie leapt towards her wardrobe the moment the door closed. She pulled out a red dress. It clashed horribly with her freckles, but she was determined to wear it anyway, knowing it would infuriate Bitsie, who had commented on the clash when Lottie had worn the dress previously.

She stepped out of her room, and paused, unease skittering down her spine. Shadows scuttled along the walls, bunching in their legions, watchful and fretful. She fled along the corridors, not daring to look back, sensing the darkness keeping pace with her.

CHAPTER 13

Edie stared at the engine in dismay. She, like Cameron, didn't know the difference between a camshaft and a fan belt.

"You wilnae fix it by looking at it, lass."

Edie swiveled to Mr. MacKenzie. She hadn't heard his approach above the howling wind that could've muffled a gunshot.

He squinted at the car, then at the storm, wiping away snow that had settled on his eyebrows. "Where's the wee lass?"

"Neve's inside," said Edie, dwelling briefly on the argument she'd had with her daughter, wanting to keep her close, but she had lost when Neve had run off. "Could you maybe have a look at the car?"

"Aye." Mr. MacKenzie tutted as he bent to fiddle about with the piping. "Mmmm . . ." he muttered. "Now there's a thing."

"What?" Edie eyed the engine with alarm. "What is it? Is it the cold? Can you fix it?"

"It's your HT lead; it's damaged."

Edie smiled slightly with a polite lack of comprehension.

"You cannae start the car without one. I'll have to order a new one from Inverness."

178

"And that will take how long?"

"A week if I get off to Haggs swiftish."

"A week!" Edie cried. "What about a taxi?"

He chortled into his beard. "Nae taxi will come over Haggs Pass, not for a million pounds. You've only two options as I see it, wait for the part, or speak to Macleod the greengrocer. He does a run down to Inverness every Wednesday."

"Hamish Macleod?"

Mr. MacKenzie peered at her in surprise. "Aye. You know young Hamish?"

"I've met him," said Edie carefully. "I wouldn't say I know him."

"Well, young Hamish will be your best bet."

"And he only goes on Wednesday? Today is Thursday!" Edie wailed. "That's just as bad."

"Aye, and that's if you can get off the island." He glowered at the snow twisting about them in a personal manner. "If this keeps up you'll be here for a guid long while. Nowt will get over the pass till the storm passes, maybe not even then."

"Shit!" Edie howled at the storm, and gave the car a kick for good measure, hurting her foot.

"Aye," Mr. MacKenzie agreed. He dropped the hood and glanced sideways at Edie. "Drink?"

She bit the inside of her cheek. Though it was only eight in the morning, it already felt like the end of a long day. It wasn't just the day; it was last night, the last week. An early drink didn't sound so terrible. But there was Mr. MacKenzie's mysterious reputation to consider. Cameron and Hamish Macleod had warned her, yet she couldn't imagine him doing anything truly dreadful. He was an old, lonely drunkard, and despite his surliness she rather liked him.

"Castle's cellar is well stocked," he added with a meaningful wriggle of his eyebrows.

Edie nodded, swallowing her misgivings. She had two options for adult company—and she did feel the need for company—Cameron or Mr. MacKenzie, but Mr. MacKenzie was the least unsettling of the two, regardless of his reputation.

She didn't bother to ask how he knew the state of the castle's cellars; no doubt the man had been helping himself over the years with no one to stop him. She hurried to keep pace when he took off through the wintry gale, surprisingly fast for a man in his seventies.

The kitchen was cold, damp and dim. An accumulation of snow on the window ledges blocked what little light dawn had brought.

Wind shrieked and whistled around the castle like an unchained beast as Mr. MacKenzie turned his glass of neat whisky in his hands.

Edie watched him in silence. He pulled at his beard worriedly, eyes flickering sideways. Outside, he always seemed so confident; in the castle he was ill at ease. No, it was more than unease; it was fear.

He caught Edie's gaze and muttered, "An uncanny place this. The auld lady, she felt it n'all."

"Lady Elizabeth?" Edie clarified.

"Nae, the young one. Alice." He squinted at the shadowed hearth as though demons of hell hid out of sight waiting to feast on his heart. "She feart something in the castle. Feart it something dreadful."

"Feared what?" Edie leaned back, worried he'd stop talking if she seemed too eager.

He took a slug of whisky. "I dinnae ken. She weren't much for a natter, but she was out more than in, and always staring up at the castle like something inside meant her harm. She was a terrified woman."

Edie didn't disregard the old man's musings, quite sure Lady Elizabeth was haunting the castle. Poor Alice. Alone all those years, terrorized by the ghost of her mother, only to die and be terrorized in death.

Mr. MacKenzie flinched when a hard gust of snow battered the windows, leaving icy fingerprints against the glass.

"It'll be the Witch," he muttered.

"The storm?" she clarified doubtfully.

"Aye, and more." He reached for the whisky bottle, and looked at her warily over his refilled glass, searching for skepticism. "She's a canny one."

"Last night Neve told me a woman led her down to the grotto. I'm assuming it was the Witch?" Edie chose not to mention that she, too, thought she had seen something in the grotto. She had been terrified for Neve, scared out of her wits generally, but with the prudence of hindsight she wasn't sure she could trust anything she had seen.

"Cannae say for sure," he conceded. "I havnae seen the Witch."

"She must want something."

"Aye," said Mr. MacKenzie, peering into his whisky glass.

Edie stared at his bowed head in frustration. She was certain he knew, or understood more about the Witch than he was letting on, but it was hard work getting anything out of him.

Awkward silence billowed between them.

"Could be it isnae the Witch," he said after another refill.

"Please tell me there's nothing else weird on this island!" Edie cried. "We've had ghosts, and shadows and bloody-minded witches. What else could possibly have a claim over this tiny island in the middle of nowhere?"

"Could be it's human," Mr. MacKenzie grumbled into his beard. "A pact with the Witch. The wee lassie maybe? She's young, could've done it for a lark."

"Neve wouldn't do something so stupid!"

"Any pact with the Witch is stupid."

"Have *you* made a pact with her?" said Edie.

Mr. MacKenzie's head snapped up. "I havnae got ferrets for brains!"

"Cameron? He told me he's done it before."

He scowled. "A right pudding that one. Could've been. Could've been another from Haggs. It isnae difficult to sneak onto the island without being seen."

"Okay, so assuming a pact has been made, what the hell does she want with my daughter?"

"The Witch be a contrary creature," he said darkly. "Those making pacts often dinnae ken the Witch takes more than blood for payment. She'll be after what's valued most, but what many dinnae ken is you cannae say what is of most value, and the Witch will read it as she sees fit. You'll need to know your true self afore making a pact with the Witch."

"That makes absolutely no sense," Edie muttered. "Are you saying someone made a pact with the Witch that is somehow affecting all of us?"

"Aye. Ye cannae outwit her. She be too contrary and canny for the likes of us." He licked his finger and ran it around the rim of his glass until it gave off a high-pitched whine. "Your lass is not the first to dream of the Witch. Them that came afore, the hotel lot and the other. Found both gibbering down in the grotto not long afore Samhain. Scared stupid, skirling about a blue woman who took over their dreams. Both left not long after."

"I saw her too," Edie admitted. "But not in a dream. I saw her last night, standing next to Neve in the grotto."

"And she was blue?" There was no disbelief in Mr. MacKenzie's tone.

"She had blue tattoos, or maybe she was painted blue. Lots of swirly patterns over her face and neck."

Mr. MacKenzie muttered, "Mmmm . . ." and drained his glass. He filled it up again before saying, "Could be one of the Pictish folk that lived hereabouts. There's a poem I read as a lad, though I cannae recall the long of it now. Spoke of a Pictish queen who was feart throughout the Highlands. But the kings beyond wisnae having any of it and massacred the queen and her people, cursed them into death for her wickedness."

"You think the Witch and this queen were—what? The same thing? A manifestation? A very old ghost?"

Mr. MacKenzie shrugged. "More happens on this island than can be explained by the likes of you and me," he said gnomically.

"If she's a ghost, which makes more sense than witches and old goddesses, maybe she wants help to find peace or rest, or find her way to the other side or whatever."

"She's an odd way of going about it."

Edie sighed in frustration and took a deep slug of whisky, then nearly choked when a click-clacking sounded deep within the castle, followed by clattering laughter.

"Did you hear that?" she asked, feeling braver now she wasn't by herself.

Mr. MacKenzie looked through the door leading to the corridor and pulled at his beard worriedly. "Aye. More ghaisties about than I remember as a lad, specially since the auld woman died. Too many ghaisties I thinking. Seen more in the past ten years than is proper."

"Alice or Lady Elizabeth?" said Edie, not always following the old man.

"Lady Elizabeth." He spat on the floor. "An evil woman that, and mad for that stone. About the only thing she did right by us was pay guid money to search for the Red when I were a lad. We havnae got much else out the Maundrells afore or since, 'cept a royal pain in our arse."

"Have you seen any of the ghosts?"

"Aye." His eyebrows drew together in a jagged frown. "Step out the house of a night and there's a baggage of them from ships on the loch to the Headless Horseman on the bridge. There's one in the auld watchtower, seen him a fair few times, though he isnae Macleod or MacKenzie. Cannae tell his clan though he wears a kilt."

"Oh," said Edie, who knew little of the Scottish clans and their individual kilts.

"And there's the baby skirling of a night. Fair put the wind up me the first time I heard the wee thing. Now I hear it every night, regular as clockwork. Hear Wully playing his pipes from the castle most nights n'all, and there's the woman in the cellars, all bloodied, holding her deid wee bairns . . . And auld Myrtle Bruce sobbing fit to burst in the grotto or mooching about in the graveyard. Too many ghaisties for my liking." He scraped his chair back and nodded at Edie. "A body cannae sit about all day. I'll be off then."

"Thank you," Edie called as he opened the door, letting in a rush of snow that quickly feathered the flagstones. "For trying to help with the car."

He paused on the threshold, half turning to her. "You got any scraps about? Perhaps a spot of milk?"

"Probably," said Edie. "Why?"

"It would pay to placate the trows with an offering of a morning. You dinnae want their sort of mischief about, what with Samhain a few days hence. Best to give the wee beasties a scrap or two to keep them sweet if the Witch is thinking to cause trouble." Then he stepped out into the storm.

Edie gaped after him in astonishment. The man was dead serious. At least when Cameron had mentioned trows, she could tell he was joking, but Mr. MacKenzie believed in trows deep down in his marrow.

The moment Mr. MacKenzie closed the door behind him *floflo-floflofloflo* echoed from the corridor beyond the kitchen, as though Alice had been waiting impatiently to catch Edie alone.

She hurried to the doorway and peered around.

I hate her! I HATE her! I HATE HER! gouged deep into the wall.

Edie recoiled in horror from the raging emotion reaching out to her across the decades.

My baby has been scoured from my womb. Mother watched Dr. Kincaid kill my baby, and said I should take this as a lesson not to share my favors so freely . . .

I cannot eat. I cannot sleep. I cannot leave my room. Days have slipped by and I don't care. At night I hear the pattering of fingers on my window, but I won't look. I know it's the Witch's pet shadows . . .

Lottie and Mungo come every day and bring me flowers. Jasper comes and goes expressing awkward banalities. Mother has left me alone and for that I am glad . . .

Vida came today and sat on the edge of my bed. I pretended to sleep, but she knew I wasn't. She told me it was a boy. Though I was glad of the knowledge, she told me in spite, and took pleasure in telling me Mother had demanded Dr. Kincaid sterilize me. After she left, I got up and dressed for the first time in months . . .

Mother has taken everything from me, what I most deeply longed for. I have no tears left, but I have hatred. I hate her! I hate her! I HATE HER! I wish Mother were dead . . .

Long after the last words faded Edie slowly slid down the wall and clutched her knees to her chest, staring at nothing. Tears slid down her face, for Alice and her terrible anguish, and for herself and her dashed hopes. She had managed to convince herself there was a personal connection between herself and the ghostly writer who had chosen to communicate only with her.

Edie didn't notice Mungo at first. He sat quietly beside her, his knees pulled up to his chest in imitation of her position.

"Hey Mungo," she whispered, her voice thick and raw, not wanting to alarm him.

She tried not to flinch when he put out a large, thick-fingered hand and stroked her hair. "Nae sad lassie," he said in a loud whisper. "Nae sad lassie."

Edie smiled through her tears. His touch was featherlight and cool, her fine hair standing up with static. "No sad," she echoed, oddly comforted by the presence of the ghost.

For long minutes they sat side by side before Mungo faded away as silently as he had arrived.

CHAPTER 14

Edie awoke with a start. She was still in the corridor outside the kitchen, curled against the wall, with no recollection of falling asleep where she'd sat. She stepped into the kitchen and drank a glass of water to get rid of the sour taste of sleep and whisky.

The blizzard still lashed the island. Dismal gray afternoon light filtered through the windows as she walked through the echoing castle. Voices drifted down to her as she climbed Blacklaw Tower's curling stairs.

"Neve?" she called. When she received no response, she approached the museum with caution. "Neve?"

"We're in here," said Neve.

"We?" muttered Edie. "Oh!" Her eyebrows rose at the sight of Neve sitting cross-legged in the middle of the room, a blanket over her shoulders. Mungo crouched beside her, his large frame folded small, knees to his chest, looking ever more like an overgrown child. He frowned at the open book Neve held with singular concentration.

"Read tae Mungo!" he bellowed.

"I *have* been reading to you," said Neve, with a long-suffering glance at Edie.

"Read tae Mungo!"

Neve bent to the book and continued reading a fairy tale. Edie stayed in the doorway watching them, a bittersweet ache in her chest for the man who was once Mungo.

"That's enough for one day." Neve snapped the book shut, releasing a puff of stale dust.

Mungo's ghostly hand stroked Neve's hair. "Neeeeeve!" He drew out the name as though testing the sound of it. "Neeeeeve. Lottie read tae Mungo. Neeeeeeve read tae Mungo."

"I could read to you, Mungo," said Edie, slipping into the room.

He looked up, wide-eyed. His round face split into a huge grin. "Sad lass!" he cried, and vanished.

"He's been here for a while," said Neve, getting up. "He's sweet. A bit demanding, but sweet . . . Sad lass?" she added.

"We met this morning."

Neve eyed her mother. "You've been crying. What's wrong? The Witch?" she asked, alarmed.

"No, but we're stuck here for another week, probably longer if this storm keeps up. And I had a chat with Mr. MacKenzie about the Witch."

"And?" Neve prompted when Edie paused to gather her recent conversation with the groundskeeper into something that resembled logic.

"He seems to think someone has made a pact with the Witch or goddess or whatever the hell she is, which is somehow affecting us."

"You don't believe in gods and devils."

"No, I don't—I didn't—I don't know." Edie grimaced. "I hope this witch isn't as vengeful as the Christian god." She had always considered herself a rational person, but what was swirling around her head wasn't even faintly logical. "We need to find out more about the Witch. She wants something."

"From me," said Neve with a shiver.

"Yes," said Edie slowly. "But why you? Mr. MacKenzie and Cameron have been on the island for years, although Cameron claims to have had a similar experience . . . Maybe she wants you to do something."

"Like what?"

"I don't know, love." She tried to smile reassuringly to wipe away the troubled lines wrinkling her daughter's face but found she could not. She was too deeply troubled herself, re-evaluating her own ideas of the world as she had always known it.

"So why were you crying?" asked Neve.

Edie told her about Alice's last communication, eliciting a whistle of horrified shock.

"Lady Elizabeth forced her daughter to have an abortion, then sterilized her without her knowing?" said Neve, aghast. "The more I hear about that woman the more I really hate her."

"So did Alice."

"I would've killed her," said Neve fiercely. Her eyes narrowed. "What made you think Alice was your mum?"

Tears slipped down Edie's cheeks. "I thought there might be a deeper, more personal reason why Alice had chosen to communicate with me. But now I know she can't be . . . Sorry," she whispered. "All I seem to do these days is cry."

Neve patted her shoulder awkwardly. "It does make sense to think that."

Edie cleared her throat. "So that leaves only Jasper and Vida as possibilities for my parents."

"I've found something about Vida, but you won't like it." Neve eyed her mother warily.

"I'm fine," said Edie, wiping her wet face and straightening her shoulders. "Okay, show me what you've discovered."

After a brief hesitation to ensure her mother could handle another emotional upset, Neve wrapped the blanket around herself and stepped into a semi-circle of boards she had set up, each with a photo in the center.

"These are all the people who were on the island when the Red disappeared," she said. "I don't really have Lady Elizabeth as a suspect as she owned the Maundrell Red, but she was here when it disappeared."

Edie peered at the photo of an angular blond woman in her sixties with a severe bob and vivid green eyes. Her startling vibrancy was undiminished by time. It was hard to consider this woman as a ghost.

"This is Jasper and his wife Vida." Neve pointed at the photo of a tall, slim man with a gentle face and a woman wearing a nurse's uniform with a severe haircut, scowling at the camera.

"I'm keeping Jasper as a suspect because he was here and he hated his mother, so he could've taken the diamond to spite her. But he's an outlier as I can't see why he would wait until 1965 when Lady Elizabeth had been horrible to him all his life. Vida I'm not so sure about, but I don't think they had a happy marriage. I found a bunch of old letters from a Gertrude Hayes to Vida—Gertrude was her mum. So the first thing that will interest you is they speak of someone at the castle they called the Sneak, and I think they were talking about your Alice. From what I could gather Vida did not like her sister-in-law, and Gertrude seemed to think Alice was jealous of Vida because she and Lady Elizabeth were friends."

"Okay, and the second thing?"

Neve hesitated again, then said, "Vida died on Samhain in 1970."

"She died the day I was born?"

"Yes." Neve eyed her mother worriedly. "She committed suicide."

A hand to her mouth, Edie gazed at the photo of Vida in her nurse uniform. "If she was my mother . . ." She paused, trying to get the words past the tears clotting her throat. "If she was my mother, she killed herself after giving birth to me."

Neve pressed her lips together sympathetically. "It could be a coincidence."

"She hated me so much," whispered Edie.

"Mum, we don't know she was your mother. There could be any

number of reasons why she committed suicide, and even if she was your mother she might have been suffering from postnatal depression for all we know."

Edie nodded, wiped her running nose and tapped a photo of a thin, faded woman who could've been anything from twenty to forty, staring nervously at the camera as though it might bite her. "This is Alice?"

Neve nodded. "I was struggling to find a motive for her, but I think you've given me one. Do you know when Alice was forced to have an abortion?"

"She never gives dates. But she mentions Mungo and Lottie, so they were still alive."

"So before Samhain in 1965. It gives Alice a motive to steal the Maundrell Red. Taking it would've been a sweet revenge for what Lady Elizabeth did to her." Neve placed a hand on the board with only a large question mark. "There's another possibility, an outlier," she said. "Dr. Kincaid."

"Who aborted Alice's baby?"

Neve nodded. "He was treating Mungo. Do you know anything about ECT?"

"It's a rather controversial treatment where electric shocks are sent through the brain."

"I hate having no reception. It sucks not being able to google shit like that," Neve grumbled.

"Poor Mungo," murmured Edie, barely noticing her daughter's language.

"Yeah," said Neve, scowling at the question mark. "I haven't found much about the doctor. The only thing I know is he wasn't on the island when the Red went missing." Standing back, she stared at the board, her head to one side. "He is a possibility though. We know through Alice that Lady Elizabeth promised the diamond to him. Maybe he found out Lady Elizabeth had no intention of giving it to him, so he stole it instead. But I have no way of knowing . . ." Neve shook her head in frustration and turned to another board.

"Okay, so leaving Jasper, Alice and the doctor aside, that brings us to the final four. Mungo and Charlotte—"

"Mungo was severely autistic; I can't see him taking the diamond," said Edie, defensive on Mungo's behalf. "He wouldn't have understood its value."

"Calm down, Mum! I'm not saying he did, but you can't discount him as a suspect. If he'd taken the Maundrell Red once before, he might have taken it again in 1965."

"Fine!" muttered Edie. "But I still don't think he took it."

"You might not think that when you see this." Neve darted across the room and came back with a box.

It was filled with bits of colored glass, interesting stones, acorns, a couple of empty shoe polish tins, feathers that were little more than a shaft and a couple of barbs white with age, a Dinky car, spoons with lovely handles, and a battalion of tiny tin soldiers.

"Now ask me where I found these?"

Edie pulled a face. "Mungo."

"Exactly. Our Mungo was a bit of a magpie and he really does have hiding places all over the castle like your Alice said. He's a bit cagey, but I've found a way to get him to show me where they are . . . a story for a hiding place." Neve rocked back on her heels, looking pleased with herself.

Edie fingered a tin soldier. "I've seen some of these. Cameron found some hidden in the woods."

"Outside? Shit! I thought his hiding places were all in the castle. How the hell am I going to get him to go outside?"

"I'm sure you'll think of something," said Edie dryly.

Neve ignored the sarcasm, put the box aside and turned back to the boards. She pulled off a photo and said, "This is Mungo and Charlotte. Charlotte's been a difficult one to pin down; there's very little about her."

The picture brought a lump to her throat. Charlotte was a freckle-faced girl with long hair in a messy plait. Mungo towered over her, his bright red hair a rat's nest above his beaming moon face.

He gazed down at Charlotte with an expression of sheer adoration. They looked happy.

She shut her eyes briefly. "We are such idiots . . . Charlotte is Lottie! That's the girl Mungo is always looking for." She peered at the photo closely, then at Neve. "You look a little like her—if your hair wasn't bright pink, of course. Maybe that's why Mungo thought you were Lottie when we first arrived?"

"That doesn't help me find the bloody Maundrell Red," muttered Neve as she came to the last board. "That brings us to Percy Maundrell and his friend Ashley Templeton. Ashley is the only one who wasn't a Maundrell or connected to them in some way like the Macleods."

"Percy, my mysterious relative who gave us the castle?"

Neve nodded.

Edie examined the photo of the two young men. They had their arms slung over each other's shoulders, their blond and dark heads a lovely contrast as they laughed in the sunshine, so carefree it made her smile. "What beautiful men," she said.

"They were gorgeous," said Neve. "It sucks that one is dead and the other would be older than you now."

"They look like a couple."

"So?"

Edie took the pinned photo off the board and looked at the back. "So they were brave beautiful men. This was taken in 1965."

Neve looked at her mum in confusion.

"Homosexuality was illegal in the sixties. If they were in a relationship, it would've been considered a crime. It wasn't accepted then as it is now."

"So that's what they were going on about," Neve murmured to herself.

"What?"

"I found this . . ." She took a letter pinned to the board and handed it to Edie.

Edie read the letter from Ashley Templeton's parents to Lady

Elizabeth with mounting horror. "She was going to use ECT on the boys?"

Neve nodded. "I didn't understand what they were going on about, talking about their son's abnormalities. I thought he might've been disabled or something, but it wasn't that; they were talking about his homosexuality. And Ashley's parents were going along with it. They seemed to think ECT could somehow cure his sexual orientation. How sick is that?"

October 1965

Lottie burst into the Baronial Hall, then shrieked when the canned witch's laughter startled her.

Scowling at Percy, who laughed at her fright, she stomped across the vast space, aware of the shadows rippling across the displays of weaponry on the paneled walls, dimming the lights from the old antler chandeliers.

Mr. and Mrs. Macleod stood next to the fireplace, their welcoming smiles fading as they looked past Lottie, to the shadows before sharing a worried glance.

The Hall was decorated in all the Halloween kitsch Bitsie could muster. Every year she shipped in more decorations from America. It might seem like a peculiarity, this compunction for a grown woman who was very aware of her status in society to obsess with what was essentially a children's holiday, but the family tolerated it, knowing it stemmed back to Bitsie's youth and the Blairs' famous Halloween ball. Tomorrow night they would all have to endure the annual party, and the trick-or-treating before. Bitsie never treated, she only tricked. Mungo loved

194

Halloween as much as their grandmother did, but Bitsie always set out to scare him unnecessarily with that dreadful costume she wore every year without fail. And Lottie hated her for it.

She shot sidelong glances at Percy and Ashley—well, Ashley mainly, who looked particularly handsome tonight, his face and arms tanned from the last few days of warm weather. Their heads close together, the boys whispered tensely as though they were planning a surprise. Or perhaps it was nerves, not knowing if Bitsie had pulled a family meeting to discuss their relationship openly.

Bitsie was the last to arrive. Seating herself on the large throne-like chair, she arranged her dark blue skirt around her thin legs before surveying the family who were all forced to stand around her like courtiers. It was so obviously contrived that Lottie rolled her eyes.

Bitsie saw it. "I apologize for wasting your time, Charlotte," she said with stinging sweetness. "Perhaps you would like another week in your room to consider your lack of respect?"

Lottie looked down at her feet, fighting the urge to cry. "No, Grandmother," she whispered.

"What was that? I didn't quite hear you?" Bitsie cupped a hand around her ear.

"No, Grandmother," said Lottie loudly. "I'm sorry, Grandmother." She felt a vicious stab of satisfaction when the shadows gathered behind Bitsie. A tendril reached out to trace the perfect blond shingle bob in an exploratory fashion before slithering back into the walls, melding with the dark grain of the wood.

"That is better."

Bitsie turned to the family, jaw tense, green eyes flashing. Something had infuriated her. Lottie fervently hoped it wasn't something Mungo had done. That sort of fury would break all agreements and have him put straight into an asylum. She glanced around the Hall, not surprised no one had thought to bring Mungo in. She tried to catch Mr. and Mrs. Macleod's attention, but the couple weren't looking in her direction.

She sidled up to Percy and Ashley to hiss, "Where's Mungo?"

"He was with us for most of the day," he murmured out the corner of his mouth. "But he ran off in the afternoon. We haven't seen him since."

Lottie's worry for Mungo ratchetted up another notch.

As though Bitsie had read Lottie's thoughts, she said, "Where's Mungo?"

Everyone turned to Lottie.

She blushed at the sudden focus on her. "Don't look at me," she said defensively. "I was in my room, remember?" She scowled darkly at her family's discomfort at her backhand rebuke that she was useful too, even if it was only to keep tabs on Mungo's whereabouts.

"It's not like Mungo to be out this late," said Mrs. Macleod with a worried look at Mr. Macleod.

"No matter," said Bitsie dismissively. "His presence is hardly likely to add anything of use or importance."

Lottie's tense shoulders relaxed slightly. If Mungo's presence wasn't needed the meeting was not about something he had done. She needn't have worried Bitsie would use the opportunity to humiliate him. The irony was Mungo didn't realize he was being humiliated so the practice was rather wasted.

Bitsie cleared her throat meaningfully. "I have called you all here this evening to tell you of a heinous crime committed against me, against our family." She paused and surveyed the watching faces speculatively.

"What is it, Mother?" said Alice, when the silence stretched to breaking point.

Bitsie took another sweep of the faces around her before announcing, "The Maundrell Red has been stolen."

Gasps of shock greeted her revelation.

Lottie happened to be looking at Aunt Alice when Bitsie made her announcement. She, too, looked shocked, but as Bitsie's words sank in, her face spread with furtive glee. It was only for a moment before Alice schooled her features into shock once more, but it made Lottie wonder if her aunt hadn't done something more than sneak about and scribble down secrets in her diary.

Alice wasn't the only one secretly delighted by the news. Beyond the initial shock, few showed dismay at the loss of the diamond. Anything that upset Bitsie would make most of the family quite happy.

"Stolen or misplaced?" said Jasper.

Bitsie's nostrils flared with irritation. "Stolen!" she snapped. "I am not in the habit of losing valuable diamonds!"

"Of course not," said Jasper mildly, "but to leap to theft before determining other possibilities is foolhardy."

"I have already considered all the possibilities! You all know I wear the Red often, and I am unlikely to loan it to someone—something I have never done before. I am equally unlikely to misplace it as I have never misplaced anything in my life. Now, if you have finished accusing me of stealing my own diamond, perhaps we can get on to the more important task of finding who stole it?"

Everyone leaned back under Bitsie's glare.

"That was not what I meant, Mother," said Jasper wearily. "I am simply—"

"Simple is right," sneered Bitsie. "I cannot believe you came from my womb! I would never have endured such hurtful remarks from your brother if he had lived. Theodore would've found my diamond already; he wouldn't have accused me like I was some common criminal!"

Everyone stared at Bitsie in horror. It was a far more vicious attack than usual, revealing the level of her agitation.

"Is it possible one of the maids could have forgotten to take it off when they took your clothing to be washed?" said Vida, raising a warning eyebrow at her husband not to say anything further.

"Nae," said Mrs. Macleod before Bitsie could leap on the idea. "My lassies know to check everyone's clothing thoroughly for jewelry and loose items afore washing anything. They've not failed me yet."

Vida started to argue, saw the fighting shine in Mrs. Macleod's eye and had the grace to back down from an argument she wouldn't win.

"Mrs. Macleod," said Bitsie.

"Aye, Lady Elizabeth?" she said coolly, showing none of the servility Bitsie thought her due from a servant.

Bitsie's eyes narrowed, sensing disrespect, but she couldn't fault the housekeeper's demeanor.

"You're to ensure the staff are before me tomorrow first thing."

Mrs. Macleod nodded, her chest rising in a sigh of resignation.

"You don't think it's one of us?" said Percy incredulously. "Why would any of us want it? We all know the bloody thing is cursed."

Everyone had views on the Maundrell Curse. The adults said they didn't believe it, except for the Macleods, who were quite open in their beliefs, yet they were all tense around Samhain, waiting for a freak accident to strike as it so often did.

Lottie believed in it fervently; bad luck had dogged the Maundrells for generations, too many horrible tragedies to be coincidence. She was almost certain the curse was somehow imbued in the stone as everyone claimed; a harbinger of doom, a talisman to fear. But sometimes she wondered if the curse came from an older time, for bad luck had stalked the Maundrells long before Ernest Maundrell brought the stone back from Africa.

And they were due some bad luck. If she didn't count the death of Aunt Alice's baby, the last tragedy had been seven years ago when her grandfather had died in a freak boating accident. Lottie had witnessed it from the cliffs, tearful because she had wanted to go out with him on the maiden voyage of his new speedboat, but he had refused, wanting to test the boat's safety first.

It had been an unusually sunny day for the end of October when Rupert Maundrell had sped across the red water, trailing a frothy pink wake. The fog had risen from nowhere, a billowing shiver gliding across Loch na Scáthanna. Sea fogs were nothing new, they came and went without warning, but it had seemed odd that day; the sun had been too bright.

A terrible crunching had echoed off the Munros. When the mist lifted, bits of wood floated on the loch with no sign of her grandfather. To this day no one knew what happened on the loch, but it wasn't long before it was put down to the Maundrell Curse.

"It's been a while since Father's accident," said Alice, thinking along

the same lines as Lottie. She surveyed the family, calculating their untimely deaths. "I feel another tragedy is coming," she added with a shiver.

"Nonsense!" scoffed Bitsie.

"Curse or not," said Vida, "it couldn't be one of us."

"It wasn't me!" said Lottie, crossing her arms defensively. "I've been locked in my room all week."

Denials and alibis quickly filled the hall. Percy was quick to stand in front of Ashley protectively, shielding his friend from accusations as the one person not tied to the Maundrells by blood.

Everyone talked over each other, putting theories forward until the hall sounded like a hive of uneasy bees.

It was entirely possible one of them had stolen the Maundrell Red if they were desperate enough, thought Lottie. She had few illusions about her family and what they were capable of if pushed into a corner. And Bitsie had pushed everyone into a corner at some stage; perhaps she had pushed someone too far.

Or . . . Lottie stared hard at the shadows squirming along the paneled walls—perhaps this was something to do with the Witch? Her shadows were unusually active this year. Had someone made a pact with the Witch? She regarded Bitsie thoughtfully. Everyone knew the Witch always took blood and what was valued most in payment. Had her grandmother wanted something else so much she had offered the Maundrell Red to the Witch? Lottie shook her head slightly. No, Bitsie would never give up the Red, not for anything, regarding it with the same obsession as a sacred religious relic.

That meant only one thing; someone in the Hall had made a pact to take what Bitsie valued most to hurt her, who in turn would lose what they most valued. It was a horrible supposition of a potentially vicious cycle, one Lottie wished she hadn't thought of.

"There's only one thief in the family," said Alice loud enough that everyone heard.

"What are you trying to insinuate?" demanded Mrs. Macleod, not

even pretending at servility. "Dinnae dare blame my grandson! He has his ways, true, but he's never taken anything of worth."

"He has taken the Maundrell Red before," said Vida.

"He returned it soon after!" cried Lottie hotly. "And Mrs. Macleod's right; he's never taken anything else of value."

"Well," said Alice, hazel eyes glittering with excitement, "that's not strictly true."

Lottie's gasp dropped into the silence that followed. She stared at her aunt with dawning horror.

"He took one of my necklaces only last week. The sapphire pendant Father gave me for my twenty-first. You remember, don't you, Mother?"

Lottie's horror bled into hatred. She knew what was coming.

"It was Lottie who gave it back to me. Isn't that right, Lottie?" said Alice, smiling encouragingly.

"Yes, but Mungo said you gave it to him," said Lottie, but her words sounded hollow, false, even to her own ears. She couldn't take her eyes off her aunt, weirdly fascinated how the most timid person in the family seemed to be weaving a web around them all, belatedly waking up to the fact that Alice was very much Bitsie's daughter, manipulative and scheming, if in different ways.

Alice laughed fondly and tucked a stray strand of hair behind her ear. "Oh, don't be silly, Lottie. We all know Mungo takes things that don't belong to him."

Lottie's gasp went unheard as everyone tried to have their say. The shadows fussed around Alice, petting her hair, her skin, her clothes, like nebulous sycophants.

CHAPTER 15

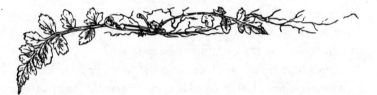

The gale died down to the occasional swift gust in the early evening, allowing the snow to fall unimpeded. Finding a pair of
old Wellingtons in the boot room that fitted her and a heavy jacket
smelling of stale lilac, Edie ventured outside.

The world was featureless and virgin white. Fat flakes swirled
in arabesques and curlicues from low clouds the hue of an old
bruise, blotting out the Munros. It hurt to breathe in the crisp,
cold air, the everyday scents purified by odorless snow, overlaid
by a whisper of woodsmoke from the fire Edie had lit for Neve in
the museum. The Brig o' Haggs had vanished under a pale quilt,
impassable by foot or vehicle to the village where lights already
glimmered to combat the early darkness.

As Edie tramped past the cairns and the graveyards with tomb-
stones and crosses poking out, starkly grim against the snow, she spied
Neve trudging in the opposite direction towards the cottages on the
north side of the island, wearing a determined expression. Assuming
she was on the hunt for Mungo's hiding places, Edie shook her head
in fond exasperation. Honestly, that girl never gave up.

Scrambling down to the dilapidated boathouse, Edie wrenched open the weathered door with the misguided notion they could sail to Haggs if the snow didn't let up soon. But one look at the three rickety boats, two almost submerged in the shallow water and the last with every appearance of joining them soon, put paid to that idea.

She slogged back up to the cliffs, then frowned down at the lonely figure on the small beach gazing out across Loch na Scáth-anna, its vibrancy muted to a ruddy flush. Not wishing to intrude on Cameron, who appeared deeply lost in his own thoughts, she turned towards the castle, then hesitated.

Sod it, she thought, and spun round to clamber down the cliff path, the snow underfoot muffling her approach.

"There's no way off the island," she said to his back.

Cameron stiffened, then faced her. He grimaced. "And just when I had a burning desire to get the hell away from this place."

"Is that because of your contrary nature or because you need to be somewhere else?" said Edie, though she rather thought it was because of his argument with Mr. MacKenzie she and Neve had witnessed that morning. There had been real anger between the two men that had felt like hatred.

He stared at Edie for so long she grew uncomfortable. "It's always my contrary nature," he said quietly, his honey-hued eyes bright with something she couldn't read. He walked up the beach towards her, saying, "Were you looking for me?"

"No, not really, but—um—" Edie's skin bloomed with a hot flush she was quite sure had nothing to do with menopause and every-thing to do with Cameron's close proximity. "Would you like to have dinner with Neve and I this evening?" The words bypassed her brain without conscious thought. "I—that is—after last night nei-ther of us want to be alone and we're all stuck here and I thought— And it won't be anything fancy, probably pasta again, but we have a fabulous cellar so—" Her breath caught in her throat as Cameron stepped into her personal space, so close she could smell the faint salty tang of his skin.

"Do I make you nervous?" he murmured.

"Yes— No!" Edie squeaked, and her self-esteem shriveled with embarrassment. She stared at his lips. "Of course not. Don't be ridiculous. I am not nervous of anything. I am absolutely fine." She leaned towards him, expectant.

"Yet you're blethering something fierce." He stepped away.

Edie quickly jerked back before she fell over. Feeling like a fool for hoping, she hid her blushing face. "I've asked Mr. MacKenzie too," she lied, with every intention of scuttling across to the old man's cottage to extend a belated invitation.

"Then I'll pass," said Cameron, his tone hardening.

"Yes. Of course. That's absolutely no problem. Um—" She turned around, her blush stealing down her body to puddle in her toes.

"I'll walk you up to the castle," said Cameron, falling in step with her. "It might not be safe walking about by yourself, especially after what happened to your daughter."

Edie gave him a sidelong glance, confused. "Thanks," she said cautiously.

"How is Neve? She had quite a scare last night."

"She's fine," said Edie, grasping the less fraught emotional ground gratefully. "I thought she'd be in a state, but she's been surprisingly fine. She's up to her eyeballs in this ridiculous search for the Maundrell Red."

"And how's she getting on with that?"

"No closer than anyone else, I don't think. She thinks it's one of ten people who were on the island at the time."

"Ten people? I thought there were only eight."

"No, ten. The Maundrells, a school friend of Percy Maundrell, and two servants, although they seemed to have been more than servants." She quickly launched into an explanation of Mr. and Mrs. Macleod. And as she had started, she told him everything else Neve had found to avoid a silence opening up in the time it would take them to walk to the castle.

"Clever lass, your Neve," said Cameron, listening intently. "And these two servants had a genuine claim to the diamond?"

"Oh yes. I think if it went to court they would win hands down. Neve found Ernest Maundrell's last will. Oh!" Edie stopped short when a shimmer in the snow-shrouded rose gardens caught her eye.

The ghostly young girl darted hither and thither, a moonbeam shiver in the gloaming. She didn't notice Edie and Cameron, too intent on her search, her face screwed up with worry.

"Jesus Christ," muttered Cameron, his eyes tracking the ghost. "Can you see that?" he whispered.

"Yes. We've seen her before."

On the muffled air came a tapping. The ghost swiveled to the castle, hand to her mouth to prevent a scream. On every window, drawn in the condensation, was a plague mask. The ghost vanished. A moment later, the windows cleared to stare blindly at the loch once more.

"It's Lottie!" Edie breathed.

"She was definitely there," Cameron murmured, rigid, staring at the spot where Lottie had disappeared. "You saw her and I saw her, right?"

"Yes. I think her name is Charlotte, but Mungo calls her Lottie. We found a photo of—"

"Mungo? Who the hell is Mungo?"

"He's one of the ghosts we've seen in the castle. He's sweet. Can't talk very well, but he's always asking for Lottie."

Cameron stared at her as though she were mad.

Taken aback, Edie said, "You've seen a ghost before. Why are you so freaked out?"

"The monks? I was pissed as a coot. I've never really thought I'd seen a real ghost!"

"Oh. Well, we're seeing them all the time. They really are everywhere here."

Cameron ran agitated hands through his hair. "You definitely saw that girl?" he asked again. "I'm not going mad?"

"If you're going mad then so am I." She smiled. "I really, really saw her," she said gently. "But she won't hurt you. None of the ghosts have tried to hurt us."

Cameron's jaw worked as he ground his teeth. "I need a drink," he muttered, and turned abruptly, disappearing down a snow-choked path.

Edie watched him go, bewildered, not sure what had come over the man. He had been quite blasé about the ghosts when they'd spoken of them previously, but he had been genuinely scared of Lottie.

Shaking her head, she continued up to the castle and went straight up to the museum rooms.

"I know who the girl in the garden is," she declared as Neve looked up when she entered. "It's Mungo's Lottie. Charlotte Maundrell!" Edie hurried across to the boards and took down the photo of Mungo beaming at the young girl. "This is her. The ghost in the garden. I'm sure of it." She darted to the Maundrell family tree and quickly found Charlotte Maundrell. It was the last name at the very bottom, the youngest of the Maundrells. "She died in 1965, same as Mungo."

Neve joined Edie in front of the family tree. "You know what's really weird? I haven't found a single thing about the night when three people died. It's like everything has been destroyed on purpose."

"You know Mungo and Lottie died that night."

"Only because we've seen their ghosts . . . So who was the third?"

"It would be simple to narrow it down," said Edie, nodding at the family tree. "You know who was on the island then. You know Vida died in 1970; Alice we know died about ten years ago."

"Jasper was still alive afterwards; Vida spoke about him in her letters to her mother after the diamond went missing. And she talks about Lady Elizabeth."

"Fine, so if Percy died last year and you take Mungo and Lottie out of the equation that leaves the Macleods and Ashley Templeton as your possible third."

Neve scowled. "I hate your logical brain," she muttered. "I totally missed that." She looked over Edie's shoulder and smiled. "Hey Mungo." Edie turned to the ghost standing in a corner of the room, watching them. He grinned at Neve. "Read tae Mungo!" he said hopefully. Then his grin faded, eyes darting to the window. "Lady is comin'!" he screamed, and vanished.

"What was that about?" said Edie, glancing at the window to see what had frightened him. Fat snowflakes rushed past the glass, but nothing to frighten him that she could see.

"He's been doing that all day," said Neve. "He seems agitated. Sometimes he does this funny little hopping dance and walks in circles. Or he asks for a story, but mostly he's been standing at the window, then freaks out and shouts, 'Lady is coming.'"

Edie nodded thoughtfully and studied the photo of Mungo and Lottie she still held. There was such love in the captured moment, in their beaming smiles, their relaxed manner that spoke of warm familiarity. "I think he knows Lottie's in the garden," she said. "He's pining for her. But I think Lady Elizabeth is keeping them apart."

Neve looked dubious. "Why? They're all dead."

"I don't know." Edie tapped a nail against her teeth, collecting impressions and recent memory together to make some sort of sense. "When I saw Lottie, plague masks appeared on all the windows of the castle. She was scared of them and disappeared. And we know Mungo is terrified of the mask. I think Lady Elizabeth is using the plague mask to scare them. She doesn't want Mungo to leave the castle, but I think she doesn't want Lottie to come inside either."

Neve looked even more dubious. "Why?"

Edie shrugged.

"It could be the Witch."

"No. Last night Mungo called the Witch his friend. He wasn't scared of the shadows or the Witch. He only got scared when the mask appeared." Edie's mind squirreled on with little coherency;

she had so few pieces of the jigsaw it was impossible to make sense of any of it.

"Everything on this island is either about the Witch or the Maundrell Red," said Neve. "So if the Witch isn't involved, then it must be the Maundrell Red."

Edie nodded. "Everyone and their sainted aunt has been searching for that bloody diamond. And Lottie is searching for something. Although why she would want to find a diamond she can't use is beyond me." She glanced up at the ceiling when the ghostly rats clattered above them. "This place wouldn't be so terrible if Lady Elizabeth wasn't here. She makes everything feel . . . tainted. If we could get rid of her . . ." She left the thought hanging, then added, "Alice, Lady Elizabeth, Mungo and Lottie. What the hell happened in 1965 that they all remained here after they died?"

"Something hellish that's never been resolved," said Neve.

Edie put an arm around her, and was ridiculously happy when Neve didn't pull away immediately. "I don't know about you, but I'm starving."

Dinner was a quiet affair. Edie pushed pasta around her plate, one of the few nonperishables she had bought at the little shop in Haggs. They hadn't touched the box Hamish had brought. She hoped it wouldn't come to rationing food if they couldn't get off the island soon. She might manage to salvage vegetables from the walled garden. She had seen pumpkins there, vast orange globes amidst the rampant wilderness.

"I saw you talking to Han Solo earlier," said Neve before shoveling a forkful of pasta into her mouth.

"I made a bit of an idiot of myself," said Edie, stabbing a bit of canned tomato savagely. "I sort of engineered a meeting, then misread his signals. But it's been so long since . . ." She smiled self-deprecatingly, cursing the treacherous prickle of tears in her throat.

"Since Dad."

"Yes."

"Has anything happened between you and Cameron?"

Edie's face flamed. "We—er—we—he kissed me in the woods the other day," she admitted.

"Then you didn't misread anything. He's playing hard to get."

"Well, it was foolish anyway. I don't know what I was thinking," she said, sensing a looming seismic shift in their relationship that she was taking advice about romance from her fifteen-year-old daughter. Did this make them friends? It was so hard to tell with Neve.

"He was never going to be good enough for you anyway."

Edie's eyebrows rose. "You were the one who said I should take an interest."

"I've changed my mind."

But Edie read the subtitles written plainly on her daughter's face; no man would ever match up to her father.

After dinner they hurried through the halls. Little feet scurried above them, keeping pace before vanishing into the echoing distance when they reached their bedrooms. Edie didn't need to insist Neve stay the night with her. After completing their ablutions in record time they hopped into bed.

Edie stared up at the ceiling, intending to stay awake in case the shadows tried something again. Neve, the covers pulled up to her chin, also stared at the ceiling, eyes narrowing when the rats scurried above them once more.

"Are you all right?" asked Edie.

"Shh! I'm listening."

"To what?"

Neve shook her head, contemplating the ceiling with a concentration it did not warrant.

Edie sighed, then muttered, "Jesus!" and jerked into a sitting position.

There was no warning whisper or scratching when the words . . . *It is astonishing that we can grow habituated to the strangest of things . . .* materialized on the wall opposite the bed.

"What is it?" said Neve, breaking her concentration. "Is it Alice?"

A finger to her lips, Edie got out of bed and whispered, "Speak to me, Alice."

Almost immediately, as though Alice had been waiting for the request, there appeared: *"I see the Witch's shadows everywhere I go,"* Edie read aloud for Neve. *"They do not come near me, but they are always watching. What does the Witch want? I fear she may take D from me. I saw her shadows in the woods when we met last night. We are nearing Samhain. She never takes a life except on Samhain; it is the one night of the year I do not meet D, for Mother still has her dreadful love for Halloween parties and they always end so late . . ."*

Edie stepped up to the wall and said, "Alice? Tell me about Vida?"

No more words appeared. Edie sighed and leaned her head against the wall. "She's gone."

Neve wasn't listening. She frowned at the ceiling, then at her watch. It was Joshua's watch and much too masculine and big for her thin wrist, but Neve hadn't taken it off since her father had died.

"What is it?" said Edie.

"Shh! I'm counting."

"Counting what? Sheep?"

"No. Rats . . . There's a pattern." Eyes locked on her watch, her lips moved as she counted. "Another ten seconds . . . Five, four, three, two, one!" She pointed at the ceiling as the scurry of claws rushed above them before receding into the distance. She beamed at Edie triumphantly. "Every half hour on the dot those rats come flying over us. Every half hour without fail."

"So? They're punctual ghost rats."

"Punctual rats my arse."

October 1965

Fog stole across Loch na Scáthanna, dulling the pale light of lanterns swinging in and out of existence across the darkened island like spunkies which, according to Mrs. Macleod you should never follow, for they led to your doom. She was never specific on what sort of doom, or if it was doom generally.

It was all a little confused. Bitsie had told them to find Mungo, certain he had taken the Maundrell Red. There was some protest; no one wanted to be abroad on the eve of Samhain. But as usual, everyone eventually obeyed.

Only Lottie and Aunt Alice weren't paired up. Lottie had been grateful no one had suggested they should. Now she wished someone had. It was lonely and scary in the dark by herself.

Mungo's name echoed off the walls of the castle, but it was impossible to tell who called and where they might be; the mist dampened sound and created dead hollows in the slinking shadows.

Holding her lantern high, Lottie squinted into the shifting darkness, *then turned quickly, her chest tightening with alarm, sensing some-one behind her. But no one was there, her fear peopling the island with ghosts.*

Loitering as long as she dared in the safety of the walled garden with the castle's friendly lights in running distance, she decided it was ridiculous the hold diamonds had over humans. Nothing more than dirty crystals when clawed from the ground, but when cut and faceted those bright stones possessed humans' souls, trapping them in unhealthy obsessions. She understood the power of diamonds all too well, for the Maundrell Red's allure was greater for its rarity, size and flawlessness.

Lottie knew she would not be the only one weighing up her options if she found the diamond. She would not give it back to Bitsie but would use it to run away with Mungo. And she had an advantage, for she knew Mungo and where he hid his treasures . . . That's if he had taken the diamond, of course, which was the one stumbling block in her opportunistic plan.

When she had studied every fruit tree, herb and vegetable bed in the walled garden, Lottie forced herself to pass through the arch and start down the path towards the rose gardens. The mist curled around her legs in sorrowful sighs. It tugged at her hair, so real she kept reach-ing up to touch her head, terrified what her hand might encounter.

Relief swamped Lottie when she saw the pendulum of a lantern ahead. She put on a burst of speed.

She stopped beside the Hercules fountain, her skin pimpling with alarm. The lantern and its holder weren't where she'd thought they would be.

"Hello?" she called uncertainly.

The mist swallowed her plaintive warble and went unanswered.

"It was not a spunkie," she whispered to herself, and sat on the edge of the fountain until the tremble in her legs abated.

Breathing deeply, Lottie had only grim thoughts about her grand-mother. She could easily imagine Bitsie pretending the Red was stolen to send everyone on a wild goose chase in the dark in her twisted desire to create drama. Bitsie thrived on drama. Unless, unless . . .

Lottie contemplated the castle. It floated above the island, suspended on the cushioning mist, lit windows little more than spectral shimmers. Could her grandmother really be that cruel?

Now she thought about it, Bitsie had been quick to leap on Aunt Alice's suggestion that Mungo was the thief. Was this her sly way to get Mungo put in an asylum with a trumped-up reason to stop the family resisting? But why now? She had been threatening an asylum for years. Had Mungo's meltdown last week been the final straw Bitsie was willing to tolerate? Was her grandmother really that vengeful? Lottie nodded. Yes. Yes, she was.

As much as Lottie wished to deny it, it wasn't impossible Mungo had taken the diamond to spite Bitsie, having taken it before. Except Mungo didn't have a spiteful bone in his body, but sometimes she had caught him staring at their grandmother with what would be a calculating expression if it had been anyone else's face.

Giving up hope of seeing someone she could tag along with, Lottie gathered her fragile courage and set off at a fast walk down the path to the boathouse.

She hadn't taken more than a few steps when gravel crunched ahead of her.

Tensing with crawling unease, she lifted her lantern high, searching for the responding light of another lantern.

When none appeared she ventured another cautious, "Hello?"

No answer.

"Percy? Is that you?"

Not a sound.

"If it's you, it's not funny!"

But Percy didn't answer. No one did.

"Who's there?" she said, hoping the waver in her voice was inside her own head.

As she listened hard to the damp silence, her unease ratchetted up to alarm. If it was family they would've responded, she would've heard them talking as they were searching in pairs . . . except for Alice.

"*Aunt Alice?*" *she whispered. Then louder,* "*Aunt Alice, is that you?*"

Alarm surged to panic. Had a stranger come onto the island and taken the Maundrell Red? It wouldn't be hard. And they might not have left.

Lottie listened for a full minute, resisting the intense urge to run back to the safety of the castle. When nothing happened, her shoulders relaxed slightly. It could also have been a ghost. She wasn't far from the grotto, perhaps Myrtle Bruce.

She relaxed a little more. A ghost who had never harmed anyone was better than a stranger who still might.

"*Silly Lottie,*" *she said in the same tone Mungo used, then startled at the sound of her own voice.*

She crept along the path, ears attuned for footsteps behind her, though her rational self knew it was her own footsteps echoing in the mist. Pushing back on the terror of a stranger on the island, she filled her mind with Aunt Alice. She had always been a sly one. Lottie knew she had been manipulated by her aunt in the Hall earlier, but she couldn't fathom the reason for it. Mungo had no reason to lie about being given the pendant. On the other hand, why would Alice lie about giving it to him? Lottie worriedly recalled Alice's smug smile when Bitsie had demanded everyone go look for Mungo. Bitsie had done exactly what Alice wanted.

The problem with Alice as the thief was why now? Bitsie had always been horrible to Alice; why take spiteful revenge now? Except there was the shift in Bitsie and Alice's relationship Lottie had recently awakened to. And what did she really know about her aunt? Nothing, she realized with surprise. Alice was secretive, yes, always scribbling in her diaries, but Lottie knew absolutely nothing of her aunt's dreams and desires. Perhaps Alice also wished to leave the island, but dominated utterly by Bitsie she had taken the desperate measure of stealing the Maundrell Red to facilitate her escape.

"*Mungo?*" *called Lottie as she entered the boathouse where three boats nudged each other gently. It always smelled of diesel and wood shavings in here, reminding Lottie of her grandfather.*

Clamping down on those horrific memories, she called again, more urgently, "Mungo, are you in here? It's time to come out."

Mungo didn't appear looking sheepish.

Lottie quickly headed back up the path and continued her speculation to distract herself from the slithering dark. She wanted to discount Percy and Ashley, but the two had been secretive recently. Understandable, considering what they were keeping secret. Could it be something else? Maybe some scheme was afoot? Lottie shook her head. She couldn't think of anything that would involve the Maundrell Red. Percy would inherit the Maundrell fortune one day, and Ashley did not strike Lottie as the thieving sort, and he, too, came from a wealthy family.

Heading along the cliff path, she considered her parents as thieves. Her father she discounted immediately. He was a good man, even if cowed by his mother and wife. She knew he would never leave the island; Greer Macleod was buried here. Lottie had often seen him in the Maundrell graveyard, standing in front of Greer's grave, separated from the others. Another act of malice by Bitsie.

Her mother, however, was a different story. Lottie didn't think Vida would steal the diamond for monetary gain but could imagine her concocting the theft with Bitsie, for those two were always thick as—

Lottie shrieked and swung around, her lantern gripped tight and raised like a weapon.

"Steady there, lass," cautioned Mr. Macleod, grabbing Lottie before they both fell over after colliding into each other. "It's no use looking to the stars when you cannae see your feet."

"You just made that up," Mrs. Macleod chided fondly.

"Aye." Mr. Macleod grinned through his beard. "But it sounded guid."

"Has Mungo been found?" asked Lottie.

"Aye. That's why we're here, to bring you in from the cold," said Mrs. Macleod.

"*Where was he?*"

"*Asleep in his bed.*" *She pulled a wry face.* "*We only thought to check not a half hour back. All this talk of thefts and diamonds scattered everyone's common sense, including our own. Fair puggled, the puir wee man. Didnae even take off his shoes.*"

"*He was wearing shoes?*" *said Lottie in surprise.*

"*Aye. Those auld boots of mine,*" *said Mr. Macleod.* "*Took them off me yesterday and I cannae get them back from him, not even for a lemon sherbet, and you know how he loves his lemon sherbets . . . Come along now. Herself upstairs will be wanting to wake the wee man to get her bauble back, and we mean to be there so nae harm comes to him.*"

And then there were the Macleods, thought Lottie as she trailed after the couple towards the castle. Even knowing the Maundrell Red had been promised to Mr. Macleod's grandfather by Ernest Maundrell, she couldn't imagine them as thieves. They certainly had just cause to steal for spite after Bitsie treated the Macleods so cruelly when their daughter Greer died and prevented them from seeing Mungo when he was a baby. But the Macleods were simply too honest and incorruptible for Lottie to even flirt with the idea.

That left Dr. Kincaid as the only other person who spent time on the island on a regular basis. She remembered the first time he'd arrived to discuss treatment for Mungo. Bitsie had met the doctor in the Baronial Hall, using its sheer size to intimidate. Lottie had hidden in the stairwell off the Hall and unashamedly eavesdropped. It had been a strange meeting, full of silences she hadn't understood. It had taken the full force of Bitsie's indomitable will to persuade Dr. Kincaid to treat Mungo with ECT. Lottie was one of the few people who knew his price had been the Maundrell Red.

Dr. Kincaid was as obsessed with the diamond as Bitsie was, but he hadn't been on the island for the past week. She still hoped it was Dr. Kincaid. She didn't want the thief to be someone she cared about . . . unless— Was it possible Bitsie had given the diamond to Dr. Kincaid and pretended it was stolen?

So intent on her speculations Lottie almost barreled into the Macleods when they stopped at a disembodied cry in the mist.

"Sounded like Miss Maundrell," said Mrs. Macleod.

"She was in the gardens last I saw her," said Mr. Macleod. "We'd best check she's not come to harm . . . Get yourself up to the castle, lass."

"No, I'm coming with you," said Lottie, who had no intention of going anywhere in the dark by herself again.

"Aye, it's best she's with us," said Mrs. Macleod. "It's too close to Samhain to walk about alone at night."

Confronted by female solidarity, the old man shrugged, and the three hurried back into the rose gardens.

Another shriek sent them running.

Then came Lottie's father's voice. "What the hell?" Followed by Lottie's mum. "Oh no! You stupid boys!"

Lottie and the Macleods hurtled into the grotto and stopped abruptly. As more Maundrells poured in, mist crept in too, haloing each lantern.

Percy and Ashley stood in middle of the grotto, chests heaving, shirts undone, Ashley's hand on Percy's bare shoulder.

Percy swallowed, not quite meeting the eye of his shocked family.

The mist was thickest around the well, shifting, nebulous, weirdly alert, as though the Witch in the Well had crept to the surface of the cold water to see who had disturbed her sleep a day early.

"I told you something terrible was going to happen," breathed Alice, bright with glee. Head cocked to one side, she studied Percy and Ashley like they were repulsive yet fascinating insects. "Didn't I say we were due a tragedy?" she said when no one responded.

"Shut up, Alice," said Jasper. He took a step towards his son.

Percy put up a hand that shook slightly. "Don't, Dad. You can't fix this. No one can fix us. We are who we are; we are what we are."

"What you're doing is illegal!" hissed Vida. "Have either of you thought of the consequences of your actions? What will happen when this comes out? You'll go to jail, Percy! You're a Maundrell! Maundrells do not go to jail, and certainly not for sodomy!"

"*Then it's just as well you're not a real Maundrell,*" Percy sneered. "*As much as you've always wanted to be one.*"

Vida jerked as though her son had struck her. "*When your grandmother—*"

"*When my grandmother what? What can she do? She can't disown me, and frankly I wouldn't give a shit if she could. I never wanted any of it.*" He turned to Ashley, tears slipping down his cheeks as he whispered, "*I'm so sorry.*" He started buttoning up his shirt. But for all his bravado, he tensed with real fear when the click-clack crunch of high heels sounded on the gravel path outside.

Bitsie stooped slightly as she entered the crowded grotto. She summed up the situation with one glance at Percy and Ashley, their lips plump from kissing, their rumpled clothing, their guilty expressions.

"*I warned you to stop this abomination!*" she hissed, her pale face reddening with fury.

Percy's fury matched his grandmother's. "*We are not an abomination! I love Ashley. But you could never understand; you've never loved anything in your life but yourself and that bloody diamond.*"

Something dark and dangerous crossed Bitsie's face. "*Do not test me, Percy,*" she said, her voice dropping with warning menace.

"*Or you'll do what?*"

Lottie gazed at her brother in horrified admiration. No one stood up to Bitsie. There would be consequences. Expecting a terrible fight, she stepped back against the rough wall of the grotto.

Bitsie surveyed the family, staring at each face until they squirmed, and found them all wanting. "*I take it no one has found Mungo?*" she said grimly.

"*He's asleep in his bed,*" said Mr. Macleod.

"*Then you'd best wake him.*"

"*No!*" cried Lottie. "*Please let him sleep. He won't understand if you wake him up in the middle of the night. All you'll do is scare him.*"

The full force of Bitsie's glare fell on Lottie. "*Very well, we'll do it your way. Vida!*" she snapped.

"*Yes?*" said Vida, startled.

"Telephone Dr. Kincaid at once. He is to be on the island tomorrow if he knows what's good for him. He'll get the diamond's whereabouts out of that idiot with a little electrical persuasion."

"That's not what I meant!" cried Lottie.

Bitsie smiled with honeyed spite. "Isn't it? Well, isn't that a pity."

"But tomorrow is Samhain," said Alice. "Perhaps it would be better if the doctor came the day after?"

"Tomorrow!" Bitsie shouted, her icy restraint cracking. She snapped her fingers at Percy and Ashley. "And make sure these two remain locked in their rooms until I decide what to do with them. They are not allowed near each other." She turned on her heel and stalked out of the grotto.

No one said a word until the tapping of Bitsie's high heels disappeared into the night.

"I'm not going to be locked in my room like a child," said Percy. "She can't make me."

"Don't fight them," said Ashley quietly. "This is your family. Don't fight with them."

Percy opened his mouth to argue, then shut it when Ashley smiled at him. It was a beautiful, intensely intimate smile that Lottie felt vaguely embarrassed to witness, revealing the love her brother and Ashley shared.

Ashley took Percy's hand and they walked out of the grotto. No one stopped them.

Alice remembered herself first and murmured, "I suppose one of us had better make sure we do as Mother demanded and lock them in their rooms." And she scuttled after the boys.

Everyone trailed out after Alice, bewildered by the night's turn of events. Lottie was the last to leave. She glanced over her shoulder at the well. Shadows clustered above the water in wary swirls. She almost didn't see something peeking out from behind one of the Pict stones.

Quickly checking her family hadn't realized she wasn't with them, she tiptoed to the Pict stone, whispered, "Sorry," to the Witch and *peeped into the hidden bag. It was full of clothes and a wad of money. A brief search didn't reveal the Maundrell Red.*

She picked it up, her heart clenching with conflicting sadness. A scheme had been afoot, one she hadn't thought of. Percy and Ashley had been running away together.

CHAPTER 16

Something weird is going on here, Mum," said Neve. She glanced at her watch and leapt out of bed, exclaiming, "It's nearly three! We need to get a wiggle on."

"Where are you going?"

"*We* are going to do a bit of investigating."

"Not in the middle of the night we're not!"

"Fine! I'll go by myself and if the Witch gets me, it will be your fault." Neve shrugged on her jacket and wrenched open the bedroom door.

"That is deeply unfair, Neve!"

Neve turned in the doorway. "I know that's why you can't sleep, same as me."

Edie puffed out a sigh of exasperation. "Fine!" she grumbled. She got out of bed and followed Neve into the dark hall.

"Well?" she demanded when Neve stopped, squinting into the gloom either way. "What are you waiting for?"

"The Grey Lady. I saw her along here the first night. You said it was three am when I woke you. And I'll bet you anything she'll be along shortly."

Edie leaned against the wall. A hot flush was building despite the leaching cold, and she needed to pee, but she wasn't going to leave Neve by herself in the dark. The events of the previous night were still so fresh and real she shivered as she sweated.

"Any time now," muttered Neve, looking at her watch, the dial lit up like a tiny constellation.

Minutes passed in silence.

"Shit!" said Neve. 'I thought I was on to something. The rats are definitely running above us every half hour. I've timed them. And I'm pretty sure live rats don't stick to a timetable, and ghost rats doubly so."

"Could be a coincidence," said Edie. "Or your mind's playing tricks on you because you're tired. We're both tired, so let's go back to bed."

"Was it exactly three when I woke you up before?"

"How the hell am I supposed to remember? That was a week ago, and I was half-asleep!"

"Shh!" Neve pointed down the hall.

Edie recoiled, a visceral reaction. The vague figure floated towards them like a puff of illuminated smoke. As it neared, the Grey Lady's outline sharpened. The ghost was rather beautiful; her voluminous dress didn't quite sweep the floor, a sheer veil revealing the contours of a wistful young woman.

As the Grey Lady reached them, Neve leapt right through her, slamming into the wall opposite. She righted herself and followed the ghost closely, swishing her hands back and forth through the transparent form, yelling, "Hello, Grey Lady!"

The Grey Lady reached the end of the hall and vanished.

Neve returned to Edie, lips pressed tight with satisfaction. "The Grey Lady's not real."

"Technically, she's not," Edie demurred. "She's a ghost."

"She's not a ghost either. When I passed my hands through her, she appeared on my skin like a projection. Someone has been pissing us about."

"Who and why?" said Edie, straightening from her slouch. "And how?" she added as an afterthought.

"I don't know . . . Come on." Neve grabbed her hand and tore along the hallway and down the spiral stairs. She switched on the lights in the museum, grabbed pen and paper and thrust them into Edie's hands. "Let's think of all the ghosts we've seen. We've got the rats and the Grey Lady. The rats run every half hour."

"I've not heard them during the day," said Edie, dutifully writing down *rats—half hour.*

"True. That's something I'll check tomorrow." She glanced at her watch. "Speaking of which, they should be along again in a few minutes . . . Okay, the Grey Lady is a few minutes after three am. But she could be at other times too."

"There's the baby we've heard. We didn't hear it the first couple of nights though."

"Probably because we were asleep."

Edie nodded and wrote down *wailing baby—night.*

"There's the Roman ships," said Neve. "I've seen them three times now, and always at night."

"And the ghostly monks. We haven't seen them, but Cameron has."

"Write it down . . . There was the maid I saw right here, and the man in the Inner Ward."

"And I saw that Highlander hanging in the Baronial Hall . . . And the Vikings. They scared the crap out of me . . . And Mr. MacKenzie said he'd seen loads of ghosts too. He mentioned the Roman ships and someone he called Myrtle Bruce who sobs in the grotto and—"

"Is seen in the graveyard in her wedding dress?"

"Yes," said Edie, surprised. "I take it you've heard of her."

"She's an old ghost. Died on her wedding day—"

"On Samhain, of course."

"Of course. But Myrtle wasn't a Maundrell, although she was marrying one that day."

"Mr. MacKenzie said he'd seen a headless horseman on the bridge."

"That's a new one to me."

"And something about a man in the old watchtower." Edie paused, then brightened. "And he's heard the wailing baby and Wully Macleod playing his pipes—"

"We've heard him too."

"And he's seen a woman with dead babies in the cellar too."

"Bloody Mary," said Neve, nodding. She took a book off the windowsill and held it up to Edie. It was poorly printed with a grainy photo of Maundrell Castle looking suitably Gothic against a stormy sky with the words *The Ghosts and Ghoulies of Loch na Scáthanna* by *P. W. Gorrie*. "According to this she killed her children and buried them in the cellar, then killed herself."

Edie nodded, not mentioning she had seen a copy in Cameron's room. "And there's Mungo and Lottie."

"And Alice and Lady Elizabeth."

"Cameron saw Lottie with me earlier this evening."

"You didn't tell me that!"

"Sorry, I forgot. I was more excited I'd managed to place her. And that was weird too. Cameron seemed genuinely frightened of her."

Neve snorted. "I can't imagine that man frightened of anything."

"Well, he was."

"That's an awful lot of ghosts we've seen or heard in the space of a week."

Edie looked down at her scribbles. "Mr. MacKenzie said there were more ghosts about than when he was a child."

"Mungo has to be real. He's been speaking to us."

"I think we can assume he, Lottie, Alice and Lady Elizabeth are really haunting the castle."

"Okay, putting them aside . . ." Neve looked up at the ceiling as a scurry of rats echoed above them. She checked her watch and grinned, darkly smug. "Half past three on the dot."

"Yes, all right. You've made your point, and I agree it appears some of the ghosts aren't real. Punctual rats, ghostly or otherwise, don't work for me either. So once again, who, why and how?"

"How is easy. Special effects."

"How is that easy?" Edie grumbled. She wasn't quite a luddite, but she was rather in awe of Neve's nonchalance with technology. "I wouldn't know where to begin."

"Cameras, projectors, sound recordings. With the right know-how it could be done."

"And a healthy dollop of credulous people in a castle that shouts haunted," said Edie dryly. "So leave the how aside; what about the who? Who would want to go to all the effort to make the castle appear more haunted than it already is when it's been abandoned for years? Seems rather pointless."

"Unless it was the people who rented the place out. A haunted castle would've pulled in the punters for the museum and the hotel. People love all that Gothic shit. I would pay good money to stay in a haunted castle with the guarantee of seeing a ghost or two."

Edie shuddered. "I can't think of anything more awful. And I doubt it was either of that lot; devices need batteries or charging up, and this place has been completely empty for years."

"Someone from the village to keep people away?"

"Why? That makes even less sense. You've seen Haggs. It's a place stuck in time."

"But they could've set up the ghosts to keep it that way," said Neve. "Maybe the villagers did it to scare the hotel people off. You did say it was weird they did all this work, then scarpered without opening the doors."

An image of Hamish Macleod's rugged face flashed into Edie's mind. She had caught him snooping on the island, and he'd seemed to know his way around the castle—well, certainly to the kitchen. Had he delivered provisions as a pretext to check his equipment?

Would he have the know-how? It was possible, of course, and yet . . .
She pulled a face. "I still can't see anyone in Haggs faking ghosts."

"That leaves Mr. MacKenzie and Han Solo."

"They both had access to the castle," said Edie thoughtfully.
"Though I can't see Mr. MacKenzie stealing about the castle with
gadgets and such. Cameron maybe. Except he's a microbiologist.
He's here to do research on the loch."

"True, which makes the why a bit tricky. Why would anyone set
up fake ghosts?"

"To scare people away."

"Obviously, Mum! But why?" Neve shut her eyes briefly. "God, I
can be stupid sometimes. The Maundrell Red!"

"Yes," said Edie slowly. "To stop people searching for it."

"Yeah."

"That doesn't work. It's not like there's been throngs of people
queuing up to search the island anymore. It would be fairly easy to
come here with some cock-and-bull story and search at your— Did
you hear that?" whispered Edie.

Neve put a finger to her lips, tiptoed to the door and darted out
into the dark hallway.

"Neve!" Edie hissed, hurrying after her.

She hadn't gone far. Standing at the top of the spiral staircase
leading to the Clan Tower, she squinted down the worn, stone stairs.

Thump . . . Thump . . . Thump . . . tapered away into the gloom.

"Sounds like a body being dragged down the stairs," whispered
Neve.

"Another recording?"

"Could be. It started on the floor above us."

Edie did not love the idea of creeping around the castle at night,
but she knew from Neve's determined expression it was what they
would be doing. Up the stairs they went to the third floor.

Two sets of shoeprints disturbed the dust brindling the floor
when Edie switched the hall light on. Geometric purple and orange

ran the length of the walls with vast purple vases breaking the pattern, casting oddly angled shadows.

Neve felt about the lintel of the stairwell of the Clan Tower and along the rounded ceiling while Edie searched around the hall, but both came up empty.

"Did you hear that?" whispered Neve, frowning down the long hall.

Edie nodded. "Footsteps."

Heavy footsteps ran towards them, trailing sobs. The Nunns drew closer together and watched the walls as the footsteps raced past them.

"That sounded like Mungo," said Neve. "He's running through the walls. He came from that direction." She started down the corridor then stopped as *click-clack-click-clack* came towards them, sucking the air dry like a sirocco.

"Lady Elizabeth," said Edie, her skin crawling into her bones. "She's after Mungo."

Mungo's sobs and heavy tread faded down the corridor pursued by a slithery echo of . . . *Pooorrr boooyyy . . . pooorrr boooyyy . . .* Then a hissed *rredredredredred . . .*

"Dinnae ken! Mungo dinnae ken!" was a distant bellow.

Redredredredred . . . rose to a high-pitched keen of thwarted fury.

Mungo's scream broke Edie's heart. But as quickly as the ghostly chase had appeared it vanished.

Silence flooded the castle. Not a single scurry or creak within, not a murmur from the blanketed world outside.

"I hate Lady Elizabeth!" said Neve in a hard, flat tone, her face twisted into something old by her loathing. "I hope she died in agonizing pain. Hell would be too good for her." She started down the corridor again.

Edie crept after her, spine stiff as a gnomon, wishing she shared her daughter's fearlessness.

Neve poked her head through each doorway they passed, revealing mostly empty rooms. She opened the last door, the top room of the Corbie Tower, and stepped inside with Edie following close behind.

A hospital bed sat in the center of the circular room, two arm-chairs faced the arched window and a trolley rested against one wall. In one corner rose a pile of boxes beside some sort of machine.

Edie opened one of the boxes. It was filled with old cardboard files. She opened a file at random and scanned the topmost notes. "They're doctor's notes," she said. "Oh! Dr. Kincaid." She opened another box. "These are all about Mungo's treatment."

"What's this?" said Neve, fiddling with the old machine. She twisted the knobs, then leapt back in fright when the machine emit-ted a crackle of electricity.

"Get away from there!" Edie cried, grabbing Neve as the machine rumbled petulantly before it exploded into a plume of sparks.

The Nunns scampered to the far end of the room and stared at the smoking machine.

"I think something's telling us to get out of this room," said Neve.

"We need to unplug it first. It's a fire hazard . . . Stay here." Edie approached the machine cautiously and bent down to follow the cable to the wall socket. She straightened and backed away.

"What is it?" said Neve. "What's wrong?"

"It's not plugged in."

The words were barely out of Edie's mouth when a scream ripped through the walls and Mungo appeared in the room. He clutched his head, his mouth wide and round, staring at the smoking machine in terror.

"Nae doc-ta! Nae hurt Mungo's heid!" he shrieked.

Edie's heart stuttered with fright as the ghost lumbered about, squeezing his head as though trying to make it burst.

"Mungo," said Neve softly, moving towards him before Edie could stop her. "It's okay. No one is going to hurt you."

He turned frightened eyes to her. "Nae hurt Mungo's heid!" he shrieked again, and ran through the open door.

"Did Mungo do that?" Neve nodded at the machine.

Edie barely heard her, her mind flashing with connections. She stared at the doorway through which Mungo had fled, at the boxes of files, the machine and the bed, noting the restraints attached to the sides. "I think this was where Mungo was treated with ECT," she said.

"More like tortured," Neve retorted.

"Yes," said Edie. She glanced at the doorway again, then smiled in relief as *floflofloflofloflo* . . . whispered from the hall, soft and secretive. She started out of the room.

'Mum! Where are you going?' said Neve.

Edie turned. "Take all these boxes down to the museum rooms. I'll meet you there in a minute; I need to find Alice."

"What? Why?"

"Just do it." Edie sped out of the room. Down stairwells and long hallways, she called softly for Alice.

She stopped in the library. The chandelier in the vaulted ceiling provided little light, but plenty of shadows. Edie eyed them warily, ready to run should they do something unshadowlike.

"Alice?" she whispered, and hurried behind the altar where she had first seen the dead woman's writing. "Alice!" she said again, loudly.

The name echoed around the library, a beat too slow, fading with a drawn-out slither. Edie stood still, breathing quietly, listening to the silence, listening for a pursuing *click-clack-click-clack*.

Minutes ticked by, the night drawing inexorably to a close.

The castle's noises slowly emerged from hiding as the dawn pressed timid fingers against the windows. Faint ticks and skitters whispered down the long halls, up stairwells and chimneys. Of Alice there was not a murmur.

Muttering curses for the fickleness of ghosts, Edie stared thoughtfully at the uppermost shelves housing the Maundrell diaries. It seemed silly now not to have checked for Alice's diaries here.

She dithered, conscious Neve was by herself and Samhain was only a day away. She had heard too many stories, too many warnings of the Witch, not to be aware that every Maundrell had died on Samhain and she and Neve were the last Maundrells.

Before she could overthink it, Edie climbed up the ladder to the top shelves and pulled out diaries one after the other; all black, leather bound with pages as thin as onionskin.

The Maundrells had been prolific diary writers. Apart from Mungo and Lottie, every single one had written their thoughts and secrets onto dry pages.

Edie opened the last diary belonging to Winifred Maundrell, checked the date and shoved it back into place. Stumped, she climbed down the ladder and stood in the middle of the library.

Not a single diary had revealed the handwriting of Alice, Gladys Maundrell. It wasn't only Alice's diaries that were missing. There wasn't a single diary after 1964, like time had vanished for Maundrell Castle the moment the clocks ticked over from 1964 to 1965.

Everything came back to 1965. The Maundrell Red went missing and three people died the next day, on Samhain. Edie's thoughts untangled with the certainty that even her birth here in the castle was somehow related.

"So that begs the question, did you hide your diaries, Alice, or did someone else take them?" Edie asked the books frowning down at her, as though angry she'd woken them from their long, unread slumber. "Or have they been destroyed? Is that why you've been writing to me? Did someone destroy your diaries and now you need to tell your story?"

Edie waited for a long while, tensed, alert for the slightest sound that Alice was nearby. But not a whisper fluttered into the air. Alice, like the castle itself, was withholding its many secrets.

CHAPTER 17

Edie ran all the way to the museum rooms to find Neve asleep, leaning against the boxes from the Corbie Tower. She lit the fire to take the edge off the cold and peered out the window. Falling snow feathered the faint dawn, the island trapped in a pale, silent world.

It was a while before Edie noticed Mungo standing beside her. He, too, peered out the window with a wistful yearning that squeezed her heart.

"You miss Lottie," she said softly. "You loved her very much."

"Aye. Mungo's Lottie." He heaved a deep sigh and his moon face crumpled. "Mungo bad. Nae hurt lassies."

Edie tensed. Her eyes flickered to Neve. She had never once thought Mungo was a danger, and yet . . . She breathed deeply and forced herself to relax. Mungo wasn't a threat. He couldn't hurt them physically. He was a ghost.

Mouth dry, she whispered, "Did you hurt Lottie?"

"Witch po-mis Mungo!" he cried, and burst into noisy sobs. "Nae hurt Lottie. Witch po-mis."

Having cared for an autistic child before, Edie knew navigating the logic of an autistic mind took patience and routine to reduce the constant fear of a bewildering world filled with emotions they struggled to express. Practically, it meant keeping everything simple, precise and unambiguous, especially questions.

"Did the Witch hurt Lottie?" asked Edie.

"Nae hurt lassies!" Mungo sobbed. "Nae hurt Lottie. Witch po-mis."

Changing course swiftly, Edie said, "I've seen Lottie in the garden."

Mungo lifted his head and howled, "Lottie!"

Perhaps Lottie heard him, for the moment her name faded away, Edie caught a glimmer of the ghostly girl darting about the roses, leaving no trace of her passing in the falling snow. "There she is, Mungo!"

He gasped excitedly, his round face beaming like the sun. "Lottie! Lottie!" he bellowed, waving madly. He turned to Edie, pointing at the ghostly girl. "Mungo's Lottie! Lottie! Look Mungo! Look!" He stabbed a finger at his chest and peered outside expectantly.

Click-clack-click-clack tapped from the depths of the castle just as Lottie looked up.

Mungo stiffened, staring not through the window but at it, then vanished without a sound.

The condensation on the glass from Edie's warmth flourished and expanded, spreading with the faint crackle of forming frost. A curved line appeared, a snail trail in the vapor, shaping and sharpening into a leering plague mask.

Edie crossed her arms defensively and forced herself to stare down the mask. Trembling from a mixture of fear and anger, she understood why Mungo was drawn to the window, hoping to catch sight of Lottie. She understood, too, that Lady Elizabeth was keeping the two apart for her own cruel and twisted reasons.

"Get the fuck away!" she hissed. "You stay away from Lottie and

Mungo. You leave us all alone!" Leaning forward slightly, she glared into the gouged eyes. "Go. Away!"

For a long, tense moment, she and the outlined mask faced each other. Edie's stomach fluttered, rather surprised at her own daring. She blew on the window, her living heat against Lady Elizabeth's deathly cold. As she blew, the mask unraveled in trickles, streaking the window until Edie could see the garden below. It was empty. Lottie had vanished too.

But Edie knew she'd only won a single battle of wills. Faint clattering laughter mocked her before it faded away.

She stayed at the window for a long while, shivering, tired and fearful what the day would bring.

"Mum?" Neve straightened and stretched like a yawning cat. She nodded at the boxes she'd been sleeping against and grimaced. "These didn't make for easy reading. Poor Mungo was treated like a lab rat. And it wasn't just the doctor; Vida Maundrell was helping him."

"I really hope she isn't my mother," said Edie.

"And my grandmother. But one good thing is the notes for 1965 are all here." Neve patted the boxes and smiled grimly. "Dr. Kincaid was on the island a few days before the diamond went missing—"

"But not on the thirtieth?"

"No, but I think he was here on the thirty-first. That wasn't in his notes, but in Vida's. On the thirtieth Vida wrote a note that she had phoned Dr. Kincaid to attend Mungo the following day at Lady Elizabeth's request. There's nothing after that. No notes for the 31 October from either Dr. Kincaid or Vida."

"Okay?" said Edie uncertainly.

Neve stood up and stepped into her semi-circle of suspects. "We've been assuming the diamond was taken on the thirtieth, right? But it could've been taken earlier. Maybe it was only discovered missing on the thirtieth." She jabbed the board with Dr. Kincaid's name as though it were a personal affront. "So that makes the nasty doctor a suspect as he spent a lot of time on the island and we know he had an interest in the Maundrell Red." She shook her head at the board and turned to her mother. "Where did you run off to earlier?"

Edie grimaced, embarrassed. "I was trying to find Alice."

"And did you?"

"No, but I checked the library and went through the diaries. You were right; everything related to that year has disappeared. There's not a single diary after 1964."

"Alice could have destroyed them before she died."

"Why would she?"

"To hide what happened," said Neve.

"Why? Everyone who might've been involved are all dead."

"But not when Alice was alive."

"Then why is she writing her diary all over the walls?" said Edie. "That doesn't make sense."

"But she hasn't said anything about 1965 as far as we know."

"Urgh! This is so frustrating!" cried Edie, throwing her hands in the air. "I need to find her bloody diaries!"

Neve's eyes narrowed. "You've never cared about finding the Maundrell Red. Why are you so upset about this?"

"I'm not trying to find the Maundrell Red. I was hoping—" She bit the inside of her cheek, determined not to cry in front of Neve, not able to cope with her scorn. She cleared her throat. "I was hoping she could tell me who my parents were."

"What does it matter now?" said Neve. "They weren't interested in you when you were a baby; why do you give a shit who they were when they never gave a shit about you?"

"It's important to me," said Edie, unable to express her desperate need to know where she had come from. She had been rootless all her life, carrying the loss of the person she might have been. Now she had a chance to give herself a history, and her place in it.

Neve eyed her mother warily. "Alice might not have destroyed her diaries," she said in a more sympathetic tone. "She may have hidden them and we haven't found them yet . . . And she might be communicating with you for another reason."

"Like what?"

"Maybe something to do with Mungo and Lottie? I think it's all connected somehow. It can't all be a coincidence of tragedies."

"Or it all centers around Lady Elizabeth." Edie gusted out a sigh and said, "Mungo was in here while you were sleeping." She filled Neve in on the brief encounter.

"He was here with me earlier," said Neve. "I'd been reading to him, but I fell asleep. There is no way Mungo hurt anyone, Mum. He's a gentle soul. He's big, but really he's a little boy." She smiled grimly. "But I managed to weasel out a few more of his hiding places. I'll check them out when it's lighter." She glanced at the window where lazy snowflakes swirled against the gray dawn. "It's Halloween tomorrow."

"I've not forgotten." Edie wrapped her oversized cardigan tightly around herself. Her chest hurt as though she had held her breath for too long. Something was coming. She could feel it in the marrow of her bones, in the saturated, poisonous air gripping the island.

October 1965

Everyone forgot to send Lottie back to her room after last night's revelations. A small reprieve, which gave her a chance to wheedle out of Mungo where he had hidden the diamond—if he'd taken it—before anyone else came with their demands.

It was after midnight when she crept into his room at the top of the Hollow Tower. She locked the door and sat on the edge of his bed clutching a brightly wrapped package on her lap.

Mungo's room was a mess. Every surface was covered in stones, leaves or pieces of strangely shaped twigs that had taken his fancy. Tin soldiers littered the floor; storybooks he had taken from the castle library and refused to return teetered in haphazard towers.

In the midst of it all Mungo slept noisily, still wearing Mr. Macleod's boots, his bed a nest of tattered soft toys Lottie had given him over the years.

She didn't wake him but watched over him, rigid with foreboding. Startling at the slightest sound, she eyed the mist's clammy fingers *pressing against the window searching for a way in. The castle always had an unsettled atmosphere that Lottie put down to Bitsie's presence, who could create atmosphere with a glance. But this felt different: an edged unease, prickly and unpredictable.*

The long, dark hours advanced towards dawn like sluggish treacle. Lottie was not the only one having a sleepless night. The click-clack of Bitsie's spiked heels paced the corridors. The more measured tread of Lottie's mother, Vida, up the stairs near Mungo's room, the doorknob twisting, the measured tread moving away when she found it locked. The sly mouse-feet of Aunt Alice, who stood outside Mungo's room for so long her furtive silence slipped under the door and Lottie's teeth ached from biting back a scream, before the mouse-feet crept away.

Twice, the tapping of her father's cane and uneven gait stopped outside Mungo's room, the doorknob turned slightly, a change of mind, before he moved on again in his own perambulation of the castle's halls.

Tired tears slid down Lottie's cheeks as she sat bolt upright, worrying. The uncertainty of her grandmother's plans for Percy and Ashley gnawed at her heart. She still clutched the bag she had found in the grotto, not sure what to do with it, knowing it couldn't be found by Bitsie. It hurt they had planned to run away without a word to her. Surely they trusted her not to breathe a word of it to anyone?

Mungo slept the sleep of the innocent, unwittingly the catalyst of the tempest Lottie feared morning would bring.

After the longest night of Lottie's short life, a miserly dawn filtered through the mist.

"Mungo's Lottie." Wide blue eyes gazed at her sleepily.

"Good morning, sleepyhead," she said, squashing her fears behind a bright smile.

Mungo sat up and clapped his hands excitedly. "Is Samhain, Lottie. Samhain fo' Mungo!"

"It's not just Samhain. What else is today?"

Mungo giggled with puzzled glee. "Wha' day?"

"Come on. You know what day it is."

"Samhain fo' Mungo!"

"And?"

Mungo wrinkled his nose, saw the bright package on Lottie's lap and roared with laughter. "Bird-day fo' Mungo! Samhain fo' Mungo!" he cried, making a grab for the present.

"They're on the same day, silly."

"Silly Mungo, aye."

"Silly is good when it's Mungo," said Lottie, smiling so hard her cheeks hurt as Mungo ripped off the wrapping paper with gusto. It took him a while to open the box to reveal the crystal wind chimes Lottie had spent weeks making for him in secret from a broken chandelier she had found in one of the spare rooms.

"Stars, Lottie! Look! Stars inna box!"

"You have to be careful with these," Lottie cautioned as Mungo pulled out the chimes to admire the light refracting off the tinkling crystals. "We'll ask Granda Ainsley to put a hook up by your window so you can see the light sparkle when the wind blows."

Putting the chimes back in the box before he broke them, Lottie set it to one side.

"Samhain fo' Mungo! Tick an' teat, Lottie." He pulled at Lottie's sleeve when she didn't show any enthusiasm. "Tick an' teat fo' Mungo!"

Lottie smiled weakly. Bitsie had introduced American trick-or-treating to Mungo, which he'd taken to with delight and now demanded everyone trick-or-treat him in the castle. But she had never liked Samhain; a day poised on the cusp of one season bleeding into another, when the world felt thin and brittle, and nothing was one thing nor the other. And she hated Bitsie's Halloween parties. It was the same every year: Bitsie dressed in that ghastly outfit, Mungo running from room to room trick and treating, and Lottie steering him onwards quickly, knowing Bitsie stalked them with the sole purpose of scaring Mungo in a twisted game of cat and mouse.

Mungo always ended the night cowering in his room in terror. Yet every year he forgot what had happened previously.

She worried her lip, hoping the usual festivities would be canceled.

But rather than upset Mungo she took the coward's way out and said cheerfully, "Up you get. We'll talk about it after breakfast."

She turned away while Mungo got dressed. Though he was mentally a child, his body had matured into a man's and there were some things Lottie did not want to see of her cousin's body. He prattled on happily as he dressed in trousers and an old shirt before picking up the padded gray jumpsuit with a long, tufted tail sewn to it and the papier-mâché head of a donkey he and Lottie had made together.

He pointed proudly at himself. "Eeyore fo' Mungo!" Then jabbed his finger at Lottie and said, "Fat Winnie fo' Lottie!" and laughed so hard he almost fell over.

Shaking her head in amused exasperation, Lottie unlocked the door, took Mungo's hand and snuck him through the castle's walls to avoid Bitsie.

They slipped unseen into the butler's pantry and entered the kitchen where Mrs. Macleod was putting freshly baked soul cakes on cooling racks. The air smelled heavenly, of cinnamon, saffron and nutmeg, laced with cloves and the vinegar of mulled wine.

"Grannie Leana!" bellowed Mungo. "Samhain fo' Mungo!"

Mrs. Macleod's eyes widened. With exaggerated pretense she put a hand to her chest and declared, "And here's me who'd clean forgot!"

Mungo's face dropped. Then he caught sight of the carved turnips waiting on a table for Mr. Macleod to string up from the doorways and windows, which in a few days would shrivel to ghastly shrunken heads. Next to them rose a heap of freshly cooked scones to be dunked in treacle later and hung from a tree while Mungo and Lottie got sticky trying to eat them without using their hands. The old tin bath for apple dooking was already at the door filled with apples and water.

Mungo burst into a great belly laugh. "Silly Grannie Leana! Look!" And he pointed at all the preparation for Samhain. "Samhain fo' Mungo!"

"So it is. And that's not all." She nodded to a present waiting on the table. "Happy birthday, lad."

Mungo pounced on it, ripped off the paper, and held up a train set below his beaming face.

"Play noo!"

"Not in my kitchen," said Mrs. Macleod firmly. "You're to wait till Granda Ainsley has a moment to help you set it up in your room. Now where's my thank you?"

Mungo grinned naughtily, grabbed Mrs. Macleod in a bear hug and danced her clumsily around the kitchen.

"Put me down, you great pudding!"

Mungo dropped Mrs. Macleod none too gently. Flustered, she patted her hair to ensure tendrils hadn't escaped her cap, and said, "Go sit yourself down."

Ignoring her, Mungo went off to investigate the treats for the evening's feast.

Shaking her head, she leaned against the table beside Lottie. "And what's the wee man's trick to be this year then?" she asked.

"Same as last year: pull off his mask and yell 'Mungo!' as loudly as he can."

They shared a laugh; then Mrs. Macleod said sternly, "Mungo! Get those great dirty fingers out of the fuarag*!"*

Mungo looked up, startled, his hands shoved deep in the mix of cream, sugar and oatmeal. "Ring fo' Mungo," he said hopefully.

"I havnae put the trinkets in yet. And lord knows I wilnae be putting another ring in. I cannae see a wedding in your future any more this year than I did the last, so we wilnae mislead fate again . . . You all right, lass?" asked Mrs. Macleod as Mungo licked his fingers, his attention diverted to the turnips, contorting his face to mimic those carved to scare away the dead.

Lottie bit her lip. "I feel strange. Like—"

"Like a terrible storm's coming," said Mrs. Macleod, nodding. "Aye, we can feel it n'all. We havnae felt it this bad since your grandad was taken by the loch, god bless him." She started picking up the cooled soul cakes and placed them on a tray. "Your aunt Alice wisnae wrong in what she said last night. We're due a tragedy. But I'm worried for our

wee man. He's had enough ill luck from the day he was born." She glared at the ceiling. "And I'll be betting he had nowt to do with that wee bittie glass bauble herself upstairs is so fond of."

"It hasn't been found?" said Lottie, not surprised.

"Nae, and not for a lack of searching. Herself upstairs has the village out this morning searching the island, and my lassies looking in the castle."

"Grandmother hasn't come to speak to Mungo," said Lottie worriedly.

They looked at Mungo, who had picked up a scone and held it from the attached string above his head to try to eat it.

"She'll be waiting for the doctor," said Mrs. Macleod, as worried as Lottie. "As if he would take it anyway. Guid riddance to it, I say. That braw bit of glass was nowt but trouble."

Lottie wasn't so sure. She didn't think Mungo had taken the Maundrell Red; he was scared of it after the repercussions he'd faced the last time he took it. But she couldn't swear he hadn't with her hand on her heart.

Her thoughts stuttered on what Mrs. Macleod had said. "Glass?" she murmured, and slapped her palm against her forehead. "I'm such an idiot!"

"I widnae go as far as idiot, absentminded maybe."

Lottie pulled a face at the housekeeper's gentle teasing. "No, it's something Mungo said a while ago, but I didn't know what he was talking about." She ran over what she remembered Mungo telling her and deflated. "And I still don't know what he was talking about, come to think of it."

"Never you mind, lass. Get some porridge in you and it will come to you when you least expect it . . . Now I'd best get on. I cannae spend all day blethering, what with my lassies still with herself upstairs."

"Have you seen Percy and Ashley?" asked Lottie as she helped herself to porridge off the stove. She placed another bowl on the table beside hers and said, "Mungo, come eat your breakfast."

"P'ridge fo' Mungo!" he bellowed joyfully as though it were a treat he'd never had before.

Lottie grinned. Mungo was going to be a delighted menace all day.

"They're fine," said Mrs. Macleod. "I took their breakfast up not long ago. That Ashley is a nice lad; Mungo has taken a shine to him; trusted the lad enough to show him all his treasures in his hidey-holes," she added like it was a badge of approval. "But I worry Ashley has resigned to do whatever herself upstairs plans. And your brother's just plain angry." She sighed. "It's all well and good for those lads in Edinburgh to be going together as I've read in the papers, but that sort of thing is not right up here."

Lottie's brow furrowed; she had not taken Mrs. Macleod for a prude. She wasn't sure how she felt about her brother's sexual orientation. She was more upset Ashley would never look at her the way he looked at her brother. That still hurt.

"I do worry what herself upstairs will do to those lads."

It was Lottie's worry too. She helped Mungo with his bib and ate her porridge in thoughtful silence.

She was still thoughtful when she and Mungo went outside. Mist held the island fast in a shroud of invisibility as Mungo led the way down to the grotto. It was stifling inside, the hazy air thick as thin gruel. The dark, seeping walls pulsed ever so slightly, in and out, in and out, like the fetid breath of a slumbering beast.

"'Lo, Witch!" yelled Mungo, with none of the caution most people had around the well. He leaned over the wall and pulled faces at his reflection. "Witch! Say 'lo tae Mungo!" he demanded.

The water remained as smooth as ever, but the blurring shadows fidgeted around him, fluid and moist, tightening into a vaporous embrace.

"Come away from there!" Lottie snapped more harshly than she'd intended.

Mungo ignored her. "'Lo, Witch!" he yelled again, his nose almost touching the water.

Lottie's nape itched with apprehension, not sure if Mungo's adenoidal breath had rippled the surface or something coming up from the depths.

"Mungo! Come away from there now!"

He looked up, startled. "Witch Mungo's friend."

"Mmmm . . ." said Lottie doubtfully, and took his hand, pulling him out of the grotto.

"Bye, Witch!" he bellowed over his shoulder, then to Lottie, "Witch sad. Nae chatter wi' Mungo."

Lottie had no response but couldn't help a backward glance at the grotto, already obscured by mist as they started up a path. A couple of figures emerged amongst the roses like wraiths. Assuming they were villagers from Haggs Bitsie had commandeered to search for the Maundrell Red, Lottie steered Mungo towards the cliff path.

They walked down to the small beach in silence, before she said, "Do you remember when you told me about the glass?"

He shook his head. "Mungo nae member."

Trying a different tack, she said, "You remember when Grandmother and Dr. Kincaid were fighting."

"Lady fight doc-ta. Aye."

"Were they fighting about the Maundrell Red? The—er—glass?"

"Aye. Glass. Mungo nae lek glass."

Used to the vagaries of Mungo's conversational abilities, she hazarded a direct question. "Did you take Grandmother's diamond, Mungo? The glass?"

She watched him carefully for the quick shift of his eyes when he was lying. He was a dreadful liar.

He wiped his nose on his sleeve, unconcerned by the question. "No' Mungo. Bad glass. Hurt Mungo."

"How will it hurt you?" asked Lottie.

"Witch telt Mungo. Bad glass."

And as with so many conversations with Mungo, Lottie had no response to that either. But she believed he hadn't taken the Maundrell Red. She doubted anyone else would, and certainly not Bitsie, who only believed what suited her.

Mungo had the attention span of a mayfly and hopscotched his way up the cliff path, yelling, "Samhain fo' Mungo!" as he went. And "Eeyore fo' Mungo noo?" with a hopeful glance at Lottie.

"Not yet," she said. It quickly became a running refrain.

He led her a merry dance around the island, unable to settle. He flitted from one thing to another, exploding into fits of excitement until Lottie caved and they went back into the castle.

"Ashy!" he demanded as they passed through the West Gatehouse and into the Inner Ward. "Mungo want Ashy!"

"He can't come out today," said Lottie, who had also been thinking about Percy and Ashley locked in their rooms.

"Mungo want Ashy!" And he suddenly darted into the Chapel Tower.

Cursing, Lottie ran after him as he disappeared up the spiral staircase to the second floor.

He skidded to a halt halfway down the hall. "Nae doc-ta!" he shrieked, and turned to run back the way he'd come.

Lottie's heart squeezed, sharing Mungo's dread. Dr. Kincaid stood in the hall with her father and two orderlies she didn't recognize. Big men who looked like escaped convicts, nothing like the two she was used to, who usually tried to treat Mungo gently. It was the presence of the new orderlies that terrified Lottie most, certain Bitsie was going to carry out her threat and put Mungo in an asylum.

Two things struck Lottie; Dr. Kincaid couldn't have taken the Maundrell Red, for she didn't think he had the guts to brazen out a return. And he was dressed as the devil.

CHAPTER 18

E die sat on the broad windowsill in her bedroom, unable to sleep. In an hour it would be Samhain. Wound up like a fiddlehead fern, she contemplated the silent world while Neve slept a few meters away. The snow had stopped and glowed like trapped moonlight; the loch lay dark and peaceful within the embrace of the smothered Munros. Not a single breath of life stirred on the island.

Midnight. Edie tensed, not sure what to expect, searching for a shiver in the shadows.

The night remained silent and still.

Midnight passed. One o'clock . . . Two o'clock . . . and still Edie gazed out, watchful, waiting. She had heard so much about the Witch and her shadows. She had seen enough with her own eyes to know they were real.

Three o'clock . . . she drooped, bone weary, nerves frayed.

A gasp. Her own. Edie jerked awake.

She squinted in the cold morning light reflecting sharply off the snow, listening hard for what had woken her. A snatch of movement caught her attention.

Nothing otherworldly, but very human in the form of Cameron stepping out of the laburnum arch. He scowled at the castle, perhaps sensing Edie's attention.

Taken aback by the fury contorting his face, she slipped off the windowsill to hide behind the concealing curtains and watched him.

Mr. MacKenzie followed Cameron from the arch, arms loose at his sides, combatant, preparing for a fight.

Edie risked reaching out to open the window a fraction to eavesdrop.

She jumped in alarm when Cameron shouted, "I will have it, dammit!"

Mr. MacKenzie muttered something she couldn't quite hear.

"Ten years!" Cameron snarled. "Ten years of my life! And that's nothing to what my father lost to those bastards. I am owed! *We* are owed!"

"You're not to hurt the—"

"And what will you do about it?" sneered Cameron. "If she wants blood and she gives me what I'm owed, then they're fair game." He stormed off across the snow, disappearing around the side of the castle.

Mr. MacKenzie pulled at his moustache, brows lowered. Finally, he shook his head, picked up a shovel Edie hadn't noticed leaning against the arch and stomped towards the Brig o' Haggs with a determined expression and started shoveling snow. A figure on the other side of the bridge trudged through the snow from Haggs, a shovel hoisted onto his shoulder. He was too far away to be certain, but Edie thought it might be Hamish Macleod.

She watched the men shoveling snow from opposite directions, puzzling over Cameron and Mr. MacKenzie's altercation. Cameron's anger had been palpable, at odds to what she'd seen of the man previously. But what did she know of Cameron, of either of them?

Tucking her consternation aside, she turned to the bed. Her heartbeat ratchetted up a notch.

Neve wasn't there.

Edie raced out of the room and flew up to the museum.

Neve wasn't there.

Panicking, she sped through the castle, popping her head through doorways, calling Neve, her voice growing high-pitched with fear that the Witch had—

She pulled up short on the ground floor of the Clan Tower at the sound of Neve's laughter.

"That's not fair!" cried Neve. "You can't have all the cannons!"

"Mungo's!"

"But you have to leave me some, otherwise I can't ever win."

Mungo chortled with dark delight as Edie stepped quietly into the room, sagging against the wall in relief.

"Mungo allus win!" he bellowed.

The circle room was filled with green felt tables, each bearing a famous battlefield. Tiny tin soldiers lined up in smart rows; mounted officers led charges towards carnage or waited amongst trees sprouting like tiny broccoli heads. The room was a boy's paradise.

Neve and Mungo re-enacted the Battle of Waterloo, complete with tiny French flags and blue uniformed soldiers opposing the red-uniformed English.

"Hey, kiddo," said Edie softly, her terror surge of adrenaline fizzing away.

Neve cast her a long-suffering glance and returned her attention to Mungo, who bent over the battlefield, tongue poking out the corner of his mouth as his hand swiped through the cannon he was trying to pick up.

"Nae work!" he bellowed. "Make work fo' Mungo, Neeeve!"

Neve placed the cannon where Mungo pointed, then picked up a box and sidled over to Edie, pulling out a tangle of cables and devices. "Look what Mungo and I found . . . Here's our ghosts. Most of them were fake."

"Most?"

"Yeah. We couldn't find anything for Wully Macleod or the Roman ships; they could be real ghosts. But the Grey Lady was fake, and the crying baby, Bloody Mary, the Headless Horseman and a bunch of others."

"But not Mungo, Lottie, Alice or Lady Elizabeth."

"No, and Mungo knew where all the cameras and projectors were."

"Did he now?" Edie gazed at Mungo thoughtfully.

"Yeah. It became a bit of a game; for each one he found he demanded a story until we came in here and he got distracted . . . And this equipment is top of the range, Mum. Many of them look new . . . Don't ask him who installed them," added Neve hurriedly when Edie opened her mouth to do just that. "He freaked every time I tried." She lowered her voice. "And that's not all. He's told me about loads of his hiding places outside."

"That's a fool's errand," whispered Edie.

"Is it?" Neve reached into the pocket of her jeans and pulled out a gold ring like she was performing a magic trick. "I found this in a small hollow in the Nine Hags this morning. The biggest one that looks like a gargoyle."

Edie sighed. "You've obviously got a theory, so let's have it."

"Maybe someone knew about Mungo's hiding places and planned to frame him. It wasn't hard getting their locations out of him, and he would be such an easy target."

"Really, Neve? That's a bit of a stretch."

"Maybe, but some of his hiding places are brilliant. I wouldn't have thought to look in most of them in a million years."

"Have you asked him who he's told?"

"Yeah. But he has his own names for people, so I'm not sure who he's talking about. Lottie knew, not surprisingly, but so did someone he calls Ash, I think. I thought maybe he'd got confused and was talking about a fire, so I've checked all the fireplaces in the castle but found sod all."

"Mmmm . . ." said Edie, and approached the ghost. "Mungo," she said softly.

He wrenched his attention from the battlefield, a quick glance, eyes sliding away. "Aye. Mungo."

"We share the same birthday. It's today."

"Aye. Samhain fo' Mungo. Bird-day fo' Mungo." It was a whisper bleached in sorrow.

The impotent urge to comfort the ghost burnt like a brand in Edie's chest. Guilt wrenched her throat; why would he wish to be reminded of the day he was born when it was the day he died, twenty-one years apart?

Clearing her throat, she said, "You see everything that goes on in the castle, don't you?"

Sorrow left Mungo as quickly as it appeared. He hugged himself gleefully. "Aye. Mungo see e'ryting."

"Do you remember Alice?" asked Edie, ignoring Neve's surprised frown. "She was your aunt."

"Ant Alice, aye. Ant Alice sad."

"Was she? Why was she sad?"

"Ant Alice fight wi' Lady." He lowered his crossed arms like he held something precious, crooning tunelessly.

"What are you up to, Mum?" Neve whispered.

Edie ignored her, and asked Mungo, "Do you know where Aunt Alice is?"

"Ant Alice hidin' fro' Lady."

"Your grandmother, Lady Elizabeth?"

Mungo's eyes widened with terror. Edie thought he might vanish. Instead he put a finger to his lips, hissed, "Shhhhh!" and glanced at the walls and ceiling fearfully. "Lady see e'ryting."

Edie followed his gaze, disquiet itching up her spine. "Why is Aunt Alice hiding from Lady?" she whispered.

"Ant Alice feart."

"Of Lady?"

"Aye. Lady."

"And you're scared of her too."

Mungo nodded vigorously, then clutched his head, and with eyes squeezed tight, he wailed, "Rrreeedddrrreeeddd!"

Edie frowned at Neve questioningly.

"He always does that when"—she mouthed *Lady Elizabeth*—"is mentioned."

"Do you think you could find Alice for me, Mungo?"

Mungo took his hands away from his head slowly and eyed her sideways. "Neeeeve read tae Mungo?" he said hopefully.

"I'm sure she will," said Edie, choosing not to see Neve's scowl. "But first let's find Aunt Alice, and Neve will come with us."

"What are you up to?" Neve asked again, hurrying after Mungo as he darted through the wall to reappear in the corridor. He waved his arms madly for them to follow him.

"If Mungo could help you find the fake ghosts, he might be able to help me find Alice. He's a ghost and so is she, and they've been in this castle for a long time together."

"You really think she knew who your parents were?"

"She was here in 1970 when I was born. She's the best bet I've got."

"Well, you'd best keep your eye on Mungo," said Neve. "He's quick when he gets going."

Mungo hopscotched ahead of them, glancing over his shoulder to check they were still following. Sometimes he disappeared, only to reappear from a doorway with a bellowed "Mungo see e'ryting!" or "Mungo find Ant Alice!" like he feared he would forget what he was doing. Then he'd hopscotch his way down another hall, another staircase.

"'Lo, Ant Alice!" he called at the top of his voice. "Ant Alice! 'Lo? Ant Alice!"

But each time he called and there was no responding whisper or a scratching on the walls, Edie's hopes sank as they traversed the castle. Each time he bellowed, she expected to hear angry click-clacking following them, but she heard not so much as a faint ticking. Yet she sensed Lady Elizabeth was near, watching them curiously.

On the third floor, Mungo yelled, "'Lo, Ant Alice!" and hopped through a door Edie recognized with a snoop's guilt.

"We shouldn't go in," she said, grabbing Neve's arm as she went to open the door.

"Why not?"

Edie's embarrassment set off a hot flush. "Cameron stays here."

"So what? This is our bloody castle," said Neve, opening the door, "and we can go where we bloody want."

Mungo was on the rug, spinning in fast circles, ensuring not to step off the edges, playing a game with himself, when they entered. "Ant Alice hidin'! Nae Ant Alice!"

Something twigged in Edie's head. "Was this Alice's room?" she asked.

"Aye. Ant Alice!"

Neve opened a window and leaned out. "This room has the best view. I can see right across the loch and all the way to the bridge and Haggs."

"Don't hang too far out that window, Neve. You know it freaks me out when you put yourself in unnecessary danger."

Neve pulled herself in, closed the window against the cold and grinned unrepentantly. She sauntered to the bedside table and picked up the photo Edie had seen before.

"Do you think this is Cameron's dad?" She held up the proud father holding his baby.

Mungo stopped hopping in circles and focused on the image. He shrieked and vanished.

Edie frowned in consternation. "What was that all about?"

"He does that a lot," said Neve. "What's wrong?" she asked when Edie stiffened and darted out into the corridor with a muttered, "Finally!"

"Oh, you beauty," breathed Edie. "Mungo did it! Alice is here," she said as Neve joined her and *flofloflofloflofloflo* whispered around her like a caress.

She pressed her hands lightly against the wall, a knot of hopeful trepidation in her stomach, hesitating to ask a direct question, yet she had so many she wasn't sure where to start. But Jasper and Vida were the two she most wanted answers to.

"Tell me about Jasper?" she asked obliquely. "Did he find happiness?" she added as an afterthought.

Words appeared too rapidly to read, flowing over each other, as though Alice was flipping through her diaries, searching. Then . . . *Jasper is a shell of himself. Though he has lived through the horrors of war, I think losing his daughter has broken him in ways the war had not. He spends most days in the orchard staring into space. Sometimes I sit with him though I do not think he is aware I am there . . .*

"Mum!" Neve hissed, squinting in vain at the wall. "Tell me what she's saying!"

Edie stepped back, and read aloud, *"At eleven each morning, regular as clockwork, Jasper still visits the graveyard. Poor Greer. I rarely think of her these days, but Jasper still loves her though she's been dead more than fifty years . . .*

"Jasper died at midnight on Samhain last night. It was a peaceful passing and not unexpected. The cancer got him just as it did my beloved D. I shall miss him, and soon Mother will join him, perhaps next year . . ."

"Jasper doesn't sound like a man having a bit on the side," said Neve, guessing the direction of Edie's thoughts. "He still loved Greer."

Edie nodded, her hope crumbling a little more as one possibility, the more palatable of the two, faded as the words faded from the wall. "Tell me about Vida, Alice."

Again a swift jumble of words swept across the wall too quick to read, then, *"It's been months since I wrote. Almost a year has passed by while I took to my bed . . ."*

"She was ill?" said Neve. "When was this?"

"Keep quiet," muttered Edie. *". . . Vida is dead!"* As the three words paled, they were overlaid with, *"Dead! Dead! Dead! And I did not know! It was the most shocking thing to wake from my stupor to . . ."* Another swirl of letters. *". . . I am glad she is dead."*

"So 1970 or '71?" Neve hazarded.

Edie nodded, her heart lurching with a lopsided terror, for this was exactly what she had been hoping for, and read, "*Vida was seen to plummet to her death off the cliffs by some of those searching for the Maundrell Red. It's not surprising stories have been circulating since that Vida was pushed off the cliffs by shadows. I do not understand the Witch's rationale for taking Vida. Perhaps she made her own pact with the Witch? Or was it remorse for what she had been party to that made Vida fling herself off the cliffs? I hope so . . .*"

"For Mungo?" said Neve. "Something else? Vida sounds like a dreadful woman."

Edie held a hand up for quiet. "*I asked D if he had seen it, but he had been searching on the other side of the island and only came running when the alarm went up. I am glad he didn't see it. I do not want my family's curse to touch him in any way . . . We have been doubly cursed. First Vida then . . . I cannot! I cannot!*"

The scratchy writing disappeared abruptly, yet Edie sensed Alice was still there in the fluttery panic infusing the air. She thought Alice had been a nervous woman when alive, perhaps not surprising when she'd lived under the dark shadow cast by her mother, Lady Elizabeth.

"Then what?" Edie prompted when Alice didn't go on.

"*. . . Even now I cannot speak of it, cannot put my pain into writing. It is too raw. Shall I ever feel anything other than the agony of loss?*"

"I thought she and Vida hated each other," whispered Neve, confused. "Why was she so upset by her death?"

"I don't think she's talking about Vida— Shhh! She's writing . . . '*My heart is broken, but Mother says she has had enough of my tears, that I must move on and face the world, that it would've been far worse for me if my little girl had lived and been loved, only to die . . .*'"

Edie and Neve glanced at each other in astonishment.

"She was sterilized," said Neve, finding her voice first. "How is that possible? Maybe she's jumped back to the past?"

"No, that was a boy. It's possible the doctor didn't sterilize her at all but told Lady Elizabeth he had."

"Or he was a quack and did a botch job," said Neve darkly.

As Neve theorized wildly, a hollow certainty dropped into the pit of Edie's stomach. Putting a hand on Neve's arm for quiet, she said, "Tell me what happened, Alice." The words were barely out her mouth when she took a step back, recoiling from the rage bleeding across the wall: *"I hate her! I HATE her! I HATE HER!"* The words were etched deep, as though Alice, when she'd written it, had pressed her pen so hard it had broken through several pages of her diary. *"I never imagined the depths of utter cruelty Mother could plumb to. I can barely write I am so furious! I HATE HER! My Florence was not stillborn! I write these words and I still cannot believe it. All these years and days and hours I have been blaming the Witch in the Well, when it was Mother who took Florence from me!"*

Floflofloflofloflo . . . fluttered around Edie like cobwebs, then drifted down the corridor as though blown by the wind.

"Don't go!" Edie cried desperately. "Please, Alice! I need to know!"

The whispering drifted back and settled around Edie, the suggestion of an arm on her shoulders, lukewarm and loving. *Floflofloft—Floreflore . . . Floren . . . FlorenceFlorenceFlorence* . . . The faint words were an embrace, a kiss, a gentle brush against Edie's cheek.

The words forming on the wall, blurred through her tears. She didn't read them aloud but kept the revelation to herself, if only for a moment.

My little girl, my miracle, my Florence, was and will always be loved . . .

Florence Charlotte Maundrell is loved . . .

Florence Charlotte Maundrell is loved . . .

Florence Charlotte Maundrell is loved, loved, loved . . .

"Mum? Mum!" Neve's voice was far away, like she was shouting from the other end of a long tunnel.

Edie dragged her eyes from the dead woman's words. "Alice Maundrell was my mother," she whispered, then to the wall, "You knew." Dazed, her voice was filled with dreadful wonder. "You knew who I was when I first stepped into the castle."

The air tightened around her, an intimate cocoon, a mother's caress. As near as Alice was able to communicate with touch what she hadn't written down when alive.

"Mum!" cried Neve. "Did you hear me? Alice didn't abandon you. She thought you were dead!"

"Yes," said Edie bleakly, her throat raw and grating, pent-up emotions swelling in her chest she dared not release.

"And she's here, Mum. Still in the castle . . . Are you all right?" Distracted from her excitement, Neve eyed her mother with concern.

Edie nodded with difficulty. She wasn't all right. She wasn't sure what she was, her thoughts were too big for her head, her chest too tight.

"You know your father could still be alive," said Neve.

Edie's gaze snapped from the wall to Neve and did the math. "He might. He'd be old, but . . ." Pressing the balls of her palms into her eyes, Edie let out a tremulous sigh and said, "Tell me everything, Alice. Right from the start."

As though Alice had been waiting for permission, the childish handwriting Edie had first seen in the library looped across the wall . . . *Alice, Gladys Maundrell, six years, seven months and twenty-three days old.*

"Mother says I'm fat and boys don't like fat girls . . ." Edie read aloud, choking on the familiar words.

She slid down the opposite wall, taking Neve with her, not wanting to miss the lifetime of words scrawling across the wall. With Alice as witness, names that had become familiar over the past week came to life; triumphs and miseries, some small and insignificant, some large and devastating.

An hour passed, then two, morning bled into afternoon as Edie read aloud until she was hoarse.

The years on the island had passed slowly for Alice until 1960 when she and the mysterious D began their secret affair. Edie read again of Alice's heartache at the forced loss of her first child. She cried silent tears for Mungo, for as Alice's illicit romance blossomed Mungo's life descended into hell with the arrival of Dr. Kincaid. She rooted for Lottie, who fought to stop Mungo's treatment as his screams echoed through the castle weekly. And through it all, Lady Elizabeth loomed, poisoning every aspect of the Maundrells' lives.

Neve disappeared briefly and came back with tea and biscuits and a, "What did I miss?"

"Lady Elizabeth has locked up Percy and Ashley. I have a horrible feeling about this."

Sitting down hurriedly, Neve stared at the blank wall, their tea growing quickly cold on the floor beside them.

October 1965

D r. Kincaid marched up to Lottie and grabbed her by the shoulders. "Is it true? Has that simpleton taken the Maundrell Red? Tell me!" he yelled in her face.

Terrified into silence, Lottie was caught in the doctor's pale smolder through the eye sockets of the leering devil's mask.

"What the hell do you think you're doing?" demanded Jasper, hobbling up to Lottie as fast as he could. "Let go of my daughter this instant!"

Dr. Kincaid released Lottie abruptly and turned to her father. "She's always with Mungo. She'll know where he's hidden the diamond."

Stiff with indignation, Jasper put a protective arm around Lottie. "I am struggling to understand your anger at its loss. The Maundrell Red is a family heirloom."

Dr. Kincaid ripped the mask off, his face ugly and snarling. He lifted his arm to hurl it down the hall in his rage.

Lottie watched him carefully. Was his anger real or the defensive *fury of someone who had taken the diamond himself and was putting on a good show?*

Remembering himself, the doctor lowered his arm, the mask hanging limply in his hand. A muscle twitched in his jaw before his expression smoothed to controlled coldness. "Ask your mother!" he snapped. "She promised it to me as recompense, and I am calling in my debts. Five years I've danced to her tune and now I am done! I will take what was promised me and you'll never hear from me again."

"My mother promised the Maundrell Red to you?" said Jasper, plainly astonished.

"On the condition my grandson be cured," said Bitsie coming up from behind.

Everyone swung around to her. She was already dressed in the costume she wore every year: a plague doctor, complete with a crackled beaked mask she'd brought back from Venice many years ago, and a black wide-brimmed hat on its dome. A black satin cloak fluttered around her catsuit that flaunted every angle and curve. Her matching high heels made her as tall as the men.

She lifted the mask to bore her ice-chip glare into Dr. Kincaid. "But you have not upheld your side of the bargain. He's still an idiot."

"What were you thinking, Mother?" said Jasper, losing the restraint he always maintained around Bitsie. "Why would you not pay the man like any other for a service rendered?"

Bitsie focused on her son. "He was certainly not my first choice, but unfortunately better doctors were squeamish with useless principles. This one, however," she sneered, "was not a complete fool and insisted on the Maundrell Red as his price. Unlike you, Jasper, I think of our family's social standing and I will use whatever is at my disposal to ensure it is not sullied." She returned her caustic attention to Dr. Kincaid. "But the doctor forgets his place."

"My place?" hissed Dr. Kincaid. "My place! You vicious auld bitch!"

"That is enough!" thundered Jasper. "You will not use vulgar language in front of my daughter and mother! Show some class, man! Have you gone quite mad?"

"*Mad?*" *For a second the doctor did look demented. His nostrils flared, eyes darting between Jasper and Bitsie, before his expression smoothed and returned with visible difficulty to controlled coldness.* "I may be mad," *he said, biting out each word,* "but I will have that diamond. You promised it to me, Bitsie, and I shall have it. I am done with this place! It is diseased! Your grandson cannae be cured. He's an imbecile and always will be. The best thing you can do is place him in an asylum as we have discussed.*"

"*That's* Lady Elizabeth *to you," said Bitsie coolly, "and you are done when I say you are done, Dr. Kincaid . . . Or should I even be calling you a doctor?*"

Dr. Kincaid grew still and wary. "What's that supposed to mean?"

Bitsie put a hand to her cheek, a mocking, wide-eyed ingénue. "I don't know the ins and outs of such things," *she said, gushing and girlish,* "but if you kill one of your patients, can you still call yourself a doctor?"

It was an age before Dr. Kincaid unfroze, hypnotized by Bitsie's poorly veiled allegation. He licked his lips, lizard-quick. "It was an accident," *he said.*

Bitsie smiled spitefully. "Is that what it was? Isn't it strange the judge didn't agree with you? I had such an interesting conversation with him a few months ago, and as I recall, it was an elderly woman. Is that right?" *she asked rhetorically.* "And she just happened to leave everything she owned to a certain Gordon Kincaid . . ." *She put a hand to her lips, eyes widening in feigned surprise.* "Isn't your first name Gordon?"

Gordon Kincaid said nothing, his long body coiled tensely, murder in his eyes.

But Bitsie was having too much malicious fun at the doctor's expense. "That nice judge kindly explained to me that you escaped a jail sentence by agreeing never to practice medicine again. And I do wonder what he would say if he found out what you've been doing these past five years . . . Or am I wrong?"

"*Is this true, Mother?*" *said Jasper, stricken with shock.*

"*Why don't we ask the good doctor? What? Cat got your tongue,* Dr. Kincaid?"

"And you allowed this man into our home, allowed him to treat Greer's boy? I—" Jasper stalled, trembling, mouthing his horror, but no words came.

Bitsie barely concealed her contempt for her son. "Jasper, I need you to go and see Mr. Macleod about tonight to ensure everything runs smoothly."

"What?" Jasper blinked at the abrupt change of topic. "Why? He knows what to do."

"Nevertheless, it's better if one of us is overseeing everything."

If Lottie hadn't known any better, she would've thought Bitsie was doing Jasper a kindness, but she knew her grandmother too well.

Jasper hesitated, glanced at Lottie. "No. I'm staying. I don't trust this sycophant of yours not to touch Lottie again."

"Oh, for heaven's sake!" snapped Bitsie. "I'm here and I assure you he won't dare touch a hair on her head without my say-so."

"I'll go with Dad," said Lottie quickly, eager to be away from her grandmother and the doctor.

"No," said Bitsie. "I need you to see to Mungo. I am sure he will need help with his costume."

Lottie regarded Bitsie suspiciously and changed her mind about getting away. Something was afoot, and she and her father were being kept apart and out of the way.

Jasper sighed, his brief flare of opposition dissolving, never a match for his mother. He kissed Lottie on the forehead and whispered, "Go find Mungo and stay with him."

He limped slowly down the hall. The moment he disappeared down the stairs leading to the kitchen, Bitsie said, "You're to do as your father told you, Charlotte. Find Mungo and stay with him. Under no circumstances are either of you to leave his room until I tell you to. Is that understood?"

Lottie took off down the hall in the opposite direction of her father, not daring to look at the orderlies who had been watching the heated discussion with interest. She stepped round the corner, pressed her back against the wall and listened for all she was worth.

"*We had an agreement, Mr. Kincaid,*" *hissed Bitsie.* "*And you will do as I say if you know what's good for you.*"

"*What are you up to,* Lady Elizabeth?" *The scornful stress of the title was clear in Dr. Kincaid's tone.*

"*It's a delicate family matter,*" *began Bitsie, her voice dropping so low Lottie inched closer to the corner.* "*I shall insist on your absolute discretion.*"

"*When have I ever not been discreet? I have been the soul of discretion, damn you!*"

A sharp crack.

Lottie startled in shock. That had sounded very much like a face being slapped. She risked a peek around the corner. Her eyes widened with astonishment at Dr. Kincaid clutching his cheek.

"*Do not think I will not speak to my friend the judge,*" *said Bitsie, shaking her hand stinging with her abrupt violence.* "*And if you ever speak to me so disrespectfully again, I will ensure you go to jail for a very long time to consider the error of your ways.*"

Lottie pulled back when one of the orderlies moved to approach Bitsie and Dr. Kincaid.

"*What would you have me do?*" *said Dr. Kincaid, voice tight with undisguised venom.*

"*It appears my grandson, Percy, and his . . . friend have developed an unnatural relationship not becoming of a Maundrell.*"

"*Speak plainly, for god's sake!*"

An uncharacteristic pause from Bitsie. "*My grandson has . . . feelings of a sexual nature for his friend,*" *she said, choosing her words with care.*

"*He's homosexual? Why are you speaking to me about this? I'm a medical doctor, not a psychologist.*"

"*That's as may be, but Vida has told me of studies on men with a similar proclivity. She claims these studies have shown electrotherapy could restore my grandson and his friend to more natural orientations.*"

"*Electrical Aversion Therapy?*"

"*Yes.*"

"*There have been studies certainly, but nothing conclusive, and I cannae treat them without their consent. This is not the same as treating Mungo, who is incapable of giving consent."*

"As they are underage, I have received written consent from the Templetons, and you will, of course, have Vida's consent and mine. I am sure as Percy's mother and grandmother that will be sufficient to quell whatever dubious ethical dilemma you may feel you have."

Lottie held a hand to her mouth to stop herself from screaming but remained rooted by her curiosity to see just how far Bitsie could push Dr. Kincaid.

"That's why you asked me to find orderlies who widnae question anything asked of them," he said. "You truly are an astonishing woman, Lady Elizabeth. I dinnae think I have ever met anyone quite like you, and I dinnae mean that as a compliment."

"I don't care what you think, I never have. Now, time is of the essence. While everyone is occupied I wish you to begin the boys' treatment. And I do not expect this to take five years as it did with Mungo, understood?"

"I am not starting them on a high dosage in their first treatment," said Dr. Kincaid firmly. "Mungo has a high threshold of pain because of his imbecility. And while you may be willing to jeopardize the lives of healthy lads, I am not in the habit of killing my patients on purpose."

"If you kill my grandson I will kill you." Bitsie's voice was quiet and intense; there was no doubt she meant every word.

A pause. A sigh. "Very well," said Dr. Kincaid, defeated.

"Excellent. I knew you'd come around to my way of thinking. We'll start with the Templeton boy first . . . and put your mask back on, Mr. Kincaid. There's a party afterwards and I insist you attend, but you must be dressed appropriately." She laughed. "And tonight I shall be the doctor, and you shall be the devil . . . Isn't that what you've called me? More than once if I remember."

Lottie snorted. Dr. Kincaid was hardly in for a treat. Bitsie's Halloween parties were dreadful affairs with the family wearing uncomfortable costumes they hated, forced to make small talk with each other when they spent much of the year trying to avoid each other.

She glanced around the corner in time to see Bitsie smile coldly when the doctor's face tautened with every appearance of telling her where she could shove her mask. But something in Bitsie's smile made him swallow his bile. He put on the devil mask.

"There!" said Bitsie, putting her hands together in a single clap. "Much better. And now we understand each other so beautifully, I suggest we get on."

Lottie pulled back again when Dr. Kincaid signaled to the waiting orderlies. She leaned against the wall, feeling ill, mind racing, not sure what to do.

Without thinking too hard about the repercussions, she breathed deeply, and slipped around the corner on tiptoe.

She froze like a hare stunned by bright light, then dashed behind a giant, bright orange vase when Bitsie stopped in front of Ashley's door and unlocked it.

"Come with me," said Bitsie into the room.

Ashley came out. "Lady Elizabeth," he said warily. He glanced at Percy's closed door across the hall from his. "Where's Percy?"

"He'll be joining us soon. If you would be so good as to wait there for a moment." Bitsie nodded at one of the orderlies. He made no threatening moves, but Ashley stepped back as though he had.

"I wish to speak to my parents," said Ashley. He looked terrible, with dark rings under his eyes. Like everyone in the castle he, too, had had a sleepless night. "I think it's time I went home."

"I spoke to your parents this morning. They are aware of the situation and insisted you remain here for your own safety for the time being."

Ashley's indrawn breath of betrayed shock broke Lottie's heart as he looked at Dr. Kincaid and the orderlies, hoping they would intercede on his behalf. Not one of them met his gaze. Helplessly, he glanced up the hall. He blinked in astonishment at Lottie lurking in the shadow of the enormous vase.

He opened his mouth, then clamped it shut when she frantically shook her head, an urgent finger to her lips.

Nodding slightly, he returned his attention to Bitsie, who was unlocking Percy's door.

Lottie touched the back of her neck, her senses in overdrive, and frowned over her shoulder. Shadows squirmed along the walls, the ceiling, the floor, like swarming snakes. Breath sharp and jerky, she watched the shadows spread in a dark spider's web, hovering, watchful, expectant. They showed no interest in her.

"Is this some sort of sick joke?" Percy's voice sounded hollow and distant from within his room. "A visit from the devil and the plague doctor."

"You should know me better than that, Percy," said Bitsie. "I never joke. I remember you once telling me I had been born with a witch's broom up my"—she didn't throw Percy's coarseness back at him but allowed it to fill the pause—"instead of a sense of humor . . . Now I want this sorted with a minimum of fuss."

"What sorted?" said Percy suspiciously. Then, "Ashley?" The relief at seeing his friend was palpable. "Are you all right?"

Lottie darted out into the open and shouted, "Don't let them take you, Percy! They're going to hurt you and Ashley! I'm going to tell Dad! He will never agree to this!"

"Grab her!" Bitsie cried as Lottie ran in the opposite direction. The shadows bunched into a twisted snarl, keeping pace with her along the walls.

Rough male hands seized her, jerking her so hard her head whipped back.

"Let go of me!" she shrieked, squirming furiously.

The orderly held on, pulling her tight against his chest, and dragged her back to Bitsie.

"For heaven's sake, Charlotte!" said Bitsie, exasperated. "There's no need to act like a child about this. It's for your brother's own good."

"Own good? Are you listening to yourself? I heard you talking to him!" she cried, trying to kick Dr. Kincaid, even as she struggled against the orderly. "Mungo's been treated for five years and it hasn't changed him at all except terrify him. This won't work! And what does it matter

if Percy and Ashley love each other? I love them and I just want them to be happy!" Then she mortified herself by bursting into tears.

"What is she planning, Lottie?" said Percy, stepping out of his room. He looked as terrible as Ashley, eyes bloodshot from lack of sleep, hair oily from agitated hands pushing through it.

"ECT!" cried Lottie. "She wants this man"—Lottie tried to kick Dr. Kincaid again—"to do what they do on Mungo on you and Ashley! I heard them! You must run and get Dad; he'll stop it."

Before Ashley and Percy could move, Dr. Kincaid grabbed hold of Ashley's arm as the other orderly took hold of Percy. It was then Lottie realized her big brother, who had seemed so adult when he came home from school, was only seventeen with a seventeen-year-old's strength, and no match for a fully matured man.

Percy fought back but was easily pinned by arms twice the size of his.

Bitsie leaned towards Lottie, the crackled mask pushed up high on her head, cold green gaze snapping with displeasure. "I'm disappointed in you, Charlotte. I thought you understood the consequences of your actions. Last week, despite your impertinent outburst, I decided to give you another chance to redeem yourself, but it appears my kindness was misguided. Now you have left me with no choice." Her voice dropped to a gentling whisper. "You realize what this means, don't you? What this means to Mungo? And you have only yourself to blame." She straightened and regarded her granddaughter dispassionately. "As you have been skulking and listening to conversations that don't concern you, you must've heard that Dr. Kincaid thinks the best place for Mungo is an asylum." Her mouth curved up into an unpleasant red slash. "Therefore, under medical advisement, I simply have no choice but to comply."

"He's not a doctor!" shouted Lottie. "You have no right!"

Bitsie leapt forward, gripped Lottie's face, long fingernails digging into her cheeks. "I have every right!" she snarled. "Now you listen to me, Charlotte! I will not have my grandson parading about as a sodomite! And if you know what's good for you—and Mungo, of course—you will keep quiet and stop performing like a monkey!" She released Lottie's face, pulled the plague mask down over her furious expression and *turned abruptly, throwing over her shoulder, "Ensure she is kept quiet. I don't want the rest of the family to hear her."*

"No! N—" Lottie's screams were cut off by a huge hand smelling of disinfectant clamped over her mouth. She was picked up bodily and carried kicking and squirming down the hall, distantly aware Percy and Ashley were being manhandled too.

Bitsie led the way to the room at the top of the Corbie Tower, high-heels click-clacking on the stone floor. The shadows coiled along the walls, the air succulent and heavy with their darkness.

CHAPTER 19

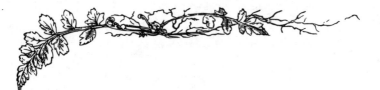

As twilight oozed into the castle, Edie and Neve sat ashen with horror as the events of Samhain in 1965 unfolded before them. Alice had recorded everything she'd seen and felt in the years that followed. The aftermath of the long trial. Her joy in her second pregnancy soured by her need to hide it from Lady Elizabeth. The island had been a constant hive of activity as Lady Elizabeth's obsession with finding the Maundrell Red continued unabated. Vida's death. Alice's devastation at the loss of her daughter, Florence, and the search for Percy Maundrell, who had left the island on the night of Samhain 1965.

Somewhere in the nineties Mungo appeared beside Neve. Unable to read, he sat quietly, listening to Edie read aloud like it was a story.

Alice's dead words flowed through the decades, her views embittered by her terrible hatred for her mother. Snippets of life beyond the island occasionally reached Alice's ears, the death of Mr. Macleod in Lochinver, and Mrs. Macleod not long after. They, too, had left the island on the night Mungo and Lottie had died; their reason for remaining so cruelly ripped away from them.

The death of Alice's beloved D in 1982 made Edie and Neve sit up, hoping for the revelation of his identity, but to the end Alice never once referred to him by his full name.

When Lady Elizabeth was incapacitated by a stroke Alice's dark glee danced across the wall. When she discovered her daughter hadn't died but been discarded in an orphanage, her elation was tainted by fury at her mother's spite. When Jasper left the island for years to search for Florence's whereabouts, Alice's frustration at remaining on the island, bound to her incapacitated mother, curdled into twisted retribution until Lady Elizabeth's death.

As Alice wrote, her handwriting changed, firm in youth, untidy in middle age, crabbed in old age.

"This may be the last time I shall write down my thoughts . . ." scribbled across the wall. *"I have sat at this table overlooking the loch almost every day to record my life. A pointless exercise for a life wasted by fear . . .*

"But these past few years, since I knew of your continued existence, my Florence, I have written each day, my words are all I can leave to you of myself. But know not an hour has passed that I haven't wondered where you were, dreaming of what you might be doing in that very minute . . .

"We have searched for you to no avail, and now I have finally received the letter from Percy I had been waiting for. He has agreed to continue searching for you, and with this I must be content. I hope Percy finds you well and happy. My greatest wish for you is happiness . . .

"Time has a funny way of catching up with you. It is Samhain once again and the Witch will take what is her due as she always does. I no longer understand what she wants. I realize now I never did . . .

"Hindsight can be a wonderful and terrible thing. As my end has drawn near, I have thought of little else but the past. And now I must make a confession to you, my darling Florence. So much of what happened on the island, what happened to you, was due to my own foolishness . . .

"There are two things I have never written down, but feel it's only right you know how things came about as they did, and the part I played in them . . .

*"D always called her the Hag of Storms, the one we call the Witch
in the Well. Though I still struggle to accept she is a supernatural being,
I've seen her hand in everything that has happened on the island. I was
not immune to her allure. So often I found myself drawn to the grotto,
whispering my heartache into the black, fathomless waters, dipping my
fingers into its icy depths, hoping to numb my pain. When Mother took
what I held most dear, I turned to the Witch. Two pacts I've made
with her, but the first came with consequences I never imagined. How
could I?*

*"I remember that night so clearly after Vida told me Mother had
engineered my sterilization. I was so angry, so full of hate, as I ran out
to the grotto. I desperately wanted Mother to suffer, to lose what she most
loved, as she had taken what I most loved from me . . .*

*"It felt like a dream. The Witch's shadows wrapped around me as I
stood over the well, expecting her reflection in the dark water, her face as
old as time. But it was not an old face that stared back at me. She was
youthful and strong and vibrant in a way I'd never been. She stood at
my shoulder, her skin painted in intricate blue swirls. She was mesmerizing and terrifying . . .*

*"I made a pact, feeling I had nothing to lose. The Witch was true
to our agreement. She took what Mother loved most, the Maundrell
Red . . ."*

Neve squeezed Edie's hand in anticipation, squinting hard at the
wall, murmuring, "Please, please, please," under her breath.

*"I laid a trail that would lead to Mungo, ensuring he would be
blamed. It was cruel, but my anger and hatred outweighed my guilt
with the sad reality that the best plans always take casualties of the
innocent. But I was not the only one using Mungo, befriending him for
their own ends . . ."*

"Mungo," said Mungo, pointing to his chest sadly, and curled up
his large body, hugging his knees to his chest. He broke Edie's heart;
he hadn't stood a chance with a family like the Maundrells.

"Who befriended him?" Neve muttered at the wall, then growled
in frustration when Edie continued reading Alice's words aloud.

"There have been numerous trespassers over the years, seeking to find the Red. They are all fools, not understanding its power. Not power like the Witch, but the power of its allure. I've seen its effect, especially on Mother. But one treasure seeker has been more persistent than the others, hiding in the woods. I saw him this morning lurking near the old cairns. The strange thing is he looks vaguely familiar, though I cannot place his face. Last night I am certain he came into the castle. I didn't go investigate. I am eighty-one and certainly in no fit state to confront an intruder in the dead of night . . .

"Forgive my digression—a curse of old age. All these years I've carried my guilt; it still twists my stomach. Because of my heartache three people died. I truly never meant for anyone to die. All I wanted was for Mother to feel a fraction of the pain she had caused me . . .

"Those years afterwards I worried what the Witch would take from me, wondering what I valued most. But the Witch is a cool and calculating creature though it took me a long time to truly understand. For she took you, my Florence. Not in death as I was led to believe, but she took you away from me nonetheless. . .

"The irony is it was you who led me to the grotto a second time, though I'd vowed never to go near it again. Even now I don't remember entering it. The ghost of D's voice was in my head, begging me to leave the grotto. I could not. D was dead, you were lost to me and the Witch had no power over you. All I had left was hatred of Mother like a garrotte around my throat . . . But the truth is the idea had been in my head ever since I'd heard you lived. For so long I had wished Mother dead, but no longer. I needed her to live. I wanted her to suffer, to feel the pain she had inflicted on me, on so many . . .

"I went outside to the nearest rosebush, and without hesitating I clasped a stem, barely feeling the thorns puncture my flesh, and watched my blood drip into the well. The water turned red as it had before. I did not beg this time, I demanded. I demanded the Witch give me a few more years with Mother and in return I offered my soul . . .

"It came easily to me, the torturing. Nothing big, no nails or blood, instead I took what Mother valued most: control. I shudder to think

what that says about me. Nothing good, but I am my mother's daughter, and her speciality was always cruelty . . .

"I reveled in the hatred I saw in her eyes, a hatred that matched mine for her. She was impotent and I had complete control over her. I manipulated her most basic urges and needs, I gave and took as it suited me, a fitting punishment for all her cruelties . . .

"On Samhain each year, I sat with Mother in the Corbie Tower, watching the Witch's shadows steal into the room and circle Mother like sycophants. One year they did not leave alone . . ."

"She was horrible. My mother was awful," said Edie, swallowing her tears, knowing if she allowed it, she would not stop crying.

"No," said Neve. "She had been harmed, and frankly, that old cow Lady Elizabeth deserved everything she got. So much fear and hatred created by one woman. All those lives destroyed because of her; look what she did to you the moment you were born? You could've lived here, in a freaking castle!"

"No. I'm glad I didn't grow up here. This is . . ." Edie looked around, her lips tight, and settled on, "Not a happy place. I don't think it ever has been."

Neve opened her mouth to argue, thought better of it, and said instead, "Is she still writing?"

Edie nodded and read in a croaky voice, *"Though I have lived these many years by myself, I often sense I'm not alone. Only this morning, I was cutting roses when I thought I saw Lottie hurrying through the gardens like she used to after Mungo, though she's been dead these past forty-five years. I found myself smiling, remembering how Mungo would come down every day to talk to the Witch, bellowing, ''Lo, Witch!' into the well, then go on his way. Often, I've felt his presence in the castle when I turn a corner to catch a flash of him running in that hopping, rambling way of his down a hall, or hear his footsteps in the passages in the walls—"*

"Mungo!" shouted Mungo excitedly. He turned to Edie and Neve. "Ant Alice see Mungo!" He reached out a hand to the wall. "Ant Alice! Mungo here!"

And Edie's heart broke a little more.

"I can't help wonder why they have remained. Or perhaps they are merely lonely phantoms of my imagination, for there have always been ghosts aplenty on the island. I hope Lottie is with Mungo. They loved each other so much—"

The writing stopped.

"Alice?" said Edie, sensing she was near, the atmosphere still thick with Alice's sadness, her regret.

It was a long moment before words slowly appeared on the wall as though Alice was stalling, not wanting the end to come. *"I fear death. I fear Mother. She has not rested easily. Often I hear her pacing the halls or smell her perfume. She is waiting for me. Mother in death is as simple to understand as she had been in life. She remains for the Maundrell Red and retribution. She will not rest until the Red is found and I worry she keeps Mungo and Lottie here too, though why I cannot fathom, unless it is pure malice. Something she was always so good at . . .*

"Of all the ghosts of my imagination, Mother is the one I feel the most. Wherever I go she is there, watching me, waiting for me on the other side. I've no doubt she will be a vengeful ghost. I fear she will torment me in death as I tormented her in later life . . .

"But perhaps it's not the dead I should fear. The intruder is in the castle again; I heard him not an hour ago, rootling about in the Hollow Tower. The fool! He will not find the Red there . . .

"My darling Florence, knowing all I have told you, it is pure selfishness on my part that I still hope you will come to the castle one day and find my diaries. It breaks my heart that I will never know you, never hold you, never hear your laughter. I wish you to know my last thoughts will be only of you and I shall be here, waiting . . .

"I must end now, the Witch's shadows are slipping through the window. I left it open purposefully though a storm rages. I hope for a swift end now it is here . . . Or perhaps it will be Mother; patience was never her strong suit . . ."

The lightest of caresses touched Edie's cheek, Alice's yearning and regret darkening the air. Edie's face crumpled with the tears she'd been holding back. She wanted to say something, but she had no words for the swell of emotion in her chest.

"So," said Neve into the weighted silence, with an uncomfortable sideways glance at her mum's tears. "Mungo, Lottie and Percy were all your cousins?"

Edie dried her face, sensing Alice's withdrawal from her, and nodded.

"And your dad was this D, but he's dead too, which sucks." Neve heaved a sigh. "I'm glad we never met them. The Maundrells were one messed-up family."

Edie's heart sank when Neve lapsed into thoughtful silence, her single-track mind picking Alice's diary apart, searching for clues to what interested her most. It wasn't long before her eyes brightened and she turned to Mungo abruptly. He hadn't moved, content to sit quietly beside them, perhaps for the company.

"Who were your friends, Mungo?" she asked.

The ghost scrunched up his face. "Lottie Mungo's friend."

"And who else?"

He hugged himself tight and giggled like he'd been tickled. He leaned towards Neve as though to confide a secret. "Ashy friend."

"Ashley Templeton?" whispered Neve. "Ashley was your friend?"

"Aye. Ashy. Mungo's friend." He started rocking back and forth, clutching his knees. "Ashy gone," he whispered sadly.

"And the Witch was your friend, wasn't she?" Neve continued to probe gently.

"Aye. Witch Mungo's friend."

"Did she—" Neve frowned when Edie muttered, "Again?" and got to her feet to peer out the nearest window. Raised voices filtered up to them, loud in the cold silence cocooning the island.

"Again what?"

"Cameron and Mr. MacKenzie. They were having a blazing row this morning." Edie's eyes narrowed on the twilit view, unable to see the men, though they should've stood out darkly against the unforgiving white.

"Mum," said Neve, coming to stand beside Edie. "I think I've worked it out."

"Worked what out?" asked Edie, though she knew the answer already.

"Where the Maundrell Red is."

Edie followed her gaze to Mungo. Her lips tightened. "He didn't take it."

"I don't think he did. But I need to go down to the grotto to check."

"The grotto? That's a terrible idea," said Edie, eyeing the window nervously, almost expecting to see shadows slithering along the glass, seeking a way in. "It's Samhain. The Witch—"

Neve picked at her sleeve, intent on a loose thread.

Edie bit her lip to hide her smile; her brave, stubborn daughter looked young and scared, needing her mum but not wanting to ask for help.

"Do you want me to go with you?" she asked, her heart softening.

Neve grinned in relief. "Would you?" Her grin faded as a faint echo of *click-clack-click-clack* raced towards them.

Edie sucked in a breath as a blast of dry air leached the moisture from her skin. She didn't need Mungo's confirmation of what came when he leapt to his feet, screaming, "Lady is comin'!" and vanished.

"I think I prefer the Witch to Lady Elizabeth," said Neve, shivering.

Edie nodded and whispered, "Let's go!"

The Nunns hurried down the Clan Tower stairs to the ground floor. *Click-clack-click-clack* followed them closely. They ran across the Baronial Hall, their footsteps a trapped echo in the vaulted ceiling, sounding once more like crows chortling at their fearful haste.

Tellltellltelll ricocheted off the walls as though the mocking crows had taken to their wings in susurrating desperation. The air withered into a mirage, spooling from the click-clacking stalking across the vast expanse, flowing and fluid, crinkling into sharp angles and softer curves until an enormous plague mask leered down at the Nunns.

Tellltellltelll hissed around them, scratching at their dry skin, their chapped lips.

Mungo hurtled into the soot-blackened hearth and shrieked in terror. The mask took no notice of him, its focus firmly on the Nunns. His gaze flickered to the doors leading to the Inner Ward.

"Get outside!" Edie shouted, wrenching open the heavy doors.

"No! I'm not going to let that cow scare Mungo."

But Edie was already pushing her daughter outside into the gray twilight with *tellltellltelll* swooping after them.

"Jesus," whispered Edie as a faint breeze winnowed through the Inner Ward on an exploratory meander, ruffling the snow up in small eddies.

The island's pulse vibrated through their feet. Humming, far louder than before, like the distant buzz of bluebottles swarming over a ripening carcass. Neve's hand slipped into Edie's as they ran through the West Gatehouse. Loch na Scáthanna sprawled before them, a rusted mirror the Munros brooded over, admiring their snow-cloaked reflections.

Edie risked a glance over her shoulder and put on a burst of speed. Behind them, cold mist rose in whispering ribbons, sculpting into the wraith of a tall woman wearing a plague mask who forged through the snow after them. Mungo stood framed in the doorway they'd escaped through, gazing at the snow and louring clouds. He shut his eyes and stepped into the Inner Yard.

Gripping Neve's hand tight, the Nunns raced into the rose gardens. Edie, desperate to see another living human, yelled, "Mr. MacKenzie! Cameron!"

"Mum! Don't shout. You'll wake the Witch."

"She's already awake," said Edie grimly, far more worried about Lady Elizabeth following them.

"I don't want Cameron or Mr. MacKenzie to know where we're going either!" snapped Neve.

Edie didn't shout again. The creeping atmosphere of the island demanded silence.

Twilight darkened to charcoal and with it came the shadows like nebulous thieves.

"Mum," Neve moaned as the shadows oozed against their skin like melting lard.

"It's okay," Edie lied, and slid herself in front of Neve. "Go away!" she tried to shout, but her voice came out as a terrified croak. "Get the hell away from us!" she cried, louder.

The shadows slunk closer, tentative, probing, molding around her face to determine the shape of her nose, her lips, her jaw.

"What do you want?" she shrieked. "Mr. MacKenzie! Cameron! Anyone! Please help us!"

Her pleas were absorbed into the bulging darkness shaping around the Nunns.

Though she resisted, Edie's feet moved, one sluggish, forced step at a time. She clutched Neve's hand, as they were bullied forward blindly, the shadows shivering around them like cold tongues, at once coercive and gentling with pinches and caresses.

Helpless tears squeezed from Edie's eyes as they were propelled along the paths through the rose gardens. Thorns caught their clothing; frozen leaves brushed against their arms; snow scrunched beneath their feet. The shadows writhed and coiled, impelling the Nunns to move without any directional pull of their own.

As suddenly as they had appeared, the shadows drifted away like cloying smoke before a shivering breeze.

Edie hugged Neve tightly, feeling her trembling, hushing her dry sobs, striving for calm and failing.

It was a moment before Edie was rational enough to take note of her surroundings. Three lanterns lit up the grotto; they hissed and spat, the stink of paraffin overpowering the underlying vegetative rot. Snow feathered the floor; the black, ragged walls dripped with pustulant lichen and moss. The shadows retreated, pooling unpleasantly, waiting to do their mistress' bidding.

Neve screamed.

She screamed and screamed, eyes wide and staring over Edie's shoulder.

Edie whipped around, took one look and vomited over the uneven floor.

Throat raw, she wiped her mouth. Her breath lurching, she forced herself to confront Mr. MacKenzie lying beside the well, his booted foot resting against one of the Pict stones.

He was quite dead. Though shadows slithered over his lifeless body, there was nothing supernatural about his death. A human hand had plunged a pair of gardening shears deep into the old man's chest.

Tamping down her own horror, Edie drew Neve back into a deep pressure hug until her screams subsided to whimpers. Unable to tear her eyes away from the old man, Edie's mind unfroze and raced to the only possibility.

Cameron had murdered Mr. MacKenzie. Like something from a lucid nightmare, she and her daughter were on an island with a murderer, a malicious ghost, a predatory witch and no way of escape.

"Shit!"

Edie and Neve jerked in unison and turned to Cameron framed in the entrance of the grotto. He glanced down at Mr. MacKenzie, then at the Nunns.

"This is unfortunate," he murmured.

CHAPTER 20

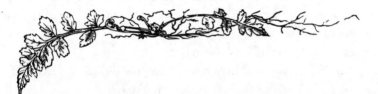

"You killed Mr. MacKenzie," said Edie. It wasn't a question.

No shame or guilt tightened the lines of Cameron's face, hollowed like a skull in the lanterns' light. "He had it coming sooner or later. Too nosy by half."

"You killed him because he was nosy?" Neve whispered, her voice raw. "You're insane."

"No," said Edie, standing in front of Neve to shield her. "He knew something." She eyed the three exits. Cameron blocked one. If she could communicate to Neve to edge towards the other two, they could run to the castle and hide. It was a short-term plan, but she had limited options. "You've been lying to us ever since we arrived, and Mr. MacKenzie knew your secret," she said to distract Cameron, giving Neve's arm a meaningful nudge. "I heard you two fighting more than once. Was he blackmailing you?"

Cameron's eyes twitched with annoyance. "That sanctimonious prick? I could have tolerated blackmail. But all he did was harp on about—" His mouth snapped shut and he glared at Edie.

"It's about the Maundrell Red," said Neve, careful not to look at

Mr. MacKenzie's body. Ignoring Edie's prodding, she stepped into the open, arms crossed, defiant. The shadows drifted towards her to listen closely.

"What about it?" said Cameron warily.

"Everything has been about the Maundrell Red and I'll bet you've been looking for it."

"That's not why you killed Mr. MacKenzie," said Edie, watching Cameron carefully. "Loads of people have searched for the diamond, but it's gone. It was stolen sixty years ago."

"I *ken* who stole the Maundrell Red!" Cameron yelled. "It was that stupid auld bitch, Alice." He advanced on them, pulling up short not a meter away.

Edie took an involuntary step back.

Not Neve. She stood her ground. "No, she didn't!" she snapped.

Feverish, Cameron turned to her. "You've figured it out?"

The corner of Neve's lips quirked into a sneer, smug, belittling. "As if I'd tell you."

Nostrils flaring, he tore his gaze from Neve to Edie and grinned, slow and wicked. "I ken who your mother was. Alice bloody Maundrell," he said, smirking when Edie flinched. "I found her diaries, blethered on something fierce about you. 'Oh my Florence,'" he said in a mocking singsong voice. "'My darling Florence . . .' Didnae ken that, did you?"

Edie swallowed the urge to hit him, not wanting Alice's last words to her sullied. She didn't have Neve's fierce courage; very aware they were in the presence of an unhinged murderer. "I did," she said. "I found out today."

Cameron rocked back on his heels in surprise. "Impossible! I burnt the stupid bitch's diaries years ago. How did you find out?"

"Alice told us." Edie watched his reaction carefully, expecting denial. Instead his eyes flickered in the direction of the castle.

"She's still here?"

"And she didn't have much to say about the Maundrell Red," said Neve. "Certainly not where it is."

"She took it. She must have," he muttered, jaw tightening with fury. "But she widnae tell me."

Edie frowned. "You said you'd never met her."

Cameron startled, caught in a lie. He schooled his expression and shrugged.

A horrible certainty popped into Edie's head. She glanced down at Mr. MacKenzie, then at Cameron. "You killed Alice."

"What?" Neve blinked at her mum in astonishment. When Cameron didn't deny it, she whispered, "Oh my god. You were right, Mum. There was a murderer on the island all this time."

"That's what Mr. MacKenzie knew," said Edie, rather proud of herself for staring Cameron down until he looked away. "He was on the island. That's why you've been arguing. He knew you killed Alice."

Hunted, seeking an escape, Cameron's gaze flittered to the well, Mr. MacKenzie, the Pict stones, the diseased walls. Then he straightened, his attention returning to the Nunns, hardened, uncaring, reckless. "He guessed. It weighed on his conscience, the pillock!" he spat. "Every time he got into the drink he'd come about telling me to do the honorable thing, hand myself in to the police. But why would I? It was an accident, another Maundrell tragedy on Samhain."

Edie's breath caught in her throat, tensing to run. She shuffled back slightly.

"Dinnae move!" Cameron yelled.

Edie jerked in fright. Rooted to the spot, she found Neve's hand, gripped it tightly. Neither said anything as Cameron breathed deeply through his nose, reaching for calm.

"You should've stayed away," he said, beseeching and earnest. "I dinnae want to hurt you, but you've left me no choice."

"Tell us what happened," said Edie in a controlled, gentle tone, belying the frantic racing of her heart. If Cameron was talking, he wasn't killing them, and they could gain precious time to find a way out of this hopeless mess. "What happened with Alice? Did it happen in here?"

Cameron shuddered with memory, unaware of the fawning

shadows tangling in his hair, slithering across his shoulders as though they, too, wished to hear.

"It was Samhain," Edie prompted. "Same as tonight."

"You must understand it was an accident," he pleaded. "I'd been on the island for a while." His eyes flickered to Mr. MacKenzie. "Fergus had seen me about and I gave him the cock-and-bull story that I was researching. I dinnae think he really swallowed it, but he didnae seem to care and he left me alone. Alice had seen me too, but she was too auld to do anything. I'd been sleeping in the castle, right under her snooty nose. It's a big place and I was careful. But that night she found me . . . I'd been down to the pub, got pissed listening to the auld men going on about the Witch. I came back here."

He reached out a hand to a Pict stone, tracing the etched pictograms unconsciously. "It was all for a lark," he whispered, focused on the same place in a different time. "I didnae believe in the Witch, not then, but I cut my hand open, let my blood drip into the water. It turned red." He scowled at the Nunns, daring them to disbelieve him. They didn't but stood still as statues, watching him with huge eyes.

"What happened?" said Edie when he didn't continue.

Cameron turned slowly to the entrance of the grotto behind him. "Alice came in," he murmured, seeing it all again. "She shouted at me, demanded I leave the island, said she'd called the police. I was pissed and she'd made me angry. I said I widnae leave until I had the Maundrell Red. She was so smug . . . then her whole attitude changed. She froze as though she'd . . ." He paused, turning the memory over in his head. "Like something had twigged. She started laughing and said, 'They were running away.'"

"Who was running away?" whispered Neve, her brow drawn low in concentration, ignoring Edie's warning glance.

"I dinnae ken. She was laughing so hard and said something about appearances being deceptive. Then she started crying. She widnae stop. She went on and on laughing and crying like a demented thing." He hugged himself tight, rocking slightly. "Something snapped in me," he whispered. "All those years without my father because of the Maundrells. I'd hated them for so long. And here was the last Maundrell laughing at me . . . It all happened so quickly. She was laughing and I was in front of her. I slapped her. It was harder than I intended; I just wanted her to stop laughing. And she was on the floor at my feet, blood leaking from her temple . . . and then the shadows came." He regarded the Nunns, disconcerted, as though he'd forgotten about them. "You've seen the shadows, how they move here like they have a life of their own?"

Edie and Neve nodded, trying not to look at the shadows skittering and coiling around Cameron.

"They came for Alice. I'm still not sure who killed her, me or the shadows. They crawled all over her, into her mouth, her ears, closing her eyes, tightening like a—a—"

"A shroud?" Edie whispered, frightened if she spoke too loudly she'd break his train of thought. She pulled Neve's hand slightly, and they shuffled a little closer to the nearest exit.

He nodded. "Aye, a shroud is fitting. I thought they would come for me next, but they disappeared into the well." He shuddered. "It was like a horrible dream, I was in no state to think quickly, but I cuidnae have the police involved, so I carried her to the castle, washed the blood off her head in the kitchen . . . and that's when Fergus found me. I told him Alice had taken a fall and I found her when she was already deid. He seemed to believe me and went off to call the doctor.

"I think the doctor had been expecting Alice's death; she was auld, and he pretty much backed up my story." Cameron snorted mirthlessly. "It didnae take long for her death to be put down to another Maundrell tragedy on Samhain. But it was only months later I realized Fergus suspected something. Pestered me something fierce for a while; then he backed off after I threatened him. And we were doing fine until you two arrived. He threatened to tell you and I cuidnae have that." He focused on the Nunns, lips curling into a snarl. "He had it coming. He and that auld baggage. Your whole bloody family had it coming after what your lot did to my father."

Startled by Cameron's Jekyll-and-Hyde switch, Edie stopped in midshuffle, her chest hitching painfully.

"Your father?" she said, croaky with fright, hoping to get him talking again.

"You really dinnae ken anything, do you? Stupid mares, the both of you! Sitting in your bloody castle, lording it over everyone. And what do you have anyway? A loch where nothing can live and a haunted castle in the middle of nowhere. Who the hell do you think you all are?" he shouted. "The only thing of value your lot had was the Maundrell Red and I am owed it." He leapt towards them, stopping just short, shoulders bunched like a bully. A gush of whisky fumes swept over Edie and Neve.

Pissed and mad, thought Edie feverishly, recoiling from his breath.

"Your family destroyed mine!" he hissed in her face. "My father went to prison because of your lot. They thought nothing of destroying his life and mine. They lied and cheated and stole without any thought of who it would harm . . . But Alice understood. I told her as she died. In her last moments she recognized my father in me. I killed Alice Maundrell and she deserved it. If she stood in front of me now, I'd kill her again and again. I would've killed that auld bat, Lady Elizabeth, too, if I'd had the chance."

"Who was your father, Cameron?" said Edie, shuffling back, taking Neve with her.

"You're just like your family," he sneered. "You never even bothered to ask my full name. You're as selfish and stupid as the rest of them. I'm Cameron Kincaid; my father was Gordon Kincaid."

"The doctor who treated Mungo?" said Edie, astonished, momentarily forgetting the danger she and Neve were in.

"Aye! He spent five years treating that cretin. Lady Elizabeth promised him the Maundrell Red for his service because no one would treat the idiot. Five bloody years. And what did my father get out of it? Blamed for murders he didnae commit and twenty-five years in prison! It was all Lady Elizabeth's doing! And I had to grow up without my father, watching my mother wither into an auld woman, moving home all the time when the whispers started up, until she gave up and died. When my father was released he and I were determined to get hold of Lady Elizabeth and claim the Maundrell Red. But she had died the year before. We asked to search for it, but Jasper threatened to phone the police and kicked us off the island like we were common criminals. For years I tried to get onto the island after Jasper and my father died, but Alice blocked my every attempt when she knew the diamond belonged to me!"

"It wasn't the Maundrells' to give," Neve piped up. "It belonged to Mr. and Mrs. Macleod. We found Ernest Maundrell's will. They are the ones who truly owned the diamond."

"And they're both deid," said Cameron damply. "Their daughter is deid, and Mungo was their grandson, and he is deid too. That diamond is mine!"

With Cameron so close, Edie dared not move again. "Lady Elizabeth had a lot to answer for," she said, hoping to appease, appear sympathetic. "She certainly didn't do me any favors."

Cameron eyed her warily, relaxed his shoulders, took a step back.

"So what was your plan?" said Edie, gripping Neve's hand, forcing her to move with her as she took a cautious step towards the nearest exit. "Live on the island until you found the diamond? Is that why you created all those fake ghosts, to scare off anyone who came here?"

"You've figured that out?" he said, unconcerned. "It worked for a while. I worked in the film industry, on crappy horrors mostly. When Alice died—"

"When you killed her!" snapped Neve, then shut up when Edie opened her eyes wide in warning.

"When I *killed* Alice," he continued with a glare at Neve, "her nephew rented the place out. I cuidnae have a bunch of idiots running about, and I hit on the idea of making the place so haunted no one would want to live here."

"But some of the ghosts are real," said Neve. "Why bother with fake ghosts?"

"I'd not seen any, not until I saw that girl in the gardens with your mum. But some of them are fake; I threw in a few extra that get attached to these old piles. I'm particularly proud of the Headless Horseman and Bloody Mary down in the cellars." He grinned smugly. "No one stayed long after that, until you two arrived. You dinnae scare easily— Dinnae move!" he yelled. A vein throbbed in his temple.

Edie and Neve froze in their furtive shuffle towards the exit, watching Cameron with trepidation, ready to run if he snapped. The shadows skittered around him, then away.

Silence bloomed in the grotto until Edie heard the faint hum from the dank walls.

Cameron breathed heavily, swaying slightly, entranced by the play of the shadows across the well's dark surface. "I've tried everything, looked everywhere," he muttered. "But she knows. The Witch has always known, I'm sure of it. Every year, on Samhain I come down here and make another pact with her." He glanced sidelong at Edie and Neve with a calculating glitter. "She's a bloodthirsty bitch . . . Maybe that's been the problem. The Witch always wants blood, but I havnae given her enough. I can give her more blood than she's had in centuries."

Human sacrifice dripped into Edie's thoughts. The idea was there on Cameron's face; there is the hiss and tangle of the shadows agitating above the well. She cast about desperately for something, anything. A weapon, a distraction . . .

"What was your pact?" said Neve, with only a slight quaver in her voice. She was more frightened than she let on, her arm trembling against Edie's.

Cameron blinked at her. "What?" he said, puzzled, as though trying to remember her name.

"What did you ask the Witch for?"

"To find the Maundrell Red. What else would I ask for?"

"You're a twat. The Witch isn't trying to hurt us; she's trying to fulfill *your* pact with her . . . Don't you get it?" said Neve when Cameron's brow furrowed, bewildered. "I'm betting you've had a few experiences like I had the other night. How many times has she brought you down here?"

"Quite a few. I thought . . . Jesus!" He spun round, staring wildly around the grotto. "But I've searched in here. I've looked everywhere."

"When she brought me in here," said Neve, "she was pushing me towards the well. The Maundrell Red is *in* the well."

"No!" He gazed at the well in horror. "No one would be so stupid," he murmured, shaking his head in denial. Then his nostrils flared with annoyance. "I ken your game. You've figured it out." He leapt forward, grabbed Neve's arm, and dragged her to the well. "Tell me where it is!" he yelled, shaking Neve hard.

"Let go of her!" Edie shrieked, and launched herself at Cameron, hitting his back with her fists. "Let go of my daughter, you bastard!"

Cameron turned too quickly, stumbled over Mr. MacKenzie's body, flung out a hand to steady himself and hit Edie on the shoulder so hard she slammed into the Pict stone beside the well. A grinding crack echoed around the grotto like the snap of distant thunder.

The Pict stone was tall, as tall as Edie. A crack ran through the pictograms. It teetered like a loose tooth, then fell in slow motion towards Cameron and the well.

Edie seized Neve and, with a strength she hadn't known she possessed, threw her daughter out of the way and dived after her.

The stone crashed into Cameron, his scream cut off by an almighty crunch and reverberating splash.

A cloud of dust and loose stone billowed out. A lantern burst in a tinkle of glass and paraffin, then another, struck by wild shards.

In the light of the surviving lantern, the shadows filled the grotto in a tight cobweb of humming darkness. Edie groped for Neve and together they shuffled back until they were against a wall.

A faint vibration came up from the dank ground, skittering along their skin like millipede legs to penetrate their ears, rising to a sheer whine. Edie held her breath, too terrified to scream.

Slowly, the whining faded. Slowly, the shadows receded, slithering and slinking to pool in unlikely places around the grotto. Slowly, silence settled on the dust still lingering in the air, waiting, quivering with expectancy. Mr. MacKenzie still lay untouched beside the well. Of Cameron there was no sign.

CHAPTER 21

"Are you okay?" Edie whispered after a long while, her racing heart slowing, her ears still ringing from the crash.

Neve nodded, her face crimping, holding back tears. "I'm fine," she said hoarsely. "Just shaken."

They stood and approached the well cautiously. Part of the Pict stone had fallen into the well with Cameron, the rest balanced on the edge of the low wall.

"Jesus," muttered Neve. "Mum, look at this." She stood on the edge of the gaping hole at the base of the dislodged Pict stone, a chunk of the grotto's floor torn away. She stepped back, ashen with shock.

In silent sorrow, Edie peered at the mass grave that had been hidden beneath the Pict stone. At least fifteen bodies, skin scraped over bones like smoked leather, tanned to almost black, mummified and perfectly preserved in the peat. They had been arrayed ceremoniously, curled on their sides as though sleeping if not for the fact that each head had been severed, then set back on a neck, with a stone protruding from each mouth.

"There's a baby, Mum," said Neve, shock tearing her voice. "Who would kill a baby and chop off their head?"

"I don't know," said Edie, nostrils twitching at the dank earthiness rising from the grave, tainted with faint vinegar. She crouched down, somewhat disconnected from the horror of the massacre of entire families, possibly a whole village. These people had died centuries ago, and a part of her was fascinated by the surviving detail: hair still intact, the wrinkles of an old woman's face like a dried apple, taut sinew stretched over long bones.

She bent closer to study the face of a woman in the center of the mass grave. A face once familiar and alien, seen for only a moment. She had been beautiful once. Full lips, strong cheekbones, defiant chin, braided hair still retaining a dull redness. She looked regal in the long sleep of death, a chieftainess perhaps, or a priestess . . . or something darker. A witch.

"Mum," Neve moaned. "The shadows."

Edie had momentarily forgotten about the shadows in the wake of their grisly discovery. She hurriedly backed away to Neve, who was pressed against the wall.

The shadows hovered above the grave, a hesitant, swirling mass. Slowly, dark tendrils drifted down, shaping into tentative fingers to brush against the leathery skin.

A visceral punch hit Edie in the chest with sudden comprehension. This was a reunion of family long parted. Intimate, private and intensely personal. Each caress of a petrified face was lovingly reminiscent, a mother touching her child's face, a wife for her husband, sisters and brothers, grandchildren and grandparents.

Slowly, the shadows sank into the mummified bodies, one after the other, settling into their corporeal forms, finding the peace that had been stolen in violent death.

Edie and Neve watched it all in silence. There was no need for words as the aura of human tragedy the island had been trapped in for so long lifted, shredding like smoke in a breeze. The shadows cast by the lantern didn't shift or crawl away as though fearing the light. Night had arrived without drama beyond the grotto and lay silent and still, peaceful in a way it hadn't been since the Nunns had stepped foot on the island.

Not wanting to disturb the hallowed atmosphere, Edie and Neve were careful as they stepped up to the edge of the grave.

"Look at her," said Edie, pointing to the proud woman in the middle. "Do you recognize her?"

Recognition bled into Neve's ashen face. "It's the Witch. From my dream."

"The Witch wasn't a witch," said Edie. "She was a ghost, a very old one. They all were." She glanced at the Pict stones, one broken, one intact. "Cameron said they were curse stones. These people were cursed."

"A week ago I didn't even believe in curses," Neve grumbled.

"They were very real for these people. They lived in a time when belief was part of who they were, as natural as breathing. If they believed they'd been cursed, they would've believed it whole-heartedly. And they believed it into death . . . The Witch wanted to be found." Noting Neve's confusion, Edie paused, rearranging her thoughts. "That night when the Witch brought you down here, I think she wanted your help to break the curse. She's been draw-ing attention to the well because she and her people were buried here. All those pacts . . ."

She shook her head, feeling her way through her forming sup-positions. Like osmosis she had been absorbing all the tales of the island, accepting them at face value, as fact, falling into the trap of other people's fears and beliefs spun into superstition. But fear and belief went hand in hand; so often people feared what they believed, and often what they believed was to be feared. It was easier to make up a story to explain the horror humans can inflict on other humans. Over the years those stories gained shape, and with each new trag-edy, the stories were embellished into legend.

"Everyone misunderstood her pacts," said Edie. "The Witch was trying to help people who came to her in the hope they would help her. We're so good at lying to ourselves, seeing what we want to see, believing what we're told even if it makes no sense. You and I were no better. We believed all the stories, that the Witch was this dreadful creature who wished to harm us."

"She *was* dreadful, Mum! She killed people."

Edie nodded. How could she possibly understand the rationale of someone who had lived millennia before? "I can't imagine how desperate she must've been to free herself and her people from the curse. Perhaps desperation twisted her motivation until she was willing to do awful things to others to achieve her own ends."

"So the Maundrells all dying on Samhain was all down to the Witch trying to break the curse? The Maundrells themselves—and more importantly, you and I—weren't cursed?"

Edie nodded slowly. "I don't think we're cursed any more than the Maundrells were," she said. "But humans love to blame something for their misfortunes. Why not a witch if there isn't anyone else to blame? Perhaps some of the Maundrell tragedies were due to the Witch and some to self-fulfilling prophecy. If you believe it will happen, quite often something will happen to fit your belief. A bit like someone who believes they're unlucky and everything bad that happens will reinforce that belief in bad luck."

Neve snorted doubtfully, her attention returning to the well.

Edie's heart sank, recognizing the obsession still gripping her daughter. She forced herself to look at Mr. MacKenzie, her throat tightening with sorrow for the old man. "Poor Mr. MacKenzie," she said. "He didn't deserve this. We need to call the police."

"How the hell are we going to explain all this?" said Neve, waving a vague hand around the grotto to incorporate all that came before.

"I don't know, but we can't leave him here like this." She straightened, sloughing off the enervation threatening to engulf her; she'd never felt so drained of emotion. "Come on, we need to get off the island. I have had about as much as I can take of its ghosts and shadows and—and—" She gulped back the sobs crowding in her throat. "Sorry," she whispered when Neve looked at her with concern. She smiled weakly. "I'm fine," she said, hating that Neve was coping so much better than she was.

But Neve's attention was drawn back to the well. She stepped to one side, careful not to stand where Mr. MacKenzie had been killed, eyes squinched, appraising, reflective.

"Neve, we need to go," said Edie.

Neve ignored her. She put her hands on the low wall surrounding the well and leaned over, so close her breath rippled faintly in concentric circles. When the water stilled, she smiled at her reflection. "I think I know where the Maundrell Red is."

October 1965

Tears dripped down Lottie's cheeks onto the hand clamped over her mouth. Never had she felt so utterly helpless as she watched Ashley being strapped to the bed in the top room of the Corbie Tower. Her hatred for Bitsie matured in her stomach like slow-release poison, the futile hatred of the captive for their jailor, twisted, bitter, bleak. If she had been free, she would've tried to kill Bitsie. Never had she wished so much for another's death, a drawn-out, agonizing death.

A stream of loathing diverted to her mother, Bitsie's accomplice. Vida hadn't blinked when her own children were manhandled into the room. It was she who strapped Ashley down, she who placed a restraint over his mouth to muffle his screams, she who listened attentively to the doctor, still wearing the devil mask, as he explained the procedure to Ashley that an electrical current would pass through his brain to trigger a seizure.

"Usually the current would pass through your feet with Electrical Aversion Therapy; however . . ." Dr. Kincaid glanced at Bitsie, who shook her head. He shrugged and continued. "There is a risk of memory *loss and some temporary confusion, and you will probably have a head-ache for a couple of days." He paused, lifting his head to Bitsie again. "This would be better if he were naked." His gaze darted to Lottie. "But perhaps Miss Maundrell should be allowed to leave the room?"*

"Charlotte stays," said Bitsie firmly. "It will be an invaluable lesson to her should she decide in the future that defiance is her best option."

Dr. Kincaid sighed, then nodded at Vida, who twisted a dial on the convulsator.

The orderly's grip on Lottie tightened as she struggled in vain. Her terrified eyes swung to Percy, whose anguished expression broke her heart when Ashley's body arched, veins popping up in his neck like enraged snakes. He, too, struggled against the orderly restraining him, trapped and ineffectual as Lottie.

The overhead light dimmed when Vida turned the dial again.

A faint hissing dragged Lottie's horrified attention away from Ash-ley's jerking body to the door, desperate for someone to come in and stop what was happening. The hissing mutated to a sly hum before darkness slid underneath the door like pooling ink.

It slithered across the floor, curled around Bitsie's black-clad legs, shinnied up her body to pet and fondle the plague mask, slinking into the eyeholes. She was oblivious to the shadows.

"Help us!" Lottie screamed into the orderly's hand, but her desperate plea was no more than a smothered mutter.

The shadows bunched up, probing Bitsie's mask as though curious to understand what manner of thing was on her face, before sliding off her and up the walls. They gathered on the ceiling like waiting vultures. A grating, predatory buzz crowding the room.

"Up the dosage," said Bitsie. She said it coolly, unemotionally, emer-ald eyes through her mask glittering with fascination.

Vida looked at her mother-in-law in surprise. "He's had enough for one day."

"Up the dosage."

Vida hesitated, lips parting to defy. She swallowed, a quick glance at her restrained children. She focused on Percy, her expression softening. "This is for Ashley's own good, and yours," she said, a faint entreaty for understanding. "I know this is hurting you, but I am here to ensure the procedure is conducted safely." And, believing her lie, she twisted the dial again.

Perhaps Vida hadn't attached the restraint over Ashley's mouth properly; perhaps the restraints weren't tight enough. His body jerked violently as the higher volt of electricity jolted through his brain; the mouth-strap came adrift, freeing a scream unlike anything Lottie had heard before. An animal howl, feral, mindless, beyond endurance.

It pierced her ears, shattered a glass on a table, crescendoed to the hunched shadows on the ceiling.

"Up the dosage." Bitsie's sharp voice cut through Ashley's scream. She no longer seemed to care if everyone heard what she'd been at pains to hide in the Corbie Tower.

"No," said Vida. "That is enough."

Bitsie lifted her mask onto her coiffed hair, her mouth rigid with displeasure at her daughter-in-law's defiance. She turned to Dr. Kincaid, her argument with Vida stored away for another day.

The devil mask disguised the doctor's expression; only his honey-hued eyes flashed his simmering fury from hollow sockets.

"You and I understand each other," said Bitsie. "A lesson must be taught . . . You will up the dosage."

Dr. Kincaid had given up free will five years before for the promise of the Maundrell Red. He hesitated for a moment, then complied with Bitsie's command.

Ashley screamed again. His body slammed against the bed with a heavy meatiness that camouflaged hurrying footsteps from the corridor outside.

The door crashed open and Aunt Alice burst in. She was dressed as a skeletal nun, complete with a realistic skull mask.

"Mother!" she cried, pulling her mask off. "What are you doing?"

Bitsie barely acknowledged her daughter. "Go away. This is no concern of yours."

"This is—" began Alice. Her eyes scuttled to the walls, then widened

in pure terror. "Can you see that?" she whispered, backing towards the open door.

Lottie's relief at her aunt's arrival dwindled, replaced by renewed fear. The walls were black with shadows seeping down like blood, puddling on the floor.

A moment later, Jasper hobbled into the room as fast as his old injury allowed. "What the hell?" he murmured. He hurried past his dumbstruck sister to Ashley twitching on the bed, eyes closed, breathing labored.

"Get out!" Bitsie's command was edged with an authority unlike anything she had uttered before, cold, pitiless, tyrannical.

Jasper ignored her and worked the ties restraining Ashley. "I cannot believe you would go this far, Mother," he said, anger stiffening every line in his body. He looked up at his wife. "And you! You allowed this to happen? Why would you countenance such cruelty?"

"Do not lecture me on cruelty!" snapped Vida. "It is better I am here to ensure no one comes to any harm."

"Harm? Look around you, Vida! This boy has been—" He leapt back from the bed.

Ashley arched at an impossible angle, then hit the bed with an audible crackle of his spine breaking.

Vida's head whipped to the convulsator. She frowned in confusion. The dials hadn't moved.

What followed was half a minute of fractured images. Vida's shocked gasp. Percy's pained moan before he slumped into the orderly's arms. Dr. Kincaid darting towards the convulsator. Jasper trying to free Ashley. Alice screaming. Bitsie frozen and frowning. The shadows hovering, slinking, cringing . . .

Lottie didn't see Mungo come into the room, but suddenly he was in the middle of it all, panting like he'd run all the way from the other side of the castle.

His round face crimped with fear, wild eyes tearing from Lottie still restrained to the seething walls. "Nae, Witch!" he bellowed, spinning round, hands clamped to his head. "Nae hurt Mungo's Lottie!"

He caught sight of Ashley on the bed and screamed. A primal, high-pitched scream. He charged clumsily towards Dr. Kincaid, who leaned over Ashley.

No one was prepared for the speed with which Mungo moved. "Nae hurt Ashy, Doc-ta!" he shrieked, arms out wide. "Nae hurt Ashy's heid!"

The room descended into chaos. Jasper tried to grab Mungo and was pushed gently aside; Alice screamed at everyone to stop Mungo; Vida stood frozen by the convulsator; Bitsie did nothing, focused calm in the confusion.

Mungo's arms closed around the astonished doctor in a bear hug, lifting him like he weighed no more than a doll, and tossed him across the room.

Dr. Kincaid slumped to the floor. Lottie, with a viciousness she hadn't been aware she was capable of, hoped he was dead.

"Mungo!" barked Bitsie.

He turned, shoulders shuddering with sobs, stroking Ashley's head. He saw Bitsie's curled lip, her loathing for him stretched tight across her face.

"Bad Lady!" he roared. "Bad Lady hurt Ashy. Hurt Mungo!" He bore down on her, mouth wide, blue eyes unfocused, heightened, unable to control the emotions within himself.

Bitsie pulled down her plague mask, stopping Mungo in his tracks. He gazed at the mask in silent terror.

Lottie bit the orderly's hand. He yelped, grip loosening. She kicked his shin as hard as she could, slipped through his grasp, and leapt towards Mungo, shouting, "No, Mungo! Leave Grandmother alone!"

He turned to Lottie, focusing. "Mungo's Lottie!" he sobbed. "Ashy hurt."

Lottie reached out her hands, palms up. "It's okay, Mungo," she said, her voice hitching. "It's okay."

"Nae 'kay, Lottie." Confused and trembling, he sobbed loudly. "Ashy! Ashy hurt!" He stumbled back to the bed and tried to pick up Ashley's limp body.

Mungo jerked, his head flicking back hard as the electrical current still passing through Ashley surged into him.

"You havnae switched off the convulsator, you stupid bitch!" Dr. Kincaid yelled at Vida. He staggered to his feet, clutching his head.

"It wasn't me!" cried Vida, trying to turn the dials in vain. "I can't stop it! Something's happened. It's broken!"

"Mungo!" Lottie screamed.

He twisted awkwardly, eyes and ears bleeding, body spasming.

He lurched towards Lottie, falling against her heavily. Together they fell to the floor.

Lottie's head caught the edge of a table. White flashes blurred her vision; a vicious pain stabbed her brain.

Blinking hard, tears squeezing from her eyes, she managed to sit up and crawl to Mungo lying prostrate beside her. She cupped his round face in her hands.

"Don't leave me, Mungo," she sobbed. "Please don't leave me."

The wide-eyed adoration Mungo had given her from the first moment she had woken up to find him standing beside her bed ten years ago flickered deep in his blue gaze. It faded as life bled from him and Mungo was gone.

Lottie hoisted him clumsily to her chest and wailed her terrible loss.

The restless shadows enveloped the two protectively, caressing Lottie's face, absorbing her heartbreak. They shivered across Mungo, pressing close to his skin, stroking his hair, and gently closed his staring eyes.

"Well," said Bitsie, gazing down at Mungo and Lottie impassively. "That's one problem solved . . . Oh, for god's sake, Charlotte, stop caterwauling and get up."

Lottie choked on her sorrow and kissed Mungo's forehead. She laid him gently on the floor; then she did as her grandmother bade and stood up.

She swayed, the room unfocused and wavering. Her head hurt, thoughts muddled. She put a hand to her temple. Her fingers came away streaked in blood. She didn't care. Nothing mattered without Mungo.

"I hate you," she said, her voice surprisingly calm, a statement of fact.

Her dull gaze roamed from her grandmother, the plague mask that had so terrified Mungo disguising her face, to the rest of her family frozen in a shocked tableau. Their eyes flicked from Mungo to Ashley to Lottie, all too cowed, too controlled, to speak up against Bitsie.

"Astonishingly, I do not care what you feel, Charlotte." Bitsie's eyes glimmered through the mask's sockets, hard as diamond, cold as the first frost. "But now you are the only one who knows where the Red is, which is somewhat unfortunate."

"The Red?" Some of Lottie's apathy slipped. "The Red?" Louder. "The Red?" she screamed. "Two people are dead and all you care about is the Red?"

Bitsie lifted the mask. "Yes," she said simply.

Lottie clutched her throbbing head; her skull felt too small to fit her brain. She worried it might leak out of her ears. Nothing was making sense. Mungo was lying on the floor, very still. What was he doing on the floor?

She laughed a little, rising maniacally, quite demented in her disorientation. She blinked at her grandmother, blurring in and out of focus. What was she forgetting?

Oh yes. The Red. "I don't know where it is." Was that her voice? It sounded odd, funny. She started laughing again. "Mungo didn't take it."

"Lies!" Bitsie spat.

A moment of clarity, the events of the past few minutes sweeping briefly into Lottie's mind, followed swiftly by a terrible rage. "You'll never get your diamond back!" she screeched. "And I will search for it, and I will find it, and when I do I will throw it in the well so you can't ever get to it!"

"Lottie!"

Her mother's voice cut into her confusion. Lottie's face crumpled. "Mungo, Mum. Mungo won't get up. You need to fix him."

Vida's usually controlled face slackened with shame. An expression Lottie had never seen her mother wear before. "I can't," she whispered.

Jasper, his brow creased with concern, took a step towards Lottie, reaching out a hand.

Confused, she took a step back.

"You had a nasty fall and hit your head," he said, his hand dropping to his side, hunching under the weight of his helplessness. "You need to lie down and Dr. Kincaid will take a look at you."

"Stop making a fuss," said Bitsie. "It was a light tap."

Bitsie's sharp voice brought everything back into focus. Lottie gasped. "You killed Mungo! You killed Ashley!"

"I did no such thing. They killed themselves with their poor choices."

"You. Killed. Mungo!" Lottie shrieked. She leapt at her grandmother, or thought she did, but it was more a clumsy stumble; her feet seemed to have grown to double their size. She reached out to Bitsie, fingers tensed into claws. She would rip that hated mask off and stomp on it; she would gouge out those green eyes; she would scratch those painted lips off; she would . . . she would . . . her thoughts tangled up in a frantic mess. She had to get out of here.

She tottered towards the door, giggling to herself. Mungo was being a silly pudding. He was hiding again. Grandmother would be furious if she didn't find him quickly.

A blast of cold stung Lottie's cheeks. She staggered into the Inner Ward. What on earth was she doing outside? Oh yes. Mungo. Had to find Mungo. Grandmother would be furious if he wasn't dressed and ready for the party tonight.

She smiled at the shadows winding around her, sleek and full of guile. "Hello, Witch," she murmured. "Where's Mungo?" She giggled to herself again, feeling oddly wild, yet apathetic. "Silly Lottie. Silly, silly Lottie."

The fragrance of late-summer roses hit her stomach. She leaned over and vomited into the nearest flower bed. She straightened, swaying. The grotto was in front of her. She had no recollection of walking here. Where had she been? Vague thoughts flickered through her mind, each more confusing than the last. Oh yes. Mungo. Had to find Mungo.

"Charlotte!"

Lottie turned too sharply, stumbled back. She tripped over her too-large feet and fell against the grotto, hitting her head. She collapsed to the ground. Vision blurring, barely able to see the plague mask looming over her. She hated that mask, fearing it almost as much as Mungo did.

"You're being ridiculous!" Bitsie gripped Lottie's face, her painted nails jabbing into the softness of her cheeks.

"Silly, silly Lottie." Lottie giggled and grabbed the beak, pulling the mask off. Her gaze drifted past her grandmother to the Witch standing behind her. Beautiful and strong, the blue swirls on her skin dulled by the darkening twilight. "Witch, where's Mungo?" she murmured.

The Witch's shadows swarmed over her. They were warming, petting her skin consolingly.

Bitsie followed Lottie's gaze, frowning. She turned back to her granddaughter, bending low until Lottie felt her breath against her face. "I know Mungo took the Red, so I shall only warn you once. Find the Red or I shall make your life a living hell."

"I will find it, Grandmother," she whispered. A surge of defiance spiked in her chest. Her lips spread in a twisted grin. "I will find it and give it to the Witch." A veil of darkness fell over her eyes; her last image was of Bitsie's narrowed green gaze.

CHAPTER 22

"Neve!" snapped Edie, conscious of Mr. MacKenzie's cold body between them. "We need to go! You are not to obsess about the Maundrell Red anymore. You need to accept that it's gone."

"But I know who took it," she said stubbornly. "And I'm almost certain I know where it's hidden."

Edie pinched the bridge of her nose; she felt a headache coming on. Frayed, all edges and angles, she breathed deeply for calm. "You told Cameron it had been thrown in the well."

Neve rolled her eyes. "I lied, Mum! I wasn't going to tell him where I thought it was. Honestly, I was hoping he would lean over the well so we could push him in, but as things turned out—"

"Neve! That's a terrible thing to say."

"Don't make out you weren't thinking the same thing."

Edie bit back a retort. She had indeed thought the same thing when she and Neve had been in danger. Now, in the safety of the aftermath, it worried her that she felt no guilt that she had considered murdering someone. "Even so," she said. Rubbing her face hard, knowing Neve wouldn't let it go. "I don't care who took the bloody Maundrell Red."

"But I do." Neve leaned across the well, careful not to look at Mr. MacKenzie, her face tight with renewed excitement. "Who was in the grotto the night it went missing?"

Edie crossed her arms, tight-lipped, refusing to pander to her daughter's obsession anymore.

"All the Maundrells and Mr. and Mrs. Macleod," said Neve when Edie didn't respond. "But who was there first? Come on, Mum! Percy and Ashley!"

Edie sighed loudly in exasperation. "Fine! You think they took the diamond."

"I do and so did Alice. I think she figured it out just before Cameron killed her." Neve dropped to her haunches and studied the walls of the well. "Percy and Ashley were in love. I think they were planning to run away before Lady Elizabeth could do anything horrible to them. But they would've needed money, so why not steal the Maundrell Red, with the added bonus that it would've pissed Lady Elizabeth off?"

The well was old. The kind of old humans struggle to comprehend as more than a number. Slimy algae clung like snot to the rounded stones. Great oozing lumps of grossness that made Edie nauseous as Neve's fingers disappeared into the squelchy green mess, prodding, poking and tugging each stone in turn.

"It would've been quite simple," continued Neve as she went around the well in a shuffling crouch. "Ashley and Percy needed a hiding place and a scapegoat if they got caught. Mungo fit both bills. He had hundreds of hiding places, some quite brilliant, and he'd stolen the Red before, so everyone would think he'd done it again."

"That's cruel."

Neve shrugged. "They were young and stupid, in love and desperate. Probably didn't think through the consequences of their actions. And if they had made it off the island, everyone would've thought it was them who took it, not Mungo."

Edie snorted. "That still doesn't mean they hid it here."

"Mum, Percy and Ashley weren't in here that night for a quiet grope while everyone searched for the diamond. I'll bet you a million pounds they had hidden it here earlier in the day, and while everyone was preoccupied with the search they came back to retrieve it. But Alice screwed everything up when she found them here and assumed they were doing something else; then they were locked in their rooms and didn't have a chance to escape and get the diamond."

"Even if you're right, you're forgetting Percy left the island shortly after Ashley died; he could've taken the diamond with him."

Neve deflated slightly, her hands deep in vile goo. "That's a possibility. But maybe he didn't."

"The grotto would've been searched afterwards."

"I don't think it was. Even if the Witch was a cursed ghost, she still scared the shit out of everyone, and Alice said it was people from the village who searched the island. I can't see them spending too much time in the grotto if they feared it."

"Others have looked for it."

"But never found it."

"Because it's not here!" Edie cried, throwing her hands up in the air. "You could be right and it was thrown in the well, or I'm right and it was sold ages ago by the Maundrells, or someone else stole it and kept schtum. It's probably been cut into—"

"This one's loose!" cried Neve triumphantly from the back of the well, with only a few inches to the wall of the grotto. She drove both hands into the algae and wrestled briefly with a stone. It popped out like a phlegmy cough. She shoved her arm back into the green slime, up to her elbow, feeling her way deep into the dark cavity. "Something's in here, Mum," she said excitedly. "Right at the back."

She withdrew her hands from the hole and held up a globule of slime.

"Is it . . . ?" said Edie, astonished.

"Clever, clever Percy," said Neve, her face flushed as though feverish, brushing some of the clinging algae away to reveal a tin soldier, a spiral shell, and a dull glimmer of red.

Edie's first instinct was to recoil from the diamond, wanting no part of it. The power it had held over its owners and those who'd coveted it terrified her. It would always be a danger to Neve and herself, when desire twisted into unhealthy obsession like it had for Cameron Kincaid and his father, and Lady Elizabeth.

But as she gazed into the Maundrell Red's dark heart, she felt its pull, its allure. Her fingers itched to snatch it away from her daughter, hold it in her hand, never let it—

She gasped in horror at her own thoughts. "Throw it in the well!" she said sharply. "It's dangerous. We need to get rid of it."

"Are you insane?" cried Neve. "We can sell it to pay to fix up the castle." Her fingers closed around the stone in a tight fist, skin white over knuckles. She tensed, hunching forward, brow lowered, preparing for an attack.

"Neve!" Edie tried again. "Throw it in the well!"

"No! And you can't make me!"

Mother and daughter glared at each other, breathing heavily, the air souring between them with the bloodied shape of the diamond.

Edie backed off first, rubbing a trembling hand over her face. Not Neve; she stood pugnacious and defiant, daring her mother to try wrest the stone away from her.

Perhaps the Maundrells were right and the diamond really was cursed; their fear of it had been real; so was Edie's as she felt the full force of its power. The danger on the island hadn't been the Witch, but the newer interloper, creating its own stream of human tragedy.

"Sorry," said Edie. "I don't know what came over me." She smiled weakly, a hand fluttering to her chest, her heart beating hard against her ribs.

Neve eyed her with distrust, edging towards the nearest opening.

She stopped, sucked in a startled breath, and hurried back to Edie. "Mum," she murmured, frightened.

But Edie had already felt it, staring at the walls of the grotto, its dankness sucked dry, the algae and slime dehydrating to a dull gray with a faint popping as it cracked. From the path beyond cold mist rose from the snow, shaping into a tall woman wearing a plague mask. She stalked towards them with a hissed *rrreeedddrrreeeddd!* A susurrus of obsession.

Farther up the icy path, a faint radiance appeared behind Lady Elizabeth.

Ephemeral as a reflection, Lottie stared after her grandmother in astonishment; then her young face darkened with remembered hatred. She darted out of sight and appeared in the grotto before Lady Elizabeth.

Lottie stood in front of Neve and held out a hand.

"Let it go." Lottie's murmur was a wounded moth, fluttering, flailing, a tattered desperation whispering out into the night to tangle in the snow-clotted roses.

Neve's mouth opened, forming a rounded denial, then widened in horror as Lady Elizabeth filled the grotto, the plague mask stretching obscenely, parching the air.

Edie's eyes darted between the two girls, the same age, the same blood, a similarity to the shape of their faces. One living, one dead. In the space between one breath and the next she understood what was needed to break the cycle of obsession.

Using Neve's horrified distraction, Edie groped for her hand, tightly fisted around diamond hardness. Prying her fingers up, Edie quickly wrested the Maundrell Red away and held it up to Lady Elizabeth.

"Has the Red really been worth destroying your family?" she said, quite proud there was only a faint tremor in her voice. Her arm swiveled to the well, holding the diamond over the water, flinching at Lady Elizabeth's piercing shriek as Neve shouted, "Don't do it, Mum!"

Edie hesitated. It was such a final act; such a thing of beauty should not be hidden at the bottom of a well. It deserved to be admired, envied . . .

As she withdrew her hand, a lightness brushed against her knuckles and a small hand appeared over hers, as fragile as an illusion. Lottie stood beside her, an insubstantial glimmer of moonlight in the gloom.

"*Let it go,*" came Lottie's plea once more.

Edie opened her fingers. The Maundrell Red dropped into the water with only a faint sound, echoed by Lottie's heartfelt sigh of relief.

"Noooooo! Fffooolishhh girrrl!" screeched Lady Elizabeth, but she was already unraveling. First her plague mask, revealing her face for a moment. Writhing like a hazed devil wind, frantic to remain anchored to the island, she shrieked in fury and snatched at Lottie, but her fingers were wisping away, then her arms until nothing was left but a shiver in the dark.

Lottie's face lit up with joy when a rising bellow swelled towards her of, "Lottieeeeeee!" and Mungo shambled into the grotto.

He stopped short at the sight of Lottie, hopeful wonder spreading across his face. "Mungo's Lottie?" he whispered, but he was already fading.

Lottie held out a hand to him. "*Come, my Magpie.*" Her words were a faint whisper as she, too, started fading.

"They've found each other," whispered Edie through her tears, her chest tight with bittersweet happiness for these two innocents who had lived in a small world filled with spite, hate and tragedy. Fear had been such a factor in their lives, subtle and constant, overlapping into death, separating them as love had held them together.

Mungo and Lottie walked out of the grotto, hand in hand, their forms hazing into the twilight.

Edie and Neve watched the ghosts until they were nothing more than a whisper of memory.

Neve broke the silence with, "I'll miss Mungo. The castle won't be the same without him."

Edie nodded, not bothering to wipe her tears away. She tried to gauge Neve's reaction to losing the Maundrell Red so soon after finding it, an apology bunching in her throat.

"Do you hate me?" she asked.

Neve didn't answer at first. She turned to the well pensively, its dark waters smooth as a mirror. Her lips tightened. "A bit," she admitted.

A tremor of foreboding crawled across Edie's skin, as she recognized her daughter's determination etched onto her face. Neve was already planning how to get the diamond back.

"Don't even think about it," she said.

With a final, shamed glance at Mr. MacKenzie, whom she'd largely forgotten about in the past few minutes, she grabbed the surviving lantern and hustled Neve out into the night, along the paths of the rose gardens. As they passed the graveyards and the old Viking cairns they broke into a run.

CHAPTER 23

In the halo of light cast by the lantern, the Brig o' Haggs looked ever more like a sea monster breaking from the still, bloody waters of the loch. The Nunns pelted across the bridge, down the narrow path Mr. MacKenzie had spent all day clearing through the snow.

Lights glittered from Haggs up ahead. Their pounding feet echoed faintly against the high Munros. Curtains twitched as they ran down the lane between old crofts straggling along its edges like weeds.

Edie banged on the greengrocer's door so hard the *Closed* sign leapt off the glass.

"Hurry up!" she muttered under her breath, and banged on the door again.

Shuffles sounded from within before the door was wrenched open with a, "Keep your bloody hair on."

Hamish Macleod's scowl sagged into astonishment.

"Could we use your phone please?" Edie gasped, breathless from their mad flight off the island. "There's been a terrible accident."

His astonishment was short-lived. He nodded, unsurprised. "I would expect nowt else on Samhain." The people of Haggs had seen their share of misfortune on the island, and this, too, would be another tragedy attributed to the Witch.

He stepped aside to allow them entry.

A woman in a faded flannel dressing gown, stood at the back of the little shop.

"It's them from the castle," said Hamish.

"I'm not blind, Hamish," she said.

"That's certain," he said sheepishly. "My sister, Lorna," he added.

"We've met, Hamish!"

"Aye." Hamish cast a long-suffering glance at Edie.

Lorna stared at Edie and Neve until they grew uncomfortable.

"Your phone?" Neve prompted, crossing her arms defensively against Lorna's continued scrutiny.

"You'd best follow me." Lorna turned to the little door behind the counter and led the way up a dark, narrow set of stairs with Hamish bringing up the rear. She showed them the phone attached to the kitchen wall.

"It'll be a fair while afore the police get over the pass," said Lorna when Edie came off the phone, having listened with unabashed interest. "I'm sorry to hear about Fergus. He wisnae bad in his way . . . It'll be the Witch," she added with comfortable acceptance.

"It wasn't," said Edie, swallowing the lump in her throat, determined not to give in to tears again. "He was murdered by Cameron."

"Is that a fact?" said Lorna. She snorted. "Always knew he was up to nae guid."

"Aye, she always did," agreed Hamish.

Lorna busied herself with the kettle, nodded the Nunns to the kitchen table and placed two steaming mugs and a plate of tea cakes in front of them. She sat opposite and scrutinized them again.

"We were hoping you'd come round all the same," she said.

"You were?" Edie regarded her warily.

"Aye . . . Sit yourself down, Hamish. They're not going to take flight."

Hamish sat beside his sister, used to doing what he was told.

"We were that worried about you, alone at the castle. Isnae that so, Hamish?"

Hamish nodded, not meeting Edie's eye.

"It was a surprise seeing you come through the village a week back," continued Lorna.

"Why a surprise?" said Neve, tucking into the tea cakes as though she and Edie hadn't discovered a dead body a little while ago.

Brother and sister shared a glance. "We only caught a glimpse, mind," said Lorna.

"*You* only caught a glimpse," murmured Hamish.

Undeterred, his sister nodded. "It isnae often we get folk coming over the pass, almost never at this time of year." She looked at Neve, at Hamish, back at Neve. "Fair took me aback when I saw the wee lass. So I sent Hamish along to the castle to make sure my eyes didnae lie."

Edie frowned. "What are you talking about?"

"Can you not see it? The resemblance?"

Her frown deepening, Edie looked at Hamish. His scowl matched Neve's, neither appreciating being spoken about as though they weren't there.

"Jesus," she muttered; they were so similar she wondered how she hadn't seen the resemblance before. It was there in the high forehead, the upper lip plumper than the lower, the eyes. She opened her mouth, then shut it, snippets from Alice's diary firing rapid connections in her mind. "The greengrocer."

"Aye," said Lorna, watching her carefully. "For generations."

"What—what was your father's name?"

"Hamish Macleod, same as me," said Hamish.

Edie sagged with disappointment, having expected a different answer.

"It wisnae our father that did deliveries to the castle," said Lorna, clearly leading Edie to figure it out herself.

The shape of possibility knotted Edie's stomach. "Your uncle," she said. "He used to do the deliveries."

Lorna smiled proudly as though Edie were a struggling student who had finally cracked a difficult algebraic equation. "Uncle Duncan."

"Mum always said I had the look of my uncle," said Hamish. "The lassie has it n'all."

"So Alice and Duncan—"

"Aye, turns out we're cousins." Hamish tugged at his beard, embarrassed. "I'm sort of sorry about that. I was a bit soft on you."

"Soft in the heid, more like," said Lorna, rolling her eyes. "Dinnae mind the great pudding. He disnae always think with his big heid." She elbowed her brother fondly.

"Why didn't you tell me when we first met?" Edie said, her throat tight with all the questions she wanted to ask.

"Wisnae sure I was right," said Lorna.

Hamish snorted his disagreement, muttering into his beard, "Thinks she's never wrong."

Lorna ignored him. She glanced around the humble kitchen. "Well, this is a far cry from a castle. It might not have been what you'd hoped for."

Edie bowed her head to her trembling hands clasped tight together in her lap. Hope. It bloomed in her chest that here, in this warm little kitchen with the night pressing close against the window, she had found family. They weren't grand and eccentric like the Maundrells, but as normal as she could've hoped for in her quietest dreams.

Lorna smiled and reached across the table. Edie clasped her hand, and the tears came.

"Uncle Duncan was a quiet one," said Lorna, unperturbed by Edie's tears. "We always wondered why he never married."

"He was in love with Alice," said Edie.

"Aye. He never spoke of it, but we remember as bairns Uncle Duncan walking across the Brig almost every night. Right to the very end he'd go across though he could barely walk for the cancer eating him."

"Mum knew," said Hamish.

"So she did. And there were the flowers at the funeral that told their own story," added Lorna. She got up, opened a drawer and returned to her seat, pushing a small card across the table to Edie.

She recognized the handwriting immediately. On the card, the top-right corner framed with pale lilies, were the words *Always yours, Alice.*

"Came with some strange flowers for a funeral," said Lorna. "I'm not much for flowers, but they were so peculiar I spoke to young Mrs. Macleod across the way, and she said they were pincushions and wormwood."

Edie, too, knew nothing about plants, and stared at Lorna blankly.

Lorna's lips quirked. "Aye. Confused me n'all, but young Mrs. Macleod put me right. Some flowers have a message, and we—" she nodded at Hamish, "believe Alice was sending a final message to Uncle Duncan. 'I have lost all with your absence.' Pretty words for those as like that sort of thing," she said with a sniff. Lorna seemed a practical woman who had little need for or interest in romantic frivolities. "Be that as it may, you were born out of love, and that's a lot more than many get."

Edie nodded. It counted for more than she had thought possible. "Do you think he—my father—knew about me?"

Lorna shook her head. "I dinnae ken. Maybe. Though whether it would've been a kindness or a cruelty for him to know . . . But he was a guid man and I think if he'd known he had a daughter, he would've done all he could to find you." She smiled. "But there's someone who'd be well chuffed to meet you tomorrow, Dad being your uncle n'all. He was that fond of his brother."

"He's still alive?"

"Aye. Ninety-four now, but he has his senses about him still. He'd be that pleased to meet Uncle Duncan's lass, and the wee one. And there's all your other aunties and uncles. They will be as chuffed to meet you."

Edie's face grew warm with pleasure. "I'd like that."

"Now you ken we're family, you'd best tell us all about your-self . . . and your lass." She nodded at Neve, who had been quiet throughout, absentmindedly making her way through the tea cakes with a faraway look that worried Edie. "And you'd best tell us what happened along at the castle."

Edie talked. Sometimes she cried, and a box of tissues was placed on the table. And in the space of a few hours the loneliness of her childhood was softened by the genuine interest of her cousins, even knowing the Nunns' frights and scares on the island would be woven into its lore by morning.

It was late the next morning before the police made their way over Haggs Pass behind a snowplow clearing their way.

Then came the endless questions. Edie told her edited truth until she was hoarse, giving a human explanation to a human murder. Like harrowing snapshots in her mind's eye, she saw again and again Mr. MacKenzie dead on the floor with the gardening shears poking out his chest, the shadows, the Pict stone crashing onto Cameron, the bodies revealed. She didn't dare mention the shadows.

Cameron hadn't resurfaced; she wasn't sure he would, his body perhaps trapped under the chunk of the curse stone that had fallen in with him. It had been an accident. A hollow defense. To protect Neve, Edie knew in her heart she would've killed Cameron with her bare hands if the opportunity had presented itself.

The youngest officer raised the question of diving down into the well. A fearsome glare from his superior quickly squashed the idea for now. The police were Highlanders and had grown up hearing stories of the Witch in the Well and accorded her fearful respect.

Mr. MacKenzie's body was removed without ceremony. Edie watched him go, sad for the old man. She hadn't known him long, but he had been kind to herself and Neve, and there was a lot to be said for the kindness of strangers.

But his murder, solved as far as the police were concerned, was eclipsed by the bodies that had lain under the Pict stone. For the first time in days, the sun poked its wary head through the clouds to watch the first archaeologists make their careful way over the snowbound Haggs Pass. They confirmed what Edie had already suspected. The bodies mummified in the peat were old; with a great deal of buzzing excitement tentative estimates of three thousand years or more were put forward.

A brief argument broke out between the police and the archaeologists as to who had first access to the crime scene, one recent, one ancient. The police won. A recent death still trumped a three-thousand-year-old mass murder that could never be solved.

That evening, the police packed up to leave with a stern caution not to go near the grotto, and put up swathes of yellow tape to push the warning home. The archaeologists were given an equally stern warning and were forced to bide their time at the pub in Haggs, which had a few rooms for the occasional lost tourists who found their way over Haggs Pass.

The castle echoed with silence after the tramping of police boots. After insisting Neve went to bed, Edie sat in the kitchen, exhausted, feeling every one of her fifty-two years . . . *Fifty-three now*, she corrected herself gloomily. Yesterday hadn't been much of a birthday, but a day she would never forget.

Unable to sit doing nothing for long, yet unable to settle to one thing or the other, she roamed the halls without direction, stepping into shrouded rooms, hoping for a warm susurration of *floflofloflo-floflo*. None came.

Sighing, she walked outside to her car. The car was still a problem, still without the necessary part and covered in snow. She was certain Cameron had tampered with the engine.

The mere thought of the man sent a nasty shiver up her spine. What a shock he must've had when they had arrived on the island, thinking he only had to contend with Mr. MacKenzie in his determination to find the Maundrell Red. Had he been planning their murder the moment he became aware of their existence?

She brushed the snow off the bonnet and lifted it to stare

helplessly at the engine. Tampering with the engine would've given Cameron time, but she wondered if the blizzard hadn't played into his schemes. A gift sent to him by the Witch.

Hindsight was terrifying if she veered down the paths of what could've happened. She had put her daughter in the orbit of a deranged murderer; it could all have ended so differently, fatally. Edie knew she would ponder the what-ifs for years to come, and take as long to process what had happened.

She startled at a sudden cry. A lonely seagull circled the island as though not sure whether to land, then swooped down to settle on one of the cairns. It eyed Edie sideways, daring her to scare it off.

She stood still, breathing in the silence, a restful quiet, the island surrounded by the bloody waters of Loch na Scáthanna at peace with its ghosts. Its humming sorrow buried in the peat had seeped away, leaving nothing more than what nature intended. In spring, she thought she would hear birdsong and insects once more.

With a start she realized she had been thinking of the island in a more permanent capacity. She gazed up at the castle with surprising fondness. Swathed in snow, it hulked above the island, grimly forbidding. Across the Brig o' Haggs was family, her father's side not tainted by the tragedy that had dogged the Maundrells for centuries. The castle and the island were bathed in her history. The ghosts of her ancestors echoed in the castle's halls, the good and the bad. And more than that, she knew Neve wouldn't leave, not with the knowledge of the Maundrell Red's location. The diamond, whether cursed or not, had a chance to redeem itself after being the source of so much grief, opening up possibilities for the Nunns.

A fragile bubble of anticipation glowed in her chest as she walked back into the castle and was immediately embraced by a warm susurration.

Floflofloflofloflofloflo . . .

Edie smiled. "Hello, Alice."

EPILOGUE

31 October 1990

Bitsie clawed feebly at her chest.

"Is your cold heart cracking, Mother?" said Alice, watching the old woman dispassionately.

"Doc-trrr," Bitsie got out, breathing labored, watery green eyes dilating with dawning horror.

"Now why would I call the doctor?" Alice tensed. Shadows slithered around Bitsie, heavy, succulent, brushing against her thin skin. The end was near.

"Can you see them, Mother?" she whispered, unable to tear her gaze away from the slick curling darkness. "The Witch is coming for you." She delighted in Bitsie's frightened whimper, her crabbed fingers digging into her chest to rip out her stone heart. The cloying shadows stroked Bitsie's white hair, so fine the pale pink skin showed through.

"All my life you kept me here under your control, never allowing me to live. You left me no choice but to live through others, in books, in stories. All those tragic tales, all on Samhain. I can't tell you how I hoped tragedy would strike you. I wished you dead with every wishbone pulled, every penny dropped in the fountain, every shooting star and rainbow I saw. But nothing ever happened to you. So often I thought how easy it would be to take a pillow and smother you, or let you fall down the stairs . . . It took me a while to realize a quick death was too good for you."

Bitsie gasped raggedly, yellowing teeth chattering and snapping.

"I hid any happiness I found from you. My Duncan—" Alice's voice hitched on his name. "My lovely, sweet Duncan who gave me a son and a daughter . . ." Her face softened with grief, then hardened with hate. "But you had to take my children away from me. You killed my son before he had a chance to live, sent my daughter away before I could hold her, not knowing she still lived." A shuddering sob swelled in her throat. "You were my mother!" she cried. "I've never understood your hatred of me. I tried so hard, hoping you'd love me."

Bitsie gave a strangled snort, shadows fretting about her, thicker, heavier. "Earrrn!" she sneered, then gasped again, the side of her face sagging and drooling. But still she clung to life with grim determination.

"I had to earn your love? Love is not earned. It's unconditional, otherwise it's not love." Alice wiped her wet cheeks, angry her mother's cruelty could still pierce the carapace she had built around herself, wounding the softness within, the inner child who had yearned for her mother's love, her approval. "It doesn't matter anymore," she said, forcing herself to calm, to breathe.

Grim-eyed and hateful, she stared into Bitsie's cold returning gaze. "You have taken everything from me, and today you will die now I've taken everything from you. But not quite yet." She picked up the carved turnip from the table and rolled it in her hands. "It was Mungo who gave me the idea . . . Remember how he used to go down to the grotto to have his chat with the Witch each morning in that gibberish of his? I would swear he was having a conversation, yet whenever I went in after him no one else was there. But it got me thinking . . ." Alice smiled at the shadows agitating around Bitsie. "I made a pact with the Witch after you killed my son, to take away what you held most precious just as you had taken away what was most precious to me."

Bitsie stilled, her breathing a wet rattle, listening to Alice as she never had before.

"Rrred . . ." she muttered. "Rrred."

"Yes," murmured Alice. "The Red. The irony is I thought legacy was what you valued most, but I was wrong. It was always the Red. The Witch understood you far better than I ever have." Alice sighed. "And in my desire to hurt you, I was complicit in the deaths of three innocents, as much to blame as you are."

"Rrred?" A strangled gasp. Bitsie stretched a hand towards her daughter, suppliant, begging for relief from the pain rippling through her tired, old body.

"Where is it?" said Alice, long used to her mother's limited forms of communication. "I have no idea who took it. I don't care who did." She watched the shadows, fascinated by their fret and pinch around her mother. "I made another pact with the Witch," she whispered. "Not long after I found out my Florence still lived. It's another irony that after wanting you to die for so long I wanted you to live with such a fierce hatred it made my stomach ache. I wanted you to live, to feel powerless, to have no control over your most basic urges."

Bitsie gurgled, still resisting death, eyes blazing.

Alice stood up and regarded her mother without pity. "It's been a sweet revenge. And now the Witch is coming for you."

Bitsie's thin lips rose in a near approximation of a sneer. "Neverrr!" she hissed. "Neverrr be rrrid of me! Want Rrred!"

The release, when it came, was not as painful as Alice wished. A twitching. A final gasp. Staring. Dead. She watched until the very end, until Bitsie's last breath was consumed by the Witch's pet shadows.

She had been expecting a lightness of being, some sense of liberation from the hatred she'd carried for the dead woman most of her life. None came, but relief that it was over. She was utterly alone now, trapped in the lonely hours with the ghosts of the past.

Alice switched off the light and closed the door softly behind her as though not to waken her mother.

AUTHOR'S NOTE

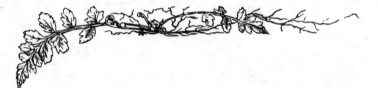

A central theme of *In the Lonely Hours* is autism. As the mother of a severely autistic boy, Mungo Maundrell was a heartbreaking character to write, drawing from my own experiences with my son. During research for *Lonely Hours*, I disappeared down dreadful rabbit holes to the perceptions and treatment of autism in the sixties. I've often wondered what would've happened to my son if we'd lived in a different era, with fervent gratitude that we don't.

Mungo sprang from a number of threaded ideas; many of his behaviors are those of my son (the hopscotch dance, talking of himself in the third person, giving people names that make sense to him, constant demands for stories), and like Mungo, my son has little concept of death, which was a springboard for an autistic ghost not understanding the transition from life to death. I've long had the idea of a ghost living in the walls of an old building. Mungo's hiding places came from a house renovation show where tin soldiers were discovered buried beneath an oak tree for decades. But what pulled those threads together was the treatment of electroconvulsive-therapy (ECT) on autistic people.

That led to branching rabbit holes about ECT. Then, as now, ECT is highly controversial. The idea that autism can be "cured" is not a new one, and so many autistic people were forced to endure ECT without their consent, uninformed of the risks, restrained against their will, without anesthesia or muscle relaxants. Autistic people on the lower end of the spectrum often struggle to even give informed consent (my son finds any form of choice difficult to understand), and the thought that parents or guardians of autistic people allowed these treatments on the most vulnerable in society is horrifying.

It wasn't only autistic people or those with other conditions (such as schizophrenia) who had to endure these treatments. Homosexual men were treated with something similar: Electrical Aversion Therapy to supposedly cure these poor men of their sexual orientation. Once again I was horrified by humans excusing their barbarity in the name of ignorance.

ECT was unregulated until quite recently, and is still used today to treat certain psychiatric disorders, though fortunately it is now done under anesthesia and with informed consent.

It is a small pet peeve of mine that so many ghost stories tend to only feature ghosts from the last few centuries. Why don't we see ancient ghosts, especially in areas that are haunted frequently? Granted, we know so little about how humans lived thousands of years ago, but I've been wanting to incorporate an ancient ghost into a story for ages, and sometimes the earth throws up astonishing snapshots of the very distant past. One such snapshot is bog bodies. These are bodies that have been petrified in a peat bog. Some are so well preserved they appear to have fallen asleep in the peat and could wake up at any moment. (Check out the Tollund Man found in Denmark!)

A final note is also an apology for my characters' Scottish accent and my bastardization of Scottish history. I love the Scottish accent, but it's hard to get just right on paper; any mistakes are my own. Scotland, for such a small country, has a long, varied and rather brutal history, and as I do so often, I have twisted history to suit my story.

ACKNOWLEDGMENTS

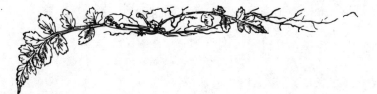

First and always, thanks to my husband, Anthony, for making sure our boys were watered and fed while I drowned in edits, and to Rory, Owen, Nathan and Luke, who keep surviving childhood despite us.

Thanks to my mum, Zoë Fourie, for driving around the Scottish Highlands with me (all in the name of research, of course!), enduring long hours and endless stops.

Thanks always to Melanie Michael, Haaniem Smith, Nicole Clark, Barbara Toich, Sumi Watters and Catherine Stainer for your friendship. A special thank you to Sumi Watters for allowing me to bounce ideas while we ate our way through Seville; I am so grateful we've reconnected.

Thanks to Karen (K.K.) Edwards, my Michigan Goose, for always reading my terrible first drafts with enthusiasm and cheering me through the feast and famine of publishing.

Many thanks to my brother-in-law, James Wright, for not laughing at my appalling Scottish accent, and tolerating my many phone calls to get the accent right so it could still be readable. Any errors are my own.

I owe so much to my incredible agent, Kaitlyn Katsoupis, who made much of my writing journey possible. I couldn't have done it without your steadfast support and enthusiasm.

My ever-wonderful editor, Elizabeth Trout at Kensington Books, had to endure terrible first drafts of this book; I am so thankful for your kindness, patience and keen editorial eye. Many thanks to everyone at Kensington Books who worked so hard to get *Lonely Hours* into readers' hands, especially Carly Sommerstein, Michelle Addo, Lauren Jernigan and Alex Nicolajsen.

A READING GROUP GUIDE

IN THE LONELY HOURS

SHANNON MORGAN

ABOUT THIS GUIDE

The suggested questions are included to enhance
your group's reading of Shannon Morgan's *In the Lonely Hours*

Discussion Questions

1. There are a number of legends surrounding Loch na
    Scáthanna; did they add to your enjoyment of the story?
    Did they add a depth to the worldbuilding and atmosphere?
    Which was your favorite?

2. Mother-daughter relationships play a large role in *Lonely
    Hours*: Bitsie and Alice, Edie and Neve, Vida and Lottie, Alice
    and Edie. What were the differences in their relationships?
    Do you think these relationships led to much of the tragedy
    that occurred on the island?

3. Some of the characters were unlikeable, especially Bitsie and
    Alice. Did you feel some sympathy for either of them? Do
    you think the reasons they were shaped into cruelty were
    understandable?

4. There's a lot of conflict in the novel. Did the characters'
    conflict create a heightened reading experience and add to the
    overall suspense?

5. There is a large cast of characters, especially in the 1965 timeline. Was the family tree useful to keep track of the characters, or were you able to keep up with who was who in the story?

6. Many of the ghosts have unresolved issues. Did meeting the ghosts as living people in the past add an additional layer to the ghosts' motivations and reasons for remaining after death?

7. *In the Lonely Hours* is told in dual timelines. Do you feel the structure worked well overall or do you prefer a single narrative in a novel?

8. The Maundrell Red is a cursed diamond. Have you heard of other cursed diamonds? Do you think there is some truth to the curses?

9. The island in Loch na Scáthanna is fictitious. Were the descriptions vivid? Did they suit the story's setting? Did they add a layer of depth to the story overall?

10. Much of the story focuses on events in the past and the way the past shapes us, who we are and our perceptions. Do you feel it would be better to forget the sins of the past or is it better to keep that history alive to ensure certain events never happen again?

11. *In the Lonely Hours* touches on a number of topics that are relevant today. Were you aware of how autism and homosexuality were perceived not so long ago? Were these handled sensitively according to character and era?